the opposite of falling apart

the opposite of falling apart

MICAH GOOD

wattpad books **w**

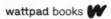

Copyright© 2020 Micah Good. All rights reserved.
Published in Canada by Wattpad Books, a division of Wattpad Corp.
36 Wellington Street E., Toronto, ON M5E 1C7

www.wattpad.com

First Wattpad Books edition: February 2020

ISBN 978-1-98936-506-9 (Hardcover original)
ISBN 978-1-98936-507-6 (eBook edition)

Library and Archives Canada Cataloguing in Publication
information is available upon request.

Printed and bound in Canada

1 3 5 7 9 10 8 6 4 2

Cover illustration by Jason Flores-Holz

To my mom and dad:

I always dreamed of dedicating a book to you.

I practiced doing it, in stapled-together pages and isolated documents on my computer.

Now, finally, this is all for you.

And to Kadin, brother and friend:

Rhys rhymes with geese.

summer 2014

1

JONAS

Jonas had done two things when he'd come home from the hospital for the first time after *The Accident*.

1. He'd taken a permanent marker and scribbled out the lower half of the left leg on his *Bones of the Human Skeleton* poster, which had hung on his closet door since fifth grade (when he'd decided he wanted to be a doctor).
2. He'd looked at the newly-altered poster and cried, for the first time after and the only time since.

He was looking at the same poster now.

"Jonas?"

His mom's tone was familiar. It was the same tone she'd been using with him for the last year. It was as if she was tiptoeing around him, walking carefully to avoid stepping on something sharp like glass shards or a Lego brick. His gaze fixated once more on the mass of permanent ink on the poster that obliterated the left tibia, fibula, patella, half the femur—irrevocable, unshakable. *It won't go away!* he'd screamed in his head, that first day, as he angrily smeared ink on the poster. *This won't ever go away!* And that was when he had cried.

"Are you there?"

Jonas sighed into his phone, the static breath rebounding in his own ear. "Yes, Mom. Here."

"Okay," she said. "Look, I know you haven't really driven since, well, you know." She paused before pressing onward, her tone diplomatic. "Your sister forgot the waiver for her summer camp, and you know they're leaving later this afternoon. I really wouldn't ask under any normal circumstances, but I have a big meeting at work today and I can't get away to bring it to her."

Jonas thought about his sister being unable to zip-line or white-water raft or any of the other things she had been going on and on about doing at summer camp since school had first let out back in May. He thought about his sister, so excited to go off and do *something*, the first thing their parents had had any extra money for, what with Jonas's stack of receipts for doctor's appointments, hospital stay, therapy, and prosthesis (which hadn't left his closet since the day he'd gotten it).

"I was just wondering if you could take it to her."

Easier said than done. Jonas frowned, massaging the place right above his nonexistent left knee, where the rest of his leg *should* have been.

"Jonas?"

He pictured himself saying no and then pulling the covers over his head to block out the outside. "Okay, Mom," he said instead. After all, he'd put her through enough, hadn't he? He could do one thing for her, right? And for Taylor, who had kind of been the forgotten one in all this mess.

"Okay? You'll do it?" Jonas could hear his mother's relief through the phone. He also didn't miss the hope in her voice. He wondered if she had expected more arguing. She'd been trying to get him to leave the house for something, *anything*, since the end of the school year (really, since Jonas's Great Tragedy). He could also hear the concern in her voice. He knew she'd be worried that she was asking too much. Jonas felt bad—the uncomfortable feeling of guilt squeezed at his insides. After all she'd done for him, she shouldn't have to worry about asking too much. She shouldn't have to worry that her son couldn't handle a little thing like a quick errand.

"Okay," he said again. Maybe she'd believe him a little more after he said it a second time. Maybe he'd believe it a little more too.

He could practically see the smile on her face. "Thank you, Bird!" she exclaimed. Jonas closed his eyes and tried not to cringe at the childhood nickname (*You're so skinny, like a bird!* his mom used to say). He could picture her smiling an actual smile (not tired or forced) and he felt a little better about himself for once. His mom was continuing, her words humming in his ear. "Taylor said the form is either on the counter or on her desk in her room. If you could just take it—they're meeting in that parking lot behind the school, you know the one."

Jonas knew the one. He didn't think he'd forget it. He and his older brother, Rhys, leaving school. That same parking lot around four thirty, post Rhys's track practice. *Crash*. The sound of crunching metal echoed in his head.

"Yes." He forced the word out. "Got it." He swallowed and closed his eyes.

"If you could just take it there and give it to her . . ."

"Yeah, all right," he said. There. All right. Something other than okay.

"All right." A pause. "I love you, Jonas."

Jonas pictured his mom. In the year since his accident she'd seemed to shrink somehow. Her dark eyes didn't hold as much light and there was a little streak of gray in her dark hair, which she always tried to tuck behind her ear. Jonas thought that maybe the worst thing of all of this was what it had done to Elise Nguyen-Avery. He held his breath a moment before letting it out and replying. "Love you, too, Mom."

Jonas hung up and dropped his phone on the bed next to him.

He stared at the ceiling's bumpy plaster for a few moments, as if gathering his strength. Then he sighed and flung the blankets back, sat up, and swung his right leg over the side of the bed, ignoring what remained of the left. *Pretend it's not there. Don't look.* (When it had first happened, there had been moments when he almost forgot. He wished he still had more of those moments—the forgetting. Of feeling nothing for a while.) Standing and using the edge of his bed for balance, he tripped over to his closet, where he hesitated, staring at the poster's ink-mangled leg once more before pulling out the prosthesis from the dark corner he had shoved it into.

He sat back down on the edge of the bed and examined the prosthetic leg. A part of Jonas hated the thing. It was a poor substitute for what he was missing. He frowned, then situated it against the stump. No, that didn't feel right. Wasn't there supposed to be a sock or something that went on before the prosthesis? A stump liner? Jonas shuddered a little; for some reason, he'd always hated that word. *Stump. Stump, stump, stump.* He had tried to get used to it, lying in the hospital bed in the pediatric unit (there were clouds and stars and stuff on the ceiling tiles; he wasn't old enough for the adult unit yet) and thinking it over and over in his head, but it didn't work—didn't sound right. Trees had stumps. Legs weren't meant to have stumps.

After a bit more digging, he managed to find the practice liner they'd given him when he'd first gotten the prosthesis. (Wear it a little every day—get used to it. He hadn't.) He put it on and refitted the prosthesis. It felt loose, and he was a little worried that the suction between the liner and the prosthesis wouldn't hold. Somewhere there was a new liner, one fitted to his leg a few months post-accident, after his leg had atrophied a bit. Shrunk. The thing—stump, leg—had actually *shrunk*.

Jonas's gaze moved to the floor, unable to look at the leg for very long. "It will be fine," he muttered into his empty room (empty house, really). "It's only for a little while, after all."

Jonas stood, wobbling for a moment, keeping all his weight on his good leg. After The Accident (Jonas's Great Tragedy was always referred to as *The Accident*), he'd gone through the motions: minor inpatient therapy, practice wearing the liner, trying on a prosthesis. He'd gone through the motions because after he did, he felt less guilty when he looked at his mom. The motions had stopped when his mom had suggested getting the permanent prosthesis. Something about the word *permanent* had made everything sink in. So he'd given up on replacing his missing leg with metal and plastic. His mom hadn't; she'd had him fitted and worked with a prosthetist to order it, hoping that once he had the leg, he might show a little more interest. He'd taken it almost as a challenge. *Think again.* It had spent most of its time in the corner of his closet, gathering dust. Jonas preferred the crutches. He'd gone to therapy long enough to learn how to use them properly. Why pretend everything was normal when it clearly wasn't?

He tried putting some weight on the leg, drawing in a sharp breath at the pain that shot up his left thigh (like his lower leg was still there and was currently being stabbed). Jonas stumbled slightly, then clenched his leg with his hand and straightened it.

You can do this, Jonas, he told himself, breathing a little heavily from the pain. Was he going to hyperventilate? *Stop it,* he ordered his uncooperative body. Had it been this painful before? He couldn't remember. His rumpled reflection in the mirror on the back of his closet door revealed a boy who was a shadow of who he'd been before The Accident—pale and a whole lot thinner. *He's back to eating like a bird!* He'd heard his mother express her frustration with him to his father in hissed whispers coming from their bedroom down the hall. He tried to smooth back his feathery dark hair (his mom's hair), which was stubbornly sticking up on one side, where it had had face time with his pillow last night. Then he tried on a smile that, when combined with the dark circles under his eyes, made his reflection look only *slightly* unhinged.

He left on his plaid pajama pants and threw on an old Washington U (St. Louis, Missouri: est. 1853) sweatshirt his dad had given him when Jonas had been accepted there (his mom and dad had met there—family tradition?). His dad was more muscular (filled out, as his mom would say), and his old sweatshirt made Jonas look a little like he was going for a swim in it.

He stopped looking at himself in the mirror when he couldn't bear it anymore. It was odd, seeing himself with two legs again. It made his chest ache a little.

He picked up the crutches again and headed to the kitchen. He tried to think of things in steps.

1. Get up. (Complete.)
2. Get dressed. (Complete.)
3. Get down the hallway.

He was thankful that he was on the ground floor, at least, and didn't have to navigate the stairs with crutches. After The Accident, Rhys had been forced to give up his bedroom downstairs and take Jonas's old upstairs bedroom (the odd space over the garage where the air conditioner didn't quite get in the summer and the heat didn't quite get in the winter). Rhys hadn't complained, and Jonas knew it was because he still felt guilty for being the one driving, and for not being injured in the same permanent capacity that Jonas was. Jonas let him feel guilty. Sometimes he felt bad about it, but most times he thought it was a poor substitute for what he himself had lost. It was complicated. He didn't exactly blame Rhys, but he didn't exactly *not* blame him either. Jonas had tried to explain this aloud to the counselor his parents had had him go to after it had first happened (until he'd refused to go and his mom, after a lot of tears, had given in) but had failed. After that, he hadn't tried to explain anything to the counselor.

There was the permission slip, on the counter.

1. Pick it up.
2. Make it down the step into the garage.

The paper crumpled when he tried to hold it and the crutch at the same time. He slowly navigated the step down into the cool darkness of the garage. The keys for the Bus were on the wall next to the door, just like always—just like they'd been when Jonas still drove, where he would pick them up almost every day. The Bus was an old Honda Odyssey with sliding doors that didn't work and a hole rusted through the door to the trunk. The air conditioner was also on the fritz, on top of the vehicle's other charms—but it was loyal, and it continued to start and run without fail. There was almost something comforting about it.

Jonas opened the driver's-side door carefully. *You can do this,* he told himself again, before opening the garage door and putting the key into the ignition, bringing the engine to life (all six minivan cylinders firing). He proceeded to give himself a pep talk that would have rivaled a football coach's rallying cry minutes before the homecoming game (well, at least what he thought that would sound like; he wouldn't know).

Jonas tried not to picture how many days had started with him grabbing the Bus's keys off the same old hook, shouting good-bye to his mom, and driving off to school or to soccer practice because he was sixteen and newly driver's licensed and he *could*. He tried not to think about how now he couldn't—about all the times he'd tried since he'd recovered from The Accident (when everyone was gone and he was safely alone), only to end up in a cold sweat, unable to leave the driveway. He could have kept trying—could have worked up to it, as the counselor had said—but he just didn't see the point anymore. *And you're afraid,* his irritating inner voice shot back.

After The Accident, there were a lot of things Jonas found himself unable (or unwilling) to do. It was too easy to be reminded of what he was before he was reduced to being a teenager with only one and a half legs. After The Accident, the way he saw the world had been skewed. To him, people were always either a) trying too hard to pretend he was normal or b) going out of their way to try to help him. Help carrying his backpack after school, help opening the door to whatever store he happened to be going into. One well-meaning friend had even offered to take his arm and help him walk, much to Jonas's embarrassment.

He was tired of people looking at him like he was less *him* than he had been before the semi hit the passenger side of his brother's car. He already felt like he was somehow less than he had been before—he didn't need other people reinforcing that.

So he withdrew from everyone. Jonas with two legs had never been incredibly social, but he'd had friends, at least. He had since distanced himself from them. It was too easy for them to make comments like, "Can't believe Coach is making us run laps today," or even the completely innocuous, "Break a leg," before a presentation at school. Jonas would give anything to run laps aimlessly around the soccer field, or for his leg to ache with something other than phantom limb pain. He was tired of being reminded. He was tired of his friends realizing he was there and then turning to him and apologizing awkwardly. Really, he could handle the comments. What he couldn't handle were the pitying looks that came afterward, or the way their words trailed off when they caught his eye, because that was what reminded him that he was different now.

Jonas always thought he would be fine if people would only act like they had before, but a small part of him, that annoying inside voice, wondered if he would really be okay if people acted like nothing had changed. *What's the point of pretending nothing has changed when everything has?* But he couldn't stop trying to pretend, at least in front of anyone outside of his family.

So he didn't go places with friends anymore. He didn't go hang out at the mall or go to the movies. He didn't watch their soccer games. He didn't drive.

He just existed, as if suspended in the moment in which he had regained consciousness only to realize he was short an appendage.

He slowly backed the Bus out of the garage and then down the driveway. He shifted the vehicle into drive and headed down his street. This wasn't so bad, right? Not so bad (he felt very much like a fifteen-year-old again, learning to drive his parents' minivan. He still remembered his dad: *Easy on the brakes, Jonas.* Then Elliot Avery would grin, even though his nervous energy was dissipating into his hands, adjusting his seat belt. *You'll give me whiplash!*).

Jonas had never been sad about the leg. The one time he'd cried was more out of anger than anything. He always wondered if it was just that the shock had been so terrible that it had yet to wear off, even almost a year later. It just . . . was. This was his situation now, and he didn't feel like being sad would help anything. Besides, Rhys had cried enough for the both of them. Jonas had never known his older brother could cry that much—could cry at all, in fact. (Rhys had gone to visit the counselor—Dr. Andy—after Jonas had stopped seeing her. Supposedly it had helped. At least Rhys didn't cry anymore.)

His mother still cried sometimes. Especially after an unsuccessful day of trying to get Jonas to show some interest in *something* other than watching the *Star Wars* movies over and over again (and wishing that there was some way he could get his hands on a robotic leg of a quality à la the hand that Luke Skywalker got after having his own chopped off by a lightsaber) or playing video games on the PlayStation his parents had gotten him after The Accident, mindlessly defeating enemies until his head emptied of all the worries about what his first year of college would bring. *I don't understand! I just want to help him and I don't know how!* he'd heard his mom cry to his father one night when he'd snuck down the hall for a drink, a phantom on crutches in the darkness. (He'd gone back to his room without the drink, and with guilt squeezing his insides *again*.)

He pulled the Bus to a jerky stop at the stoplight. This was it. The last thing between him and the main road.

The light turned green and he shakily accelerated, turning rather ungracefully but managing to stay in his lane, which was a plus. Jonas mentally added another point to his first-time-driving-again score.

After several turns, he was about ready to convince himself that this really was okay after all. His muscle memory was starting to kick in, and his braking and acceleration weren't so shaky and halting. (Plus, his hands weren't as sweaty.)

In hindsight, maybe he'd spoken—or thought—too soon.

At that moment, a semitruck passed in the left lane. Jonas held his breath. His vision wobbled a bit, sparking in and out of static, like a radio with a bad signal. He imagined that the truck was coming into his lane and ended up swerving dizzily, only to find that the truck was firmly where it belonged, and it was just the spinning of his head that was warping things. It was flashes—a semitruck; the shocked face of a man named Paul Whitford; Rhys crying and saying Jonas's name over and over again, like the more times he said it, the more likely he'd be to get a response.

Was he dying? Or just having a panic attack? The horizon line was wonky, and Jonas desperately pleaded with himself not to pass out. He was so busy holding his breath and vise gripping the steering wheel as he watched the truck, trying not to give in to a flashback to the moment when everything had gone black, that he didn't notice the red light in front of him.

When Jonas did notice the light, he panicked. Everything went from slow motion to 2x speed—he went for the brake with his right foot, which seemed abnormally sluggish for the speed at which everything was happening, while his left foot, the one belonging to the unwieldy prosthetic leg, somehow got stuck under the pedal. *Shouldn't have done this. Shouldn't have done this,* was all he could think, over and over as he slammed down the brake, pressing it as far as it would go with his shoelace caught around it and his prosthetic foot jammed up under it. His thoughts switched from *Shouldn't have done this* to *I'm going to die now; this is it* to *What if I lose my other leg? No-legs Jonas?*

The van came to a stop, but not before bumping into the car in front of him, jolting it slightly.

And everything stopped but the ringing in his ears. *Shouldn't have done this.*

2

brennan

Brennan hadn't felt like going to work today.

Not that she felt like going to work any day. Her last summer before college was speeding by, the days blurring together, too slippery for her to grasp hold of the time and *hold on*.

Brennan would have spent the entire summer holed up in her room, writing. Instead, she was spending the summer working, trying to save money for college expenses. She glanced at the pennant she'd pinned to the wall above her desk in hopes of rousing some excitement—some sort of spark—for school. *For college*. SIUE. Southern Illinois University Edwardsville. Brennan felt a little sick thinking about making it her new home. It was a nice school—really nice; on visits, she'd almost felt like she could *belong*. Back at home, though, the feelings faded in the wake of anxiety.

Brennan pulled her hair up into its usual knot on top of her head. She could almost hear her mother. *I wish you'd actually put some effort into your hair, for work at the very least.* Brennan, the disappointment. If she saw herself that way, would her parents see her that way too?

Sometimes she wondered. She stared at the stubborn flyaways around her ears that refused to be tamed. It wasn't that she didn't care at all about the way she looked. She did care, somewhat. It was just that she had come to the conclusion, at the start of high school, that people weren't worth her putting extra effort into dressing herself up and hiding who she really was. Her black leggings and T-shirts were easy to grab even on an anxious morning; they didn't take thought. *Thoughts* were something that tended to cause trouble for Brennan. *What if I look silly in this shirt? Is this skirt too short? Will people notice that my sweater has creases where it was folded?*

Letting the thoughts lead her around by a leash hadn't helped when she'd been a freshman, after all. After her family moved when she was in middle school, Brennan had left behind her school and the friends she had made. Instead, she was homeschooled. It was sort of a relief—Brennan had always found it hard to make friends, and after having all the effort she'd put into it at her old school wiped away, she was perfectly fine with being at home.

That was when her love of writing had started. She'd had so much time to write what she wanted and how she wanted. Her mind was filled with stories—with fantasy worlds, half-formed. Without a laptop, she wrote by hand, her handwriting growing more sloppy and slanted the faster she wrote, as she tried to keep up with her racing mind.

Then she'd been a freshman, they'd moved back, and her parents wanted her to go to "actual school," as her then-best friend had called it. She was reenrolled at her previous school.

Brennan had been excited. She'd gotten new clothes, new binders, and new notebooks. She'd daydreamed for days about being able to see all her old friends. Then she'd shown up on the first day of class only to find that everything was different. Her friends had gone on with their lives without her, because *of course* they had. What had she expected? It wasn't as if they'd just stop time in their sixth-grade year and everything would be the same now that Brennan was back.

Her best friend from the homeschool group her mom was a part of had enrolled in school as well. Brennan took comfort in this; at least she'd have a *person*. But when they showed up on the first day of school, her friend met someone new and they hit it off, immediately leaving Brennan the awkward plus one. You know, the one who had to walk ahead or behind when the sidewalk wasn't wide enough for three people.

That year had been when the anxiety had started. The first time Brennan had had what she later discovered through some Googling must have been an anxiety attack, she had thought she was having a heart attack. She'd stood in the bathroom stall, back against the cold metal door, her breath coming quick and shallow, her hand on her chest in an effort to press away the deep ache and keep from falling apart. *Can fourteen-year-olds have heart attacks?* she wondered. And then *I can't get a breath. I can't breathe.* Eventually, it had settled in long term as a knot in her stomach, where it liked to make her feel like she was about to throw up. It gnawed at her stomach every day, for seemingly no reason. She was sick, she told her mom. *You're fine,* her mom would say, after pitying Brennan initially. Brennan didn't blame her; she had to be tough; had to force Brennan out of her comfort zone lest she become a total recluse. And so Brennan was grateful to her mom, at least somewhat—even when her mom forced her out of the house and into a job the last summer before her first year at college.

So Brennan scraped together all her anxiety, tied it into an ever-present knot of sick in her stomach, and went to work behind the deli counter of her local grocery store. Needless to say, she wasn't one of those people who left for work excited, loving her job. By the end of the day, she'd be dirty and food splattered, feet aching from standing for hours with only one break. On top of that, she was usually starving, because the anxious demon in her stomach wouldn't allow her to eat in public. *What if you get food poisoning?* She would counter with *I can bring my own food,* to which it would reply *But you*

feel SICK. If you eat, you'll THROW UP and everyone will think you're
D-I-S-G-U-S-T-I-N-G.

For now, Brennan tried not to focus on how she'd feel at the end of
the day. She was too busy gathering strength for the beginning of it. And
it took *a lot* of strength, carefully gathered, to push down the nausea at
the back of her throat and get out of the car, slam the door, and speed
walk into the store before she changed her mind and turned to run.

Currently, Brennan was trying to write a summary for a novel.
There was only one problem: How could you write a summary for
something when you didn't know exactly where it was going? When
you didn't know the ending?

She was stuck. She'd written the beginning of Ing's story about ten
different times (in first person, third person, present, and past tenses)
and she still couldn't tell exactly what was going to happen. *When are
you going to just pick something and soldier on?* asked Brennan's friend,
Emma, via Facebook Messenger. They'd met sophomore year. Emma
liked what Brennan liked. Emma had her life on track—she wanted to
be a chemist someday. Sometimes, Brennan wondered if she'd maybe
thought some of Emma's on-track-ness might rub off on her. Brennan
hadn't had any idea what she wanted to do until the last week of her
senior year, and she still wasn't entirely sure.

You should shadow your aunt, her mom had said. Brennan's aunt
(her mom's youngest sister) had just recently graduated with a doctor-
ate in physical therapy. It was an idea, and Brennan grabbed hold of it
like a lifeline.

Really, Brennan didn't see how choosing your major before going
off and actually experiencing things made any sense. And sure, you
could go undeclared, but that just felt like too much pressure for
Brennan when everyone else seemed to know. Left and right, everyone at her high school was declaring majors. Brennan had felt like the
weird one whenever people asked her what she was going to major
in. She'd always tried to avoid the subject. She would have gone for

English if she thought she could make a career in fiction writing. There was the problem, however, that Brennan couldn't bring herself to post anything for people to actually read, other than the carefully culled bits of scenes that she sometimes sent to Emma when she was feeling especially brave. There was also the problem of the luck involved in writing—you might make it or you might not. Brennan didn't know if she had what it took to make it, and no one else could tell her if she did or didn't, since she wouldn't let anyone actually see what she wrote.

Physical therapy was convenient because SIUE had a bachelor's program to prepare for physical therapy school, and Brennan had a scholarship for SIUE.

Brennan had written to her aunt last night.

> Dear Aunt Kim,

Too formal. Aunt Kim was family.

> Hi, Aunt Kim!

Better; at least more friendly, like maybe she actually wasn't nervous at all about shadowing.

> I'm interested in pursuing physical therapy when I go off to college. I was wondering if I might be able to shadow you a few times before I go down to school for the fall. I'd love the chance to see what a physical therapist does, and how they interact with their patients.

That had seemed all right.

> If you have any time available, please let me know. I'm off Mondays and Wednesdays, so those would be good, but if

you need to do other days or times, you can let me know
and I can try to work something out with my boss.

"Hit send," Brennan whispered. "Don't freak out."

That had been when she messaged Emma, trying to distract herself by talking about the logistics of her novel. (Or *story*, because Brennan wasn't quite ready to call it a novel. Something about that seemed too real.)

When are you going to just pick something and soldier on?

Emma, like Brennan, was an introvert, and so both were con-tent to have occasional in-person meetings supplemented by hours of Facebook chatting. Not sure, Brennan had typed back, partially offended by Emma's blunt questioning, and partially feeling called out because Emma was right.

I feel like I'm almost ready,

she finally responded.

I just want it to feel right, you know?

She couldn't explain how important it was for Ing to be *just right*, because she was the antithesis—the opposite—of Brennan in every way. She was what *Brennan* wanted to be, if she were a character in a young adult novel.

She sent Emma little scenes sometimes, but never anything full—fleshed out. Emma would send them back, editing the little typos that her friend was very prone to making in her all-fire hurry to get the words from her head to her computer (it was so much easier typing than writing by hand, but sometimes Brennan's hands still couldn't keep up with her mind).

Today, for no particular reason, Brennan was especially nervous about going to work. Even the drive from her house into town hadn't managed to calm her down. *Your pulse is RACING,* her mind said. *CHECK IT.* Brennan didn't want to check her pulse. It felt like giving in. So she breathed in and breathed out and clenched the steering wheel so tightly her fingers cramped. *Check. Your. Pulse.* Her mind was screaming now, and her breathing was speeding up. She imagined that her mind was laughing at her, standing next to a sign proclaiming 34 Days Since Last Incident and preparing to flip it to zero.

Brennan pulled to a stop at the light. She adjusted the air conditioner so it was pointed straight at her face, cooling the heat in her cheeks and calming her a little. The voice was a little less loud, but still there. *It can't hurt,* she argued with herself. *It isn't giving in. It's just proving your mind wrong, because the pulse will be normal, and you'll know you're fine.* She tried to focus on the color of the light. It was one of the busier intersections in town, and she knew the light would stay red for some time. She sighed, forcing herself to unclench her fingers, stretching her hands before clenching the wheel once more, despite her efforts to relax. Even with the air conditioner, she was sweating. *Better put on more deodorant when you get to work,* inner Brennan chided her. *Wouldn't want your co-workers or customers smelling how nervous you are.* She tried picturing the GIF with the ever-expanding and constricting circle, breathing in time with it. In, out. In. Out.

She thought about her summary. *In a world of Extros (people with physical or strength powers) and Intros (people with abilities based in the mind), Ing is an Ambivalent. She's normal, and normal isn't wanted in Santos.* Brennan frowned. Too much explanation? *Solve the puzzle. Defeat the queen. Kill the king. Welcome to the Santos Game.* The problem was Brennan hadn't quite decided what exactly the Santos Game entailed. Her mind was filled with vague images of riddles and challenges, intrigue and trickery—but none of it was solidifying into anything concrete. She knew she wanted Ing (Ingrid Wei, hero of the story) to trick the Superioris (Santos's government—ten houses and a king) and enter the game to win, basically, her freedom to exist in Santos, all while proving that those without powers were just as powerful as those with. Maybe the game contestants were drawn by lottery, and Ing didn't have a choice? Brennan just couldn't find a plot where the pieces fit together perfectly. It was frustrating. It had been a *year* since she'd started working on this idea.

Brennan focused on the stoplight again. Still red. She left the summary behind in favor of thinking about the scene she was currently working on—in which Ing, newly-chosen contestant in the Santos Game, attends the Celebration of Beginnings, which was basically the send-off for the entire Game Season in the story. In the scene, which was a masquerade ball complete with lots of gilded and ornate masks and dresses, Ing meets a mysterious stranger. She is unsure if he is an investor in the game or a contestant, but something about his eyes—somehow nothing and everything, brown, hazel, green—captivates her. *"Trust no one," he said, leaning ever so slightly closer to Ing. "The Game isn't a game after all . . ."*

The car jolted forward, and Brennan's hands, which had started to relax, immediately clenched around the steering wheel once more. Had her foot come off the brake? What had happened? It took her a moment to make sense of things.

The light was still red but she knew it would be green soon. She glanced in the rearview mirror at the minivan behind her. It was close; abnormally close. Then she got it.

She'd been in a car accident. She, Brennan Davis, was part of a fender bender. A bad one? No, probably not, she guessed. No airbag—she'd only jolted forward a bit.

Brennan figured she could do one of the following things:

1. Drive off. Better to do that than to face the embarrassment of talking to another driver.

2. Get out and yell at the other driver. It was their fault after all, and the tension inside of her was just begging to be let out, unleashed.

3. Sit. Wait. Let the other driver lead.

She tried to remember what they'd said in driver's ed about what to do in a car accident.

She vaguely recalled something about not moving, in case of neck or spinal injury. Brennan glanced down at herself. It wasn't that kind of accident. She was all right. No injuries. No intrusions into the driver's compartment. She undid her seat belt. At worst, a slight case of whiplash that would leave her sore tomorrow morning.

But then the anxiety demon clenched her stomach. *What if it's internal? What if your liver is lacerated and you're bleeding out into your abdomen? You should CALL AN AMBULANCE. Just in case. Better safe than sorry.*

Brennan shook her head. *Be logical,* she told her demon. *Next. What next?*

Probably she'd have to talk to the other driver. Inspect the damage. Get his name and insurance information. She glanced in her rearview. The other driver seemed to be staring forward in shock, making no move to get out.

Okay, okay, she thought. She remembered being told not to admit fault in an accident. Leave it to the cops, the insurance company, the lawyers—anyone else. But in this case, she didn't think that mattered. It wasn't her fault. He—she?—the other driver, whoever it was, had rear-ended *her.*

She wondered if they'd been texting. Sleeping. Looking out the window?

She saw the light turn green and people started moving forward without Brennan. In her peripheral vision she could see passersby glancing sideways, watching her with curiosity and concern. *Oh, an accident? Interesting. That's not something you see every day.* Her chest tightened. *They're STARING at YOU,* her brain yelled. *MAYDAY MAYDAY.*

Please shut up, Brennan begged her mind. She glanced at the dash clock. It seemed like hours had passed, like everything was happening in slow motion. In reality, it had been mere minutes. Hours or minutes, she was going to be late to work.

So she took out her phone and, people outside forgotten in the wake of a million other things to worry about (like the fact that she could currently be, at this moment, bleeding out), she called her boss.

The phone rang in her ear a few times before her boss picked up.

"Hi," Brennan said. "I'm going to—I'm going to be a little late."

3

JONAS

Jonas put the car in park as soon as it had stopped, bumper to bumper with the car in front of him. He didn't try to back up from the car; the thought didn't even cross his mind (or maybe it did but got lost in the rapid fire of his brain's synapses).

With the car stopped, it was easier to extricate his foot. He glared at it in disgust. He imagined shoving it back into the corner of the closet. Or better yet, under his bed, where it could gather dust, completely out of sight. *Prosthetic piece of crap,* he thought, his hand massaging the point where the remaining part of his left leg met plastic. Jonas ignored the pins and needles sensation in his leg and turned his gaze back to the car in front of him.

Whoever he'd hit wasn't getting out. Jonas could tell it was a she, but nothing else about her. Would she be angry? *Most likely. I'd be angry if someone hit me,* he thought. *Well, I was angry when someone hit me.*

Jonas wondered whether or not he should tell the truth about what caused the accident. He decided he would just say he hadn't been paying attention. What was he supposed to say? *Um, sorry, I have a fake foot and mental issues with semitrucks, and I rear-ended you because I was trying to decide if I was having a panic attack or dying.* Better Jonas look like an incompetent driver than tell her the truth and watch her expression morph into that look of pity that people inevitably got whenever they learned that he was an eighteen-year-old with only half a left leg.

He saw the other driver turn her hazards on and decided that he should probably do the same.

After doing this, he steeled himself to the inevitable conversation that would have to occur between him and the girl. So he slid over to the passenger side (having enough sense left to know that it would be inconceivably stupid to open a door into oncoming traffic, no matter how slow it was going) and opened the door. Jonas felt like every other driver on the road was watching him. He tried not to think about it. *Who cares?* he told himself. *Not me. If anything, I'm used to being stared at by now.* He almost laughed at the ridiculousness of the lie. Carefully placing both feet on the ground, he got out. With his pants covering his prosthetic leg, the view looking down was almost normal; there was no way to tell that one of his feet was plastic, except for the way it felt. *Like it's dead.* He wished that he was wearing almost anything other than plaid pajama pants and a too-big sweatshirt.

Jonas stepped forward. He stumbled when his left foot hit the ground. Instinctively, his arms went up, to catch himself if he fell. (Parachute reflex. He remembered reading about it when he still wanted to be a doctor. It developed sometime during infancy—you fall, the arms go out.) He regained his balance and limped onward, hand pressed against the Bus for balance. He tried to match his walking as close to normal as possible, ignoring the discomfort and pain that shot through the *missing* part of his leg with each step. *A majority of amputees have phantom pain following limb loss,* Dr. Andy, his counselor, had said, back when he first went to see her. She'd brought out a mirror. He'd obliged her, sitting on a couch in the office and holding the mirror in front of his left leg so that it reflected the right. He'd pretended he had two whole legs—normal. *Be normal, be normal,* he told himself as he made his way along the side of the Bus. Jonas told himself to watch where he was putting his feet, due to lack of sensation in his prosthesis, so that he didn't step too hard or trip forward. Still, he tripped a few more times, fighting his parachute reflex in order to avoid flailing his arms any more. It was like he was stumbling around with impaired depth perception or something. He couldn't help but feel like the leg might buckle; might not hold him up.

When she saw Jonas coming toward her car, the girl rolled down her passenger-side window.

"Um, hi," Jonas said, rather lamely in his opinion. He leaned one hand against her car, holding himself up, running the other shakily through his hair before gesturing toward the back of her car. "Look, I'm really—I'm really sorry," he choked out, fixing a half smile on his face like a piece of armor and hoping he didn't look as unhinged as he had in the mirror that morning. "I just . . . I looked down for a second and then I looked up, and the light was red—" *Half truth.* He had been looking at the semitruck. *Don't think about it,* he mentally ordered himself, trying to ignore the way his heart sped up at the memory.

"Oh," stammered the girl. "It's fine. You know, accidents happen. I just need your insurance information I think? And your name, probably."

It struck Jonas that she wanted to be anywhere but here, talking to him. She looked like, if she could, she would have just driven off. She was staring forward as if it might kill her if her gaze deviated from the windshield. When she *did* look at him, it was at a point slightly to the right of his head, off in the distance.

"Of course," said Jonas, keeping his lips fixed in the contrived smile, although he was now sure that his eyes weren't cooperating with his mouth. He wondered how he wasn't better at fake smiling by now. Rhys always said he frowned too much, even before The Accident. Afterward, Jonas wasn't sure when the last time he'd *really* smiled had been. He glanced at the traffic that seemed to be backing up as more and more people slowed down to see what was going on or to let the cars stuck behind the accident into the open lane.

Jonas shifted his weight on the hand propped against the car—the metal was hot under the sun. Uncomfortable. He turned back to the girl in the car. She was still refusing to look directly at him. "I think that both vehicles look moveable," he said calmly, hiding his discomfort behind a veneer of pretend confidence. "I think if we pull into the parking lot over there"—he gestured to the mostly empty parking lot of a nearby Walgreens—"we should be able to inspect the damage a bit better, and I'll give you my information. This really is my fault, and I apologize."

The girl had been staring at Jonas until he made eye contact to apologize, at which point she blushed even redder and looked away once more. "You're not supposed to admit fault in an accident," she mumbled under her breath, almost so Jonas couldn't hear her. "I think it can be used against you or something." Her voice trailed off.

Jonas frowned. "What?" he asked. What was wrong with this girl? Logic would say she'd be glad to have him admit to being at fault.

"Nothing," she mumbled even more quietly.

"All right," he said. "You go ahead, and I'll follow you."

She nodded, then turned her hazards off and shut her window.

Jonas turned away, allowing his shoulders to slump and the fake smile to disappear. The few steps back to the Bus seemed like a mile. All he wanted to do was sit down and remove the stupid prosthetic leg. The remaining part of his leg was clearly not used to having to bear weight, and every step was painful. He was also regretting not taking the extra time to find the newer liner, as the inside of the ill-suctioned plastic socket was starting to slicken with sweat. Jonas took a deep breath and a quick step forward, just enough to get his hands back against the Bus, back against support. He made it back to the still-open passenger-side door and slid across to the driver's side.

He broke things into steps:

1. Start the car.
2. Keep his left foot as far from the brake pedal as possible.
3. Put the car in drive.
4. Go into the parking lot.

He turned in and stopped behind the girl—perpendicular to her so he could see the back of her car. She had gotten out of her vehicle and was inspecting the damage.

It didn't actually look that bad, Jonas realized with relief. Maybe the cost to his parents wouldn't be too much. He was still on their insurance. He'd have to pay them back of course—but how would he earn the money? Jonas tried not to think about how the monthly insurance bill would increase after an accident. He shook his head. *I'll worry about that later,* he thought.

He got out of the Bus once more, relieved not to have to slide over to the passenger side again. He leaned his back against the side of the van, alternating between putting his hands in his pockets and crossing his arms. He settled on hands by his sides and tried to stand as straight as possible while still leaning against the side of the vehicle.

The girl came around her own car to meet him. Now that she was out of the car, he had a better look at her. She was the type of girl who most people wouldn't really remember if they passed her on the street. Quiet and unassuming. Not trying to stand out. Not that that was a bad thing. She had brown hair, the majority of which was tied up into a haphazard knot on top of her head, except little pieces that frizzed around her ears and forehead in little wavy tendrils. And glasses—round glasses that seemed a bit too big on her round face. They made her eyes look bigger, like she was afraid or nervous. *An animal in the headlights,* Jonas thought. She was dressed in a slightly-too-big-for-her blue collared shirt and black pants; tennis shoes completed the outfit.

Jonas's eyes went to the badge pinned to her shirt. *Brennan.* He resisted the urge to tell *Brennan* that there was a hole in her left sneaker, right where the side of her little toe would be. It might be weird for her; it was weird, right? The way he subconsciously noticed people's left legs now?

"I'm making you late for work, aren't I?" he said instead, somewhat worriedly. It was bad enough that he'd crashed into her, now he was making her late. *Inconvenience. This leg is always an inconvenience.*

"It's fine," Brennan said, blushing again. She always seemed to be blushing. Her glasses were fogging up around her nose too. It was humid outside. She took them off, awkwardly rubbing them clear on the corner of her uniform shirt. Kroger. She worked at the grocery store. Jonas's mom did all their weekly grocery shopping there. "I called my boss, anyway," she said.

"Okay," Jonas said. He didn't know what else to say.

He wanted to walk around to the front of the Bus and see what damage had been done to his own car. He wanted to, but his leg didn't want to, so he stayed where he was. Whatever it was couldn't be worse than any of the Bus's other attributes. Whatever it was would probably fit right in.

Jonas noticed Brennan looking at him strangely and redoubled his efforts not to slouch against the Bus, ignoring the painful rubbing of the sweaty liner against his residual limb as he straightened his left leg. *Blisters,* he imagined, already dreading the thought. He didn't need blisters on top of everything else. *Where in the world did I put the new liner?*

Jonas bit back a frustrated curse and inspected the back of Brennan's car more closely. There were some scratches in the paint, but it wasn't noticeable with the light blue-gray color of her car. The most concerning thing was the dent in the back of the vehicle.

Brennan was standing next to him now, having come forward quietly. The heat was starting to get a little oppressive in the Wash U sweatshirt, and Jonas held his breath, hoping he didn't smell like sweat.

He tried to remember when he'd last showered. A day ago? Two? He couldn't remember. The last two days had been gray days, as his mom called them. *Bird's having a gray day,* he'd heard his mom tell his dad yesterday. Gray days meant that Jonas locked himself in his room and alternated between playing video games and staring at the wall or the ceiling.

He brought himself back to the present when Brennan spoke. "I think it's really fine," she said a little breathlessly. "I thought it would be much worse. This isn't even as bad as the time my mom backed into one of our cars with the other one." She took a deep breath. "And that dent popped out within a week. I don't even think I need to take your insurance information." She said all of this too quickly, with only the one breath between, as if she had to get it all out before she lost the nerve.

"Are you sure?" Jonas asked, frowning. "If I've damaged your car, I should really pay."

She looked like she'd rather be anywhere but there; as if letting Jonas off was the fastest way to get away from him. It didn't ease his conscience.

"It's fine," Brennan said, shifting her weight from one foot to the other. "You can't see the scratches in the paint and the dent is hardly noticeable. Not worth the rise in your insurance premium, is it?"

He shrugged. She was watching him. He tried not to think how he must look to her: messy hair and pajamas, like he'd just rolled out of bed. *You* did *just roll out of bed,* Jonas reminded himself.

She turned to leave. "I'd better get to work, though," she said.

"Wait!" Jonas pulled out his wallet, opening it and taking out a lone twenty-dollar bill that had been there since before The Accident. It wasn't much, but it was all he had at the moment. "At least take this." He held it out to Brennan, and when she didn't make any move to take it, he inwardly groaned in frustration and took a stumbling step forward. He pressed the bill into her hand, admittedly a bit roughly.

"For the trouble," he said. "For the work you missed. For—" For something; he just couldn't let her leave. It felt too easy.

"I don't need . . ." Brennan spluttered weakly. Her glasses were half fogged up again.

"Take it," he said.

"It's really fine."

"Take it!" he demanded, frustration creeping into his voice, "I don't want it!"

She looked startled by his change in tone, and she took the bill. "Okay," she said, still watching him carefully, brown eyes wide behind her glasses.

"Okay," he said, letting out a breath. *Unhinged. Calm down.* "All right. I'm sorry. Again." He just wanted away—away from here, out of the heat, back in his room.

"I'm really not upset about it," she said quietly. She looked a little uneasy, and made eye contact even less than she had before (if that was possible). He wondered if she was just shy.

"All right," he said. "I guess I'd better head off then. I've got something I need to drop off for my sister."

"Okay," she said. "Just pay a little more attention to the road." She laughed uncomfortably, as if she had been trying to make a joke or a witty comment.

Jonas stared at her blankly for a moment and then forced an awkward laugh, not because he found it funny, but because he felt awkward on her behalf.

He got back into the Bus and pulled forward enough for Brennan to get past him. She got into her car and pulled out of the parking lot, driving away, on her way to work. He sat there for a few moments, letting the Bus idle. Eventually, he shook his head and put the van into gear.

Taylor looked absolutely shocked to see him when he pulled up to give her the form. Jonas had expected her surprise; why should she expect her brother—who never left the house except for visits with his doctor, his prosthetist, or his rehab therapist—to actually be out and about? She would have made a big deal about it, but Jonas shut her down with a frown and a shake of his head.

So Taylor just thanked him quietly and took the permission slip.

Jonas drove home and locked himself in his room, throwing the fake leg back into the corner of his closet and settling in to play video games, trying to drown out the pain in his missing left foot.

He didn't leave the room for the rest of the night except to use the bathroom down the hall. His mom brought him a plate of dinner (homemade pizza, his dad's specialty), but Jonas just muttered, "Not hungry," from his place in the bed, staring at the wall. His mom set the plate on his desk and walked over to the side of Jonas's bed. He didn't turn over. She hesitantly touched his forehead with the back of her hand. "No fever. Are you feeling okay?" Her words were laced with concern. Guilt squeezed his stomach again.

"Yeah, fine," he said. "I'm just not hungry. Thanks, though. I'll try to eat some in a little while."

Elise Nguyen-Avery was quiet. She sighed and gently ruffled his hair (that was how he'd woken up in the hospital after it happened—to his mom ruffling his hair). "Okay," she said. "I love you. I'm here, okay?"

"Okay," he whispered. Whispered because he was afraid that if he spoke any louder, some of the churning inside him might escape and he might cry again. He didn't want to cry right then. *You're angry, not sad,* he chided himself.

His mom's hand stilled, entwined in his hair. She seemed like she might say something, but she just turned and left the room.

Later she peeked in again. "Thank you for taking the permission slip to Taylor."

Jonas hadn't told her about his fender bender. He wouldn't tell her;

she'd just feel bad about asking him to go in the first place. She'd think it was her fault, and it wasn't.

"You're welcome," he mumbled. He heard the door shut and turned over so he could see the poster on the closet door, with its sloppy mass of black ink. *Irrevocable. Un-take-backable.*

4

brennan

"Can I get a pound of the honey roasted turkey, sliced on a two?" Two. Deli speak for sandwich slices.

Brennan flashed a smile at the customer on the other side of the counter. "Sure!" she said, feigning cheerfulness. Her feet were hurting again. She hadn't sat down since she'd gotten to work. *Keep busy*, her brain demanded. *Distraction is key.*

She glanced at the clock as she opened the deli case and grabbed the turkey in question, slapping it down on the slicer and laying a piece of tissue paper down for the meat. She sliced back and forth, the rhythmic hum of the slicer creating background noise.

Finished, she picked up the piece of paper with the turkey and weighed it. One pound on the dot. Brennan always felt lucky if she got the exact measurement she'd been aiming for. She put the turkey in a plastic bag, sealed it, and slapped on a sticker with the price. Thanks for shopping! it said. Then Brennan said the same, out loud. She handed the bag to the customer, who smiled, thanked her, and went on about their shopping business.

Brennan sighed, turning and leaning back against the deli case. She eyed the clock once more. One minute until four, and then she'd go on break. She wasn't used to working in the evening; she normally worked in the morning and afternoon. She'd picked up a shift for a co-worker who was having back pain, apparently so badly that he couldn't even walk. Brennan doubted the validity of this excuse, however, since she'd seen said co-worker out at the movies with his girlfriend on one of the days he was supposedly in so much pain that even sitting up was an effort. He had seemed to be sitting up just fine. Snogging his girlfriend just fine.

Kissing, Brennan reminded herself. *This isn't Harry Potter.* The big hand on the clock finally hit the twelve and it was four o'clock. Brennan took off the protective hairnet that made her look like an extra on the set of a medical drama.

Leaving the deli and entering the world of grocery that existed on the other side of her counter always seemed like a breath of fresh air. Even her feet were glad to be able to be walking rather than just standing there, holding her body weight in one place for so long. They hurt a little less.

She bought a bottled water and a package of peanut butter cups, and headed to the break room.

There were a few other people there, but they mostly minded their own business, other than occasionally making a passing comment about the news that was playing on the TV mounted on the wall. They didn't even acknowledge Brennan, other than to look up when she walked in. Brennan was totally fine with that. She didn't really know any of them. Maybe she just hadn't been there long enough to *bond*.

She claimed the break-room couch, thankful that, for once, there was no one else sitting there. If there had been, she would have had to sit at the tables, because *You can't sit on the couch if someone else is THERE. What would they think if you just sat down at the other end without saying anything?* And asking was out of the question, because

Brennan's mouth had a bad habit of drying up like a desert whenever she opened her mouth to ask people questions.

She opened her water and took a sip.

She thought about the boy who had hit her car earlier. He had looked to be about her age; maybe he was even getting ready to be a college freshman, just like her. He was somewhat skinny *but not unattractively so,* she defended him in her mind, embarrassed. *Ha-ha,* her brain seemed to laugh at her. *What are you embarrassed about?*

He had nice hair. It looked soft, and kind of like he'd just gotten out of bed that way. A crazy part of her wondered if it was as soft as it looked. She'd watched him for a while, until he had noticed her looking, and then she'd turned away, blushing (always blushing). Brennan had an aversion to eye contact. No matter how hard she tried, she could never tell if she was holding it for too long, which resulted in a lot of glancing around and awkward attempts to meet the other person's gaze. She'd stared at a lot of ears and feet in the process of avoiding eyes.

She thought about the twenty-dollar bill in her pocket. From him, whomever he was. He never had told her his name after she let him off the hook with the insurance thing.

Brennan sighed and shoved her candy into her pocket. *You should wait to eat until you get home,* her brain muttered. *What if you feel sick again? Eating will make it worse.*

She thought about the boy again, because he distracted her from herself. He had seemed kind of odd, she had noticed. He looked dreadfully uncomfortable, for one thing. Maybe he felt sick or something. Whatever the case, he also walked kind of weird. Not quite a limp, but not quite a normal gait either. Sprained ankle? Pulled muscle? And he seemed glued to the side of the silver minivan he was driving. *Why do I care?* she asked herself. *Because you don't know anything about him. Because he's a mystery, and you spend all your spare time making mysteries out of people. Is it creepy? Maybe it's creepy. It's creepy, right?*

She did—make mysteries out of people. She watched customers over the deli counter, going about their shopping, and made up stories in her head about what each one was there for, and what they would do after they left the grocery store. Sometimes they were elaborate (he's an undercover cop and one of the workers here is a suspect in a murder) and others were simpler (it's her anniversary today and she's picking up frozen pizzas for the kids so the two of them can go out to eat at a fancy restaurant and have some alone time).

She glanced up at the clock. Thirty minutes had already passed. *Break over.*

She sighed (*You sigh too much.* Her brain. Again.) and tossed her empty water bottle in the recycling.

Four hours down, four to go.

Plenty of time for something to go wrong. Do you feel like your pulse is fast? Brennan self-consciously brought her fingers to her neck, as if she was just brushing her hair out of the way. She watched the clock for thirty seconds and then multiplied by two. Seventy. Two beats more than her normal.

You're fine, Brennan told herself. *Fine.*

5

JONAS

Every week Jonas's mom asked him to go on some errand or another with her. Every time before, Jonas had declined. Since school had gotten out, he'd only gone to the follow-up visits with his doctor and on yesterday's ill-fated excursion to deliver Taylor's permission slip.

This was why his mom was somewhat surprised that he said yes when she asked if he wanted to go to the grocery store with her for the weekly shopping.

His residual leg was relatively sore from the overexertion yesterday. The last time it had had to bear any weight was when he'd first been fitted for the permanent prosthesis, and he hadn't used it since then. Jonas stood in front of the mirror on his closet door, hunched over his crutches. *Fake leg? No fake leg?* He shifted his weight. He'd always hated the way it felt, like he was standing on one leg, even with the crutches. He'd had crutches once before, when he'd twisted his ankle during soccer season. Then there was still the feeling of a leg there, no empty space throwing off his balance. As much as Jonas hated the prosthesis, it felt less like he was hopping around on one leg.

He decided to wear the prosthesis but to still use the crutches. If anyone asked—if *she* asked—he could say he'd sprained his ankle or something. He'd found the good liner, at least. Stuck in an old box of winter sweaters at the back of his closet.

Jonas hoped she—Brennan—would actually be at work today. Otherwise, bringing along the sixty dollars currently in his pocket would be for nothing. What did dents cost to fix? He didn't know, but the twenty dollars he'd given her yesterday certainly couldn't be it. Would sixty more? He hoped so. He'd spent the morning digging through his sock drawer, his desk drawer, and a stack of old birthday cards, pulling together every bit of cash he had. He didn't have anything else, and talking to his parents wasn't an option.

Once Jonas was actually in the passenger seat of his mom's minivan, he regretted agreeing to come along. *What was I thinking?* Brennan hadn't wanted money; maybe if he'd listened, he wouldn't be forcing himself out of the house again. He massaged his leg absentmindedly— that pins and needles sensation there *again*, this time in his toes (his toes that weren't really there anymore). He hated the phantom sensations. It was bad enough to feel pain, but to feel pain in a limb that wasn't there? It was creepy. At least with the proper liner the prosthetic leg felt like it would actually stay on.

"Jonas?" His mom's voice was hesitant. "Are you all right?" They stopped at a stoplight and she turned to look at him with concern.

Jonas snapped out of his thoughts, recognizing the stoplight as the one from the fender bender. He thought about how easy it would be for one driver to not be paying attention—one driver to hit them. One driver—an old man in a semitruck—to hit him.

"Fine, Mom," he said, giving her a small smile. He thought this one might look a little more real than usual.

She seemed satisfied and continued on when the light turned green.

Jonas thought about the Act of Leaving the House. He was oddly proud of himself for leaving yesterday, even if it had been a disaster.

He'd *left*, gone *out*, and that was what had mattered. It felt good, which was surprising. Jonas had mentally promised himself to try again sometime. He just hadn't expected to be trying again so soon. But his mom needed groceries, Brennan worked at the grocery store, and he was tired of feeling like he was getting off because of the leg (even though Brennan didn't know about it, so it couldn't be the reason she was letting him off the hook for his role in the accident).

His mom parked the car, and they walked in together—or rather, Jonas crutched inside while his mom walked. He received a few glances, but not nearly as many as he would have if he had just left his pant leg empty and the prosthetic leg at home. His sweatpants covered the metal, and he almost felt normal. *Almost.*

By the time they reached the end of the second aisle, his mom crossing things off on her list as she got them (Jonas's mom always wrote her lists by aisle number—milk, eggs, cheese: aisle one; canned beans, corn, tomatoes: aisle two; etc.—he thought it was rather smart, actually), he had begun to notice her casting glances sideways at him as they walked.

"What?" he asked, furrowing his brow.

"Are you tired at all?"

Jonas's frown deepened slightly, but he sighed and said, "No, Mom. I'm fine." He was always *fine*. What did fine even mean? *Fine* was such a lie.

But his mom nodded and resumed her list-crossing-off.

Truth be told, Jonas was getting a little tired. The last time he'd been on the crutches this much was when he'd been in school. Even then he'd had a wheelchair for when he just couldn't take the crutches anymore (he'd used it as little as possible, but there had been days, especially at the beginning, when he was in so much pain that he'd given in). After the school year had ended, he'd gotten around mostly by hopping on one foot, propping himself on the wall, if he had to get somewhere in the house, and occasionally using the crutches when he was feeling particularly lazy or when his mom was watching. Using crutches for a prolonged amount of time was more uncomfortable than he had remembered—wrists aching, arms tired, wanting to sit down.

His mom seemed happy to have him here with her, though, and that was worth the discomfort.

Jonas wondered what department Brennan worked in. Was she a cashier? Did she stock shelves? Bakery? Then again, was she even at work today? *You're an idiot. She said it was fine. Why can't you let it be fine?* Nothing was fine, so this couldn't be fine.

Farther down the aisle, his mom came across something on her list that she hadn't ever bought before, and therefore didn't know where in the store it was.

Chipotle peppers in adobo.

Jonas would have just looked for the peppers until he found them, heaven forbid he ask anyone before he'd exhausted every effort on his own. His mom, however, had no problem flagging down the closest sales associate.

Jonas stood a little way behind her, kind of wishing he was farther away, because she was gesturing at him suspiciously. What in the world was she telling this stranger?

He suddenly realized the stranger had a familiar messy bun (familiar wild tendrils escaping at the ears) and blue uniform shirt–black pants combo. Jonas's eyes widened before he immediately returned his gaze to the floor, hoping she—hoping *Brennan*—wouldn't recognize him right away. He needed to separate from his mom somehow if he wanted to keep the accident a secret. He stared at the little hole in Brennan's left sneaker.

Meanwhile, his mom was chatting Brennan's ear off, telling her about the recipe she was making, as if that was required background information in the search for the canned chipotle peppers. Jonas would have just said, "Excuse me, do you have canned chipotle peppers in adobo?" That was, if he had asked at all. His mom was turning it into Elise Nguyen-Avery and the Quest for Chipotles in Adobo.

Finally, Brennan found enough of a pause in the conversation so that she could insert her reply without accidentally interrupting Jonas's mom. Jonas had been watching her and the way she kept going to say something and ending up just smiling and nodding at something Jonas's mom had said. When he looked at her more closely, he could see what appeared to be panic growing in her eyes. She looked trapped. *Go ahead, interrupt her,* Jonas mentally urged her. *It's okay. Do it now. One, two, three, now!* "I know we have them," Brennan finally said. "I'm just not sure where they are." Jonas wondered if she hadn't been working there long. "I can find someone who knows for you, though, if you come with me." Brennan was continuing, and his mom was smiling.

Of course Jonas's mom followed her. Brennan kept turning around and making comments to his mom, as if trying to fill the silence on the walk to wherever they were going. She laughed awkwardly after most of the comments. Jonas wanted to say *It's okay. You don't have to talk. It's all right,* because it seemed like she wanted to be anywhere but there, leading them around the store. She walked too quickly, and no matter how hard he tried, he realized (with frustration building within him) that he couldn't keep up.

His mother glanced back at him. He gestured for her to keep going, but slowed down, following them at a distance.

Eventually, they must have found someone who was able to tell his mother where the chipotles were because Brennan departed (as quickly as possible, Jonas noticed, and frustratingly before he could say anything to her about paying for the dent in her car).

Calm down, he thought, relaxing a bit. He wasn't sure if he was relaxing on her behalf or letting go of the unspoken worry he'd had that she'd somehow reveal their fender bender to his mother.

They visited every other aisle of the store. Jonas wondered why they hadn't just looked in every aisle for the chipotles as they shopped instead of asking someone (instead of asking *her*). Of all the people. He felt a little bit bad that he still hadn't told his mom about the accident, but he *still* thought it was for the better. He wouldn't be able to stand it if she felt any more guilt because of him. A small part of him whispered *Or do you just not want to feel any more guilt over all the things she now worries about because of you?*

After the aisle shopping came the specialty shopping, which meant that Jonas's mom went to buy fresh ground beef (*How much fresher can it be than what they have in the packages? It's not like they butcher a cow in the back of the store,* thought Jonas, who would rather have spared himself from the conversation that ensued when the guy behind the counter asked what had happened *Sports injury? Sports injury.*) and salmon fillets.

The next stop was the deli. His mom ordered a pound each of sliced ham and turkey, and a pound of provolone cheese (Jonas's favorite because it didn't really have a strong cheesy taste) and then left Jonas to wait for the cold cuts while she went off to order a cake for Taylor's birthday (*A week away, but better to get the order in early,* she'd said). He'd been trying to find a way to separate from her and go find Brennan, but it seemed like maybe she'd given him a chance all on her own. He could get the order and then wander the store a bit and find Brennan again.

Jonas zoned out, watching the deli worker slicing the meat for the person who had been in line in front of him—back and forth, back and forth. He was rather amazed that the worker hadn't managed to slice off his own fingers. Jonas wondered what it would be like to be finger-less *and* legless. He also wondered if his mom was relieved to leave him behind for a bit and walk at a normal pace over to the bakery.

"So you're pretty accident prone."

He started and turned to face none other than Brennan. She was wearing a ridiculous hairnet that looked like a mesh shower cap.

She seemed to mistake his blank look for his having not understood her statement. "You know," she explained, awkwardly (everything about Brennan was awkward). "First the fender bender, and now the crutches." She frowned, pushing her glasses up her nose a bit and studying him but not making eye contact (she always seemed to end up looking off to the side at his ears. He suddenly felt self-conscious about them.) "What'd you do anyway?" she asked.

"Soccer injury," Jonas blurted, trying not to think about his ears and whether or not they stuck out. "Tore my ACL and meniscus." Back before Jonas's Great Tragedy, one of his friends had been out for the season because of that same injury—good enough as any for Jonas to borrow.

Brennan raised an eyebrow. "You've certainly had a rough week."

"Yes," he said. "You could say that." *Rough year, but who's counting?*

"So," she said, silent for a moment before continuing. "The dent really isn't noticeable. My dad didn't even notice it, until I told him about it." She smiled slightly. "My dad was just happy I wasn't the one who actually *caused* my first car accident."

"Really?" he said, shifting his weight from one crutch to the other. He tried not to picture her telling her parents, because a little fender bender—a tiny car accident—didn't hold any larger meaning for them (didn't hold memories of blood and hospital rooms and waking up lacking). "That's good, I guess."

"Yeah," she said. Silence reigned once more. The other deli worker was just getting to his mom's order. "So what brings you to the grocery store today? You'd think most people with torn ACLs would be at home, relaxing."

Jonas shrugged. "I came to the grocery store for the same reason most people do," he deadpanned. "To get groceries."

Brennan rolled her eyes, but he caught the small smile that turned her lips. It almost made *him* smile. *Almost.*

"Brennan," called the other deli worker from up the counter. "Slice one pound of provolone, sandwich slices."

"Sure," said Brennan, taking the block of cheese and heading to the other slicer along the counter.

After a few moments, Jonas moved down the counter to watch. "Uh—I might have lied a bit about the groceries thing," he mumbled. "I wanted to pay you back. For the dent. I mean, pay you more." His cheeks heated a bit and he mentally cursed his sudden awkwardness.

Brennan paused a bit in her preparation of the cheese. After a while she spoke, looking at him like she might be trying to make eye contact but was finding just his ears again. "Do you—do you know how much a dent costs to roll out?"

He shook his head, a little dumbly.

She shrugged, smiled a little. "Me neither. So let's forget about it."

She moved farther down the counter and Jonas, after a moment of frustration, followed her. He watched her put the cheese on the slicer and position it carefully.

"That's for me," he blurted, inclining his head toward the cheese.

"Provolone, eh?" she said. "One of the less distinctly flavored cheeses."

"I know," he said. "That's why I like it."

"You need to expand your cheese horizons." She moved the slicer back and forth. Somehow, the risk of sliced-off fingers seemed more real when the person doing the slicing was someone he knew—could put a name to—albeit someone he'd known for only about twenty-four hours.

He swallowed. "How so?"

She finished his cheese and bagged it up, slapping a price sticker on it. Jonas's mom wasn't back yet.

"I mean, try something new."

"Why try something new when I know what I like already?" he said, frowning. *Which isn't much lately.*

Brennan laughed softly as she reached for two cheeses from the deli case. "Live a little," she said, slicing a piece of each cheese and handing the slices to him. "I'm authorized to give you a free sample. Try these."

Jonas tried the first cheese. It was surprisingly good, although the orange on the outside edge was kind of suspicious looking, at least in Jonas's opinion. "It's decent," he said, nodding as if in approval.

"Don't be stubborn; you liked it," said Brennan. Jonas shrugged. "It's Muenster," she added. She handed him a second cheese. "This one is Baby Swiss."

Jonas liked that one pretty well, too, and he told Brennan so, somewhat begrudgingly.

She smiled. "I thought you might like them. They both have milder flavors, not too unlike provolone."

"Well, aren't you a regular cheese expert," he said sarcastically.

She shrugged, handing him his order of meat and cheese, now finished. "You pick things up working in the deli. Have a nice day, I guess. Hope I don't run into you again. Or rather, I hope you don't run into me."

Jonas rolled his eyes. "Har, har, har. Aren't you hilarious."

Brennan's smile left her lips, but Jonas could see that her eyes were still laughing. They were kind of nice that way, brown and shining.

"Let me pay," he said.

"You pay up front."

"Not for the meat and cheese," he corrected, furrowing his brow. "For the dent."

"I'm probably just going to leave it if it doesn't come out on its own," Brennan said. "It's really tiny. Really."

Jonas stared at her. Then he frowned. "I don't understand."

"I just don't want to make you pay for something that was an accident. You hit me. You didn't mean to. You apologized." She shifted uncomfortably. "If it was really noticeable, it might be one thing, but it's not."

He wanted to argue. He opened his mouth to say something, but his mom was back then, taking the meat and cheese from him. So he nodded at Brennan, who gave him another small smile, and then followed his mom away from the deli.

In the dairy section, his mom stopped to compare a few different shredded cheeses, one of which was on sale. "Do you think this is a good deal?" she asked Jonas, holding up a coupon from the little coupon dispenser attached to the shelf. "One dollar off, but less cheese than this other one."

"I don't know," he said.

Jonas distractedly pulled one of the coupons out of the dispenser, trying to ignore the pain that was just starting again in the nonexistent left toes. Variety shredded cheeses. One dollar off. He frowned at the coupon.

Before The Accident, a lot of things were different. His dad had been going to teach him to drive stick shift. After The Accident, Jonas's dad had traded that car in for one with an automatic transmission. One pedal, one leg needed to drive it. He hadn't said anything to Jonas, and he hadn't grieved as visibly as Jonas's mom, but Jonas knew why he'd done it all the same. Elliot Avery was trying to fix one little part of everything, the best way he knew how.

But what happened to Jonas couldn't be fixed. This could be, though—*for once,* Jonas wanted to *fix* something.

He grabbed the pen his mom had been using to cross things off the grocery list, flipped over the coupon, and carefully wrote out a few words: *Text me and tell me the total.*

He signed his name and then carefully printed the ten digits of his phone number.

"I'll be back, Mom," he said.

"Mm-hmm," she hummed.

Jonas crutched quickly back to the deli counter, scanning the employees for familiar big glasses and hair-netted brown hair. He saw Brennan when she came out of the back cooler.

"Back so soon?" she said. Her glasses had fogged up a bit in the corners from the temperature change between the walk-in cooler and the counter. Her fingers twisted the edge of her apron, transferring her nervous energy to the fabric.

"Hi, again," Jonas said. He didn't know what to say next, exactly. He sighed. "Look, just take this." He handed her the coupon face up.

She studied it. "One dollar off shredded cheese?"

His mom was calling to him from a distance. "Jonas! I'm ready to leave!" Jonas's gaze flicked rapidly to his mom and then back to Brennan.

"Look, I—"

"Jo-nas!" His mom was getting closer. "Time to go."

Jonas forced a smile in Brennan's direction, eye contact as poor as her own in the moment. "Expand your cheese horizons?" he said, shrugging against his crutches. He cringed at his own joke. When he spoke again, his words were frustrated. "Flip it over. I have to go."

Then he turned and left, but he glanced back at her one time to make sure she flipped it over.

She did.

He felt a tiny bit better.

6

brennan

Brennan took off her hairnet and tossed it in the trash, simultaneously untying her apron with her other hand and pulling it over her head.

She was exhausted. Tired of deli meats and cheeses and putting on her I'm-totally-together face and talking to customers.

Brennan trudged out to her car, immediately getting hit by a wave of humidity as she exited the air-conditioned store. *Nice,* she thought, taking off her glasses, which had immediately fogged up. *I love Illinois summers.* For some reason, the past couple had been particularly bad.

Or at least, worse than she remembered them being as a kid. Maybe that happened when you grew up—the things you used to like (like warm sunny summers) became somehow less exciting and more of an inconvenience. (Maybe adulthood was the age of inconveniences.)

She sighed, got into her car, and put the air conditioner at full blast.

At least she was getting off earlier today. She hadn't had to close.

At home, her mom was making dinner. Brennan made it upstairs to her bedroom with nothing more than a mumbled hi and an okay when her mom asked how her day at work had been.

In the safety of her room, she changed into shorts and an old T-shirt before flopping onto her bed and staring at the ceiling.

She felt bad; she hadn't actually sat down and written anything out for her book. No one would know; since she was too much of a coward to post it to the writing website she'd found, allfixx.com, no one could read it. Even so, she felt the familiar punch of failure in her gut. Like she should be being more productive and had instead given in and, well, not been.

Brennan was conflicted because she thought that maybe writing was this big journey, like an adventure of sorts, that should be enjoyed one step at a time. You would work hard and then, one day, look back and realize where that hard work had led. However, she also wanted to feel like what she was doing mattered now, at least to someone. *Give up*, her brain scoffed. *You can't even read your own writing without wanting to change it. That means no one else will like it either.*

In high school, Brennan had written Harry Potter fan fiction. It had been a running joke. Eventually, somewhere along the proverbial road, she'd stopped telling people what she enjoyed, because she got too excited, and most people looked at her like she was crazy. You could like Harry Potter, but you couldn't *love* it the way Brennan did—to the brink of obsession, to the point of writing fan fiction. That was just odd. Once she started toning down the fangirl part of herself, Brennan became the most boring person ever. She was lucky Emma had even taken the time to get past her walls and see anything there to like. The Walls kept most people out.

Even when Brennan eventually started writing her own original work, she didn't tell anyone, because the Act of Telling was exposing herself, somehow. All of this came from her mind, after all. There had to be some psychoanalytical crap buried in there somewhere that said something about Brennan. She didn't want to know what it said about her. She didn't want to give people the chance to think about it.

At dinner, Brennan was mostly silent. Her brother, Ayden, talked a bit about his day. Eventually, he fell silent, too, and Brennan knew that would mean her parents would look to her next.

"How was work today, Brennan?" Her dad, from the head of the table. Brennan's hair was the same color as his, but that was about where the similarities ended.

She shrugged. "Okay." One word answers; keep it simple. *Actually, work was awful. I basically had an anxiety attack in the cooler and felt like throwing up for half my shift.* She choked down a bite of food and took a sip of her milk.

"Did you email Aunt Kim about shadowing?" her mom asked. Rose Davis pushed her glasses up on her nose. Bad vision was the thing Brennan had inherited from her mom. Brennan remembered being little and asking her parents what parts of her looked like them—did she have Dad's nose? Mom's smile? The older she'd gotten, the less she looked and acted like them. Sometimes she looked at her family pictures and imagined being adopted as a baby—she didn't *match* in the pictures. Ayden, Rose, and Dan all matched. Then there was Brennan.

She nodded in answer to her mom's question but didn't offer anything more. She felt a little guilty. Maybe she didn't match because she didn't put enough effort into it—into being part of dinner conversations and outings to Ayden's scholastic quiz games or track meets.

When Brennan had come down the stairs and into the dining room for dinner, her dad had widened his eyes in pretend shock. "Well, well, well. Look who decided to join us!"

Brennan hated when he said things like that. She knew he was joking but part of her wondered if he really would like a different daughter—one who showed up to family dinner and talked about her day and didn't have anxiety eating her up at any given moment.

After dinner, Brennan was tired. It was like she had a meter—full at the beginning of the day but depleted by every interaction between her and any other person.

She headed back upstairs, turned out the ceiling light in her room, and crawled into bed. She left the lamp on her nightstand on for the moment, not quite ready to plunge the room into total darkness yet.

Brennan sighed, turned on her side, and faced the wall, pulling her blankets up to her chin. In bed, trying to turn her mind off, it was easy to start worrying about college again, because her room at college would smell different and there would be the shadows of different trees dancing on her wall. The familiar sick nausea twisted her stomach. She shut her eyes and tried to fall asleep. She *was* tired, after all.

It was one of those nights that, no matter how tired she was, Brennan couldn't sleep.

She wondered if college would be like high school. Everyone (her parents, her guidance counselor, the old guy she worked with at the deli) constantly said that it would be nothing like high school; people wouldn't be so fickle, or people would be more accepting. They were more themselves. Something like that. Brennan wasn't quite sure that she believed them.

She hoped it would be different, but she didn't want to get her hopes up. Too many times she had gotten her hopes up only to have things fail to meet her expectations. Then she bottomed out, mentally, for a bit. It was discouraging, to say the least.

Brennan sighed, giving up on sleep, and pulled out her phone, opening the Messenger app and shooting a quick message to Emma. Hey.

She wondered if Emma was still awake. Sure enough, moments later: Hey, what's up.

Brennan propped herself up on one elbow and typed back. Worrying about school. The usual.

It was a few minutes before Emma typed back. Don't be. It will be fine.

But I have a random roommate! What if she absolutely hates me but we're forced to live together? What if she's superpopular and she's ashamed of me because I'm a dud.

What even, Brennan? A dud? You're gonna be fine. My sister has been off at college for three years now. She loves it, and she was totally shy. People are different in college. You're gonna find friends who are just as nerdy as you, and they won't think you're a dud even if, God forbid, your roommate does.

Brennan sighed, because Emma was right, she knew. So why did it still feel, deep down, like Brennan's life was about to fall apart? At least her Aunt Kim had messaged her back. She would shadow. That was doing something—that was taking steps toward not being a total and utter failure.

Who knows, Emma typed. You might even meet some fellow writers, so you can have those coffee-shop writing meetups you've always wanted to have. You can sit there and write with each other but never actually share what you're writing about. Just revel in the camaraderie. You never know. There're all kinds at college.

Brennan smiled a little at the thought. Maybe you're right.

I am right.

Brennan sucked in a breath and bit her lip, heat stinging the backs of her eyes and threatening tears, before typing back. It's just so easy to spend time worrying about it. I have to be in this strange room that will smell strange, with a strange roommate, and strange suitemates next door.

Strange, Emma retorted.

Brennan continued, unable to stop until she got it all out, like her life depended on somehow explaining the tumult inside of her. And I have to eat cafeteria food. What if I get food poisoning and I'm sick in front of my roommate? And where do you sit in the cafeteria? Do you meet up with people or go yourself? I'll probably end up at a table by myself, watching Netflix on my phone or something. That, or I'll have a stash of ramen noodles hidden under my bed so I'll never have to even go to the cafeteria. I'll just creep out of my room, hiding inside a blanket, and sneak down to the lounge to heat them up before skulking back to the depths of my cave.

She could picture Emma rolling her eyes. Find the cafeteria or I'll drive to Edwardsville and drag you to it.

Maybe that's not a bad thing. Then I'd have you. You should have come to SIUE instead of going off to Missouri.

I wish I could have, but my scholarship is in Missouri, and I have to go where it's best for me. You know that.

I do. Maybe I should come to Missouri.

For the same reason that I can't go to SIUE, you coming to Missouri would be a bad idea. One word: SCHOLARSHIP.

I don't have a full ride like you, though.

Brennan.

I know, I know.

:)

You have to still message me, you know.

I know, replied Emma. And I will. I need my daily dose of Vitamin B.

And I need my daily dose of Vitamin E, so promise that you won't forget. Promise.

All right then. I guess I'd better be going off to sleep. Brennan yawned then, as if on cue. The sick feeling had subsided somewhat. Good night, Emma. And thanks for calming my nerves, as usual.

raises wand, Potter style Farewell, Brennan. Sleep well.

Brennan put her phone on her nightstand. Her eyes caught the coupon resting there. Variety shredded cheeses, one dollar off. She reached over and flipped it.

Text me and tell me the total. Jonas.

And then, his number.

Should she text him? Or should she just let him fade into the background of her story, forgotten and unimportant? He was just the guy who had rear-ended her car.

Brennan opened Messages. She carefully typed in the ten digits of Jonas's phone number, checking and double checking a few times. The dent had popped out of her car yesterday anyway. She should let him know that, right?

After typing a quick message, she turned off the lamp and rolled onto her back again, staring up at the ceiling through the dark.

Maybe college won't be so bad after all, she told herself, turning her thoughts back to the future. Her voice was cheerful in her head, pep-talk-like. *Maybe you'll love your roommate. Maybe she'll love you. Maybe she writes. Maybe you'll be best friends.*

Maybe.

She closed her eyes. *Or maybe,* anxiety whispered, *it will all be awful, and you should prepare yourself.*

She squeezed her eyes shut so tightly that little stars sparked across the backs of her eyelids.

PS, anxiety added. *You definitely should not have texted Jonas.* She pictured her inner demon shrugging. *Too late.*

7

JONAS

By the time the weekend passed and Monday rolled around, Jonas was in a bad mood that he couldn't come up with one single definable source for. It was more of a medley of frustrating things.

For one thing, his leg was still sore from using the prosthesis last week. When the amount of phantom pain he usually had increased, his mom lectured him about how he needed to build up to wearing the prosthetic leg more slowly.

So he sat and half listened to her lecture, growing more frustrated by the minute. It wasn't as if *she* knew anything about missing half of one of your limbs, so how would she know how it felt?

Jonas almost wanted to put the leg on again and walk all the way around his neighborhood, just to spite his mom (who was just trying her best really, he conceded eventually) and his own body (weak, weak body that couldn't cooperate with what he wanted to do). But he'd heard his mom last night, talking to his dad in hopeful tones. He hadn't heard her hopeful in quite some time. He still hadn't told her about the accident. *Let her be happy. Let her be hopeful.*

While his mom was happy, Jonas's bad mood wasn't helped by the arrival of two letters from Washington University, one with his housing assignment and one bearing the news that the labs for the anatomy and physiology class he had tried to sign up for were full and he had been put on a waiting list. Regarding the A&P letter, he wasn't that upset. He supposed it was what he got for signing up for classes long after everyone else had. He'd just take A&P next semester, if he took it at all. He still hadn't decided what he was going to do now that he'd given up on being a doctor. Maybe he wouldn't even need A&P. The housing assignment itself also wasn't that bad, but the big deal that his mom made over it was. There were tears, lots of them. His mom had been excessively overprotective since The Accident, and she hadn't been too sure about him going to a college that was out of town, even if it was only a few hours away (far enough to be away but not far enough that it was unreachable should there be an emergency). The letter brought on a whole new round of her trying to convince him that it might be best just to stay home (*I can take care of you, Bird*), and Jonas insisting that he'd be fine (*I'm not your little Bird anymore, Mom*) and then him trying to comfort her because he hadn't meant it that way, he just needed *away* from anyone who knew him *before*, because then maybe he could become someone else without the pressure that came with having everyone from before watching him now.

Eventually his mom had just broken down and kissed his cheek and hugged him, saying how proud she was of him, while ruffling his hair.

Now Jonas was back in his room, watching *Star Wars: A New Hope*. Outside, the humid air lay over everything like a hot, wet blanket. Inside, the air conditioner seemed like it was constantly running, struggling to keep up.

He was wearing the prosthesis. His gaze kept gravitating to his left foot. He stared at the sock. It was a knit sock (his grandma had made it), but he couldn't feel it—the knitting was rough, uneven, but for all his fake left foot would know, it could have been the most luxuriously soft sock in the world. He stared at it some more, as if that might make him magically regain feeling in the plastic toes. At least they looked normal right now—with the prosthesis on and covered, he could pretend. The prosthesis was a good one. His mom had done all the research on features, compared all the prices, and come up with a final wish list, the result of which was the current leg. (*I think we want a dynamic response foot, and something called a cosmetic shell that lets you wear shoes and socks like normal,* she'd said, squinting at the notes she'd made on her phone, and then at Jonas. That was how she'd woken him up that morning, sitting on the side of his bed with squinty-tired eyes and messy hair, hunched over her laptop. He would later find out that she hadn't slept the previous several nights, instead sitting in the living room and pouring herself into reading about prosthetic legs and feet. So he let her bring her list to the appointment with the prosthetist.)

Jonas dragged his gaze away from his left foot and picked up his phone. Unlocking it, he opened his texts. A number without a name, but still no doubt who it belonged to. The texts had arrived last night.

The first message: Is this fender bender Jonas?

Jonas's brow furrowed and he frowned at the screen.

The second message: Anyway, I just wanted to tell you the dent popped out of my car. No harm done. No need to pay.

He squinted at the phone a bit, in thought.

The third message: This is Brennan, by the way.

Of course it was Brennan. Who else would it be?

Jonas sighed. He debated over whether or not to respond to her. He had what he needed, after all—the dent had popped out of her car. That was as much as he needed to know. Should he say something back? (Did anything need to be said back?)

He would probably never see her again anyway. He'd go off to school in a month. She'd go off to school. Or at least, he assumed she was around his age. She'd had graduation tassels on her rearview mirror. Recent senior, just like him? Maybe.

So to text Brennan or not? He wasn't really looking to form any new attachments to people in his hometown. It just got awkward once you went off to college and then, eventually, you'd fall out of touch. He'd seen it happen with Rhys, although it was a bit messier for his brother because there were not only best friends (several) and sports buddies (many), but there was also a girlfriend (Madison, whom Jonas generally tended to hide from, especially since her intended major in biomedical engineering made her way too interested in Jonas's prosthetic leg— *What kind of foot did you choose? I mean, there are lots of options. If it was me, I'd want something that allowed for more movement.*).

No, attachments weren't for Jonas. For him, friends he'd had in his hometown were a before and the friends he'd (hopefully) make at college would be an after.

So why did he feel like saying *something* to Brennan, even if it meant she might say something back?

8

brennan

Sometimes, it was just as hard being off work as it was actually going to work.

Especially when your impending freshman year of college was taking up the majority of your thoughts every time you had a nonbusy moment to fill with anxiety.

It was a hot and sunny Wednesday. Brennan tried to concentrate on writing. Ing was standing out front of the pristine (too pristine; blindingly white) House of Games in Santos, preparing to put her name in for the Game that could decide the rest of her life. *If she didn't think too hard about it, Ing could almost imagine that this was just any other September first . . .* Not thinking too hard. That was the key. That was what Brennan was missing—what she *couldn't* do.

She squinted at her laptop screen. She couldn't get the words right, much like in real life. Ing had gone inside, where she was to write her name on a slip of paper, drop it into a bowl, and . . . and . . . Ing should say something, probably, in response to the good luck proffered to her by the attendant at the entry table. Brennan sighed. Maybe if she was better at talking, her characters would be better at talking.

She closed her laptop and pulled her phone out. She opened the allfixx app and pulled up the draft of her story. She thought about publishing a summary—just a taste, to judge interest. Then again, she didn't even have a title yet. She closed allfixx and opened her Messenger window with Emma.

Hey, can I bounce some novel ideas off of you?

Nothing back. Emma was probably at work.

Brennan sighed again and swung her legs over the side of the bed. *What to do, what to do.*

She thought about her few encounters with the boy who'd rear-ended her. Jonas. It was kind of nice, knowing his name instead of just thinking of him as the guy who ran into her car. It had been weird, because she had actually managed to talk to him—like somehow he'd made her actually want to speak, which was an entirely new level of weird that she wasn't ready to deal with yet. *The Walls,* her brain whispered. *Keep the Walls up.* Brennan's Walls had been up at least since high school, if not before then. It felt safer with them up, like she was less vulnerable.

Anyway, something was off about Jonas. She didn't quite know what, but whatever it was, it didn't seem like something bad. It was almost easier to talk to him since he seemed like he was irritated 100 percent of the time. If he was already irritated, Brennan couldn't be the one to make him grumpy.

Easier to talk to or not, you shouldn't have messaged him. Her stomach twisted just thinking about it, and her brain threatened to pull her into an anxiety spiral. *Down and down and down.*

She sighed and checked her email again for the hundredth time (not an exaggeration; she'd likely checked it at least that many times since the message came last week). There it was. The dreaded roommate email from SIUE. For the hundredth time, Brennan read it over (as if she didn't already know it by memory).

Important Information about Your Fall 2014-Spring 2015 Housing Assignment.

She read on, the words blurring into one another in black and white lines. Prairie Hall, room 165, PRS. And then the abbreviation key: PRS = shared bedroom. Shared. *Shared.*

Your roommate is Ambreen Saluja.

Ambreen. Brennan liked the name.

She wondered how Ambreen would be. Was she social? Extroverted? Or could it be possible that there was someone out there even more reclusive than Brennan? Would she have lots of people over? Stay up late? Would she play loud music? Would she like having music played at all? And most importantly, would she even like Brennan?

Brennan pulled her phone out again and opened Facebook. She searched for Ambreen.

She held her breath and hit Add Friend. *Friend request sent,* it said. Brennan sighed and hit the Message button.

She stared at the screen for a moment. What was she supposed to say? *Hi, I'm Brennan! I'm your totally wigged out roommate who is really afraid you'll hate her. Will you hate me?*

Instead, she wrote,

Hi, Ambreen! I got an email saying that you are going to be my roommate for the upcoming school year! I just wanted to say hi, and maybe get to know you before the school year starts. I hope your summer is going well!

She hit Enter, and the message sent. There, it was done. Whatever happened, she'd at least made the effort.

Jonas hadn't texted her back. *Don't be stupid. He won't. He'll give up now, like any normal person would. Maybe you should have just taken his money. If it made him feel better about things—you had to go and be all noble.* Then again, most normal people probably wouldn't care that much about paying her back.

She tapped on the Facebook search bar. She wondered if she could find Jonas. Did that make her creepy? For some insane reason, she wanted to keep talking to him, even though he clearly didn't seem to like *her* very much.

Jonas Avery, Brennan typed. She wasn't a stalker (or maybe she was, since she was looking him up on Facebook); she just knew his mom's last name since his mom was a frequent customer at the Kroger deli and had introduced herself one day in an attempt at friendly chatting with Brennan.

She found him. Right hometown, a high school name she recognized. She couldn't match his face with the one from his profile picture, but the profile hadn't been changed in a while, and the picture was taken from a far enough distance away that she couldn't study it anyhow.

She turned her phone screen off. *What is wrong with you? First messaging him, then sitting here looking at his Facebook page like a stalker.*

Brennan stared at the black screen of her phone, feeling like an idiot. Every few hours, she'd kind of forget about the messages she'd sent Jonas, and other times they would come back to hit her with a load of self-deprecation. *You're an idiot, such an idiot. Why would he text you back? Why do you want him to? He barely knows you and probably doesn't even like you anyway.* It had been a few days and still no response. He was probably ignoring her. He'd heard what he needed—that the dent had popped out—and that was that.

And then there was her message: *Is this fender bender Jonas?*

God. Why had she even sent that? She groaned just thinking about it. She had been trying to be chill and carefree, like someone you might want to be friends with. It had failed. *Epically* failed. Now Brennan wanted to crawl into a hole (a deep one) and not come out for a long, long time (until the memory of this humiliation faded, which would probably be never, considering how often her past humiliations came back to haunt her).

She'd almost decided that she could never bear seeing Jonas again when, suddenly, her phone buzzed with a new message. Are you constantly going to remind me of that? Brennan stared stupidly at her phone. What did one do next, after having one's weird message answered by a boy one hardly knew who somehow made one feel like talking?

She opened her messages and read his message again. *Are you constantly going to remind me of that?* Jonas sounded as irritated as he would have been in real life. Brennan almost laughed at the thought.

She tried to think of a witty reply, but couldn't, so she settled for ignoring the question. I just wanted to let you know that the dent popped out.

Silence, and then the three dots that meant he was typing. He typed for a while, then stopped. Then just sent: So you said.

Well . . . I guess now you know.

It took a few moments before Jonas responded again. She had started to think he really was ignoring her now. Look, what do you want?

What did she want? She wanted to feel like she had the other day at the deli, when she'd talked to him about cheeses. Maybe she didn't particularly want to talk about cheeses again, but the part where she had held a normal conversation in which she thought she *might* have been even one iota more witty than usual; she wanted that part.

I'm not really sure, she typed. Backspaced. I just wanted someone to talk to. Lame, right? Delete. She didn't know what to type next. How's your knee injury? she sent.

He didn't respond for a while, and she wanted to curl into

herself—shrink smaller and smaller until she just wasn't there anymore. She read her text over and over a few times. *It's none of your business!* her anxiety shouted.

Look, a new message from Jonas made her phone buzz. To be honest, why does it matter to you? You don't actually know me. You don't need to feel obligated to ask how I'm doing or anything.

Well, you kind of did rear-end my car. And we've talked a couple of times since then, so I would say we know each other a little bit. Actually, I'm Facebook friends with some people from my high school who I know less than that about.

Again with the car thing. I offered to pay. I'd love it if you'd stop throwing it back in my face.

She frowned. It was a joke. Send.

No response, but he'd definitely seen it—read Monday, 8:42 p.m. It was as if he was taking his time to think of a response. *If* he responded at all.

The dent came out, she sent, unable to sit there with the yawning digital silence.

From downstairs her mom yelled, "Brennan, are you on that computer again?"

"No, Mom!" Brennan yelled. "Talking to a friend!"

"Online again? You need to get out of the house more! The more you stay barricaded in your room, the worse that anxiety of yours will get." Brennan squeezed her eyes shut.

Eventually, Jonas replied and her phone buzzed. So you said. Again.

Brennan sighed, unsure how to continue the conversation. From downstairs her mom yelled again. "Do you hear me, Brennan?"

"Yes, Mom!" Brennan's mom didn't yell again, so Brennan deemed it safe to send Jonas another message. What are you doing?

Jonas typed back quickly this time. Trying to ignore you so I can concentrate on *Star Wars*.

And then I guess that could be construed as rude. Sorry. Let me try again. I'm watching *Star Wars*. Brennan liked that he knew how to use *construed* in the proper context.

You enjoy *Star Wars*? she typed. I've never watched it. My dad and my brother, Ayden, are huge fans though.

You should watch it. You don't know what you're missing.

Just out of curiosity, how many times have you seen the *Star Wars* movies?

A few minutes later: Too many to count. Let's just say that I've had a lot of spare time on my hands this past year.

Brennan was curious as to what that meant, but she shrugged and responded with I guess I'll leave you to your *Star Wars*.

After she thought he'd stopped replying for good, she got a response. Thank you.

She liked the fact that she could picture him, his face completely deadpan, his tone flat and sarcastic. In-her-head Jonas was wearing the plaid pajama pants and Wash U sweatshirt he'd been wearing when they first met, and his feathery hair was sticking up in the back the same way it had been that day.

She closed out of her messages and just stared at her phone for a while.

It was weird, Brennan thought, how just talking to someone, outside of work or school, made her buzz. It made her feel normal. It made her feel like there was hope for her making friends in college.

It was also weird that she wanted to keep talking to Jonas, even though he came across as being rather uninterested and unimpressed with her attempts to converse. *Why do you always do this?* her brain chastised her. *You can't just let people alone. You'll try to fix the way they think about you, and you'll push and push and push—pursue their good opinion until they just see you as stubborn. Clingy. A-N-N-O-Y-I-N-G.*

9

JONAS

The next day found Jonas spending his time moping around the house. His brother was gone (as usual), Taylor was still at camp, and his dad was at work. That left his mom, who was off for the day. That didn't stop her from working, though; she was scrubbing the entire house from top to bottom, her hair tied up and apron on. Jonas watched her. She used to dance in the kitchen when she cleaned the floors, radio on and arms swaying in time to the music. Jonas couldn't help but think it was his fault that she didn't anymore. So he sat on the couch, frowning moodily at the turned-off TV.

Jonas's mom seemed to pick up on his bad mood and didn't really engage him, whether to remind him of his doctor's appointment later that day (the one he didn't want to go to at all) or to suggest some other activity (that involved leaving the house).

He didn't feel like being in his room all day, which was strange, because there was usually no place he enjoyed being more. He didn't really feel up to going out, and his leg hurt, but he didn't feel like doing nothing.

It was strange. Since he had gone out, since he had given himself the chance to see that he could indeed successfully leave the house, he'd stopped being completely content to stay inside. Like, since he'd given it a chance, it had ruined his contentment with doing nothing.

The only problem was that he wasn't quite ready to admit that to himself yet, so here he was, camped out in the living room, his own personal compromise between hiding in his bedroom and going out.

Eventually, his mom put away her apron and grabbed her purse and keys. "Time to go," she said hesitantly, watching him from the door. Jonas wordlessly got up and retrieved his crutches. He'd chosen to wear the prosthetic leg—he'd been wearing it more and more lately because he'd become almost addicted to the visual representation of having two legs; taking the leg off at night was kind of depressing now—but he still wasn't going to actually walk on it.

"I've got to go to the grocery store afterward," Jonas's mom said. "If you don't want to go, you could always drive yourself to the doctor's?" She sounded like she'd rather take him to see the doctor and then drag him around the grocery store as well.

"No," Jonas shook his head. "I'd rather not drive."

"All right," she said, nodding and heading out the door. Jonas followed her and got into the passenger seat of her van (which was nicer than the Bus: newer, and with air conditioning). He stared out the window as they drove, the trees and the buildings blurring into smears of color as they eventually picked up speed on the highway and headed downtown.

When they reached the doctor's office, his mom came around to open the passenger-side door for him.

"I'm not an invalid," he snapped, probably too harshly, he thought, judging by the hurt look in her eyes.

"I know, Bird," his mom said, backing off. She suddenly looked tired again. Jonas hadn't realized she'd been starting to perk up over the past couple of weeks, but the change in her now made it evident. "I was just trying to help," she added softly.

Just, just, always just. "I'm not going to break, Mom." Jonas avoided meeting her eyes as he got out and positioned his crutches, making his way to the door of the doctor's office.

The building was home to many doctors, and many specialists, several of whom Jonas had become familiar with over the last year. It was big—too stark and too clean for Jonas's taste. And it smelled like a hospital, which he hated. (*Funny, since you* were *going to be a doctor.*)

There was a list of things Jonas thought about when he thought about hospitals, and none of them were pleasant:

1. Flashes of lights on the ceiling.
2. The faces of doctors and the sound of his mom crying.
3. The sensation of finally giving in to darkness because that was all his body wanted to do and he couldn't fight it, couldn't fight it anymore.

He hadn't always hated the smell of hospitals; it was an after The Accident thing. A side effect. (Like the not driving and the noticing of people's left feet.)

Back in the present, Jonas eyed the people using the stairs with a frown. He would have used the stairs if he could have. *You should eventually be able to walk almost as before,* his prosthetist had told him when he was first fitted. *With practice, you could even conquer stairs.* Jonas hadn't wanted to conquer anything. He hadn't wanted to *have* to. He had wanted to have his leg back.

They got into the elevator. He pushed the button for the third floor. It was all familiar, all robotic movement. Go through the motions; go home afterward.

They signed in at the front desk.

"Jonas!" The nurse called his name eventually. Jonas wanted to do anything but stand up, force a smile at the nurse, and begin to walk back with her. His mom stood, too, making her way to his side.

She always came for his appointments. She was always there, ready to support him, willing to help if she was needed. He wondered, suddenly, if maybe that was a small part of his problem. Too many people to help him, to pity him; too easy for him to just let them. Maybe he really just needed to help himself. He was leaving for college, after all.

"Mom," he muttered, stopping short. "I-I'd really just rather go alone this time."

"Oh," she said, drawing back her hand from his arm. "Are you sure?" She was frowning, worry in her eyes. Her voice wobbled a bit.

"Yes, Mom," he mumbled. "It's not a big deal. I just want to go by myself. All right? Please don't make it a big deal. It isn't; I promise."

"Yes, all right. Of course." She swallowed and patted his arm in what was supposed to be a gesture of comfort, but really just conveyed to Jonas, along with the glistening of her dark eyes, how upset she was. She wanted to go with him; she wanted to feel useful. He wondered if maybe sometimes she felt like she'd somehow failed as a mother, although that was really the furthest thing from the truth. None of this was her fault. Guilt squeezed his stomach again.

He wanted to comfort his mom, so he turned back at the last second, crutched back to her, and kissed her on the cheek, squeezing her arm. "Okay, Mom?" he asked her.

She smiled slightly, swiping at her face with shuddery hands. "Okay, Bird," she said. "I'll be just out here if you need anything."

"I know," he said, giving her a little smile before turning and following the nurse.

———

Dr. Akeson, Jonas's orthopedic surgeon (aka the one who'd neatened up what remained of Jonas's leg after the metal from the car door had finished with it), was a short man with a balding head and a white beard. He was like Santa Claus, if Santa wore a lab coat and smelled like antiseptic.

"I've been—I've been trying to walk some," Jonas started, uneasily. He'd tried to imagine how the words would feel, how they would taste, when he finally said them. He couldn't quite decide yet if they felt good or bad to say. He looked down at his lap, his fingers absentmindedly tapping his leg just above the prosthetic socket, a nervous tic that came out just about every time he was at a follow-up appointment. He was self-conscious in the hospital gown they always had him wear. He knew it was so they could examine his leg more easily, but he felt cold and a little exposed. He quit tapping and crossed his arms tightly across his chest.

"Really?" said Dr. Akeson, peering at Jonas over his glasses from his chair next to the computer. He made a note of something in Jonas's chart. "That's good news. How is that working out? Are you having any problems with the socket fitting?"

"I-I'm not really sure," he muttered. "It's all a little much. I haven't worked with a prosthesis much since the practice one I wore during those first weeks in physical therapy. To be honest, the main thing that's bothering me is that I've had an increase in pain since I started trying to walk."

"Does the pain mostly happen when you're using the prosthesis or do you have it other times as well?"

Jonas thought about it a bit. "Mostly when I'm wearing it. Occasionally when I'm not, but I always had occasional phantom sensations before, so I guess that's not really new. My leg's been a bit sore; I think it's just because it's not used to bearing weight."

"That would most likely be correct," Dr. Akeson said. "It's usually best to start slow with these things. Work up to it. Can you describe the pain you feel when you wear the prosthesis?"

"It's sort of a shooting pain. Sometimes it feels kind of like a burning sensation, almost. But only when I'm putting weight on it, or sometimes just when I'm wearing it. I don't know if maybe I'm walking wrong, or something. Like a misstep."

He tapped his fingers on his leg again. In the ceiling, the air conditioning kicked on, ruffling Jonas's hair. Dr. Akeson was making another note.

"There are a few possible explanations, but one stands out to me at this time, based on what you've said." He scooted his stool forward a bit and gestured to Jonas's leg. Jonas was used to this, even if it was his least favorite part of being in the doctor's office. He stared straight ahead, refusing to look at his leg as Dr. Akeson shifted the gown and examined the fake leg and the socket, and then took the leg off, examining Jonas's residual limb. He massaged a few places, stopping when Jonas winced in pain. "There it is," the doctor murmured, as if to himself.

"What?" asked Jonas, massaging his leg again. Still not looking at it. *Never looking at it* (if he could help it.)

"I'm thinking it's most likely a neuroma," said his doctor, moving back to make another note on the computer. "Amputees are known to get them, especially in traumatic amputations, as yours was. Think of it like a tangle of hair, except in this case, it's a tangle of nerve endings. It can be sensitive, especially to pressure."

"Can it be fixed?"

"Usually it's as simple as adjusting your prosthesis. In this case, you'll just need another visit with your prosthetist. It would explain why the pain has only started now that you're working on walking. It usually takes a few months after an amputation to show up, and if it hadn't been exposed to pressure, it wouldn't be a cause for concern. But since you've started wearing your prosthesis, it's starting to put some pressure on it."

He nodded toward Jonas's leg. "Does that help?" he asked, watching Jonas massage a particular spot.

"Yes," said Jonas. "It usually does."

"That's good," he nodded. "Massage is one of the ways to relieve pain from a neuroma."

The doctor stood, preparing to leave. "Just make sure to make an appointment with your prosthetist to get your socket refitted. Not only for the neuroma but, as time goes on, the residual limb atrophies a bit and the prosthesis can be too loose." He paused, meeting Jonas's eyes. "Additionally, if you're going to start walking more frequently, it may be a good idea to see a physical therapist again."

Jonas started to protest, but Dr. Akeson held up a hand. "Now I know you didn't like the therapy when you did it after the initial amputation, but it's something I would recommend now. It can be very helpful for amputees to work with someone."

Jonas frowned. Dr. Akeson smiled. "I'm honestly glad to see that you're starting to work toward walking, Jonas," he said. "It's always a good step." He chuckled a little at his own pun, then picked up his papers and opened the door. He stopped one final time. "Follow up in another month," he said. "I'd like to see you one more time before you head off to school."

"Okay," Jonas said. Dr. Akeson left the room, and Jonas got dressed once more, grabbing his crutches and making his way out to his mom, who immediately put down the magazine she was reading and came to his side.

"How'd it go?" she asked, smiling widely.

Jonas forced a smile. "Fine," he said. "He says I should make an appointment with the prosthetist to get the socket fitting adjusted on my leg."

"All right," she said. "We'll do that."

They turned to leave. Once they were on the elevator, his mom turned to look at him. "Are you okay, Jonas?"

"Fine, Mom," he said. Always fine. He was always fine. And then: "Dr. Akeson also thinks I should start physical therapy up again, before I go off to school."

"Really?" she said. "Are you going to try to start walking again?" Jonas could tell she was trying not to sound too hopeful.

"Yeah," he said, nonchalantly, as if this was nothing of consequence. He watched the floor number change as they went down. "I think I might." His mom suddenly stepped forward and wrapped her arms tightly around him, almost knocking him over. He hadn't realized how much taller he had gotten compared to her until she was there, standing a head shorter than him. Everything was so different now.

"Mom?" he asked her hesitantly. "Are you all right?"

"Yes," she said, stepping back and shaking her head, still smiling. "I'm just so proud of you."

He almost rolled his eyes, somewhat embarrassed, but this was his mother. So he smiled instead, hesitantly. The most real smile he'd smiled in quite some time.

They went to the grocery store and he helped her get things off the high shelves instead of just following behind her like last time. When they went to the deli, he nonchalantly glanced around, looking for Brennan—for messy dark hair and big round glasses—but she wasn't there.

10

brennan

Today, it was horrible.

It was on days like these that the anxiety would rise up and grab Brennan by the throat, choking her, making it seem like she couldn't even breathe, let alone open her mouth and force words to come out. She worried that if she did open her mouth, all the sick feeling in her stomach would come out. It washed over her like waves, suppressed one moment, then overwhelming her the next, pulling her back into herself.

So she didn't—open her mouth, that was. She was abnormally quiet, pacing back and forth in her bedroom, trying to distract herself from the churning in her stomach. *Let me GO,* she begged the anxiety that lived in her stomach, her mind. *NEVER,* it retorted.

In these moments, Brennan felt like she was just a body controlled by some parasite inside of her that fed off her emotions. She mentally ticked the counter in her head—Days Since Incident—back to zero.

Anxiety. Brennan hated it; hated the word. She hated when people said it, like it was just her being shy, or nervous, and not something that caused her to lose sleep, to feel sick, and to feel like she couldn't breathe. They said it like they were characters in a story and it was a word that was italicized, emphasized. *Oh. You have* anxiety. Like there were air quotes around the word and it wasn't a real thing. Then they would nod as if in understanding. *This is why she's like this. Weird.* Maybe, in her head, she talked to the wrong people. Someone out there had to understand how she felt.

She wished her body didn't have to have a fight or flight misfire whenever she found something little to be nervous about, because it was destroying what little confidence she had.

She was lucky she was off work today, because it was one of the bad days.

It was a vicious cycle too. Every time she got nervous about something, Brennan started to expect that she would be nervous the next time that circumstance presented itself. She was nervous about being nervous.

And it never ended; it only repeated itself.

Fingers twitching, she yanked open her nightstand drawer and dug around inside, pulling out the white bottle with the paper label firmly affixed to it. *Brennan Davis. One nightly.* Solazepram, or Sol-ER. Only a few of the pills were missing.

TAKE IT, I DARE you, her brain taunted her. *Remember the side effect of nausea? Remember how you got nauseated last time you took it, and then you couldn't sleep that night? And you threw up?*

Brennan set the bottle on the nightstand and squeezed her eyes shut so tightly that she saw little flecks of stars spark across the backs of her eyelids. *That's only because you worked yourself up so much in anticipation that you'd be one of the ones to feel that particular side effect,* logical Brennan retorted. *You expected it, so you felt it. It was all in your head.*

Maybe she should try it again—take the time to get on a schedule and go the weeks required for the levels of the drug to build up and be effective—before school started. But what if it didn't work, and then she had to stop and try to find another med? And it would take a while, because you couldn't stop abruptly; you had to taper your doses over quite some time.

Go on. It doesn't help. I. DARE. YOU.

Brennan smacked the pill bottle off the nightstand and back into the drawer, which she slammed shut. She yanked her covers over her head and curled into a tight ball, pressing a hand to her roiling stomach.

How will I ever be able to survive college? She sniffled. *For that matter, how will I ever be able to be normal? I'm crazy.* Certifiably *crazy.*

She'd never told anyone the *full* extent of her anxiety. It felt okay to mention that sometimes she was nervous about work on random days, for seemingly no reason in particular. It felt all right to say that she was nervous in large crowds, or when meeting new people. She had told her doctor all these things.

What she hadn't told her about was that sometimes she just felt like she couldn't breathe, even if she was just going to the store. Or meeting someone for a lunch out. Or on an elevator alone with someone. Her friends didn't know, because she didn't tell them how she constantly worried about getting food poisoning and throwing up in front of people, so she tried not to eat in public. She didn't tell them how it was depressing to think about the *what if it never goes away* and the *what if nothing changes.*

She couldn't tell them; they'd lose any good opinion of her that they had, wouldn't they? They'd realize how insane she was. They'd look at her strangely, or they wouldn't understand, or both. They'd say, "It's okay! I get nervous sometimes too!" They'd say, "Don't worry! You have nothing to worry about!" Some might shake their heads. "There are people with real problems," they might say. Or, "Just tell yourself not to worry." They didn't understand that she couldn't just shut off her brain. Couldn't just stop her stomach from churning. Couldn't just stop the part of her that was crazy from taking over.

Brennan had always been this way, since she was seven. Off and on, she'd get the anxious periods. Usually, she'd be anxious for about a year, and then it would pass and she'd be fine—maybe for a year, maybe for a year and a half.

Now, in the middle of what had been the longest anxious period of her life so far, Brennan was holding on for the light at the end of the tunnel that had always come before.

The only problem was that it just seemed like it was much farther away than it had ever been.

Brennan felt hot tears burn at her eyes. *Don't cry. Don't cry.*

She was supposed to shadow her aunt tomorrow. She tried not to overthink. And yet, what would she wear? Would she talk to her aunt's patients or just listen to her aunt talk? What would she do with her hands? Fold them in front of her? Or behind her?

Tomorrow, at nine o'clock.

She thought about messaging Emma. Then she thought Emma might think she was crazy for being so nervous about, basically, when it came down to it, spending a day with a family member.

And really, she was crazy.

So messaging Emma was out.

Brennan thought about texting Jonas again, but immediately chided herself for the thought. She wanted to talk to him, but at the same time, she didn't want to be the one to message him first, considering it had been a few days since they'd talked.

She had typed up a message a few times but had always ended up abandoning it, backspacing until all evidence of any attempt was gone.

Besides, an impulse message born of anxiety probably wouldn't make the best impression anyway. Nothing good came out of her anxiety.

She closed her eyes and pictured the expanding circle GIF. *Breathe in. Breathe out. Slow your breathing.*

She heard her door creak open from underneath the covers.

"Brennan?" It was her mom.

"Yes?" she said after a few seconds, her voice tight and quilt muffled.

Brennan heard her mom sigh, and then she sat on the edge of Brennan's bed, the springs creaking a bit. "Are you okay?" she finally asked softly.

Brennan's throat constricted, and tears threatened anew. "Okay," she forced out. "Just anxious." The word tasted bad on her tongue. *Shouldn't be anxious. Shouldn't be.*

Brennan's mom was silent for a few moments. Then, "It gets better, okay? You just take one day at a time. You do what you have to." A beat. "Are you taking your meds?"

"Yes," Brennan lied.

"Don't think about all the bad stuff," said her mom. "Don't think about the worst thing that could happen. Just let life come. Thinking about that stuff won't change anything."

"Okay," Brennan mumbled. She wanted to say she couldn't stop thinking about the bad stuff. About the worst scenario.

But the words stuck, and her mom was leaving the room anyway.

11

JONAS

Jonas sat on the couch while his mom talked on the phone. He'd asked her to call the therapy place that Dr. Akeson had referred him to. His fingers were tapping on his leg again, a rhythm-less pattern on the hard plastic of the prosthetic socket.

The office was located at the north branch of the hospital Dr. Akeson worked at, closer to Jonas's house. The building, from the outside, looked about ten years older than the hospital it sat next to. He'd asked his mom to drive by it on the way home from his appointment the other day.

"She's very good," Dr. Akeson had told him about the therapist. "She's worked with a number of amputee patients recently, with good results, and I think she'll be very helpful."

Jonas had seen the prosthetist earlier that day and gotten the socket adjusted slightly, just enough to take some pressure off what Dr. Akeson thought was a neuroma. So far, so good. A few steps, and pain free—other than some soreness.

"You have a cancellation tomorrow?" his mom said loudly, as if for

Jonas's benefit. She covered the phone receiver and gestured at Jonas. "Is that okay?" she mouthed.

Jonas shrugged and then nodded.

"Great!" his mom said. "Tomorrow at eleven thirty." Jonas zoned out again as she finalized details. Bring crutches, bring the prosthesis, blah, blah, blah. He was tapping again.

He looked out the window and frowned.

He really hoped he wasn't making a mistake.

You have to start sometime. You can't stay here and do this forever, after all.

He sighed and propped his chin on his hand, watching as a neighbor jogged by, earbuds in, oblivious to the world. Jonas followed him down the road with his eyes for a few moments before looking away.

———

The therapist's office was nice, or at least as nice as any other doctor's office Jonas had been to (and surprisingly nice compared to the dated brick of the building's exterior). The walls were decorated with pictures of patients, smiling and happy, assisted by therapists and various physician's assistants. Some were in wheelchairs; some were using walkers. Some were being helped with various exercises. Most of the patients were elderly.

Jonas frowned, looking around, before making his way to the receptionist's desk and signing in on the offered clipboard. He filled out the new patient paperwork and brought it back to the desk, then returned to his spot on one of the sofas in the waiting area.

He'd had his mom drop him off but requested that she not come in with him. He was half afraid that he'd fall or that he'd not be very good at balancing without the crutches or something to lean on, and he didn't really want his mom to be there for that.

He felt a little like there was an extra heart in his throat at the thought of starting therapy again. He tried to stop himself from tapping his fingers against his leg but eventually gave up when he realized he just kept going back to doing it, like his mind wouldn't let him stop.

He got out his phone and absentmindedly checked his email. There were a few from school, a painful reminder that summer would end sooner rather than later. At least if he could walk, people would stare less. His head hurt.

"Jonas Avery?"

He got up, forcing a tight smile as the physical therapist greeted him. He kept his grip tight on his crutches.

"Hi!" she said. "I'm Kim Richards. Dr. Akeson sent your chart over."

"Hi," Jonas said in return, rather lamely. She led him back into the office and to a spacious room set up with a couple of chairs, some parallel bars that Jonas recognized from his first post-accident therapy sessions, and various equipment pieces that he'd never used before.

"I thought we'd start with some basics today," she said. "I know that you've had some therapy sessions before with a temporary prosthesis, but I think that it's best to look at this as a sort of fresh start. I don't want you to come into it with any expectations of yourself based on that previous therapy. It's been quite a while since then and, from what Dr. Akeson has told me, you've mostly just used the crutches."

Jonas nodded. "What do you want me to do?"

"First, I want to talk about what your ultimate goals for these sessions are."

Jonas looked at her in confusion. "I want to walk?" he said, almost like it was a question.

She smiled slightly. "Is that all?" she asked.

He frowned. "What else is there?"

The therapist laughed softly. "Jonas, if you want it badly enough, the sky really is the limit. You can run again—there are even amputees who play sports."

Jonas thought about it for a moment. His head felt a little fuzzy. The therapist was wearing perfume that, ordinarily, wouldn't have bothered him, but which was starting to compound the headache he'd come in with. He decided against getting his hopes up. "Just walking for now," he said. "I think I'll focus on that first."

"That's perfectly fine," she said, not pushing him.

She stood and walked over to the parallel bars, gesturing for him to follow.

Once he did, she took his crutches and leaned them against the wall, letting him use the bar in front of him for support.

"All right," she said. "I assume that you've already learned to balance—to sit and to stand—without the prosthesis on, and without the crutches."

"Yes," said Jonas. "Although I thought we were starting from the beginning?"

Kim smiled. "We are," she said. "With the prosthetic leg. No sense repeating the sitting and standing lessons if you already use them in your day-to-day life."

She brought a walker over and gestured for him to turn so he could face her, and then take hold of the walker, balancing himself with it. She instructed him to transfer his weight from his good leg to both legs, including the prosthesis. He did.

"How does that feel?"

"Okay," he said. "A little sore, but other than that, it feels okay." He'd done this part a few times at home since his visit with Dr. Akeson. Put down the leg, stand on both feet, try to get used to the feeling of dead space from his left thigh down.

"Okay!" Kim bent and adjusted the walker a bit until it was correct for his height. "This is great. Do you ever feel nervous about putting weight on the prosthetic leg?"

"A little," Jonas admitted. He felt like an old person, holding on to the walker. "Sometimes I get this feeling that it won't hold me up, or that it isn't stable enough, like it might buckle." *I can't feel it,* he wanted to say. *It feels dead. It is dead. It's not a leg. Prosthetic. Fake. Not a leg.*

"That's perfectly normal. A lot of amputees need to learn to trust their new leg." (*Leg, leg, leg.*) "It's something different; it takes getting used to." She turned to face him. "Eventually, putting weight on the leg will be second nature."

She picked up her folder. "I think that's all we're going to do today."

"What?" said Jonas, unable to stop himself from sounding incredulous. "That's *it*?"

She smiled, turning to look at him once more. "Learning to walk again is a slow project," she said. "It's important not to go at it too quickly, to avoid injuring yourself. Best to practice putting weight on it and learning to trust the prosthetic leg. I'm going to give you some homework too—I'd like you to start taking some supported steps. Do you have a walker at home?"

Jonas shook his head.

"We'll have you take this one, but you can use your crutches as well." She moved his crutches closer to him, leaning them against the parallel bars so he could reach them. "Basically, you'll support yourself with the walker or your crutches, and practice taking some steps, a few times a day. I also have some pamphlets with some exercises you can do to strengthen your upper body and remaining limbs. It's important that the rest of your body serves as a balance for what's not there anymore. If you'll just wait here, I'll have my assistant bring them in for you, and then she'll take you to the front desk. Same time next week?"

"Yes, I suppose," said Jonas, a confused frown fixed on his face.

"Okay," she said cheerfully. "Just wait a few moments."

Jonas watched over his shoulder until she left the room. When the door closed behind her, he turned back around and looked down at his feet. He had thought maybe he'd leave the office today having at least taken a few steps. He moved the walker forward an inch, then two, stepping in behind it, each step looking more like a limp. He didn't have pain anymore—the prosthetist had fixed that—but it was like walking when your muscles were sore; there was still an ache.

"Jonas?" He heard a surprised voice from behind him.

He hadn't heard the door open, and the voice made him jump, his heart picking up, blood thudding in his ears. He whirled around instinctively, forgetting about his prosthetic leg. He slipped, and reached to grab the walker but missed, falling ungracefully to the floor instead.

He sat there for a moment, eyes closed, his face pricking with heated embarrassment. *First day of therapy—already made a fool of myself. What a precedent.*

"I'm sorry for startling you. I just—I was just surprised to see *you* here."

Jonas opened his eyes to see Brennan leaning over him and watching him with an expression of concern.

"B-Brennan!" He half scuttled backward, bumping into one of his crutches where it leaned against the parallel bars and knocking it to the ground with a loud clatter. His embarrassment mixed with frustration, churning in a potent mass deep in his chest. "What are *you* doing *here*?"

She hesitated, looking slightly hurt. Her eyes found his left ear again. "My aunt," she said. "She's a physical therapist. Well, *the* physical therapist here. Kim Richards? I was shadowing her today, but I was taking a break during your visit. She sent me to give you some pamphlets . . ." Her voice trailed off.

She frowned, looking down at the various materials in her hands. "About exercises for amputees?" Her eyes traveled to Jonas's, the confused look still fixed on her face.

brennan

Jonas glared at her. His eyes were angry and his face was red. The bottom of Brennan's stomach had dropped out, leaving the anxiety free to invade her entire chest. She shouldn't have startled him, shouldn't have even come in.

He reached up and grasped one of the parallel bars for support, pulling himself clumsily up until he was standing, ignoring her when she offered him her hand to help.

Brennan studied Jonas. He didn't *look* like an amputee and hadn't the other times she'd seen him. Her eyes darted to the sweatpants he was wearing. Then again, he'd always worn long pants—if he *did* have a prosthetic leg, she wouldn't have known it. And it would make sense; it would explain what was off about him.

"Jonas?" she said, so quietly it was almost a whisper. He had turned his back on her and didn't seem to hear, so she cleared her throat, eliciting an angry "What?" from him.

"Are you, I mean, are you—" She was tripping over her words. She didn't want to say it aloud because she got the feeling that this—finally, the explanation—was the reason he was so frustrated all the time.

Jonas whirled to face her, much better balanced now that he was back on the crutches. "Am I what?" he snapped. "An *amputee?*" He said it like he was disgusted by it.

Brennan didn't even nod; she was too mortified that she'd created this situation in the first place. She took a step backward. *Stupid, stupid, STUPID,* her brain shouted, until the word rang in her ears like someone was actually shouting into the stillness of the therapy gym.

Jonas was directly in front of her now, glaring down at her. She hadn't quite realized before how tall he really was. It made her want to shrink even more than she already had. "Yes," he snapped. "Yes, I am." He forced a short, bitter laugh. "Now you know my little *secret.*" He shook his head, looking annoyed. Brennan wasn't sure if he was annoyed at her or at himself. *Probably both.*

"Why didn't you tell me?" she said falteringly, as he turned to leave.

"Did you think it would have mattered?" Her mind went to the car accident, and she realized suddenly. "And the fender bender—it wasn't really because you weren't paying attention, was it?"

"No," he said darkly, over his shoulder. "It *was* partly because I wasn't paying attention. But probably not for the reason that you think. And yes, partly, the leg thing. But don't you get it? I didn't want you to know that! I'm tired of the leg being the first thing people notice about me! I'm not just the guy with the missing leg!" Brennan stopped short as his face went slack, like he'd said a little bit more than he'd meant to.

His features hardened, his dark eyebrows drawing low over his eyes. He continued on his way out, and she followed him, trying to convince him not to leave, her words spilling out, one attached to the other in a long stream of blather that felt sort of useless (but she had to try anyway). "You still have to make your appointment for next week! I was supposed to show you to the front desk." She was holding his walker and the pamphlets.

Jonas shook his head, continuing doggedly onward. "I'm not making an appointment for next week. I'll go somewhere else—if I go at all. This has all been a terrible idea. It was a mistake."

"Please." Brennan was begging now, her voice wavering. Tears threatened to spill from her eyes, which was stupid, because she was angry. Angry at herself. Angry at Jonas for giving up so easily. Angry at the fact that she was losing one of her aunt's clients on the first day of shadowing. *ANGRY, not sad,* she yelled at her stupid brain. "My aunt is lovely," she tried. "It's all my fault. Don't blame her. I'll never be here again. If you come back, you can count on that—"

Jonas whirled around once more, causing Brennan to have no choice but to stop short or run face first into him. She tried not to be distracted by all the things she could notice when she was this close to him, like the little crease that formed on his forehead between his eyebrows when he was irritated (always) and how soft his dark hair looked up close. "Listen," he said, his teeth gritted. "Your aunt is fine. But this—this walking thing—it's clearly a mistake. I'm not going to embarrass myself again. So I'm not coming back. Okay?"

Brennan didn't say anything; she didn't trust herself to. She swallowed.

He turned around once more and called for the nurse going down to hold the elevator, before disappearing onto it.

The doors closed with a ding, leaving Brennan standing there, with the pamphlets and the walker in her hands and half the office occupants staring at her. At some point, she became aware of how she must look, watching the elevator like maybe if she watched hard enough, Jonas would step back out.

She snagged a nurse and managed to get out that her aunt's last patient had left without his walker and pamphlets, shoving them clumsily into her hands and watching as the nurse headed off to the stairs to hopefully intercept Jonas.

Her face flushed even hotter as she muttered "Sorry" to the still-watching waiting room occupants and disappeared into the back offices, going immediately to the bathroom to hide from everyone. She closed the lid on the toilet and sat down, hugging her arms and staring at a crack in the tile flooring. She wasn't ready to tell her aunt that she'd just lost one of her patients.

12

JONAS

Hey.

I'm really sorry about today.

Jonas's grip on his phone tightened, the words blurring in a haze of anger. He tossed the phone onto the mattress next to him, ignoring Brennan's message, before turning back to the PlayStation, pressing the controller buttons harder than usual in his frustration. He kept feeling the sensation of sitting on the floor in the therapy gym, hot embarrassment flooding him.

His phone vibrated again. He hit Pause on the game and threw down the controller, picking up the phone and furiously typing back a response, not bothering to read Brennan's last message.

Nothing you can do about it now, so leave me alone. Please.

He tossed the phone down and was just about ready to hit Play once more when it buzzed again. He sighed and picked it up, reading her message.

Are you going to give up on walking just because of me?

Jonas frowned before typing back, None of your business. Leave me alone.

Brennan responded immediately, and he gave up on the game, irritated. That's stupid, she sent him. Then, immediately after, I'm sorry. I just mean . . . you can't give up.

He didn't respond so she sent another message. You're giving up on the chance to walk again because you embarrassed yourself?

I walk just fine. And I'm not embarrassed.

His brow furrowed. *Wasn't embarrassed,* his mind repeated.

You mope around on crutches. It's not the same. And you were embarrassed.

Why have you made it your mission in life to annoy me?

Maybe because you seem like someone who has to be annoyed before they finally decide to do something that's good for them.

Then You should come back to physical therapy.

Jonas rolled his eyes. Why was she so persistent? No, he sent. He glanced at the walker currently leaned against his closet door. He'd thought about using it, but each time he'd pushed the thought away.

If you don't, Brennan sent, I guess I'll just have to send you messages every day until you do. I'll just interrupt your . . . what is it you spend your hours doing . . . watching *Star Wars*?

If you do that, I might have to block your number. And don't insult *Star Wars*. Have you even seen it?

No, I haven't. I'm more of a Harry Potter girl.

Of course you are.

What's that supposed to mean?

Everyone's a Potterhead.

Because they're the best books. You aren't?

I've never read them.

WHAT.

You heard me.

There was no response for a while, and Jonas wondered if maybe she'd finally left him alone. He also wondered why he kind of missed her replies when they didn't come. He had just grabbed his controller again when she messaged him back. He read her message: How have you never read Harry Potter? I just can't believe it. It's like a rite of passage.

You haven't seen *Star Wars*, Jonas pointed out.

You changed the subject though, she typed out. We were talking about you walking.

If I'm content to not walk, who are you to try to change my mind?

Yes, but are you content?

Jonas frowned slightly, his grip on the phone turning white-knuckled. That frustrating little voice inside of him was shouting *No*.

She sent him another message. Did you get your walker?

He didn't respond to either question, and Brennan didn't send him any others the rest of the night.

brennan

The next morning, Brennan rolled over in bed and picked up her phone. Jonas still hadn't responded to her most recent message.

Good morning, she sent him. Have you reconsidered therapy?

A few moments later, sounding just as grouchy as he would if he was sitting across from her on the bed, he typed back. Is this how you normally greet people in the morning?

She let out the breath she'd been holding since she'd seen the three dots indicating that Jonas was typing his response. No. That's just reserved for you.

Lovely, I feel so special.

Brennan turned onto her back, pushing her pillow up against her headboard and adjusting her blankets. She took comfort in the semi-darkness of her room, the morning light filtering through the edges of her blinds.

How'd you lose your leg, anyway, if you don't mind me asking? Now that I know, I've kind of got a thousand burning questions here. She was genuinely curious.

You can't just ask a legless person why they're legless.

Can't you? He didn't respond. Come on. You didn't answer my question.

I thought you said, "If you don't mind me asking," in which case, I do mind. Very much.

Come on. Please? Technically, I could just ask my aunt when I shadow with her later today.

Pretty sure that's some sort of violation of patient privacy.

I won't have to break any privacy laws if you just tell me.

Okay, he sent. And then, It was bitten off by a shark.

You have got to be kidding me.

I was.

Hardy-har-har.

You know how some kids cut their hair when they're little, kind of just to see what happens?

What??

I did that with my leg. I thought it would grow back.

Brennan stifled a laugh, not wanting to interrupt the early-morning quiet and wake her parents. Wow, she typed. You actually have a sense of humor?

Apparently. I'm as surprised as you are. I thought it got cut off with my leg.

You're avoiding my question.

Which one? The "Are you content with not walking" one, or the "What happened to your leg" one?

Both.

Jonas didn't send anything back for a while after that, and Brennan wondered if he'd gone back to ignoring her. She started to feel bad about pressing him. *Stupid Brennan. You can't just press people like that. You'd freak if it was you.*

Finally, the little bubble popped up that showed he was typing. It started, then stopped, then started again—a few times.

She sent him a message instead. I'm sorry for asking, she said.

You're not really going to give up, are you?

One corner of Brennan's mouth quirked up, and she quickly typed her reply. I can, if you want me to. She held her phone, waiting.

She could picture Jonas, with that little crease between his eyebrows, phone in both hands, thinking.

Fine.

Fine?

1. I lost my leg in a car accident.

2. Maybe I'm not.

And a few seconds later

Content, that is.

JONAS

Jonas wondered what Brennan would say. It took her a few minutes, but then, If you're not content, do something about it.

Jonas stared at his phone for a long time before setting it down and looking up at the ceiling, staring at it as if it might give him answers.

Why did Brennan have to be right?

I can't, he typed back. Sent. He put his phone facedown on the nightstand and closed his eyes tightly, pressing into the black static behind them.

brennan

I can't make you walk again. But I think you're lying to yourself if you think you could be happy if you never tried.

Jonas didn't respond. Brennan sighed. She didn't know what else to say. She had all these words spinning around in her mind, but none of them seemed right. The entire conversation was out of her comfort zone. She thought too much. She *always* thought too much. Sometimes she never ended up replying to her messages because she overthought the things she wanted to say, turning them over and over in her head until nothing sounded like it was supposed to. This time—*this* time—she'd told herself not to think; told herself to just respond.

But now that Jonas wasn't messaging her back, she didn't know what to do. Messaging him was good; that was fine. She could usually think of something to say, and she didn't have to make eye contact. Now that everything was going wrong—

She took a breath. In. Out. *Anxiety is a wave. It will recede.*

Another breath. This would be as much of a leap of faith for her as it would be for Jonas.

She typed quickly, not giving herself time to second-guess the words. If you decide that you want to do something other than mope around in your room, come to 418 W Westmor Drive tomorrow morning at eight.

She hit send before she could reread it.

JONAS

Later that night, Jonas scrolled back up to see what the message from Brennan that he hadn't read had said. If you thought it would matter. You know, that you're an amputee. If you thought it would matter to me, I just wanted to let you know that it doesn't.

The internet revealed that 418 West Westmor (a street name that was somewhat comic, in Jonas's opinion) was just about a block away from the library on the north side of town. Was it her house? He couldn't imagine she'd have any reason to send him any other address, but even sending her own felt like a leap, since they hardly knew one another.

Jonas spent the rest of the evening debating whether or not to actually show up. Why could she possibly want him to? *Why does she care so much about this?*

He changed into his pajama pants and a T-shirt and turned the light out, lying on his back and looking at the texture-speckled ceiling. There were still glow-in-the-dark stars stuck there, from when Rhys had put them up as a child. Before Jonas's Great Tragedy. Before he was a teen with one and a half legs. Jonas hadn't taken the time to remove them; now, with the plaster specks, they were their own constellations.

He stared at them, the only pinpoints of light in his otherwise pitch-dark room. To go or not to go?

Most everything in him said not to go. He hardly knew Brennan, anyway. He'd run into her a couple of times, yes, and she'd messaged him, but did he really know anything about her? Enough to trust her with the most vulnerable part of himself?

He finally fell into a restless sleep.

13

brennan

Brennan woke up at seven, unable to sleep. She wondered if Jonas would come. She wondered how she'd feel if he didn't, which was the more likely outcome. She put that one at 90 percent, and the odds of him showing up at 10 percent, lessening by the moment.

Still, she tried to prepare herself for what she'd do if he did show up.

She didn't really know how to act around him. So far, their in-person encounters had only managed to make her look like a bumbling idiot (she had the irrational worry that he might think she was on drugs or something) and had probably served to make him think she was crazy.

She pictured herself making eye contact with Jonas and frowned. She wasn't good with eye contact. She worried that she glanced away too many times when she was involved in conversations. Back and forth, never sure where to direct her gaze.

And then there was the awkward laugh thing. Jonas had probably already noticed that from their other meetings. Brennan had a bad habit of laughing awkwardly at things that weren't funny to either:

1. Fill awkward silence. (Her brain had this annoying habit of trying to fill any silence it came across.)

Or

2. Make up for a lack of response to a comment she had made that she thought was witty. (As if her laughing at her own joke was *less* embarrassing than no one laughing at it.)

Brennan glanced at the clock: *8:03 a.m.*

She sighed. He wasn't coming. In a way, she was disappointed. But in a different way, she was relieved. It took a lot of pressure off of her, at least.

She picked up the stack of library books she had to return, and headed downstairs and out the front door. She had just turned around to lock the door when she heard a car pull up along the street behind her. The van was a familiar dinged Honda Odyssey.

Brennan froze.

She watched in silence as Jonas got out of the passenger side, retrieving his crutches. He said something to whoever had dropped him off, and the van departed. For a few moments, Jonas just stood there, staring at her house with a frown on his face.

Then he seemed to notice her.

The frown didn't go away. If anything, she imagined that his expression soured.

"Um, hi!" she said awkwardly, doing the laugh thing, and a slight wave (she wasn't sure what to do with her hands). *Stop it, Brennan!* her brain scolded her. *Idiot.*

Jonas didn't return her greeting, choosing instead to continue frowning at her. "Well," he eventually said. "I'm here. Now would you consider telling me what I've dragged myself out of bed early and come halfway across town for?"

"To go to the library with me," Brennan blurted. Word vomit. It was about as attractive as it sounded.

She hadn't really thought about what they'd do if he did come. At the moment, it was just a half-formed plan to get him to walk somewhere. She had thought that could be a good start, especially since it was so close that she could see the building from her house.

Jonas's frown deepened. "You're kidding me, right?"

"No," she said, a little more firmly. "I'm not. You're going to walk to the library."

He scoffed. "Yeah, good luck with that," he said, turning back to the street. "I told Rhys to drive around the block to make sure I wasn't going to need a ride home immediately," he muttered.

"Come on!" she begged, feeling a little desperate. She had to fix this. Had to fix the version of her in his mind that, right now, was no doubt very poor. "Just give it a shot. And if you don't like how you feel afterward, then you never have to do it again. And I'll—" She hesitated. "I'll never bother you about it again."

He turned around slowly and raised an eyebrow skeptically. "You'll never bother me about walking again? If I walk to the library."

Brennan bit the inside of her cheek and nodded, anxiously awaiting Jonas's response. He seemed to be considering this. Finally he nodded slowly. "Okay," he said flatly. "I'll walk to the library. On two conditions." He gritted his teeth, a muscle twitching in his jaw. "One, you keep your promise to never bother me about the whole walking thing again. And two, I don't have to walk *back*."

"That's fair," she said. "Walking there would be enough. You can't wear yourself out on the first outing, anyway."

The silver minivan drove back down the road. Jonas waved it on. "First and last," he immediately corrected her before frowning again. "All right," he said slowly, as she came to stand next to him on the sidewalk. Up close, she could see how tense he was in the clench of his hands around the crutches and the set of his jaw. "I guess—I mean—"

Brennan recognized the expression on his face—the I'm-about-to-internally-combust look—as the same one she wore when she started running scenarios in her mind, trying to find the *out*.

Jonas met her gaze for a few moments, and she found that she couldn't look away. She briefly wondered if she should look away, reduce the awkwardness between them. As quickly as it began, it ended, and Jonas looked away, frowning, before carefully extending his left foot—the one Brennan now knew was a prosthesis—to rest on the ground next to his right.

For the first few steps of their venture, they were silent. Jonas stared straight ahead, continuing doggedly onward, one foot in front of the other. She noticed that his gait was slightly uneven, like limping, and he favored his remaining good leg and tended to lean on the crutches, as if he didn't quite trust the prosthesis to carry him.

Their progress was slow, and the silence between them was as heavy as the humidity. Brennan wanted to say something, only for the sake of filling the space, but she couldn't think of anything that wouldn't sound stupid. *So, how's your day*, and *What do you think of the weather* seemed like dumb conversation starters in this instance.

Suddenly, one house down from hers, Jonas stopped short. "Stop making it so awkward!" he snapped, shooting a sideways glare at her.

"I'm not trying to!" she said.

"You keep staring at me like I might trip and fall or something if you don't! I don't *want* you to watch how I walk! That's half the reason I hated physical therapy when I did it after the accident!"

"I'm sorry!" she apologized. "I was just—" She couldn't think of any excuse. He was right. She looked away even though she still wasn't convinced that he wouldn't trip over a sidewalk crack or something.

Jonas rolled his eyes before continuing on. He seemed to be trying to make his steps more even, imitating the way his right leg moved with his left. He stared at the ground, watching his feet carefully as they moved.

Brennan found herself watching her own feet, suddenly aware of them. She tried to imagine not having one of them. They went on in silence for a few more steps before she spoke. "So I thought that once we got to the library, I could convince you to read Harry Potter."

"Ha, no." Jonas sounded slightly breathless. She wasn't sure if it was because his leg was hurting or just that walking with two feet was tiring.

"Why not?"

"I'm just not that interested. It's always seemed to me like something everyone just reads because it's just what everyone does. For the *experience* or something."

"You're horrible."

"Because I won't read Harry Potter?"

"Because you're so skeptical of everything."

Jonas's jaw tightened again. "Being skeptical of Harry Potter translates to everything?"

"Harry Potter, the walking thing, me." Brennan glanced sideways at him. There was that tuft of hair sticking up from the back of his head again. She really wanted to smooth it down.

She heard his breath catch as he stepped on a rock with his prosthetic foot and stumbled a bit, catching himself with the crutches and stopping. He closed his eyes for a moment, his jaw tightening.

"Are you—"

"Fine," he cut her off and continued doggedly onward.

"Okay," she said, just as she tripped a bit over her own foot, too busy watching him again. Her face flamed. "I guess maybe I'm not the best-qualified person to help you walk again."

She thought he might have almost laughed.

JONAS

Jonas hadn't really been sure how he'd feel after the walk to the library was over. He hadn't been sure about going in the first place; part of him wanted Brennan to make good on her promise to never bother him about walking again, but another part of him figured that this was a chance to try walking with no strings attached. After all, he'd just made the condition that he didn't have to walk again if he went this once.

What he was sure of, however, was that he had *not* expected to *want* to do it again. He almost felt *giddy*.

And sure, he could look back and see Brennan's house from the library, and it wasn't that long of a distance, but it was *something* and he'd walked *the whole way there* (albeit with the crutches for support, but still—*both feet on the ground*).

They were inside now. The air conditioning felt good on his sweaty face, cool fingers brushing away the humidity from outside. Jonas didn't want to admit how much of an exertion the short walk had been for him, so he followed Brennan around without complaint.

Right now, they were walking through the teen fiction aisles, and Brennan was trying to pick out a book for herself. Or at least that was what Jonas thought she was doing—until she came to a stop and pulled a book off the shelf, whirling around and handing it to him proudly.

He frowned, taking it from her. He met her eyes and raised an eyebrow.

"Come on!" she coaxed. "Give it a chance?"

Jonas rolled his eyes. "All right," he sighed. "I give in."

Brennan turned around, heading on her way, pulling a book off the shelf here and there to read the back cover.

He stood there, holding *Harry Potter and the Sorcerer's Stone* and watching her. She looked so happy here, among the books, like she was in her element. Like she could shrug off the layers of awkwardness and the shyness that seemed to hang over her and feel comfortable. Like at the fender bender, the grocery store, and the therapist's office, she was Brennan shining at half wattage, and here she was, Brennan at full brightness.

And Jonas knew that she wasn't one to feel comfortable easily. He could tell how awkward she was walking with him. It was like she didn't know how to react to him, whether to watch him, to offer him help, or to simply pretend everything was normal even though they were walking down the sidewalk at a snail's pace. She didn't know, and she wasn't good at hiding that.

The weird thing was, Jonas didn't actually mind, with her. He'd minded before, with other people at school he used to hang out with, if they didn't know how to react around him, or what to say to him. It made him feel out of place, lacking. With Brennan, for some reason, it wasn't like that. He got the impression that she acted like that with everyone. It was weird, because it was almost *endearing*. He shook his head, dazedly. Brennan had *endeared* herself to him.

Brennan had also left him behind, too engrossed in picking out books to recognize that he'd stopped.

Jonas, left alone in a back aisle, slumped down in the chair at the end and waited for her, stretching out and resting his legs, crutches propped against the wall.

Soon, Brennan returned, holding a pile of five or six books.

"Wanna sit for a while?" she asked him, seeming to perceive how tired the expedition had made him. He wasn't conditioned for walking on two legs yet—or one and a half plus the crutches, whatever.

"Sure," he said, as if it was just as much for her benefit as his own, and grateful that she had asked. He wouldn't have said anything, or complained, but he was happy for the chance to have a break.

She sat down, leaning against the wall and setting her pile of books next to her.

"So," she said. "Walking—was it okay?"

He shrugged, trying not to show her how much he'd actually enjoyed it, but no longer able to keep a small smile from tugging at the corners of his mouth. "It was okay," he said.

And Brennan smiled.

14

brennan

Brennan thought she might write the summary today. She felt better about her story than she had in a long time. She'd even decided on a name—*Superioris*—Latin for superior, and the name of the oppressive government in the story.

She started to read over the scene she had just written.

> The first time Ing realized that Ambivalents were once considered the normal ones was when she was at Thorn's shop and found a box of old comics in a broken refrigerator. Since most of Thorn's regular customers couldn't read, he'd given the beat-up cardboard box with its treasure trove of stories about heroes like Batman, Thor, and Iron Man to her. She'd carted it home to her apartment on the twentieth floor of the building with the blue door, on the corner of Memorial and Twentieth.
>
> She'd read through all the stories, using a flashlight and batteries she'd gotten from Thorn two years ago, to comb over them even after the power went out for curfew. Afterward,

she stuck the covers of her favorites up on the wall of her tiny, squarish room.

In all the comics, it struck her that the people with abilities weren't the ones who were normal in the stories. They were sometimes even feared because they were *different. And all the citizens of Earth who were "normal," the ones who populated the cities that the heroes saved, didn't seem to have powers. They seemed Ambivalent, like her.*

Brennan's phone vibrated and she lost her place in her document.
Hey.

Jonas. Brennan couldn't think of anyone else it would be anyway; she could list the people who texted her on one hand (her mom, her dad, her brother, Emma, and her grandma).

Hi, she sent, ignoring the fact that his text had set her stomach on edge. What are you doing?

Being bored, he typed back. I don't have Wi-Fi right now, and my parents think we can survive on three gigs of data a month between five people. So anything online is out.

Where are you that doesn't have Wi-Fi?

The doctor's office, Jonas said after a while. And they do have Wi-Fi, but you need a password, and I didn't really fancy asking the receptionist for it.

You sound like me. I hate places where you have to ask for the password.

Talking. Ugh, am I right?

Brennan smiled slightly. Why are you at the doctor's office? We didn't hurt your leg by walking, did we?

No, leg is fine. This is a different doctor, not my orthopedic surgeon. It's just for a physical. You know, the annoying ones you have to get every year before you go off to school.

After a moment, he sent another message. So. About Harry Potter?

Yes? Brennan held her breath, somehow anxious to know what he had thought about the first book in her favorite series. She didn't know why, but it really mattered to her what he thought. It always mattered to her what people thought of the things she liked, but for some reason, this mattered more—like Jonas's opinion mattered more.

I concede defeat. Brennan liked when he talked like that—when he used words any other person might not use in a mere text. Maybe it was stupid of her. It was good. Finished it just a few minutes ago. Which is why I'm texting you; I no longer had anything to do but sit and stare at my feet, of which I'm short one. So, as you can imagine, that got boring pretty quickly.

So you're going to get the second book then?

Yes.

And then: A resounding yes. Right after this appointment.

He didn't say anything after that, and Brennan wondered if he was waiting for her to say something. Finally, he sent her another message.

I was kind of wondering if you wanted to meet me at your house again and, you know . . . She liked that he used ellipses in texting. It reminded her of herself. She loved ellipses. They were like the equivalent of the breaths between phrases when you were talking in real life.

Walk? she asked, as if she didn't know. She could picture him rolling his eyes. It made her fight a stupid grin.

Yes, that.

She really grinned then. Of course. Tomorrow? Same time? 1432 N. Winchester.

Tomorrow, he agreed, not even questioning the new address. Maybe he trusted her.

And then, I hate the doctor's office. It always takes them so long to call me back.

And, in quick succession: What are you doing right now?

I was writing, but you sort of put a stop to that.

Writing? Like . . . stories? Or to-do lists? There were those ellipses again. She almost wanted to tell him how much she liked them.

Stories, she said.

About what?

She should have known he'd ask that. *You can't tell him,* anxiety argued. *You can't tell him, because he'll think it's weird. Or he'll say it doesn't sound good.*

About . . . well, it's a book I've been thinking about for a long time. You know like . . . extroverts and introverts?

Yes.

Well, one day I just had this idea of extroverts having physical powers. Like strength or superspeed. The introverts would have mind powers, like mind reading and telekinesis. I've moved away from personality types though. They're Intros and Extros. That's just how I came up with the idea. Anyway, I know it's kind of a weird idea, but that's what I've been working on for a while now.

No, typed back Jonas. Then, I don't think it's weird. I think it sounds cool. Tell me more.

And she wanted to, for the first time. The main character, Ingrid Wei, is an Ambivalent. In the story, it means that she doesn't have any powers. But Ambivalents are suppressed by the government—the Superioris. So Ing has pretended to be an Intro for her entire life. And now she's reached the age where she has to put her name in for the government's Santos Game . . . sorry, it probably sounds silly. She wondered if he thought it sounded weird. In her head, it was great, the stuff of literary prizes. But outside of her head—in the open—it was like a freaking kindergartener's attempt at putting words on paper.

I promise I don't think it sounds silly, Jonas's reply interrupted her thoughts.

It's okay if you do. Sometimes I think even my parents do. They have this kind of smile-and-nod-and-pretend-to-be-supportive face that they get when I talk about it.

I really don't. I think it's cool. That you write.

You do? You actually do, and you're not lying to me?

Do I strike you as the type of person to lie?

Well, you did sort of lie to me the first few times we met. You know, I went around thinking you were a normal person with two good legs, but here you are, with one and a half.

That was a low blow.

Brennan's smile faded. *Oh no,* she thought. She quickly typed a response. I didn't mean it that way, she said. I only meant to joke about the fact that you did lie to me the first few times we met.

Calm down, he replied. I wasn't being serious. I knew what you meant.

Like she was supposed to know that—to read between the electronic words and somehow gauge what Jonas was thinking when he typed them. She had a hard time telling when he was being serious or when he was just kidding; his dry sense of humor and sarcasm confused her. *He* confused her. At that moment, she was terribly conscious of the great space between their brains—the totally-differentness of her and Jonas.

Brennan?

Brennan shook her head, clearing it. Yeah?

You all right? I really wasn't upset.

Yeah, she said. I didn't think you were.

15

brennan

1432 North Winchester was a Walmart.

Brennan tried to tell her brain, which was currently telling her stomach that it should be sick and that the world was somehow ending, to *shut up*.

"What am I supposed to be seeing?"

Brennan stared at the Enter sign above the door. *Can't let him see how nervous you are; it's just a store. You'll be fine, you're always fine, YOU'RE FINE.* She cleared her throat. Aloud, she said, "You're not supposed to be seeing anything, necessarily. It's just a Walmart. It's like any other Walmart in America."

Jonas frowned. "Then why are we here?"

She finally smiled, just slightly. "Because Walmart is, like, the least judgiest place in the world. *And,* before you ask, I do know that judgiest isn't a word."

Jonas scoffed. "You're the writer, after all," he quipped.

Brennan turned to look at him. "Anyway, I thought we could walk places other than the library."

He shrugged. "Lead the way." She couldn't help but notice the tense set of his shoulders today, even through her own haze of anxiety.

They went inside. Brennan was a little distracted. She was busy thinking about college, thinking about it more than usual. Her mom was taking her shopping for stuff for her dorm room later in the afternoon, after she got back from her trip with Jonas. *I'm hanging out with a friend this morning,* she'd told her. *Would the afternoon work?* Really, it was the last thing Brennan wanted to do. Her whole college application process, the whole summer up to this point, had felt like it was happening to someone else. Now it was starting to feel real, and she hated it. Ambreen was even messaging her.

From Ambreen, just that morning: ONLY A COUPLE MORE WEEKS. I'M EXCITED. ARE YOU EXCITED?

Brennan had sent back YES, even though her mind was shouting *NO.*

She thought about telling Jonas but she reminded herself of the Walls. When she put them up, no one could truly get through, and she was safe. She couldn't be constantly worrying that she'd drag someone else into her mess, so she kept the Walls up, because the Walls meant that she didn't have to feel guilty.

Speaking of Jonas—"What's with you today?"

She turned absentmindedly, and frowned at him. "What?"

He rolled his eyes, concentrating on his next few steps. He was using the walker today (Brennan didn't have the heart to tell him it made him look like an old man, because he would probably think of it as an insult, even though she thought it was kind of cute). She could tell he was a bit more tired and sore than the last time they'd walked, but as he wasn't complaining, she didn't suggest that perhaps he was overdoing it (too much too soon, or whatever it was her aunt would say). "You look like you're not quite all here," he finally said, turning slightly to look at her.

She sighed. "I'm just thinking." She was carrying the crutches so that after he'd walked a bit he could go back to using them and rest his leg. She put them underneath her arms and swung forward a step.

He remained silent, but she got the feeling he was waiting for her to continue.

"About going off to college," she said. The sick feeling was gnawing at her stomach again, having escaped its neat little knot. She tried to push it away and not think about it. She knew if she did, she'd only feel more sick, and she didn't want to ruin their Walmart run with her nerves.

"I guess that's pretty normal," he said. "I worry about it too."

"Not like me," she mumbled.

"How do you worry about it then?" he asked.

"Sometimes—sometimes I worry so much that I feel sick," she muttered, embarrassed. She was always embarrassed when she tried to describe her anxiety. It always sounded stupid when she said it out loud. *Sorry, I just have to check my pulse because right now I can't breathe and it's freaking me out; I have to make sure everything is okay.* That was the problem. Everything big and unconquerable inside her seemed insignificant when she put it out there. She didn't want to let people know how crazy she was on the inside, but she hated that if she, for some reason, wanted to tell them, she couldn't find the words to express it sufficiently.

Jonas looked like he was trying to understand. "Like how you'd feel sick before a sports game if you were nervous?" he said.

"Yeah," she said. "Kind of like that." She swallowed hard. "Except all the time." She didn't want to tell him that it wasn't a normal day for her if she didn't feel nervous at least once.

"All the time," he repeated, as if attempting to wrap his mind around it.

"It's never going to be as bad as you think," he finally said, turning his head slightly to watch her. They were in the men's T-shirt section. Brennan halfheartedly pretended to examine a T-shirt with a bowl of ramen noodles on it. Send noods, it said.

"I hope that's the case," she finally said.

"Where are you going to school?" he asked her.

"Southern Illinois University Edwardsville," she said. "I'm planning on working toward getting into physical therapy school."

"Can I give you a suggestion?"

"Yeah, I mean, I guess. What is it?"

Jonas deadpanned. "Don't sneak up behind your patients when their backs are turned." His face read *serious*, but his eyes read *teasing*. Brennan wondered how someone's face could be so contradictory.

She laughed shortly, picturing the surprised look on his face when he'd seen her at her aunt's office. "I'll keep that in mind."

She picked up a shirt. "Here," she said, handing it to him.

"What's this?" Jonas unfolded the T-shirt Brennan had placed in his hands.

"A commemoration," she said. "For going into Walmart *walking* for the first time since your accident. I guess I thought you should celebrate it somehow. Have something to remind yourself of what you did." Jonas was staring at her. Brennan's face hummed with heat. "Or don't. Whatever." She shrugged and turned away, her hands tight on the crutches.

Jonas held up the shirt. It was a nice shirt, decorated with a retro-ish *Star Wars* logo.

Brennan wondered if she was imagining that his face turned a little red. "It's just going to a Walmart, you know," he said.

She shrugged. "It's more than that for you."

He was silent for a few moments as Brennan busied herself looking at the other T-shirts. "I don't think you have anything to worry about, you know?" he finally said. "For school? You're persistent enough. You got me to walk, after all. Well—sort of. Not many people can go off to school and say they've already had a real patient."

Brennan blushed. "You're not my patient."

"What would you call this then?" he asked. "This thing."

She thought about it. She'd started out thinking of him almost as (and she hated to admit it) her charity case. Like she'd taken him under her wing, convinced of her ability to give him a new outlook on life. But now?

She was surprised at the answer.

"You're my friend," she said simply. Which was weird, because Brennan didn't have many people who she genuinely thought of as friends. It felt nice. It felt like she was almost normal. The Walls, however, seemed like they were shouting at her, reminding her of why she'd put them up in the first place. And her mind was screaming *WHAT ARE YOU DOING. You're making yourself vulnerable! You can't admit things like this!*

Jonas watched her face for a moment, as if he was thinking, and then he smiled. Then he turned away so she couldn't see his face and continued on. The fact that he had actually smiled made her smile, too, and she almost forgot about the Walls for a few moments.

16

JONAS

The next day was a workday for Brennan.

Which, for Jonas, meant no address in his messages. No walking. At least, not with her. He supposed he could do it by himself, if he really wanted to. Did he want to?

Thinking about the implications of walking on his own instead of someone else making him do it was hard, so he instead spent the first half of the day in his room reading *Harry Potter and the Chamber of Secrets* until he finished it and there wasn't anything left to read.

He sighed and set the book next to him on the bed, looking at the ceiling (suddenly conscious of how often he found himself looking at the same ceiling—at its constellations of stars and plaster). Before, he'd have been fine with this. This would have been a good day.

Now, however, it was like his eyes had been opened to the possibility of *more*—of walking places, of going places, of doing *things* outside of his own house.

He had this thought, which he liked to push down and hide— it was basically that he wondered about the implications of reaching normal again. Like, now that things were different (and they were so vastly different than before), normal might not be so good, because it would never be the normal of before.

New normal < Old normal.

Plus, he had this choking feeling that reaching normal just gave bad things another excuse to happen. Like finding normal and being content with his life was just *asking* for something to come along and mess it all up. But at the same time, he ached for it (for normal). *Normal, normal, normal.*

Dumb Brennan, making him discontent with his life.

He didn't need friends.

He needed a new start, off at college.

So why was his mind saying *Forget fresh starts* and telling him to go to the dumb grocery store?

First, he convinced Rhys to give him a ride. Then he texted his mom: You know how you were going to get stamps after work today? I can stop by the store and get them for you.

She texted him back in surprise. Really? You'd do that?

Sure, he said.

She sent back a heart emoji and a smiley face. There's money in the top left drawer of your dad's desk.

A pause, and then—Be careful, okay? I love you, Jonas. She didn't say anything else, and part of Jonas knew that she didn't want to say anything that might discourage him from going out.

He rolled his eyes a little but smiled all the same. She hadn't called him Bird. Before The Accident, she hadn't called him by his childhood nickname in a while. He had been growing up. After The Accident, Jonas and Bird were synonymous. Maybe she was letting him grow up again. Maybe that was good. I love you, too, Mom.

brennan

Coming back to work after a weekend, or after being off for a few days, was always the worst. Brennan felt especially sick on those days.

Right now, she was having a hard time forcing words out past the sick feeling in the back of her throat. Her heartbeat pulsed, thudding against her ribs and in her ears. It was almost her break. Just twenty more minutes she had to get through, and then she could escape out to her car for fifteen minutes, away from people. She could calm herself, put herself back together somewhat for the rest of her shift. *Just twenty more minutes.*

So she smiled as she greeted customers and forced her voice to sound seminormal when she asked how she could help them.

She got a brief moment's respite when she went into the back cooler to get a new block of Muenster cheese. She shut the door until it was open just a crack, and then she closed her eyes, breathing in the frigid air. The sound of the cooling system filled her ears until it was all she could hear. Cold air always helped her, like it brought her back to reality. She could have stood there in the cooler for hours, if they'd let her.

Well, maybe not hours (it was pretty cold), but a long time. Long minutes, maybe.

Brennan steeled herself once more and exited the cooler carrying the cheese, her smile pasted back on her face once more. Brennan, packaged pretty to hide the mess inside.

"Brennan!"

She jumped at the sound of her name, hoping it wasn't some person from high school, come to pretend they'd been the best of friends even though said person had hardly bothered to get to know her. At least they couldn't awkward hug over the deli counter.

It was Jonas, standing at the counter, eyeing some salad or another in the deli case with a look of displeasure. She was surprised to see him, especially without his crutches. He had the walker, though, and she noticed he looked vaguely uncomfortable with the idea of being out in the middle of the store, alone, with it.

"Jonas?" she breathed, her anxiety momentarily vanishing in her surprise at seeing him here, at the deli, *and without crutches.* At that moment, she thought she might have been okay with awkward hugging him.

"You sound surprised," he said drily. "Who'd you expect? The queen of England? Harry Potter in the flesh?"

Brennan rolled her eyes. "I just didn't expect you to come here." *To come see her.* Had he come to see her? "You know." She cleared her throat. "Without the crutches."

Jonas frowned at some kid who was staring at the walker curiously. Brennan almost wanted to tell him to be nicer but refrained. Jonas was just being Jonas. At least his old-man grouchiness matched his old-man walker. "Well," he said, turning back to her. "Yeah." She wondered if she imagined the uneasiness in the way he glanced around at the surrounding customers. It reminded her of, well, her—like he was suspicious that everyone around was looking at him.

Brennan was about to ask if he was all right when she noticed the line of customers that was forming behind him.

Her smile faded, the nerves coming back suddenly, like they'd only retreated momentarily and were now waging a full attack once more. "I'm still on duty," she said. "I've got to help customers. I have a break in ten minutes though—"

"And you've got a customer now," Jonas interrupted. "One pound of honey-roasted turkey, sliced on a two—that's what you deli folks say, right?" She nodded, trying her best not to stare at Jonas. He continued. "One pound of Black Forest ham, sliced the same, and a half pound each of provolone and Muenster. Sandwich slices."

"Couldn't you have made it *more* complicated?"

"Hey, now," said Jonas, pretending to admonish her. "It's only four things. It's what my mom always gets."

"Sure enough," she said as she started to slice the turkey.

By the time she finished with his order, it was time for her break.

"Now keep it in the deli case until I'm done shopping," Jonas ordered, feigning importance. "And by shopping, clearly I mean bothering you on your break."

Brennan half laughed and placed the packaged meats and cheeses in the deli case, out of sight, where they stored things for customers who had ordered and then gone off to shop while their order was being prepared.

She came around the counter then, and they walked toward the front door of the store. She still needed to get out of the building.

Jonas seemed not to question why she was making a beeline for the front doors. He walked along with her and she slowed her pace to match his better, trying not to rush ahead in anticipation of being outside. She hadn't realized before how slowly he was actually moving. Before, it hadn't mattered. Now, her mind was screaming at her to bolt.

They left through the sliding doors, crossing the divide between the cool air conditioning inside and the heat outside. Brennan collapsed into a chair that was part of a patio set for sale in front of the store. She felt better outside. Less panicked. Like her mind opened up with the space around her. Jonas sat down in the other chair, stretching out and resting his arms on the chair's armrests.

Brennan found herself watching him out of the corner of her eye. His hair looked shorter and less messy, like maybe he'd gotten a haircut. He was watching the other people in the parking lot with a frown on his face (but not a frown-ier frown than normal, Brennan observed).

Eventually, he picked up an abandoned store advertisement someone had left on the patio table and started fanning himself with it. "As if ninety-degree heat wasn't enough," he complained, "today we had to have ninety percent humidity as well."

Brennan sighed, swiping a hand over her forehead, which was already sweaty. She felt Jonas kick her leg, and she looked up, startled. He handed her half of the ad. She started fanning herself.

"Why don't you sit inside?" he asked her, like he'd been waiting to ask her for a while but had been trying to be tactful. "Do they not have a break room for you?"

"They do. It's nice. It's just that sometimes I need to get *out*, you know?"

He looked like he didn't quite know, but he nodded anyway. "I finished the second Harry Potter book," he told her, after a few moments.

"Oh? Did you like it?"

"Yes. I need the third one now, but I don't have anyone to make me walk to the library."

She sighed. "That's a shame. I work the rest of the week. And then I'm done." She swallowed hard, suddenly aware of the fact that college really was almost here. It was that terrifying feeling that college was *real* and she was about to have to face it. "I have the next week to prepare for school and then I leave," she said a little flatly, like she couldn't believe it. She bit her lip, absentmindedly tapping her foot. It was really just a week? It seemed like she should have longer.

"I can't believe it's time already. I feel like just yesterday, I was in middle school," Jonas said, frowning. "It feels like there should be so much more time. Like life should have so much more time. But we just sit here and wonder where it goes." He caught her gaze then, and his frown faded. "Time," he clarified. She wondered if he was trying to make her feel less alone or if he really did have introspective thoughts about time. Either way, it was nice to feel like it wasn't just her.

"Where are you going?" she asked him, leaning back in her chair and propping her feet up on the table. She tried to relax—to uncoil her wound-tight muscles—but she couldn't quite get all the way there. She wondered if she ever would—maybe she'd be this tightly wound her entire life.

"Washington University in St. Louis." Jonas was tapping his fingers against his thigh—the left one, where his prosthetic leg was. Now that it had caught her gaze, she was fixated on it—like, for some reason she couldn't look away from the way his fingers moved. Long, graceful—with purpose, even though he was just occupying himself with tapping.

"So you'll be close by," she said, sounding a little too eager. She could feel him watching her. He seemed like he was thinking about something. Brennan just hoped it wasn't about how disappointed he was that he wouldn't be able to escape her at school. She looked at her own hands.

She checked her phone. Already time to go back to work. She sighed, the enjoyment of talking to Jonas fading. "I have to get back," she muttered.

She turned to go but stopped when she felt Jonas's hand on her arm. She froze. A crazy part of her wanted to take it, his hand, and see how her fingers fit with his. But as soon as she turned around, he let go. He was watching her closely, frowning—again. She couldn't quite meet his eyes, so she looked at the little frown crease between his eyebrows. Weird, how it was one of her favorite things about him.

The list, so far:

1. Frown crease.
2. Text ellipses.

And now

3. His hands.

She was a mess. (More of a mess than usual?)

"You all right?" he asked her.

She shrugged. "Fine, I guess," she said. "Just tired," she lied.

He seemed like he didn't believe her, but shrugged and straightened. "Okay then," he said. "Have a good few hours until you're off."

JONAS

It was probably stupid. Was it stupid? He shouldn't have ordered the deli stuff. His mom had just bought the deli stuff for the week. He'd just wanted an excuse to go farther back in the store than just the register, where the stamps were. So it wouldn't go to waste, he made himself a turkey sandwich for lunch.

The house felt empty. Taylor was back from summer camp, but not home currently, and Rhys had been up in his room since they'd gotten home, holding court in that corner of the house, where he might as well have not been home either.

After his sandwich, Jonas sat at the kitchen island for a few moments, thinking. *A few steps? Without the crutches?* He'd traded the walker for the crutches as soon as he'd gotten home. They were leaned against the counter next to him. *But what would it feel like to take a few steps without them?* Just to put his plate in the sink. Just a tiny test.

He pushed back from the counter and stood, gingerly transferring his weight to both legs. *Okay. Okay, okay.* Sore, but okay. A tiny bit of warmth took hold in his chest. *No crutches, no walker.* He let go of the counter. Took a step away from it. A step back from it.

1. Pick up the plate.
2. Turn.

But when he turned, his left leg buckled. He let go of the plate to grab the counter. The plate hit the ground and shattered, and his right arm just about tore out of socket as it took the full force of his weight against the counter and kept him from fully hitting the ground.

God. His left hand was bleeding. The sound of shattering ceramic felt like it was bouncing around his skull.

Footsteps. He pulled himself up to lean against the counter.

Rhys came down the stairs just enough to peer at Jonas. "You okay?" he asked, frowning at his younger brother.

Jonas looked away, hid his left palm against his left thigh—fingers pressed against plastic. "Dropped a plate." He tried to ignore the sudden pain in the stump—the ache from the leg twisting and his fake knee hitting the ground. (There was literally a dent—tiny but there—where the metal knee had hit the laminate wood.)

Rhys's eyes went to the plate on the ground. "Crap, is that one of the good plates? Mom's gonna freak."

"I'll clean it up."

Rhys looked from Jonas to the plate, then back at Jonas again. "Do you want help?"

"No, I'll get it."

"Are you su—"

"I've *got* it."

When Rhys was back upstairs, Jonas slowly lowered himself to the ground next to the plate. The pain in his right arm faded. His left palm stung. The stump was throbbing, syncing up to the beat of his heart pumping blood through his body. *Beat-throb. Beat-throb. Beat-throb.*

For a few moments, he let himself drown in it, feel nothing but pain.

He thought about walking with the walker—feeling like everyone was watching him. *Look at that. A teen with a walker. I wonder what's wrong with him?*

He thought about Brennan. *Yeah, all the time,* she'd explained the other day. He wished he could have explained to her that he knew what it felt like to feel something all the time, inescapably. He gritted his teeth. Kicked the prosthetic leg into the cupboard across from him. Nothing, until the force reverberated up the prosthesis and into the *useless, useless* remaining part of his left leg—pain, delayed, and then there, overwhelming. Anger.

His eyes stung. *Stop it. Stop it.*

Eventually, he forced himself to pull the pieces of the plate into a small pile. Then he opened the cupboard across from him—the one under the sink—and pulled out one of the plastic bags his mom kept there (all the plastic bags nested into one singular plastic bag). Piece by piece, into the bag. Then into the garbage can—clunk, at the bottom, glass on glass.

———

When his mom got home that night, she didn't ask about the dent in the laminate, or yell about the broken good plate, or frown at the blood on Jonas's T-shirt. She just asked if he was okay, worry in her eyes. "What happened?" she asked.

"I'm sorry," he said. *Be angry. Yell a bit. I deserve it. It was your good plate.* She didn't yell. She just mussed Jonas's hair and frowned.

Jonas couldn't help but think she would have been angrier if it was someone else who'd broken the plate.

17

JONAS

It was the next week. Brennan was officially off work. They were walking to the library again—one final end-of-the-summer walk. Out of some odd loyalty to Brennan, Jonas hadn't gone to get the next Harry Potter book until she could go with him. She'd sent him the address last night: *418 W Westmor.* Meet at her house, just like last time.

He leaned against the crutches a little more today; the residual part of his leg was hurting. His left palm still stung. He'd put a bandage over it but didn't know if it was really doing anything—every time he clenched his left hand or wrapped it around his left crutch, the bandage wrinkled and unstuck from his hand just a little more.

He didn't say anything to Brennan. He didn't want to. He didn't want to ruin everything with the pathetic story of him sitting in broken glass and kind of feeling like crying. They were having a nice walk.

Or at least, he was. Brennan looked like she was lost in thought. She was staring down at the sidewalk, frowning. Jonas noticed that she kept tugging at a loose thread on her jean shorts, somewhat absent-mindedly, like she didn't realize she was doing it.

"You okay?" he asked her after a moment, concentrating a little more on her and a little less on where he was putting his feet. He was surprised to find that his left foot still moved forward the same way when he wasn't watching it. (He tried to take this as a good sign.)

"Fine," Brennan said briefly, looking up. She looked like she'd rather look anywhere else than at him. She was staring at a spot left of his ear again, like she had when they'd first met. Her fingers continued to tug at the thread.

"So," he began, trying to make conversation, "there was this anatomy and physiology class I signed up for that was full. I had this thought last night—you know, since I can transfer credits between schools—" He stopped talking, as it was clear she wasn't listening. He halted in the middle of the sidewalk for a moment, watching her.

"Brennan," he said, startling her. She whirled around. "You're clearly *not* all right." She looked like she wanted to make a run for it.

Jonas sat down on the bench next to the bus stop. It was an old bus stop, Brennan had told him; the buses didn't even come this way anymore. The colors of the ad printed on the back of the bench were muted, the sun having sucked the life out of them. Right now, it was just a convenient place for Jonas to rest and try to figure out what was up with Brennan. She didn't make any move to join him.

"Come on," he urged, trying to ignore the pins and needles in his leg. "Tell me what's bothering you. I may not be able to walk very well, but at least my ears work."

Brennan hesitated before coming toward him. She didn't sit down, however, but walked a few steps one way and then the other, pacing.

"For God's sake!" Jonas exclaimed, getting annoyed. "*Sit!*"

She sat down, clasping her hands in her lap and avoiding eye contact.

They were silent for a few moments. Sighing, Jonas turned his head slightly to watch her. "Brennan, is there something you're not telling me? Is it your anxiety?"

She shook her head, glancing at him helplessly. Her eyes were huge behind her glasses. She looked like she was trying to plaster on a normal expression, a smile. "I'm fine," she said. "Just on edge a bit."

Fine. There it was. The biggest lie in the English language. He would know. He raised one eyebrow. "Seems like more than just being on edge."

Brennan frowned. "What does it matter, anyway?" she challenged him defensively. He wondered if he had imagined that, for a moment, she looked scared. Scared of what? That he'd figure out something about her? That she'd give something away? What? He knew she wasn't 100 percent comfortable around him, which he had to admit stung a little, even though he tried to ignore that feeling.

"Brennan," he sighed. "Half the time I see you, you look like you'd rather you never left your house. Sometimes—like now—you look like you might be sick."

She frowned, shaking her head a bit too emphatically. A few strands of dark wavy hair escaped their knot and fell on her neck. "Nothing is wrong," she said, somehow firmly but with a falter in her voice all the same. "I'm just anxious about school starting in a week."

"Brennan," he said, like a parent trying to explain something to their child. "I'm anxious about school. You seem like you're somewhere beyond that." He watched her, concerned, but not really sure how to proceed.

She picked at the thread on her shorts. Jonas realized he was tapping the prosthetic socket again. Nervous. "It's nothing," she mumbled. She stood and started to make her way down the sidewalk.

brennan

"It's clearly not nothing," argued Jonas. Brennan closed her eyes. Her mind was looking for an out. How could she get out of this conversation? How could she end this? She *couldn't* tell Jonas about how bad her anxiety really was. *You'll lose a friend,* her brain taunted her. *He'll think you're crazy. C-R-A-Z-Y.*

"I don't want to talk about it, okay?" she said, turning away. "Let's just walk." *Walk. Just walk. Please stop asking about it.*

Jonas was silent, but eventually she heard him stand and resume walking, crutches clunking against the ground. However, he didn't stay quiet for long. (She wondered, vaguely, if it served her right for being so annoyingly persistent about getting him to walk again.) "You can't just lie to me, Brennan," he said. "I'll keep asking because I'm worried about you. Maybe . . . maybe you have an anxiety disorder," he offered.

Brennan whirled around, eyes flashing, nausea forgotten for a few seconds as she faced Jonas. "I do *not* have an anxiety disorder!" she snapped. "I don't! I told you, I just—I just get nervous. Sometimes." Saying it made it real. Real meant scary. Even with her doctor she'd only referred to it as an anxiety problem. Disorder meant there was something wrong with her. A label. She tried not to think about the fact that, if she looked in her chart, her doctor had probably entered those very words in her problem list, right before she'd prescribed Brennan the solazepram. She pictured them. Anxiety. Disorder. Right next to each other.

Jonas looked surprised at her defensive reaction. Why shouldn't he be? He'd only made a statement. He was *worried* about her. *This is why you have the WALLS!* her brain was admonishing her. Why was she so angry at him? Because it was true. It was true and saying it would make it real. So she couldn't say it. Maybe she should take her medicine. Even if it made her feel sick, maybe it would make her normal. She wanted normal. She wanted herself to be normal.

Jonas was frowning more than usual, but not in an angry way. He looked concerned. His eyes still frowned, his brow still furrowed, but there was a certain downturn to his expression that wasn't normally there. "Brennan, I'm sorry," he began, at last. "I didn't mean anything by suggesting—"

She turned around again, so he wouldn't see the tears that she was trying to hold back. "Please don't, Jonas," she said quietly. "I don't . . . I can't . . . I'm sorry." She stumbled over her own words. She tried to remember the breathing GIF, the one with the circle. In. Out. Slowly. But in her head, the circle expanded and contracted faster and faster. *You can't breathe!* her brain was shouting. *Check your pulse!* She couldn't do this, not in front of Jonas. Crazy Brennan was fighting to get control over normal Brennan, and it was only a matter of time before she was in full-on anxiety-attack mode. She whirled around and began walking more quickly, back toward her own house. If she could just get ahead of Jonas, get a few deep breaths, gain control of her thoughts, maybe she could salvage this.

"Brennan, wait," she heard Jonas call to her. He sounded far away through the pounding in her ears. She glanced back, surprised to see him picking up his own pace, attempting an awkward crutch-walk-limp that didn't look very comfortable. She didn't stop, couldn't. The tears pressed harder, pressure building in her sinuses. *You've embarrassed yourself. You've done it this time.*

This always had to come up with people eventually. Her stupid anxiety. Dumb nerves. She had thought she would have been able to control this situation better, but it turned out that she couldn't. Not with Jonas, because she *wanted* to tell him. That was the difference; she *wanted* him to know.

But she was too afraid that telling him would ruin everything. *BEAT, BEAT, BEAT,* her pulse thudded in her ears and her throat. *You disgust me,* her brain scoffed. She slammed her Walls back up, because they had started to come down, which wasn't right. They needed to stay up—needed to protect her, needed to . . .

"Brennan!" Jonas sounded slightly irritated now. Angry with *her.* She hadn't meant to make him angry. She kept her head down and continued on. *Now he hates you,* her brain pitched in. *Hates you, hates you, hates you.* Sing-songy. Mocking.

"Brennan, will you hold on a min-—" Jonas's voice cut off jerkily, and she turned around just in time to see him fall.

"Jonas!"

He looked flustered and embarrassed. She saw the reason; he'd tripped over a large crack in the sidewalk. His face had turned bright red, and now he really looked angry.

"So *now* you turn around!" he snapped, trying to work out how best to get up. She offered a hand to help him but he ignored her, pulling himself up on his crutches.

"Are you—are you okay?" she asked him, horrified. *You made him fall.*

He continued past her, limping more now, ignoring her concerned questions.

"Jonas, please just—"

He turned around and faced her. "Just *what* exactly, Brennan?" he said angrily. "I tried to, you know, be there for you. Help. Whatever. I was not trying to *insult* you when I said you might have an anxiety disorder. I was just showing concern. Trying to help you. I have my own issues. Why do you think I got dropped off? Why do you think I rear-ended you in the first place? The other day when I came to see you—my brother had to drive me, because I basically have a breakdown every time I try to drive. Because I can't handle cars, Brennan! Which"—he laughed, sounding a little unhinged—"is so *stupid*, considering I wasn't even the one driving when the accident happened!"

"Jonas, I didn't—"

"You know, this is stupid. My leg is sore today. I shouldn't have even come out. But, you know, I thought it would be nice to go on a walk together to the library. To chat with my *friend*." He said *friend* like they weren't anymore. He shook his head, turning around. "Clearly I was wrong. I'll see you some other time."

Jonas started to pull out his phone to call his ride to come get him. Brennan wanted to yell *You're right*. Two words. All she wanted to say.

And yet she couldn't get them out because her throat kept constricting around them, boxing them in.

"Jonas, come on! Please!" She felt desperate. Like this was her last chance to stop herself from losing him. "You have to come. You have to get the third Harry Potter book, remember?"

"I'll buy the eBook," he said, not turning around.

"But you're getting so much better at walking!"

"Yes," he said, finally turning around, only to glare at her. "*So* much better. Because that's what this was about all along, wasn't it? Some challenge for you, getting the bitter cripple to walk again. Maybe it made you feel better about your own issues?" He laughed shortly. *Issues*. Her throat constricted a bit more. "Well, you can stop trying now. You're not going to succeed at *fixing* me, Brennan." He spit the words out like they tasted bad. "You can't fix me!" He shook his head, frowning.

He met her gaze then, finally. She wondered if that—that moment and the way he was looking at her now—might be the thing that killed her.

"So stop trying," he said flatly. His eyes held hurt and frustration, whether at her or at himself, Brennan couldn't tell. Had he always felt this way? Had he always felt that that's what she was trying to do? *Fix* him? He was looking at his phone again, getting ready to dial.

"I'm not trying to fix you!" Brennan blurted impulsively. *What are you doing?*

Jonas stopped, his finger inches away from hitting dial. He didn't turn around but he seemed like he was listening.

"I'm not trying to fix you," she said again, clearing her throat to get past the lump that was choking her. "Because there's nothing to fix," she finally said. "You're not broken, Jonas. You're fine. You've always been fine. More than fine. I was just—I guess I was just trying to help you see that."

He stood still for a moment more, then called Rhys. They stood silently until his brother pulled up. Jonas didn't look at her again as he got into the van and shut the door. They pulled away, leaving her standing in the middle of the sidewalk, like an idiot.

A really sad idiot.

18

JONAS

Hey. Jonas, I'm really sorry.

Jonas read Brennan's message over several times. Then he turned off his phone and rolled over in bed, turning off his lamp and plunging the room into darkness punctuated by the weak light of the glow-in-the-dark stars.

He felt humiliated. He wasn't good at this stuff, whatever this was. Trying to be a friend. Trying to help someone. For the past year he'd spent his time withdrawing further and further from everyone he might have considered his friend before. Did he even know how to be a friend anymore? Why couldn't Brennan just let him help her? Why did he *want* to help her? He hadn't *wanted* to do anything in a long time. Wanting hurt. Walking hurt. *Hurting* hurt.

He closed his eyes, trying to make sense of everything.

His face got hot when he relived the events of earlier in his mind. He couldn't believe he'd *run* after her (or half limped, half run; whatever it was, it was more effort than he usually put into using his own two feet). He couldn't believe he'd fallen in front of her. *Again. That* was embarrassing.

He called her words to mind, replaying them over and over. *I'm not trying to fix you, because there's nothing to fix. You're not broken.*

Nothing to fix. Not broken.

Was she right? Jonas *felt* broken. He felt like something had changed in him since The Accident, like something had snapped and he'd been falling apart ever since. But had it? Or had he changed because he felt that that was the only right way to respond to such a traumatic event? Had he only changed because he expected himself to? You expect something so it happens? Maybe it was like homeostasis, and his life had just tried to find a new set point in response to the change.

The worst part was that he'd gotten his hopes up, and he hadn't even realized it until they crashed down again with his third fall in the past month. *What if it works this time? What if you walk again?* he'd asked himself in the mirror on his closet door as he'd stood in front of it the other night (the one he'd fallen in the kitchen). His self responded with *What if it doesn't?*

Jonas squeezed his eyes more tightly shut, trying to block everything out. He didn't want to think about Brennan anymore. Because when he did, he only thought of a hundred things he wished he'd said differently. He just wanted to sleep. He just wanted to escape. He begged for it. Sleep. *Sleep.*

When he did sleep, he dreamed that he was in the passenger seat of the semi with the driver. The man who'd hit him. Paul Whitford. From the semi, he watched The Accident. When Rhys's car turned, he saw, for a split second, himself, completely unaware of what he was about to lose. Jonas wanted to yell something—a warning of some kind. But when he opened his mouth, nothing came out. When the two vehicles collided, pain shot up Jonas's left leg and he woke up, a cry in his throat and real-life pain gripping like a vise—toes, shin, knee—what wasn't there anymore.

He heard his mom's startled Vietnamese from the room next door, and then she was waking his father up—"Elliot. *Elliot.*"

Then footsteps and his door cracked open. His dad, in rumpled pajama shorts and an old Wash U T-shirt. "Jonas?" he whispered hoarsely. "Are you okay?"

Jonas didn't sit up. He just tried not to grit his teeth too much when he answered. "Yeah."

Elliot Avery ran a hand through his hair, nervous energy dissipating through his hands like always (there was something comforting in that *like always*). "You—you cried out. Are you—are you sure you're okay?"

"Bad dream," Jonas breathed. "Fine. Really."

When his dad was gone, Jonas sat up and whipped the covers off his left leg, looking at it—just the stump: no prosthesis, no liner, no sock—for the first time in a long time. He forced himself to stare at it. *Stop it!* he yelled at his brain, willing the pain to stop. *There's nothing there! See! THERE'S NOTHING THERE.*

fall semester 2014

19

brennan

Brennan swallowed and tried to keep from throwing up. Her stomach was tied in knots. In one hand, she clenched an envelope containing two keys: one for her mailbox and one for her room. (*The keys to the rest of your life*, her dad had joked, which hadn't helped the ball of sick that sat like lead in her stomach.) In her other hand, she clenched the handles of a duffel bag.

She swallowed again. Her mouth was dry. Her throat felt like something was caught there. She felt like hyperventilating. She wanted to run, although she didn't know where to. They were currently stuck in the tight maze of the dorm hallway, other students and their families crowding the corridor with carts full of plastic bins—it was like everyone had tried to pack their life up and take it with them. Brennan's mom came to her side.

"Well?" she said. "Are you going to open the door?" Brennan nodded, forcing her feet to move forward. She set down the duffel bag and removed the key from the envelope, unlocking the door.

The room smelled weird. That was the first thing she noticed. It didn't smell like home. In fact, it was distinctly *not-home*. Like cleaner and all these other scents layered on top of one another until Brennan couldn't separate and identify them.

Her roommate had already chosen the bed by the window and had already moved in her things. She'd texted Brennan twice earlier: the first asking if Brennan minded if she took the window bed (Brennan said she didn't mind because either bed brought the same level of anxiety to the table) and the second letting her know that she'd finished moving in and was going to be out at the welcome events. Ambreen's wall was filled with pictures—Ambreen smiling with friends. Ambreen in Europe. Ambreen being a lot more exciting than Brennan.

Brennan was glad her roommate wasn't here to watch her have a panic attack. She nervously took a few more steps into the room, displacing some of the weird air. She almost wished she had taken the window bed so that she could at least open the window—let the fresh air in—and pretend she felt less claustrophobic than she actually did.

"It looks nice!" said her mom cheerfully, carrying in a box and setting it down to survey the room.

"Yeah," Brennan said halfheartedly. "Nice." Like prison was nice. Like any number of not-nice things were nice.

One desk. One dresser, with three drawers. One lofted mattress on a squeaky metal bed frame. One half of a closet that was smaller than her one at home.

Her mom left the room to help her dad carry in the rest of Brennan's things.

Brennan just stood there, staring.

She briefly wondered if Jonas was moving in today also, down at Washington University. He really wasn't that far from her. Somehow, the thought made her even more nervous. Jonas hadn't texted her back since the day they'd had their falling out. She'd sent him messages but he hadn't responded. She kept going to the library, like maybe he'd come to get the next Harry Potter after all. She'd eventually given up.

She had decided that maybe she just wasn't built for having friends. Brennan, solo, was the only way she was manageable.

"Do you want to start unpacking?" her mom asked her.

Brennan shook her head. "I'll unpack later. It'll help distract me and give me something to focus on. Right now, I just want to get out of here."

"Okay," said her mom, giving her a side hug, squeezing her arm gently. "Let's go get dinner."

Brennan didn't know how she was going to survive a year here, let alone her first night. *I mean,* God. *I can't even hug my mom without getting teary eyed.*

JONAS

Jonas sat in his desk chair and watched his mom bustle about the room, putting away clothes, making the bed, dusting the desk (not that it needed it), and, in general, making sure the room was up to her standards. (*Spick and span*—she proclaimed when they had gotten there—*by the time I'm through with it!*)

Jonas would have protested, except he knew how worried his mom was about him going away to college, so he let her have her way with everything. It wasn't that he really cared how the room looked or how things were put away. If he needed to move something later, he could.

"Man, you got lucky," said Rhys, flopping down on the bed admiringly (and jealously, Jonas thought). Since Jonas had gotten a private bedroom, it had come with two of everything—two beds, two desks, two dressers. It was really just a shared bedroom called a single, with no one bothering to remove the extra furniture.

Jonas's mom had pushed the two beds together and made them into one big bed, which Rhys was currently stretched across.

"Rhys! Get up!"

Jonas rolled his eyes as his mom shooed his older brother off the freshly made bed, smoothing the comforter and the sheets until they were flat again. Rhys grabbed a pillow and tossed it at Jonas, gaining him an angry glare from both Jonas and their mother, who immediately snatched the pillow back and returned it to the bed. "Take your shoes off in the room!" she admonished Rhys, smacking him with a duster.

Now she was stacking Jonas's textbooks on the shelf above his desk.

"Man, you're certainly getting the royal treatment, Jonas," grumbled Rhys as he bent to take his shoes off and add them to the line of the rest of the family's shoes next to the door. "When I moved in, mom and dad helped me unpack a few things and were out the door." Jonas wondered if being away at college had rubbed off on Rhys (more and more, his brother forgot to take his shoes off at the door even though it had been a long-time house rule), and he wondered if it would rub off on him too. He decided it wouldn't. He would get a shoe rack or something for inside the door. It would make his mom happy.

He thought about what Rhys had said. His brother sort of had a point. His mom, especially, was making a huge deal of this. A huge deal that wouldn't have been a huge deal if Jonas had had two good legs.

"Mom," he said. "Don't you want to go out to dinner or something before you guys head home?"

"Yes," she said. "I just want to make sure everything is nice for you."

Rhys rolled his eyes. Jonas glared at him. "It's okay, Mom," he said, turning to her. "I'll be okay. Everything looks great now."

"If you're sure."

"I'm sure, Mom. It's really okay." He smiled at her reassuringly. "Let's find somewhere to eat."

She grudgingly gave in and, sighing, picked up her purse, stepping back to survey the room. "All right," she said, finally giving it her seal of approval. "Let's go."

They each put on their shoes and filed out of the room one by one, Rhys and Jonas coming last. "Spoiled," muttered Rhys, under his breath.

"What was that, Rhys?" asked Jonas, knowing full well what that was.

"Nothing," huffed Rhys.

As he hunched over his crutches in the elevator, Jonas wondered if Rhys had a right to be angry with him. For a while, Jonas had blamed Rhys for what happened, even though it was in no way his brother's fault. He'd just happened to be driving. He'd been the easy scapegoat for Jonas's blame. Now Jonas was mostly mad that his brother thought he was milking it—getting as much mileage out of it as possible. He clenched his fists, his left palm stinging where his fingers pressed against his still-healing cut. *I'd like to see* him *lose a leg,* thought Jonas. *See how he likes it.* He immediately felt bad for the thought.

He wondered how it would be, being down at school with Rhys. He knew it made his mom feel better having Jonas be near someone who could help him if he needed it, but Jonas almost wished it was anyone else in the family but Rhys.

He thought about texting Brennan, telling her he'd gotten all moved in. Asking if she had.

He almost did. He got his phone out and opened the conversation between the two of them. He still hadn't deleted it, like having the messages was proof that the last month had happened after all.

He stared at his phone for a moment before shaking his head and putting it back into his pocket.

20

brennan

She was alone now.

Finally.

Brennan took a deep breath and looked around the small, cramped room. It was smaller than her room at home, and yet it was supposed to hold two people. Brennan felt claustrophobic. She busied herself with unpacking in order to distract herself from the tight feeling in her chest and what felt like an extra heart in her throat.

She made her bed and methodically hung up her photos and posters. She set her books up on the shelf above her desk, starting with her Harry Potter books and finishing with the numerous other books she'd brought with her. *You won't have time to read!* her dad had said. She knew that, but something about seeing them lined up on the shelf over her desk was *reassuring*. She stacked her textbooks on her desk and filled her desk drawers with supplies.

Suddenly, everything was done. Brennan no longer had anything to distract herself with. She was hit by how isolated she felt. Her parents were on their way home now, already a couple of hours away from her. The distance seemed huge.

She pictured them getting home, going inside their home-smelling house without her.

She felt a little bit like crying. *Suck it up,* she told herself. *You're gonna be okay. It's just for a semester. Take it week by week. One day at a time.*

She felt like hiding under her blankets. She didn't know when her roommate was coming back, and she was on edge, waiting for the door to open, ready to switch on performance mode.

Brennan grabbed her pajamas and her towel and crossed the hall to their bathroom, shutting the door behind her and locking it.

Safe in the shower, encircled by steam and hot water, Brennan did cry. As the choking tears flowed down her cheeks with the water cascading from the showerhead, the knot in her stomach gradually loosened itself, and her heart returned to its normal anatomy in her chest, where it thudded a little faster than normal, but was otherwise fine.

By the time she was finished with her shower, she felt a little more confident about meeting her roommate for the first time.

She got out and dressed in her pajamas before standing in front of the mirror and looking herself in the eye. *Okay, Brennan,* she told herself. *Get out there and get ready to meet people. You're going to make friends. You're going to be normal. College will be fun.*

She grinned at herself in the mirror, like she was practicing. Cheesy, too much teeth.

JONAS

Jonas could finally breathe.

He missed his parents a little bit (he knew he'd probably miss them more later), but at the moment, he was just glad to no longer be the center of attention. His mom had doted on him the entire night, and then she had cried in the hour leading up to the time they'd finally bid him good-bye and left. He hadn't wanted to feel irritated with her because he knew how hard it was for her to let him go. However, it had gotten to be a bit much. He'd started to feel a little overwhelmed. Like he was carrying it all—his mother's worries, Rhys's bitterness—by himself.

Now he was lying in bed, looking at the ceiling, just as if he was at home. He almost missed Rhys's dumb glow-in-the-dark stars. He closed his eyes, listening to the music playing through his headphones.

His suitemates were in now; he could hear them, loudly celebrating the beginning of their freshman year. He briefly considered going out to greet them, but he quickly decided against it.

He unlocked his phone and opened his email. He scrolled through, opening a particular email from several weeks ago.

Jonas Avery,

I've reviewed your academic records and I think it would be perfectly fine for you to take an equivalent course for Anatomy and Physiology (BIOL 4580) at nearby SIUE due to our labs being full. The credits are transferable. The course number there is BIOL 240A.

He stared at the words until they blurred into one long line of text. He'd wanted to tell Brennan *that* day. He had been about to. What if he had? What if he hadn't pressed her about *the other thing*. He'd thought it would be nice to tell her he'd registered for a class at SIUE. He'd take the bus there on the days he had class, and maybe he'd see her. Now it felt stupid. He considered dropping it—why take A&P anyway, if he wasn't going to be a doctor?—but he supposed he had to just soldier on. They'd already paid tuition.

Jonas dropped his phone on the bed and pulled out his chemistry textbook, beginning to read the first chapter, as an email from his chem professor (already!) had requested.

After all, he really had nothing better to do.

At nine o'clock, he was hungry, and so he ate the leftover pizza he'd brought back from dinner. At ten o'clock, he crossed the hall to the bathroom and brushed his teeth. Then he crossed back over to his room, shut the lights off, and got into bed.

He lay down and pulled the comforter up to his chin. *First night of college, only ten o'clock, and already in bed,* he thought. *I have to be just about the most boring college student ever.*

21

brennan

Ambreen returned to the room at around ten. Brennan had been lying on her stomach on her bed, reading the first Harry Potter book over again. She was inwardly debating the pros and cons of having the first pack from the ramen stash under her bed. Pros: fulfilled hunger, soothing warm broth, finding the microwave in the student lounge for future reference. Cons: one less ramen = one meal sooner that she'd have to visit the cafeteria or find a ride into town with her roommate to buy more. It was a big enough con that she decided not to have the ramen.

Ambreen banged open the door enthusiastically, making Brennan jump a bit. She could hear the sound of people laughing and chatting in the hallways, and the scent of hairspray, perfume, and men's body spray drifted in through the open door. Ambreen shut the door, which cut the noise off for the most part, but Brennan could still hear people, like a low hum in the background. She wasn't used to this much noise. She wished the walls were thicker.

"Hey!" said Ambreen as enthusiastically as she'd opened the door.

Even though getting down was the last thing Brennan wanted to do, it felt awkward to be up in the lofted bed, talking down to Ambreen. So she reluctantly hopped off and greeted her roommate. She wondered if a handshake would be appropriate. For being a young adult female, Brennan wasn't very familiar with young adult females.

Before she could give the matter any further consideration, Ambreen was hugging her. Brennan's eyes widened, and she tried not to give any indication of how uncomfortable she actually was. *She's hugging me,* was playing on repeat in her mind. *Personal space invasion!*

Ambreen stepped back, her hands still on Brennan's shoulders. "I'm *so* excited for this year!" she said.

"Uh, yeah!" said Brennan, forcing a laugh and grinning cheesily, despite her earlier mirror practice. "Me too! How was the welcome back bash?" Brennan had heard about the bash and had steered clear accordingly.

"Oh, it was wonderful!" gushed her roomie, already shuffling through the top drawer of her desk looking for something. "So much fun. Why didn't you come?" she asked curiously, finally pulling out the phone charger she'd been looking for and plugging her phone in.

"Oh, I just had kind of a headache from reading in the car on the drive down here," lied Brennan. "Just felt like getting settled in and relaxing." She watched her roommate. Her dark hair swished when she moved. It was so smooth. Brennan was self-conscious about her own (currently very humidity-frizzy) mop.

"I hope you're feeling better!" Ambreen said, already picking up her wallet and keys once more. She almost bounced, never still.

"Much," muttered Brennan. "Better, that is."

"Great! Hey, I'm going next door if you wanna come? Figured we could meet our suitemates."

No, Brennan wanted to say. *No, thank you.* "Sure!" she said aloud, grinning. Was she grinning too much? She didn't know how much was too much. Her face kind of hurt.

"Awesome, come on!" Ambreen grabbed her arm and pulled her into the room next door. Brennan felt weird about being in her pajamas already when everyone else was still dressed up. Then a magical thing happened—no one seemed to care. Still, she awkwardly hugged herself and half hid behind Ambreen.

She tried to inject her way into the conversation occasionally, but eventually gave up and just sat back, listening.

She learned that her suitemate, Jennifer, a tiny five-foot whirlwind wrapped in warm brown skin and colorful fabrics, was an amateur fashion designer who made some of her own clothes and was at SIUE to major in English. Her other suitemate, blond and equally as short as her roommate, Mattie, enjoyed photography and loved anime. "Undecided major," she said, shaking Brennan's hand enthusiastically. (Why had Brennan been so afraid of being undecided? Mattie seemed totally at ease.)

Ambreen herself had the most interesting background story of all of them. She was born in India, apparently, and then her family had lived in England for a while before they came to Illinois. Brennan wondered who'd give up India or England for Illinois. Apparently it had to do with Ambreen's father's job. Over the summer, Ambreen had told Brennan she was also majoring in physical therapy.

There were also two other girls in the room who weren't even from their dorm; they'd apparently just tagged along after the bash. Brennan's suitemates were practically giddy. "Let's go meet everyone else!" Mattie suggested excitedly. Brennan thought it would be bad if she just excused herself to her room immediately, so she faked a few giggles (she hoped they didn't sound tortured) and followed the rest of them.

They checked out everyone else's dorm décor, gushed over other girls' outfits, and met their RA.

And collected phone numbers. Apparently you were required, by some unspoken rule, to gather as many phone numbers as you could.

Girls *and* guys, which Brennan thought was weird. She'd never had a guy's number in her phone before (well, other than her brother, her dad, *and Jonas,* she remembered with a pang), but now she had one more (Calvin, a tall black guy whose bookshelves full of books made Brennan a tiny bit jealous). Still not many, but *still.* She'd mostly just tagged along, not really comfortable with having a bunch of numbers for people she didn't know. Tonight she only added her suitemates and Calvin.

Finally, she was able to excuse herself to go back to her room. Ambreen was still out and about. Brennan lay on her bed and looked at the ceiling. *One day down.* She closed her eyes. Pretending was hard. Pretending to be *normal* was the hardest thing of all.

Brennan picked up her book again and started where she'd left off. Reading distracted her from the knot in her stomach.

22

JONAS

Someone was knocking on his door.

Jonas groaned and rolled over, picking up his phone off the night-stand. Seven o'clock.

Whoever was at the door knocked again. Jonas's original strategy had been to ignore the knocker until they went away. After all, he couldn't exactly answer the door legless. (Well, technically he could, but he wasn't *going* to, so that option was out.)

He forced himself out of bed and hurriedly fitted the prosthesis, pulling the leg of his pajama pants down over it before stumbling to the door, half tripping over his crutches and gritting his teeth when he put more weight on the prosthesis than he wanted to.

"Hello?" he said groggily, opening the door. He wondered if his hair was sticking up and if his breath smelled as bad as his mouth tasted.

"Hey, man!" greeted the invader of Jonas's sleep, too loudly for it being seven in the morning. "I'm Travis. Me and Sam are your next-door neighbors." Travis had shaggy blond hair and dressed like he was half hipster, half hippie.

"Hi," said Jonas lamely, his mind not quite awake yet. It was awake enough to want to correct Travis's grammar though, *Sam and I.*

"Anyway, we were just getting ready to head to the cafeteria for some breakfast. Want to join us?"

No, absolutely no. Jonas forced a tight smile and leaned on the crutches. "Sure," he said. "Just let me get dressed."

"Awesome, we'll be waiting inside," Travis said, gesturing at the door to his own room. "Just knock when you're ready!"

Jonas shut his door, leaning against it and transferring his weight to his right leg. He supposed it was better to meet his neighbors now rather than later. He'd just have preferred to sleep longer beforehand. Yesterday had tired him out.

He sighed and got dressed in his usual jeans and T-shirt. *At least they'll have coffee at the university center,* he thought. He'd already made up his mind that he was going to have to start a relationship with coffee in order to survive college. He grabbed the crutches again—*like a little kid's security blanket.* His hands gripped the crutches more tightly.

Jonas exited the room, heading next door and knocking hesitantly on the door to Travis and Sam's room. Someone who he assumed was Sam opened the door. Sam was about a head shorter than Jonas, a little pudgy, and was wearing a *Super Smash Bros.* T-shirt. "Ready, man?" he heard Travis yell from somewhere in the back of the room.

Um . . . "Yeah!" called Jonas, directing his voice back toward Travis.

Soon enough, Jonas, Travis, and Sam were headed downstairs and on their way to the cafeteria.

"What's with the crutches?" asked Travis as they waited for the elevator, his voice curious.

"Er," Jonas hesitated.

Two options:

1. Tell.
2. Don't tell.

"Torn ACL," he said, kind of halfheartedly. His leg responded with that painful pins-and-needles feeling.

"Dang," said Travis. "That had to hurt."

"Yeah. Lots."

They all got on the elevator.

Once downstairs, they made their way outside, leaving Umrath House behind and heading toward the Danforth University Center (or as Sam had already taken to calling it, the DUC, pronounced *duck*, like the bird).

After they had their trays of food in hand and had found a place to sit, Sam and Travis immediately launched into a description of the festivities last night. They'd been up until three o'clock, apparently. Jonas wondered how they were functioning a mere four hours later. Travis was busy talking about a girl he'd met, and Sam was nerding out about *Smash Bros.*, talking about the tournament he'd had in his room (which he had won, of course).

"Where were you last night?" Sam asked.

"Studying for my chem class," Jonas admitted. It sounded even lamer when he said it out loud.

"Oh man," moaned Travis. "Someone's getting into the grind early."

"My chem professor sent an email—he wanted us to get started on reading the first chapter."

"Do you actually think he expects you to have read it?"

"I—"

"I read it two weeks ago," Sam broke in, saving Jonas from having to respond.

"Dude," said Travis. "You're such a nerd." Sam just grinned and pushed his glasses up his nose, like he was proud of his nerd status.

Jonas went back to eating his pancakes.

"Hey, man, check out that girl over there," said Travis, nodding in the direction of a brunet who was currently paying for her food. "I met her at a party last night. She's really nice—and single. You into brunets, Jonas?"

Jonas almost choked on his pancakes. "I'm not really—" He coughed and took a drink of his water before finishing his statement. "I'm not really looking for a relationship right now. I need to get settled into college." Besides, Jonas figured it was less about him being interested in a girl than it was about her being interested in him after learning that he didn't have a left leg.

"No time like the present," Travis muttered. "Speaking of which—" He turned to Sam. "Mandy and I have a date for tonight." Mandy was the girl Travis had met at the party yesterday.

"Hey! Congrats!" said Sam, high-fiving Travis. They launched into a conversation about where Travis should take Mandy on their date.

Jonas thought about Brennan. He wondered how she was doing. For about the hundredth time he seriously considered texting her but he decided against it, yet again.

Fresh start, anyway, he thought.

Still, when he went back to the dorm, his thoughts were occupied with wondering how Brennan was doing, and then with how his mom was doing. He wondered if she was still worrying about him or if she'd relaxed since he was away—unwound, now that the thing winding her up was gone.

That night he searched online *Vietnamese restaurants nearby.* He found a place just down the street from the university. He waited until Travis and Sam had left for the cafeteria and then left Umrath to crutch the block or so to the restaurant. The *bánh mì* wasn't as good as his mom's, but it was close.

23

brennan

Brennan was messy, she had decided. Not just outwardly messy (though she was that, with wrinkled clothes, and frizzy hair, and glasses that fogged in the corners), but emotionally messy. Complex.

> That's why I'll never get married,

she explained via Facebook message to Emma.

> Never say never, Brennan.

Brennan smiled a little, holding her phone in both hands. She was sitting on a bench inside Peck Hall, waiting for her psych class to start. Except psych was on the third floor, and Brennan was sitting on the first floor. She just hadn't quite made it up the stairs yet.

So she was messaging Emma.

I'll probably just live in a tiny apartment with like . . . three dogs.
Three is a lot for an apartment, isn't it? And I'll write every day, but
always be too afraid to post it anywhere, so it will just sit on my
laptop for people to discover when I'm dead.

A stream of chatter and bodies surrounded Brennan as a big group
spilled into Peck from outside. Not freshmen, Brennan decided. They
didn't look like they were trying too hard. Most were in sweatpants or
leggings, because they were comfortable, not because they were worried about first impressions. Her phone dinged.

You're posting the summary and the prologue, though, remember? You set a date. This Friday. You have to do it now. You told
your followers.

My four followers?

Brennan rolled her eyes.

Five now. I made an account, finally.

Aw, how nice of you.

I am nice. Have you gone upstairs yet?

Not yet. I like it here, on my bench.

Go upstairs. You'll never be a physical therapist if you don't go to
any of your classes.

Okay, okay. I'm going.

Smell you later.

Nice.

Brennan tucked her phone into the front pocket of her backpack,
which she shouldered, tightening the straps. She took a deep breath in.
Then let it out.

Her hands gripped the backpack straps tightly, like if she let go she might pass out. Swallowing the lump in her throat, she pushed her glasses up her nose and trudged up the stairs. One floor. Two floors.

Third floor. She turned down the hallway and counted the steps it took to reach the psych classroom, immediately losing track of the number upon reaching the door. She was a half an hour early, yet everyone else was earlier.

Brennan's heart rose up into her throat again. She could feel herself starting to sweat.

There weren't any seats in the back, next to the door. The long tables meant that if you were anywhere other than the aisle edge, you were stuck.

She hadn't prepared for this eventuality. She had thought a half an hour would be early enough—had thought she'd be there well before anyone else.

She considered her options.

1. Ask girl-in-the-back to move her backpack so she could sit there. Pros: seat in the back. Cons: seat between two people; girl might be saving seat and might hate her for asking.
2. Find a seat in the front. There's a trash can there. At least if she threw up, she'd have somewhere to do it. Pros: her stomach was feeling queasier by the moment, the blueberry muffin she'd had for breakfast sitting heavy in her gut. Trash can = security. Cons: if she did throw up, everyone would have a great view.
3. Sit in the middle. Pros: pretty much none. Cons: no trash can; no door; sitting between people. Basically, everything.

She swallowed before taking an open seat one row from the back, all the way against the wall. *Pros: none.* She tried not to think about all the people who were between her and the aisle, should she need to get out.

Her phone vibrated, reminding her that she needed to put it on silent before the lecture started. Her phone was always on silent or vibrate; she didn't even know what her ring tone was.

She looked at the text. Jonas. They hadn't talked since the Incident— Brennan's breakdown—so it was surprising that he'd text her now.

Happy first day. It's going to be okay.

Jonas. She stared at the words, all eight of them. She pressed her finger against the screen, like maybe she could touch him through it. *It's going to be okay.*

Maybe it was.

JONAS

Jonas wasn't entirely sure what had made him text Brennan. He'd gotten up, dressed, and packed all his textbooks into his backpack. Then he'd texted her, because it felt right, and also maybe because his inhibitions weren't quite all there that early in the morning. Maybe his own nervous energy needed somewhere to go.

As he headed to Louderman Hall for organic chemistry (whose stupid idea was it anyway to stay up until one in the morning playing *Mario Kart* with Sam and Travis), he thought about whether or not he regretted it, sending her that text. He wondered what Brennan thought. After all, he hadn't texted her since *the Incident*. She probably thought he was nuts for texting her now. Plus, he'd meant to be getting a fresh start. Yet here he was, drawn back to Brennan as if by some invisible string. So did he regret it?

No, he decided. Even if she would think he was nuts, on the slight chance that the words *It's going to be okay* were what she needed to hear, he'd open himself up to potential accusations of craziness.

Screw fresh starts, he thought as he trudged into Louderman with the other huddled masses of students bound for organic chemistry.

He picked an outside-edge seat and leaned his crutches against his chair. *Besides, here you are, off at college, and still not walking. Not exactly a fresh start.* He shook off the thought.

———

The feeling of guilt over his lack of fresh starts set Jonas's stomach on edge all through his chemistry lecture.

Afterward, instead of going back to Umrath, he crutched to Rhys's dorm and found their car—a 1990-something Honda CR-V named Gus. Gus was meant to be shared by both of them, but there was sort of an unspoken understanding after The Accident that the car was Rhys's car and Jonas would never drive it.

He got the key out of the front pocket of his backpack (where he'd put it, just for emergencies) and unlocked the door. He got into the driver's seat.

For a while he just stared out the front windshield. Then he put his hands on the steering wheel.

Okay. Okay. Hands are sweaty, but you're here. You're fine. Could you start it, do you think?

He started it.

Then he sat like that, for a few minutes—until he started to feel like the car was closing in on him, and a feeling of dread took hold of his throat. He swiped an arm over his forehead and it came away wet with sweat. *If you drive, you'll crash. You crashed last time you drove. You'll crash.*

Jonas didn't know why, but he felt so strongly about this that he immediately turned the car off and got out. His entire body was tense—teeth gritted, hands on the crutches, what was left of his left leg.

He tried to force his muscles to relax, one by one. *It's stupid,* he thought. *The car didn't even move. You weren't even going to drive anywhere.* He tried not to think about what had happened the last time he'd tried.

He went back to Umrath and changed his T-shirt because the old one was sweat soaked. Plus, changing out of it felt a little like leaving behind the feelings he'd felt while sitting in the car.

24

brennan

I told Emma that I'd post the summary and the prologue of my story Friday.

But I'm scared.

Do I back out? Or do I go for it, even if it isn't that good?

Brennan didn't know why she'd texted Jonas that. It was Wednesday now, which meant that it had been two days since Jonas had told her it would be okay, and she had lamely responded, "Thank you." Since he hadn't sent anything after that, she sort of doubted he'd respond to her now.

Except, then he did.

I have a feeling it's better than you think.

Will the world end if you post it? Will you suddenly dissolve into dust and cease to exist in the memories of all who met you?

Subsequently, if you did, I wonder what it'd be like to exist in a world where you didn't. Would I go back to not walking at all?

A giggle bloomed in Brennan's chest, warm and a little crazed. She pressed a hand to her mouth, stifling it. Across the room, Ambreen's breaths were still deep and slow. The yellow glow of the lights lining the path running from the back of Prairie Hall to the rest of campus bathed the room through the open blinds. Brennan alternated between hating when Ambreen left the blinds open (what if some pervert decided to peek in; they were only on the first floor after all) and loving the surreal amber edge everything took on when the light came in.

She pulled her comforter over her head, forming a barrier between her and her sleeping roommate.

1. No. Obviously not. But it feels like it might, you know?

2. You're still walking, then.

It only took Jonas a moment to respond.

Yeah, sometimes . . .

And then, I use the crutches mostly, but sometimes I put weight on it, like over the summer.

Brennan rolled onto her back, stretching her arms up above her, phone in hands. Are you going to try without the crutches?

She wondered if Jonas fought smiles in his own dorm room like he did when he was in front of her or anyone else. He didn't respond to her text for a while.

Then, finally: I don't know. But we're talking about you, not me. Post your story. This is like . . . your thing. Post it. The world won't implode. Promise.

Promise.

You know, she sent. Trying a few steps without the crutches would be okay. The world wouldn't implode.

Are you going to post it? He'd ignored the part about walking without the crutches.

Was she going to post it? Writing was part of who she was, after all. It had been, for forever. She opened the allfixx app and went to the My Stories page. She'd had *Superioris* saved as a draft since the summer. *If anything, you can unpublish it,* she thought. So she hit Publish, because, well, *forget* deadlines.

Then she stared at her screen and waited for something to happen. Nothing did. *They won't read it right away,* she reminded herself. *No upvotes or comments yet but even though nothing good has happened, nothing bad has either.*

And Brennan felt lighter.

I'm a writer, she thought. *Brennan Davis, author. It's out there now.*

Jonas texted her again. Brennan?

I did it, she sent him.

You did it?

She typed back, fingers flying over the touch screen: I did it. I published it. It's a thing now. It's out there.

Now you just wait for all your fans to start rolling in.

I have four followers.

She amended that message with Actually, five. My friend Emma follows me now too.

Before you know it, five will be fifty, and fifty will be five hundred.

Brennan snorted. In my dreams. Hey, sorry to cut this short, but I've gotta go to sleep. 8 a.m. psych.

Gross. But go on. Be a responsible student.

Night.

Night.

Brennan shut off the home screen on her phone, pitching herself into darkness under her comforter. For a few seconds she stayed there, until the starbursts of light flashing in front of her eyes in the sudden absence of the phone's brightness. Then she pulled the comforter down and looked at the splashes of yellow and orange that the lights outside cast onto the wall.

She thought about Jonas. About him not walking. Then she thought about the text she wished she'd sent him, because she had to know, and they hadn't actually talked about the-thing-that-happened-at-the-end-of-summer. *Are you mad at me?*

"It's all a game."

In a world of Extros (people with physical or strength powers) and Intros (people with abilities based in the mind), Ing is an Ambivalent. She's normal, and normal isn't wanted in Santos.

Ing isn't supposed to exist in anything other than the background of the world the Superioris, the governing body of Santos, has created. She definitely isn't supposed to be in the Superioris's Santos Game. When her name is drawn to play, it's even more important that her secret stay hidden.

But she's smart, and she's going to win the Santos Game (or at least, that's what she tells herself). She's going to win and prove that Ambivalents are just as valuable to society as Extros and Intros.

Of course, as her newfound kind-of-ally, Cas, tells her, it's a lot easier to say she's going to win than to actually do it.

Welcome to the Santos Game.

—

Brennan Davis

@b-rennan

5 followers

—

Hi, all! Brennan here!

I hope you're as excited for Superioris as I am! Hopefully updates will be semiregular—I did just move down to

college for the first time, so things may be a little spo-
radic. Wish me luck with the whole college thing (and the
whole first novel thing). I'll let you know how things are
going once I get settled in! Thank you for your support.

—Brennan

———

The next morning, she had three upvotes and a comment on her prologue: This is amazing! Can't wait for more!

It was small, but at the same time, Brennan felt like the heavens had
opened and shone down upon her (not to be dramatic).

I have votes! she sent Jonas. And a comment!!?

She wondered if he was even up yet. It was seven in the morning,
after all. She didn't know if he had class this early. Actually, she didn't
know anything about his schedule.

She got up, got dressed, and took her time trekking down the path
to campus.

By the time she got to campus, the high of having people actually
read her story had dissipated, replaced by the heavy feeling in her stomach. She was too early.

As soon as she walked in the door, the tight feeling advanced to
include not only her stomach, but her throat in the torture.

Brennan sat down. People weren't as early today. Throughout the
week, the number of people who arrived early had shrunk; as the days
had passed, the mass of people straggling in right at eight had increased.

She nervously twisted a piece of her hair that she'd missed when
she'd thrown it up that morning.

Her heart *thrum-thrummed* in her ears. She wanted to run. *It's only class,* she argued with herself. *You've made it every day this week so far. Don't mess that up now.* But she really felt like she was going to throw up. *You're going to throw up,* her brain whispered.

I'm not, she mentally replied.

You are.

Not. No. Nope.

Yeah-huh.

Brennan pressed her fingers against her lips and tried to judge how in control of her nausea she was. *Very,* she told herself. *You've got this. You aren't going to throw up.*

Nope nope nope, her brain mocked her. *You* are *going to throw up. You can't open your mouth or it will all come out, everything inside you. Run run run.*

I won't.

You have to.

Why?

You have to. Something is going to go wrong. That's why you feel sick, because something is going to happen. Obviously, there's something to worry about, right? Or you wouldn't feel this way.

She couldn't take it anymore.

In. Out. *Picture the GIF.* The circle in her head expanded and contracted. Too fast, too fast.

She *really* couldn't take it anymore. She stood up, mumbling a slurred excuse me to the students she bumped into on the way out the door. Eight o'clock. Straggler arrival time. Time for class to start.

Brennan felt heat on her cheeks, in her ears, behind her eyes—like fire in her veins.

When she was outside, she left Peck Hall behind and walked a wide oval around Founders and Alumni, over and over until she was calmer, five times.

Then she texted Jonas.

Everything is going to be okay, right? I mean, I know you already said it several times, but can you say it again? Please?

She wondered if he would even text back. He hadn't texted her back yet. Maybe he was in class. Maybe he was sleeping in. Maybe he had remembered he was mad at her for *stuff*.

He texted her back. It's going to be okay.

———

She cried on the way back to Prairie Hall. Then she took a solazepram. *I'll be better this time*, she promised herself.

25

JONAS

It was mid-September. Brennan had texted him again. Everything is going to be okay, right?

Jonas tried calling her.

After class, he'd headed down the street to the Vietnamese restaurant that he went to at least twice a week. The waiter had just delivered a fresh bowl of *pho bo*, steam rising from the hot broth when Brennan had texted him.

He scrolled through their messages. She'd sent him the same one several times now, the first back at the beginning of the semester, and then a few more times. He thought about finding her when he went to his anatomy class at SIUE but decided that if she really wanted to see him, she'd say so.

She didn't answer the call, but she texted him.

Hi, she sent. I'm sorry. I'm just really bad on the phone. He assumed she didn't mean that she was bad at using the phone, but maybe bad at talking on it.

She clarified, anyway: I just can't judge how things are going as well as

I can in person. If that makes sense? I mean, it's not that I can judge very well in person, either, but better, you know?

It's okay, he replied.

Can we text though?

Yeah. He fixed the crutches next to him and adjusted his position on the patio seat, folding his good leg underneath him and shifting his weight. What's wrong? The weather was already starting to hint at fall. A cool breeze pushed through the warmer air and Jonas had to hold down his napkin to keep it from blowing away. He put it under his bowl.

Just stuff . . . things are complicated, you know?

Sure. Life's complicated. I probably know that better than some people.

My roommate is letting people sit on my bed while I'm not there.

He had a feeling she was sort of changing the subject, but he let her. He twirled some of the noodles around his chopsticks and took a bite of the pho. Hot. Good. Like home, when his mom decided it was time for a pho day (as Jonas had liked to call them when he was younger).

Some of them keep their shoes on, Brennan added.

Uncouth, Jonas sent.

I'm glad you understand. You'd take your shoes off if you came over, wouldn't you?

Jonas thought of the shoe rack by his door, and of Rhys not taking his shoes off without their mom reminding him. It used to be habit. Of course, he told Brennan. I would.

Good.

Jonas snapped a picture of the pho and sent it to her. Lunch, he said.

She sent him back a picture of a half-eaten granola bar. Lunch, she said.

He could feel himself crack a smile.

So you like pho, huh? Ha-ha. Say that out loud.

Pho, huh. Rhyming. He smiled again, or maybe he hadn't stopped.

I love pho. Then Fun fact: I'm a quarter Vietnamese. My mom's dad—my grandfather—is Vietnamese. Maybe pho was the stereotypical Vietnamese food choice. But something about it just reminded Jonas of his childhood, and of his mom—it was comforting.

I guess I should give you a fun fact about me. A fact for a fact.

I guess you should.

I have this weird thing with the number three. Like, when I was younger, I used to do certain things three times, like rinse my mouth three times after brushing my teeth or take three bites before being done with supper. Now, it's kind of like my lucky number.

He pictured Brennan, doing things in threes.

I went superweird, didn't I? she sent.

Nope. My turn. When I was younger . . . actually, there's been sort of a resurgence since my accident . . . my nickname was Bird.

Why Bird?

My mom always said I ate like a bird, or that I was all skin and bones like a bird. I don't know. She said it once and it stuck. My dad has mostly stopped, but she still calls me that.

Do you miss her? Them? Do you miss your parents, I mean?

Jonas looked at his half-eaten bowl of pho. He thought about how when he'd first had it, he'd mentally compared it to his mom's. He thought about how when he'd had a hamburger at the DUC, he'd compared it to his dad's homemade ones. Yes, he typed. But it's gotten better the longer I've been down here. Your turn now.

When I was younger, I wanted to be a veterinarian. Then we had to put our dog down and I decided I could never do that.

That took a dark turn. I'm sorry about your dog.

It's okay. It's been a while. I still miss him sometimes, though, like randomly, when I least expect it.

I think missing people—missing anything—is like that. Jonas thought about the times when it randomly hit him that he only had one and a half legs now.

What about you? she asked. What did you want to be when you grew up?

Jonas swallowed. A doctor.

What do you want to do now?

He took a breath. I don't know.

Did you just not want to be a doctor anymore, no second thoughts? Is there something else you want to do?

Not exactly, he sent. It's hard to explain. It was when I lost my leg. I guess I just thought . . . that what I wanted had to change, you know? Because I had changed.

I get that, she said. It makes sense.

Jonas looked at the seat across from him. He wished Brennan was actually here and not just living in his phone.

You still could, you know. Be a doctor. Maybe you have changed, but maybe that means you'll just be better than you would have before.

He hadn't thought about that, at least not really. He tended not to think of anything related to his leg in terms of better. Besides, he still wouldn't walk without the crutches. He'd thought about it, the other day in his dorm room, but when he'd leaned them against the wall and transferred his weight to the prosthesis, he had just been reminded of the hot shame that had burned through him when he'd fallen in the kitchen over the summer. You sort of had to walk to be a doctor, right?

Anyway, sent Brennan. Thanks for talking with me. Got to go to class now.

Okay, have a good time.

Jonas sighed as the screen on his phone went black. He finished the last bit of broth from the pho. His phone lit up again. It's going to be okay, you know? You still have time. You'll figure out what you want to do. Maybe it's being a doctor. Maybe it's something better. You never know.

He smiled a little before replying.

Yeah, you never know, I guess.

When Jonas got back to the dorm, he kept thinking about how maybe being a doctor wasn't so out of reach after all, and that the only thing stopping him was himself.

But then, when he thought about it, the whole walking-without-anything-to-hold-him-up thing seemed even bigger and scarier. Like he wanted to do it, yes, but it also scared him.

He dug his fingers into his hair and then twisted until his head hurt. *You can't even look at the freaking stump. You still call it* the *stump, like it's somehow not a part of you. How the hell would you walk?* He turned his left hand over and spread the fingers out, the skin on his palm stretching where a white scar cut it in two. Broken glass and embarrassment. What if Jonas tried to walk and then failed, and everyone saw that failure?

He grabbed his crutches and left his room. Travis and Sam's door was open. Jonas crutched to the doorframe and stopped, shifting his weight awkwardly to his good leg.

Sam was sitting on his bed, eyes focused on the TV, but when he noticed Jonas in his periphery, he turned around and smiled. "What's up?"

Jonas shrugged, then opened his mouth like he might say something, before giving up and closing it.

"This college thing gets to be a lot sometimes, doesn't it?" Sam scooted over on his bed and picked up an extra controller. "Travis isn't here, so it's just me, but you're welcome to play some video games. *Excellent* for taking your mind off what ails you."

Jonas took the controller and awkwardly lowered himself to the ground, leaning his back against the dresser.

He turned his controller on and settled in. *Distract, distract, distract.*

26

brennan

"Brennan? Don't you have psych today? Did you sleep through your alarm?"

Brennan pretended to be just waking up, turning over and peering at Ambreen through fake-squinty eyes, as if the light was too much. This was the first time she'd skipped class that she hadn't even made it out the door. The worst part was, she'd been doing better. She hadn't skipped for five days. Mentally, the counter ticked back to zero.

Brennan put a hand to her forehead. "I have an awful headache," she moaned. "I'm just gonna stay here today. Thanks for checking on me, though."

"No problem," said Ambreen, frowning at Brennan a bit. "Do you need anything? Medicine? Anything?"

"Nope. I'm fine. I took something earlier when my alarm went off."

"Okay. Feel better." Ambreen left then, shutting the door more quietly than she normally did. As soon as she was gone, Brennan threw back her covers and got down from her bed, pulling out her laptop. Only one thing could distract her from the anxiety today. Writing. She had to write.

She opened her document and picked up where she'd left off yesterday.

> *Cas shoved a shaky hand through his dark, feathery hair. Ing took note of the place where it stuck up in the back. His face was pale, all cast shadows and angles in the moonlight. His nothing-and-everything eyes refused to meet hers—*

Brennan wondered what color Jonas's eyes were. She'd never really paid attention. Maybe it was because she was so nervous every time she was around him. But not like her normal nervous. Something different, like electricity—a nervous hum somewhere deep in her veins, in her arteries, carried along with the beating force of her heart. She both hated it and wanted to feel it again, every time it happened.

Cas was starting to look more like Jonas. When Brennan realized Jonas was bleeding into her writing, she almost laughed at herself. Dark, feathery hair, sticking up in the back. She supposed she couldn't help it that some of her best descriptions were of Jonas. She wondered if she could tell him; if they would laugh about it. *You're* almost *in my story,* she might say.

Or maybe it would be weird. Since he wasn't a writer, he might not get it.

———

She went to class the next day and the next day, but the day after that, she couldn't quite get inside the door. So she stood outside of Peck for a few moments, trying to convince herself to go in.

She saw someone who looked like Jonas, from a distance. Dark hair, sticking up in the back. She thought about what he might think if he knew she wasn't always going to class—that, in fact, she probably *didn't* make it in as many days as she did.

She went inside. While her teacher lectured about anxiety (*Ironic*, Brennan thought), she wrote, in tiny handwriting so no one else could look over her shoulder and read it, a scene for *Superioris*, in which Ing first meets Cas. They were all out of order, the scenes she was writing. Then, somehow, they fit together.

She wrote until the end of class.

Afterward, she texted Jonas. Four days down, one to go.

Can't wait to be done with this week, he sent back almost immediately. A&P practical, organic test, and a crap ton of homework due. But tomorrow after class, I'm going to go over to Travis and Sam's room and play *Smash Bros.* until my brain starts to atrophy enough to forget the pain.

Sounds fun.

You could come hang out, you know. Sam and Travis would be fine with it, I'm sure.

JONAS

Jonas didn't know why he hoped she'd say yes. Why he half held his breath while he waited for her to answer. Turning his phone's screen back on every time it went off, as if he'd miss her message if it was off.

Somehow, he thought he might feel better if he saw her. Like maybe that slight hopefulness that had come with her in the summer might come back.

brennan

Brennan's stomach flipped. It felt like it was tying knots, and the sudden nausea made her feel like running for a bathroom, just in case. *Are you getting sick?* Her face flushed. *What if you're getting sick?* (Did she have a fever?) *What if you go to Jonas's dorm and get sick there? Puke is the most disgusting thing ever. He'd never see you the same way. DON'T MESS THIS UP!* her brain shouted.

She left Peck because she was starting to feel claustrophobic.

Wish I could, she texted Jonas. I have way too much to do this weekend.

She stared at the message. It kind of sickened her, the way she immediately felt better after sending it.

JONAS

He didn't really know why her response made him feel deflated.

That's all right. Have fun being a studious student.

. . . She was typing.

His phone dinged. Have fun rotting your brain!

27

brennan

Mid-October, Brennan decided she wanted a change. She normally spent about five minutes in the bathroom each morning, throwing her hair up into a bun, but one day, when she looked in the mirror, she imagined herself cutting it off.

So she'd gone to the hairdresser in town and told them that she wanted it chopped to just above shoulder length, in a long bob. (She wasn't going to go too crazy and ask for a pixie or anything.)

Afterward, she'd come back to Prairie Hall to a room full of people. Ambreen had friends over again. It was starting to get old, this whole thing where Ambreen invited everyone in their hall over to the room to hang out. It made Brennan feel anxious and claustrophobic when everyone was over. She didn't tell Ambreen because she wanted Ambreen to like her. If only she was normal, she wouldn't have this problem.

She halfway didn't mind the company this time, though, because they all made a big deal over her hair and how nice it looked. For a few minutes, she felt an indescribable warm feeling settle over her—if she had to give it a name, she might call it *belonging*. She was getting used to it, this college thing. The dorms didn't smell weird when she walked in from outside anymore, she'd figured out how to do her laundry and pay with her student ID, and she'd learned her class schedule by heart.

"We should celebrate!" said Ambreen, sliding off her own bed and clapping her hands together, gaining the room's attention, like a professor about to lecture. "There's a big party over at Road's Edge!" Road's Edge was an apartment complex that catered to college students. Upperclassman territory. Brennan hadn't been there before.

"Yes!" seconded Jennifer. Brennan's suitemate was always up for a party. Dressing up, dancing, and having drunk conversations about literature was a good Friday night for her. Brennan always thought Jennifer looked like she was having fun, and Brennan sometimes wished she could feel that free. But she was also gripped with anxiety at the thought of losing her inhibitions. *What if you say something stupid? What if you throw up on someone? HANGOVERS.*

"I don't know," Brennan began, hesitantly. "I really need to study tonight." Only a partial lie. She did need to study. She also needed to calm her suddenly twisting stomach, and a party wasn't the way to go.

"Oh come on, party pooper!" said Ambreen, grabbing Brennan's hand. "It'll be fun! You look great, and you should really get out there and experience a party, at least once. It's part of college!"

Brennan still hesitated, her anxiety tying more and more knots in her stomach. "I just—"

"It's Friday night! You'll have tomorrow to study, and the next day. Live a little!" This from Calvin, the guy who held the distinction of being one of only two nonfamily guy contacts in Brennan's phone. He adjusted his glasses and grinned reassuringly.

"You never do anything, Brennan," pouted Ambreen. "Let us dress you up and show you off for once. You could take off your glasses, keep your hair down, wear something other than leggings and baggy sweaters."

"But I like sweaters. And I need my glasses—"

"You don't have contacts or anything?" Ambreen was already shooing out the guys, shutting the door behind them and turning her attention to Brennan.

"No."

"Hmm. Well, we can work with the glasses, but you'll need to wear some makeup."

They were talking like it was a done deal that Brennan would go.

"I never said I wanted to go," she muttered, pretending she was still in control and forcing her tone to be light, almost as if she was joking. Fake smiles. She hoped they'd take the hint.

They didn't. That, or they completely ignored it.

"Just this one night," coaxed Jennifer, turning Brennan around to face the mirror over the back of the door and resting her hands on Brennan's shoulders. "Please come with us?"

"I-I guess," Brennan finally mumbled, worried that she'd disappoint them. It was her greatest fear, that she might disappoint someone. She always tried not to worry about it, but she always did. Inevitably. The knot in her stomach tied itself tighter but she tried not to focus on it.

"Yay!" cheered Ambreen, going to the closet. She pulled out a short skirt. "How about this?"

"No," said Brennan. "That is where I draw the line. I'm wearing jeans."

"Fine," huffed Jennifer, but she grinned, tossing Brennan a pair of dark-wash skinny jeans.

Ambreen handed her a flowy, off-the-shoulder top. Brennan looked at it with hesitation. She didn't like showing off her shoulders because

1. (and only) Keratosis pilaris. Little red bumps that her doctor had called chicken skin. Ugh. There could be nothing attractive about something called chicken skin.

"Can't I wear something that doesn't, you know—"

"Nope," said Jennifer. "You drew the line on jeans. I'm drawing the line on this."

"But isn't it cold outside?" It was rather cold for mid-October. "Can't I just wear a sweater?"

"Come on, Brennan. Don't be a spoilsport."

Brennan sighed. "Okay." She relented.

Then commenced the awkward affair of having to change in front of her roommate and suitemate, who were apparently not going to leave. Brennan knew that a lot of the other girls in the dorm dressed in front of one another, but she never had, always crossing over to the suite's bathroom to change.

Reluctantly, she turned her back to them and put the jeans on first. She didn't turn around, not wanting to show them the places where she had curves instead of edges. She'd seen Ambreen change, at least. Ambreen was perfect. All glowing brown skin that never seemed to be too oily or too dry, dark-brown hair that was straight like Brennan only wished hers could be. Defined in all the places Brennan was blurred— at the waist, elbows, and chest. Brennan had hips that could be called *sturdy* and scatterings of freckles in places where she thought freckles shouldn't be—her stomach, below her collarbone (but only the right one, oddly).

She quickly pulled on a black tank top and then the flowy patterned shirt that Ambreen had given her.

She hesitantly turned around for their approval.

"Whoa," said Ambreen, hand to her mouth. "You look amazing. This calls for a picture."

"Wow!" Jennifer smiled widely as Ambreen dug around in her purse for her phone. Brennan felt that ache of *belonging* again. "You almost look like a different person!"

But do I want *to look like a different person?* Brennan asked herself. *Yes*, her brain told her. *Of course. It's better.*

So she smiled even as Ambreen got out her phone and held it up to take a picture of the three of them.

She kept smiling because that was her defense, and her defense couldn't fail now.

———

At first, Brennan let herself be swept up in the good-natured camaraderie that existed between Ambreen, Jennifer, and the rest of the people in their hall. It was like she'd always been a part of the group, and not just Ambreen's lame roommate who never went anywhere and was just now tagging along. They all laughed and chatted as they piled into cars and made the short drive to the party.

Brennan was squeezed into the back seat, stuck in the middle because she was the smallest. Calvin was on one side of her, and another guy named Luke was on the other side. She tried to make herself as small as possible, feeling kind of awkward about sitting so close to two guys she didn't really know that well. She always felt awkward around guys. Around everyone, for that matter. (It was just worse with guys.)

"You okay?" Calvin asked her. "If you need me to, I can ask Ambreen to turn around and take you back." He chuckled a bit, awkwardly. "You seem nervous. I feel a little bad about pressing you to come now."

"No!" she said quickly. "No, I'm fine." She grinned and tried to focus on breathing in and out, calming the anxiety in her stomach. She pictured the GIF. For once, it worked. *Maybe for one night, I can be normal,* she thought. *I just want to be normal. Is that too much to ask?*

Eventually, they made it to the party and everyone exited the vehicles. Brennan took in a breath of the crisp fall air, feeling relieved to no longer be cramped between the guys in the back seat. She felt immediately better, freer. She shivered a bit, wrapping her arms around herself.

The jovial group continued on to the apartment where the party was, making their way upstairs and banging on the door. The loud music issuing from the room ceased and a guy Brennan didn't know opened the door, greeting them and letting them in. The guy gave an all-clear to the student behind the makeshift DJ station (a few speakers and an iPhone) and the music resumed. Brennan awkwardly followed the rest of the group, trailing behind, laughing uneasily and too loudly whenever someone made a joke and hoping it sounded like she was having fun.

She immediately regretted coming. She wanted to go back in time and tell Calvin to tell Ambreen to turn around. Or better yet, to the dorm room, where she could say no on her own.

Someone offered her a drink and she took it, moving deeper into the party. She felt a bit claustrophobic. The apartment was packed. Someone bumped into her arm, and whatever was in the cup she'd been given sloshed sloppily over her hand. She grabbed Ambreen's arm anxiously. "Ambreen." Almost yelling above the chatter and music.

"Hey, don't worry!" yelled Ambreen, putting her arm around Brennan. "I'll stick with you. It'll be all right. Okay?" Ambreen was beaming. She seemed so sure. Maybe if Brennan relaxed, she'd have fun too.

"Okay," she responded.

However, it didn't take long for Ambreen to be swept off into the festivities, leaving Brennan alone. Brennan swallowed, her hand clutching her drink. She eyed it suspiciously. *Never take drinks from people at parties; pour your own drinks so you know what's in them.* She set the plastic cup down on the counter, distastefully, remembering the words from the little pamphlet they'd given her at the doctor's office on party safety.

She hugged her arms nervously, glancing around at the other people in the room. Her stomach was starting to tie more and more knots. She felt kind of like puking. She felt claustrophobic. Her chest felt tight. She needed to get away. She needed to run. Her hand was sticky from where her drink had spilled earlier. Maybe she could find a sink to rinse the feeling away.

"Hey."

She jumped and whirled around, only to see the drunk-looking guy behind her wink at her and then look her up and down, like he was sizing her up. She hugged her arms again, covering herself protectively, nervous. "Hi," she said back, already backing away.

The guy definitely smelled like alcohol. Her eyes widened as he stepped closer to her.

"Dance with me," he said. His words were sloppy, falling over one another.

"I-I don't dance," Brennan said, laughing and half fanning her face. When had it become so hot in here? She looked around in panic. Where was Ambreen? Where was Jennifer? Or anyone she'd come with, for that matter.

"Aw, come on," said Drunk Guy, grabbing her wrist too tightly. It felt like the bones in her wrist were grinding against one another. She tried to pull away, but he caged her in. She thought she saw Ambreen through the crowd, waving, and thought that she maybe heard her name, but her roommate disappeared as the bodies shifted, weaving and gyrating in a crazed, feverish dance.

Drunk Guy dragged Brennan onto the dance floor, seemingly oblivious to her protests. Once out on the floor (which was really just the middle of the apartment's living room), he turned and grabbed her, beginning to dance, getting way closer to Brennan than she liked.

Something about the alcohol smell and the closeness of him drove her over the edge. She panicked. She didn't *want* this. She wanted to get away. She *had* to get away, because *she couldn't breathe*.

Her mind was racing in a million different directions. She was starting to hyperventilate. The guy was still trying to get closer, pressing against her. Her mind said *Fight* and *Run* at the same time.

So she kicked him. She aimed low but must have missed, because he was still standing. However, it was enough to make him lose his balance, drunk as he was, and let go of her wrist.

And she ran.

She pushed her way through the other people in the room, not caring if she stepped on anyone's feet, not noticing if she bumped into someone's drink.

She had one goal, and that was the door. *Outside,* Brennan repeated in her head. *Outside. Get outside. Get outside.* Her heart was beating hard: short staccato bursts, hammering in her chest.

She opened the door and shut it hard behind her, stumbling down the stairs like she was drunk herself, then flinging open the door to outside. The cold air chilled her to the bone.

And she ran.

She didn't really know where she was. She'd never been to Road's Edge before, even though others in her dorm frequented it for parties. She must have run in the wrong direction, because instead of finding the car, she seemed to be going deeper into the expanse of apartment buildings.

She ran until she couldn't run anymore, because there was a lake. There was a little playground there for the children who lived in the apartment complex.

Brennan halted, out in the open now, shivering. The flowy shirt wasn't warm at all. She missed her sweaters.

Hide, her mind told her. *Hide from everything.*

So she fled to the playset, climbed up the ladder, and crawled into the slide, where she curled up in a ball at the place where the slide turned, effectively keeping herself from sliding down.

And then she cried.

With shaking fingers, Brennan pulled out her phone. Three percent battery. She needed to call Ambreen. Why hadn't she charged her phone before she left? *Stupid, stupid.* She never left without her phone charged. But tonight had been spur of the moment. *It was a bad idea in the first place. It was a bad idea. I should never have agreed to come.* She was still hyperventilating. She couldn't catch her breath.

She felt dizzy, her vision blurry through her tears and fuzzy around the edges as she opened her contacts and jabbed at the As, numb fingered. She held her phone to her ear, listening as it rang and rang.

And rang.

28

"The caller you are trying to reach is currently unavailable. Please leave your message after the tone."

29

JONAS

Jonas groaned and rolled over in bed, attempting to grab his phone from the nightstand, where it was plugged in, charging. What time was it?

He hadn't quite reached the phone, so he sat up on one elbow and fumbled for it with his hand. He ended up knocking it off the table and onto the floor. By this time, the phone had stopped ringing.

Crap, he thought, feeling for the switch to turn on the lamp next to the bed. He winced at the bright light that flooded the room. He reached down and retrieved the phone, pulling it toward him by the charger cord still attached to it.

Phone now in hand, Jonas switched the light back off.

He frowned. Why would Brennan be calling him? She didn't call; she texted. Jonas looked at the time then. Ten minutes past midnight. The phone display went dark in his hand, and he stared at the blank screen.

Why would Brennan be calling him this late? *Why would she be calling me at all?*

The phone dinged and lit up once more.

One new voice mail.

Jonas unlocked the phone, wide awake now, and opened Voicemail, hitting Play and putting the phone to his ear.

The first thing he registered was the panic in Brennan's voice. It kind of sounded like she was crying.

"Ambreen! *Please* look at your phone!" She sounded like she was pleading. Jonas's frown deepened.

"You *said* you wouldn't leave me alone. You said we could stick together. But you left, and some guy tried to make me dance with him, and he was getting too close—" Brennan's voice broke, interrupted by a hiccoughing sob. By this time, Jonas was sitting up in bed, his grip on the phone tightening.

"Please come get me. I need you to come get me *right now*. I'm at a playset somewhere in Road's Edge. It's by a lake? I don't really know where it is other than that. *Please*, Ambreen. I need you to—"

The voice mail cut off. That was it. That was the (heartbreaking) end.

Jonas swung his good leg over the edge of the bed, already hitting Call Back. The call went straight to voice mail.

Jonas's mind was racing. Had her phone died? What party had they been at? And Brennan was outside now, at night?

Jonas tried the phone again. Again, straight to voice mail.

He was fully out of bed now. His fingers fumbled as he put the prosthesis on, forcing himself to slow down and get it on properly after dropping it twice. He hunched over his crutches and tried the phone again. Voice mail. *Again.*

Crap. Crap, crap, crap. He crutched across the room, then back a few times, trying to figure out what to do. His body hummed with nervous energy. *You've got to go get her. What if her phone died and she's alone? If something happened? What if something happened? What if it's happened already? Come on.* He tried to talk himself into it. *Let's go.*

Remembering how chilly it was outside, he put on a jacket before grabbing his keys and wallet and heading out the door.

It took an eternity for the elevator to climb to the third floor. *Come on. Come on, come on. Why didn't you learn to take the damn stairs?*

In the elevator, Jonas tried Brennan's number again. *The caller you are trying to reach is currently unavailable. Please leave your message after the tone.*

He was already sweating by the time he made his way across campus. He dropped the keys twice trying to unlock Gus's driver-side door. His hands were shaking now. (He tried to convince himself it was because of the cold.)

He turned it into steps:

1. Start the car. (He started it.)
2. Put it into Reverse. (Wait, back into Park. Seat belt on. Then Reverse again.)
3. Back out.

He hadn't adjusted the rearview mirror. When he glanced up, he saw himself instead of the rear window and it really hit him then. *You have to drive. You have to drive; there is no other way you can make absolutely, 100 percent sure, that she's safe. You're going to drive.*

Rhys had one of those solar dancing animals on the dash (it was from his girlfriend, Madison) and, even though the sun wasn't out, it rattled all the same. Jonas tried to focus on that instead of his own rapidly beating heart. He didn't want to drive on the highway. He always took the Metro and the bus to his class at SIUE, to avoid it. But this was more important than being afraid of driving.

He picked up the phone again. Voice mail, *again.* "Brennan," he said, as the voice mail tone sounded in his ear. "If you get this, hold on, okay? I'm coming."

———

Jonas had never gone this fast. Even when he'd driven before The Accident, he'd never gone above five over. He'd just never liked driving fast.

Now, however, Jonas was going around eighty in a seventy-mile-per-hour zone (at this point, he didn't think he could move his foot anyway, he was so tense). He had two prayers at that moment:

1. That Brennan wasn't coming to any harm.
2. That there weren't any cops along Interstate 55.

Thankfully, he made it to his exit without any flashing lights turning the darkness blue. It was around twelve thirty now. Jonas wondered if Ambreen had come to get Brennan. He doubted it, if Brennan had called him by mistake. Maybe she'd managed to get out one more call before her phone died—realized her mistake and called Ambreen. Maybe his phone had only reached her voice mail the first time because she was *already* calling Ambreen.

He accelerated onto Interstate 255, hands gripping the steering wheel like he might crash if he let go, as he watched the speedometer climb.

He passed eighty and forced himself to slow down. He grabbed his phone, swerving a little and having to consciously tell himself it was okay, he'd driven with one hand before. *Nothing is going to happen; it's fine.* He fumbled a bit before managing to unlock the phone and call Brennan.

Voice mail again.

Jonas hung up, and then accidentally dropped the phone on the floor instead of returning it to the passenger seat. He gripped the steering wheel with both hands. Tightly.

He passed a semi, and his grip on the wheel went white knuckled, his breathing speeding up until the truck was left in the distance. His head swam. His foot felt leaden on the gas. He could practically feel the sweat gathering on his forehead and the nape of his neck.

Following his phone's muffled-against-the-floor directions, he took Exit 3 for Edwardsville. *Why is it taking so long? It feels like it's taking forever.* He looked at the dash clock, the numbers glowing in the darkness. Only 12:40 a.m. Only ten minutes since he'd last checked.

The road was mostly empty, save for a few stragglers out late. The GPS directed him to make a right, and there it was, after a lone stoplight. *Road's Edge.* The newer development was still lit up, and Jonas wondered which light in the darkness was the party Brennan had been at.

He slowed down, peering out the window and trying to see past the lighted apartments, looking for a playset. She'd said the far end—it probably wasn't bad to keep going.

The road stopped, running into another parking lot, with a sort of roundabout for drivers to turn around. Jonas was about to go all the way around the roundabout when he saw it.

A playset, the moon shining down on plastic and metal from a gap in the cloud cover.

Jonas couldn't help but think it looked like a horror movie.

He parked the car and let it idle, frowning. The playset looked empty. Perhaps Brennan had been picked up already. Perhaps she was fine. Okay. *Okay.*

Jonas turned off the car and got out, retrieving his crutches (and his fallen phone) from the passenger side. He locked the car, which chirped in the silence, headlights flashing, and put the keys in his jeans pocket.

He made his way slowly toward the playset, looking to the left and right as he approached it. It appeared to be deserted. A chilly breeze blew, rocking the empty swings gently back and forth. Up in the sky, clouds filled in the gap, covering the moon.

Jonas's frown deepened as he approached the play area. "Brennan?" he whispered quietly. No one answered, but in the silence after he'd spoken, he heard shuffling, and then what sounded like sniffling.

Maybe she was afraid to come out?

The noises had come from the slide.

Jonas reached the ladder and (after a few moments of hesitation—*Climbing a ladder?? Can you climb a ladder?*) climbed up it, half dragging his left leg and finally struggling onto the platform at the top. The stump hurt after his clumsy journey up the ladder, and the breeze tugged at his hair and cut through his jacket. Below, it knocked over his crutches from where he'd leaned them against the playset.

He stood by the entrance to the slide, leaned forward slightly, and peered into the darkness, trying not to topple over.

"Brennan?" he asked again. He pulled out his phone and turned on the flashlight, illuminating the tunnel to reveal her. *Brennan,* huddled in the place where the slide turned, curled into a ball. She looked up, squinting into the light. He almost dropped the phone again.

"Jonas?" she said, her voice hoarse and small. "Wh—what are you doing here? Did you drive? Are you okay?" She was asking *him* how he was? She was shivering, her teeth knocking against her words. Jonas was suddenly conscious of how cold it actually was. She was wearing jeans and some insubstantial flowy top. "How did you get here?" she kept saying. "How did you know *I* was here? Were you at the party too?"

Jonas set the phone down and went down onto his good knee, ignoring the ache of his remaining left leg protesting the new positioning, and holding his hand out to her. "Never mind that," he said. "Get up here first, okay?"

She looked hesitant.

"Come on, Brennan!" he snapped, irritated. At the crumpled look on her face, he immediately wished the words hadn't come out that way. He'd just been so worried. Now that he had her, and he knew she was safe (was she safe? had anything happened?), all the nervous energy was dissipating into impatience, unfortunately.

He closed his eyes, letting out a shaky breath. "Okay," he breathed. "I'm sorry. Just come up, all right? It's freezing out here. You're shaking."

Brennan gave him her hand. It was cold as ice. (His own hand was probably clammy, thanks to the drive over.)

Jonas helped her up and then stood, pulling her to her feet next to him.

They both climbed down from the playset, Jonas doing his best not to fall on his face. He picked up his crutches and studied Brennan, looking for any signs of injury or struggle, before pulling off his jacket and wrapping it around her shoulders. She was still shivering and crying, and now her nose was running, too, her cheeks and upper lip pitifully wet.

"Geez, Brennan, what happened to you?" he muttered. He moved both crutches under his left arm before putting his right around her and pulling her into him, rubbing her arm, trying to warm her up.

She didn't answer, just leaned her head against him as they started to make their way slowly to the car. Jonas helped her into the passenger seat and then made his way to the driver's side.

He got in and started the car, turning on the heater and pointing it at Brennan, who was still wrapped in his jacket. She stared straight ahead, not speaking, hardly blinking.

By now, the clouds that had gathered were unleashing their burdens. The rain-blurred reflections of streetlights bled over the pavement, and the *thwick thwick* of the windshield wipers filled the silence in the car. Jonas forced himself to breathe normally, like his brain wasn't having a mini meltdown over driving in the rain.

Brennan stared straight ahead, shell-shocked. She held on to Jonas's crutches like she was holding on for dear life.

"Where are we going?" she asked suddenly.

"We're just going," Jonas said, glancing sideways at her. "For however long you need." It felt right to say it. It felt less right after he'd said it, and his brain caught up and realized it meant more driving.

"Nothing happened, you know," she finally said, after another few moments of silence. Jonas glanced sideways at her again. She looked like she was shrinking, shoulders hunched and curled inward, arms around herself like a shield.

"But it could have," he finally said. "And that's important. It doesn't mean any less just because it didn't go that far." Jonas sucked in a breath at the potent mixture of rage and fear that shot through his veins at the thought. "It doesn't mean any less, Brennan," he said again, firmly. "You are still allowed to feel this way."

She looked at him then, finally, her eyes red and bleary. She nodded, and then lapsed back into silence, returning her gaze to the window. Even when his accelerating and braking were shaky, she didn't say anything.

Jonas drove around for a while, until the rain stopped, then pulled into a mostly empty parking lot, his entire body slumping in relief as he turned the car off. *Jenny's Diner. Open LATE: till 3 a.m.*

Brennan looked around before frowning. "What are we doing here?"

"We're getting breakfast," he said, shrugging and turning off Gus. Jonas gestured to the clock, which read 1:37 a.m., glowing in the dark for a moment before shutting off now that the car wasn't running. "Good morning, Brennan."

He took the crutches (trying not to hit her in the face as he moved them to his side and got out) and came around to Brennan's side. When she got out, she halted by the car and refused to take another step forward. "I-I can't," she said. "I-I let them put makeup on me. I cried . . . mascara—"

Jonas frowned, observing her now that the lights in the parking lot let him really see her. Her hair was a little messy (and shorter than it had been when he'd last seen her) and her makeup *did* look a little smudged. He didn't care. "You look fine," he said. "Come on."

She still didn't come, so he sighed, moved his crutches to his left side again, and stuck out his hand, offering it to her. She stared at his outstretched hand for a few moments before giving in and taking it. He led her inside, trying not to think about how small her hand was in his, even though he'd never thought of his own hands as particularly large.

They found a booth next to the window and sat down. Brennan didn't let go of Jonas's hand, like she was stuck there, so they sat on the same side of the table.

A waitress came by and handed them menus and glasses of water. Jonas asked Brennan what she wanted, but she just shrugged.

So he ordered a pancake breakfast to share, and asked for an extra plate.

30

brennan

After the waitress was finished taking Jonas's order, Brennan excused herself and bolted for the bathroom.

Once inside, she stood in front of the mirror, taking deep, shaky breaths. What was Jonas doing here? How had he known where to find her?

She must have hit the wrong contact. Ordinarily, Jonas and Ambreen wouldn't have even been close in Brennan's contact list. However, she'd put his name in, first and last—JONAS AVERY (all caps, just like that)—and Ambreen in only as Ambreen, leading the contacts list to categorize them both as As (her only two As). Plus, it wasn't like she had that many contacts anyway.

Brennan gripped the edge of the counter, leaning forward. She'd been so glad to see him. *Too* glad to see him. Relief had overwhelmed her and she'd started blubbering like a toddler, falling apart. And then he'd put his arm around her, and she'd really lost it, leaning against him. She didn't know what it felt like to be drunk and lose your inhibitions, but she imagined it was like that—warm and less conscious of the rest of the world.

You're such an idiot, her anxiety admonished her. She'd embarrassed herself. It would be bad enough to have to admit that she couldn't even handle a party to Ambreen and Jennifer, but to admit it to Jonas? She suddenly felt like a child, too incompetent to even deal with a social event. And here he was, showing up in the night like a *knight,* like a responsible adult—

And what did he think of her? He hadn't really said anything yet. *And he drove. He drove to get* you. *You made him drive. You* know *he doesn't like to drive. YOU IDIOT.* It was an accident. *STUPID.* Please, stop.

Brennan looked up at the mirror once more, staring. She looked like a blurry version of herself. Her makeup was smudged all over her face, and residual wetness on her upper lip made her look like a child.

She splashed cold water over her cheeks and forehead, letting it calm her before taking a paper towel and wiping her face clean of any and all makeup. She put her glasses back on. Now her eyes just looked wet and huge.

She'd have to go back out sometime.

Brennan exited the bathroom, slowly making her way back to the table, where Jonas was sitting, looking at his phone.

This time, she sat down across from him. If he noticed, he didn't say anything. *If?* her brain teased. *Of course he noticed.*

Once Brennan sat down, Jonas turned off his phone and leaned back against the seat, studying her. "Are you okay?" he asked eventually.

Brennan's fingers, still white, wrapped around the just-forming purple bruises on her wrist. She almost started crying again, just over the fact that Jonas had asked.

"Fine," she managed to get out. She couldn't help but notice the slight tremor in Jonas's hands as he folded and unfolded them, and the wetness of sweat around the collar of his T-shirt. *God, you made him* drive.

The waitress brought the food and a steaming pot of black coffee.

Jonas busied himself with moving half of the pancakes, hash browns, and bacon to an extra plate.

He passed it to Brennan, then began to eat his own portion.

Brennan's anxiety gathered in her stomach again, like the storm clouds in the sky earlier. Ominous. Jonas must think of her as a nuisance. After all, he'd *driven,* all the way from St. Louis, just to rescue her from a kiddie slide.

And it sounded really, really dumb when she put it that way. She thought of herself, crying in the slide. She wished a hole would open up in the ground and swallow her, saving her from the embarrassment.

She picked at her food before setting down her fork and looking at her hands in her lap.

"Why did you come all the way to Edwardsville for me?" she asked Jonas quietly, not quite meeting his eyes. She was staring at his chin now, and couldn't seem to bring herself to raise her eyes any more than that, for fear of meeting his, and what she might see there.

She heard him drop his fork, which clattered against his plate.

"I couldn't get a hold of you, and I needed to make sure you were all right. It's the middle of the night, Brennan. Anything could have happened to you, for all I knew."

"You didn't have to, you know," she muttered.

"Brennan," he said, his tone admonishing. "All I knew from your voice mail was that some guy was giving you problems. Since I couldn't get a hold of you again, I had to make sure you'd gotten away all right. You didn't sound too good on the phone," he pointed out.

"What would you have done if the guy was still hanging around?" she asked him curiously.

"Kicked him. Hard. With the metal leg."

Brennan almost cracked a smile at the image of Jonas beating up Drunk Guy with his fake leg. He smiled too. She wondered if she imagined that it didn't quite reach his eyes. She swallowed. "I'm sorry," she began.

"What for?" he asked her.

"For putting you through all this."

"Brennan, if I hadn't wanted to come, I wouldn't have come." He was silent again.

"Did you want to drive?"

It was his turn to avoid eye contact. His hands were *folding and unfolding*. Perpetually.

He didn't say it, but she knew.

She felt like crying. "I had a panic attack," she blurted out. "I couldn't breathe properly. I ran because I couldn't—I didn't know what to do. Ambreen had said she'd stay with me, but she left, and not even after we'd been there for a while and I'd gotten more comfortable but, like, right away. So I was stuck there, with some drunk guy who was trying to get me to dance with him—" Suddenly everything was rushing out of her. Word vomit, as unattractive as it was, again. *Gross,* her brain said. *Look at you, making everything about you.* But she couldn't stop.

"He grabbed me by the wrist and pulled me along with him. I managed to get away . . . got out. I went to the playset. I didn't really know where else to go. I didn't really know quite where I was. I—"

She paused, on the verge of crying again. "Jonas," she said. "I have anxiety. Really bad anxiety. I always tried to hide it because I'm crazy, Jonas," she said, a tear falling down her cheek. "I really am. Because I have this—this thing. I'm not normal, right? I mean, this can't be normal. It can't be normal to feel sick almost every day of your life, usually for unexplainable reasons." She shook her head, trying to keep herself from crying more, but failing.

She closed her eyes. "I couldn't even handle one party." She laughed bitterly. "Now everyone's going to know me as crazy Brennan, who panicked and bolted. Brennan who ran." She didn't even know how she'd face Ambreen and the rest of them again. "I just . . . I panicked," she repeated, dazedly. "I didn't know what else to do but to run."

Jonas hadn't said anything the entire time she'd been talking. He'd just watched her, that little crease between his brows.

"And now," she added, "you'll probably go on back to St. Louis thinking how crazy I am."

He cleared his throat slightly. She chanced a glance up at him. He didn't say anything, so she tried to fill the yawning silence.

"I just—I should go." *Where are you going to go? You don't have a car. You don't have money for a bus. Where are you going to go?*

She was standing now. (Panicking again. Running again.)

So was Jonas. He grabbed her arm. It was weird how different the motion was coming from him than it was coming from Drunk Guy, who had grabbed her arm like he was trying to latch on—sink claws in. Jonas's grip on her arm was light, hesitant, just enough to stop her but not enough to keep her there if she didn't want to stay. She wanted to stay. "Brennan," he said, pulling her back to the booth and gesturing for her to sit back down. She did, obediently, her stomach busy tying knots of anxiety.

Jonas sat back down across from her. "Look at me," he said.

She did, even though it was the last thing she wanted to do. She was afraid she'd see some kind of annoyance in his expression, some kind of frustration at having to deal with her. She met his eyes and managed to maintain eye contact for once. Not just maintain it, but hold it, like a lifeline.

"I want you to listen, okay?" he said.

She nodded dumbly, staring at him. Dark, that was what color his eyes were. Not black, absent of color, but not brown, not anything definable. Dark like the night sky—endless, but with light in them. Like stargazing.

Jonas continued, "You shouldn't expect that people will leave just because of your anxiety. Yeah, it makes things different. And yeah, it makes things harder. But if people leave you just because you have this thing that you have to deal with, then that's their fault, okay?"

He looked away for a moment before saying, "I know what it is to be the one who feels like they're making everything more difficult. I know what it is to feel like you're the one who has a problem that inconveniences the people around you."

Jonas met her eyes again. "I can't drive, Brennan. I mean—" He looked skyward like he was searching for the words. "I *can* drive, but I don't. Because it feels like I can't. I can't explain it. I get this . . . it's dread. Like, I get in the car and I'm convinced I'm going to die. Or lose another limb. I just *know* something bad is going to happen."

Brennan blinked, unable to look away.

"I hate it. I hate the feeling, but I can't make it stop. It feels like I should be able to, because it's *my thoughts*, so I should be able to think *Hey, now, brain, let's stop this*. But I can't. I'm a huge inconvenience.

"The point is, Brennan, that it's okay. For the people who matter, you aren't an inconvenience." He looked like maybe he was trying to believe his own words. "For the people who matter, they aren't going to care if you don't want to go out, even if they don't always understand exactly why. They'll hang out with you anyway. They'll make things work. They aren't going to care if you leave a party early. They're not going to care if they get a call at midnight and end up driving eighty miles per hour down the highway just to get to you and make sure you're okay. Okay? Because I know you have anxiety, Brennan. I've known, really, since the summer. And I'm still here; I still came. Even though I didn't want to drive. I *really* didn't want to drive. Driving was scary. But you—this, you, your anxiety—that didn't scare me. It doesn't scare me. Your anxiety didn't scare me away, Brennan."

Brennan nodded, tears welling up in her eyes.

"And no matter what, no matter how bad it gets, remember this: just because you have this thing to deal with that's different from some of the other people you know, it doesn't mean there's something wrong with you. It doesn't make you broken, Brennan."

She was really crying now. Jonas was watching her with concern. "Okay?" he said.

"You," she said, half laughing, half crying. Hiccoughing. "You know, it doesn't make you broken either, Jonas."

He didn't look like he quite believed her, but—there. The corners of his mouth pulled up just the slightest bit.

31

JONAS

Rhys was mad at him for taking the car.

"It was an emergency," said Jonas. He noticed that Rhys hadn't taken his shoes off when he'd come in the room.

"I needed to go to a study session with Bryce." Bryce was Rhys's friend from his calc class. "I couldn't because *you* took the car without asking me first."

"At midnight?"

"It was a late-night study session. We have a test on Monday." Rhys stopped his angry pacing and faced Jonas, who was sitting on his bed trying to read his chemistry textbook. The boxy dorm room seemed even smaller when they were both in it, like the walls were closing in. It made Jonas even gladder that he didn't have a roommate.

"Besides," continued Rhys, "what did you need to do at midnight anyway? You don't even drive anymore. That, and the fact that you go to bed at, like, ten o'clock. So where'd you go?"

Jonas glared at his brother, giving up on chemistry and slamming the book shut. "Is it really any of your business?" He wondered what

Rhys would think of the new Jonas who stayed up playing video games every weekend.

"It's my car," said Rhys, crossing his arms.

"It's ours to *share*," retorted Jonas. Rhys rolled his eyes and fixed an angry gaze on his brother's face. It wouldn't have been a problem before; Gus pretty much *was* Rhys's car. And Jonas was fine with that. Rhys could do whatever he wanted with the car. Jonas had a set of keys for emergencies.

Last night was an emergency. Big enough for Jonas to drive again. His heart rate still picked up when he thought about it. *Eighty miles per hour down the interstate.* And nothing happened. He didn't die. He still had all his limbs. (Well, the three that he'd been left with, at least.)

Rhys was pressing onward.

"We both know you never leave your room unless you absolutely have to. You don't even *drive* anymore," he repeated. "I took you to your little meetups this summer, remember?"

"That's not true," said Jonas, getting defensive. "If you'd paid any attention this summer, instead of being out of the house the majority of the time, you'd know I drove. Once, I mean. When you weren't there." He winced. It sounded pathetic. It *was* pathetic.

"Ooh," said Rhys, raising his eyebrows, mock impressed. "What do you want me to do? Give you an award?"

Jonas clenched his fists at his side, trying not to let his fingers shake from all the talk about driving. (*God, you're just* thinking *about it!*) "What's your problem, Rhys?"

"You're my problem, Jonas," Rhys snapped. "I've spent all this time feeling guilty for what happened and not *once* have you cared whatsoever. You act like you're the only one who has to deal with what happened. What about that guy—Paul—the guy who hit us? Mom? What about *me*? So you lost your leg. It's getting to the point where you just need to get over it and move on."

Rhys's words were like a slap to the face. Jonas had known that there'd been tension between them since The Accident, but he hadn't known that Rhys was *this* angry. Rhys turned around and started to make his way to the door. "So, yeah, take the car. Get out, whatever. It's great and all that you're finally moving on. Maybe I can too. Just let me know when you're taking the car. Give me some *notice* or something."

Rhys left.

Jonas let out a deep breath and allowed himself to fall backward until he was lying on the bed, looking at the ceiling. He closed his eyes. What had he even been doing last night? What had possessed him to get out of bed at midnight, drive (*drive*, of all things!) to Edwardsville, and find Brennan?

She was in trouble, he argued with himself.

She probably thought it was weird, another part of him said. *You really didn't have any place. I mean, sure she called you* (accidentally), *but you're not exactly best friends or anything.*

He sighed and picked up his phone from its place next to him, shifting so that he could prop his head up on his pillow. He opened the text again.

Thank you.

From Brennan, that morning. Or rather, that afternoon, when he'd actually awakened after his late night. It had all seemed like a dream—half-fogged in his mind—until he had read the text.

He hadn't responded. He wasn't sure what to say. *You're welcome* seemed too simple. However, in the time that had passed since she'd sent the text, he hadn't thought of anything better to send.

So, reluctantly, he typed You're welcome and hit Send.

32

brennan

You're welcome.

That was all that Jonas had responded with. Brennan wondered if he was trying to forget about the whole situation. If it had been her, she probably would be trying to forget.

The wire frame of the dorm bed squeaked beneath her as she shifted uneasily, holding her phone in both hands.

I'm sorry, she sent him. I really didn't mean to call you and get you all caught up in my mess.

There was nothing for a while, and then she could see the dreaded three dots. He was typing a reply.

She lay on her bed, staring at her phone, at those three dots. Then they disappeared.

But no message.

And then her phone buzzed. *Incoming call.*

Jonas!

Brennan panicked. She didn't do phone calls well. Jonas knew that. So why was he calling her? Her brain was stuck; she couldn't think with

Jonas's name shining up at her from the screen. JONAS AVERY, all caps, just like that. She remembered typing it in like that over the summer. She didn't answer. She set her phone facedown on her bed and sat up, staring at it like it was a ticking time bomb.

The buzzing stopped eventually. Brennan held her breath.

And then her phone chimed with a text.

She stared at it for a few more seconds before picking it up and opening the message.

Answer your phone, Brennan.

It vibrated again, as if on cue. Brennan took a deep breath and hit Accept. Should she say "Hello, this is Brennan," on the very slim chance that it wasn't Jonas and the caller didn't know who she was? (She still had this worry, even though it clearly said JONAS AVERY on the caller ID.) Should she just say hello? Unable to decide, she opened her mouth and no words came out.

"Brennan?" said Jonas's voice after a moment. Jonas had a nice voice, not too deep and not too high. Rather, it was somewhere in the middle. Nice. Comfortable.

That was Jonas, to Brennan. He was comfortable. She was comfortable with him, or at least as comfortable as she could be. It was weird, thinking about it, because she was hardly comfortable with anyone.

"Hi," she said after a moment, forcing her voice past the lump of nausea in her throat. It sounded like a croak. She *really* wished he would have texted, but she did like to hear his voice. It was oddly soothing, and it reminded her of last night. Of him walking her from his car to the front door of her dorm and asking if she'd be okay, his shaky-from-driving fingers turned sure and steady as he traced the bruises at her wrist, worry in his dark eyes. Telling her good night, good-bye, and walking away, hunched over his crutches.

Jonas was silent for a few seconds, and Brennan pictured him frowning, his forehead getting that little crease between his eyebrows.

"Hi," he finally said. "Okay, look." He paused before going on.

"I was *going* to send you a text, but I actually really hate typing long messages, so this is better."

"Okay?" she said.

"All right. Brennan, you really don't have to apologize for last night, okay? You were scared. Maybe you didn't mean to call me, but it's already done. You did, and *I* was the one who made the choice to accept the responsibility of making sure you were safe. What if I hadn't, and something had happened to you? I don't know if I would be able to live with myself, honestly. If I'd ignored your call and turned over and gone back to sleep."

"I just feel like I put you out or something. I always—" She choked out a fake laugh. "I always feel like I'm putting people out."

"Well then, trust me, as someone who knows very well what it feels like to constantly feel that way, you weren't putting me out."

Brennan sighed. "I just wish I could tell, you know? I wish I could tell if I was putting people out, bothering them."

"You're just going to have to trust me," said Jonas after a while.

"Trust is hard," she said. "It's hard for me. I just can never tell—" *Can't let it go,* anxiety said. *Have to know.* Her fingers picked nervously at her shirt hem. "I'm always second-guessing myself, replaying everything over and over in my mind, trying to analyze what I've done wrong because it seems like there's always something. I drive myself crazy." Brennan closed her eyes, mentally berating herself. This was too much. This was too deep. She didn't want to share herself with anyone, and yet when anyone gave her the opportunity, she immediately spilled her worries and fears. She was way out of balance, swinging between sharing too much and not sharing anything at all. Amoebic, constantly shifting. No true form.

"I'm sorry, again," she said. "I said too much. I don't even—I don't even know anymore." She shook her head, frowning.

Jonas didn't say anything for a while. Finally, he spoke again, his words slow and thoughtful. "All right," he said. "That's okay. So you ask me. If you think you've said something wrong, or if you think you're bothering me, ask me. I promise not to lie to you."

She let silence hang between them, undisturbed, for a few moments. No one had ever offered this to her before. And sure, she'd probably still worry, but it would take a lot of stress away from her. She'd worry less, and the less worrying she had to do, the better.

Brennan breathed in, fingers stilled against her hem now, no longer anxiously picking at the thread. "Yeah?" she finally said. "You'd do that for me?" For once, her brain was quiet.

"I promise," he said. "Try me."

She swallowed before going on. "All right," she said. "Have you ever found me annoying?"

"Yes," he said. That stung a bit. He continued on. "You were kind of a pain at first, insisting on the whole walking thing. But you make me think about things." She heard him suck in a breath. "Like I think, what if I did walk? What if I decided not to? I'm in an English elective this semester—the other day, we had an essay assignment to write an alternate ending for one of the stories. Brennan, you make me think about alternate endings."

She laughed slightly, a brief spurt, before catching her breath. Her laugh. Too loud. Too breathy. She was silent then, but Jonas put words into the empty space of his own volition.

"I need to finish reading Harry Potter." Like he hadn't just been talking about massive life choices.

Brennan smiled, almost against her will. Talking to Jonas felt so nice, like having a normal conversation—like *she* was normal. Just that sent a thrill through her. "You still haven't finished?" she said.

"I don't have anyone to force me to the library anymore."

"If I had a car, I'd drive straight to St. Louis and give you my copy right now. You ought to be ashamed, starting and then leaving off like that."

"I know, I know," he said. "I'm a failure."

"You don't just stop reading a series in the middle."

"I concede your point," he said in mock surrender. He sounded relaxed, at ease. She wished she could be like that. She wished she always knew how to respond to people. Why was conversation so hard for her when it seemed so easy for Jonas?

"Brennan?" Jonas interrupted her thoughts. "You still there?"

"Yes," she said. "I was just thinking."

"About what?"

She sighed. She tasted the words, testing them in her head, before actually saying them. "About this. About talking to you. I don't do well with conversations. I can't ever think of the right things to say."

"Then don't think," he said.

"Easier said than done," she muttered. "Sometimes I can't shut my brain off."

"I know your brain can't just turn off," Jonas amended his earlier response. "I just mean that you can go ahead and tell it to shut up when you're talking to me."

"Shut up," she said.

"Excuse me?"

She grinned. "I was talking to my brain."

"Shut up," he said.

"What?" she asked, just *kind of* jokingly.

She could hear the smile in his words when he spoke again. "That's for your brain," he said. Then—"It sounds so cheesy when I say it out loud."

Her face heated as she smiled. "*But,* it works a little bit. Even if it's cheesy."

33

brennan

So anyway, I have something to tell you.

Brennan stood outside her psych class, waiting until it was a little closer to time to actually walk in. She was going today; she'd psyched herself up appropriately, telling her brain to shut up and picturing that Jonas was telling it too (even if it was cheesy, her telling herself that in the mirror that morning).

What is it? she replied to Jonas's text message. It was nice texting him; it distracted her from the impending psych class.

I actually have a class at SIUE.

WHAT?

Remember before the end of summer, when I started to tell you something about an anatomy class?

Vaguely/not really, I guess. I'm really sorry about that.

It's okay. I know you were distracted. When we weren't talking, it was kind of convenient that you didn't know about it anyway. It was better for you, I think. And maybe me too.

She didn't ask him to expound on why; she already knew, and she liked that he knew enough about her anxiety to have left her in the dark at first.

So when do you come here?

Tuesday and Thursday at noon. Tuesdays after class, I have lab for three hours.

You've been driving here twice a week??

Give me some credit; I'm very good at avoiding driving.

Not that good. You did just drive all the way here to get me out of a kiddie slide.

Touché. Sort of good.

How do you get here normally?

By foot, train, and bus.

Brennan smiled. That sounds complicated.

A little. And it takes more time than I'd like, but I don't mind it much. Riding the Metro is kind of fun, actually. I get a lot of time to think, which is good.

Do you ever wish you drove?

He didn't reply for a few minutes, and she wondered if her asking was too much.

Sometimes, he finally replied. Yeah. Sometimes.

Hey, she said. You save miles on your car. That's good.

Rhys would probably have a cow if I took Gus anyway, he said.

Gus?

The car.

The last-minute stragglers were showing up for psych, hair thrown up haphazardly, and clad in sweatpants and sweatshirts. One guy was literally wearing pajama pants. Plaid ones, in SIUE colors. The joys of college. Brennan snapped a picture of the bottom half of the guy's legs and sent it to Jonas. You, the first day we met, she captioned it.

Ladies and gentlemen, Brennan brings it up again.

Brennan smiled at the screen. She was glad everyone else waiting had gone inside the classroom and didn't have to see her grinning at her phone. Sorry, she sent.

It's okay. I'm beginning to think of that day with a lot more fondness than before.

Brennan was a little afraid to ask what he meant, because it could mean exactly what, deep down, she wanted it to, or it could mean something else entirely. She went inside and sat down, not really caring, for once, that the seats in the back were already full.

She was just preparing to turn her phone to silent when it vibrated once more with another text from Jonas.

I took that class so I could see you, you know. Because you were my friend, and at first all I wanted to do was leave everything from home behind and start fresh at school, but you forced your way into my life, and you're probably the first thing that's made me really happy since The Accident and I didn't want to leave that behind, you know?

Brennan didn't know how to respond to that. She'd never been that for anyone; everyone always had something else that made them happier than hanging out with the nerdy writer who never wanted to go out. Her psych teacher was in front now, greeting them all and pulling up the slides for the lecture. Brennan slipped her phone under the table, into her lap, before responding. She sent a smiley face emoji. *That's my face right now,* she said.

———

"It's weird. This is weird." Brennan sucked in a breath, trying to stop grinning. "But not *weird* weird. Good weird."

Jonas smiled crookedly at her from his spot across the table on Lovejoy Library's third floor. It was post psych class.

"I still can't believe," she repeated, "that you've been taking a class here this entire time—like, a couple of buildings away from me."

He shrugged, still smiling. She opened her laptop and listened to the hum of the old PC booting up. She shook her head again. "I just can't believe it."

Brennan watched as Jonas looked around at the shelves surrounding them. The third floor had that comforting smell of old books; it enveloped you as soon as you came out of the elevator or the stairwell, like *home* (at least to Brennan).

The table they were sitting at was in a far corner, so far back that when Brennan tried to return to it after finding it for the first time, it had taken her several wrong turns before she stumbled upon it again. Only after a couple of weeks of visiting it every day could she come straight to it, the convoluted maze of shelves between it and the stairs keeping it generally free for her use.

"What do you do up here?" Jonas whispered, as if the quiet of the library demanded some reverence.

"I write, mostly. Avoid my roommate." Brennan rolled her eyes. She was distracted by the fact that she kept bumping into Jonas's foot with her foot, which she was nervously swinging underneath the table.

"How's that going, by the way?"

Brennan smiled wryly at her computer screen. "Writing or avoiding my roommate?"

Out of the corner of her eye, she saw Jonas smile. "Writing."

She sighed. "It's going okay. I've got a few more followers. I'm up to about fifty now. It just feels so tiny compared to other authors on the site. Some of them have, like, fifty thousand."

"What did I say back when you first posted it?"

"About?"

"About five becoming—"

"Fifty," she acquiesced. "And fifty becoming five hundred."

Jonas nodded. "So five has become fifty already, and before you know it, you'll end up with fifty thousand too."

"How do *you* know? It's not like you've read my work. You don't actually know if I'm any good."

He shrugged. "Well, let me read it then."

Brennan's heartbeat picked up and her cheeks flushed. "I don't know if—"

Jonas smiled slightly. "It's okay," he said. "I kind of guessed you weren't ready for that yet. But when you are, I would *like* to read it, if you'll, you know, if you'll let me."

They lapsed into silence for a few moments, Brennan's hands hovering over her laptop. For some reason, the words were stuck. She couldn't think, not with Jonas sitting across from her, even if he'd now turned his attention to his A&P textbook. He was just so close, and he made her mind stick, unable to work.

"I feel bad," she blurted suddenly. "It's like you've been so good and perfect"—she blushed redder at the word perfect—"and *nice* to me. But we never . . . I messed up, you know. At the end of the summer. I messed up. When you suggested I might have an anxiety disorder. I was so focused on keeping my walls—because I have these walls that I've put up ever since high school—that I let you get hurt. I hurt you, in an effort to protect myself." She chanced a glance at him. He was watching her (and there was that crease between his eyebrows). His slightly hooded eyes had narrowed a bit, like he was thinking. "I just—I wanted to talk about it, but you haven't said anything, so I kept letting it get buried, because talking about it was going to be uncomfortable."

"We did talk about it," Jonas interrupted her. "I mean, kind of. We kind of talked about it. You told me, at Jenny's that night, that you did have an anxiety disorder. It's not like I didn't know you were lying about it. And it's not like I don't get it. You know, lying to protect yourself." He awkwardly rubbed the back of his neck with his hand, avoiding her gaze. "I lied to you for the same reason. About my leg? Making up a fake injury just seemed easier than letting myself be vulnerable."

"So you get it?"

"I get it."

"That doesn't mean it didn't hurt you."

He nodded. "It doesn't. But I'm okay."

"And I'm sorry. I'm really sorry."

Jonas smiled then, patiently, and lowered the screen of her laptop a little so that her face wasn't so blocked by it. "Brennan," he said. "It's okay. We're okay."

"We're okay," she repeated. "We're both okay."

For a moment, all her missed classes, the solazepram that she wasn't taking again in the bottom of her backpack, and the voice in her brain didn't matter.

All that mattered was the way her chest felt in that moment, like it was somehow constricting and expanding at the same time, like she couldn't just feel her heart beating, but she *was* her heart beating—like she was alive, and a college student, and maybe even just a little bit normal.

34

JONAS

Jonas pressed the heels of his hands against his eyelids until stars flashed across his vision. He stayed like that for a while. Better the darkness than the blank, unforgiving document that sat before him on his computer screen, demanding that he fill it with words. At this point, he wasn't even sure what he was writing about anymore.

He was supposed to be writing an analysis of a poem for his English elective. The problem was, he didn't understand the poem. He was also overtired after spending several late nights studying for midterms; his brain was too fried to actually process anything about English—like there was a short circuit somewhere.

He would leave if he could. Go somewhere. In that moment, he *really* wanted to go somewhere else. He'd had a meeting with his A&P professor to talk about the most recent lab. Rhys had driven him (they were silent the entire time, Rhys staring ahead at the interstate and Jonas keeping a mental tally of the number of semitrucks they passed). Rhys had gone to Bluff Hall to visit a friend who went to SIUE, so Jonas was left to occupy time until Rhys was done.

If you drove, you could go somewhere. Anywhere. Do it. Drive. He'd told Rhys he'd be fine studying for the evening.

His phone buzzed, and he shut his laptop, hiding the still-unwritten English paper.

Brennan. What are you doing?

I'm on campus. Had a meeting with my A&P professor.

Where are you at?

Morris University Center. He leaned back in the armchair and stretched his feet out on the ottoman. Upstairs by the coffee shop.

Five minutes later, Brennan was there. She flopped into the chair next to him and sighed heavily. "Just registered for spring semester today," she said. "As a physical therapy major, I get to take A&P too." She looked at him. "Should have taken it with you this semester." Her eyes wandered off him. "Look at all of them," she said, pointing at the students who were packing up their things and leaving the MUC. "Getting out of here. Off to take part in Friday plans, or at least to be away from here." She pulled a hair tie from her wrist and wrangled her hair into a haphazard bun. Jonas watched as the too-short pieces in the back inevitably flopped out.

"What if we—" Jonas watched Brennan swallow before she continued. "What if we did something? I have this thing—"

He opened his mouth to reply, but she interrupted him. "Never mind," she said. "It's actually a stupid idea. Forget I said anything."

He caught her eye.

"Okay, fine. Do you want to go to the Saint Louis Zoo?"

"That's—" Random. Unexpected. *Terrifying. Freaking terrifying.* His brain immediately jumped ahead. *Brennan doesn't have a car. Does she expect you to drive? You can't drive.* Didn't he do it the other night, though? *You don't drive.*

"Silly, right?" she finished, staring at him for a few seconds and waiting for an end to his sentence that didn't come. "It's extra credit for my bio class if I go to the zoo and take a picture to prove I was there."

He hated the fact that he was trying to think of an excuse. *Not enough gas, low tire, Rhys might want to leave early.*

Brennan seemed to sense his unease. She shifted awkwardly, like it had transferred to her (maybe unease was like static electricity). "Maybe," she said, "maybe we could get there via a complicated combination of bus, train, and foot?" She smiled a little then.

He forced a smile of his own and then moved his gaze to his left foot, propped on the ottoman. Pins and needles in toes that weren't there. And pain, more as time went on. (Was the neuroma making itself known again?)

"Forget it," she said. "It's a dumb idea. You don't drive." She glanced sideways at him like she wanted him to talk about it. He didn't want to talk about it.

"No," he said. "Let's go. If you . . . would you drive?"

"You drove the other night," Brennan said hesitantly. Then quickly, "Not that I won't drive, I just—you came to get me."

"That was different."

———

They got Gus from the University Center parking lot, and Brennan drove them back to Prairie Hall. "I just want to pick up a scarf and hat," she explained. "It's a little chilly." It was one of those fall days when the air was crisp and clear, biting—pricking your lungs so you knew you were alive. Brennan came back out bundled up in scarf and hat, hands shoved into her pockets as she made her way to the driver's side.

They left the dorm behind, and then campus, and then they were on the highway. Jonas kept his gaze trained straight ahead, left hand clenching his prosthetic socket, where what remained of his leg ended.

They drove in silence for a bit, Brennan's hands tight on the steering wheel. Jonas wondered if she was a little nervous to be driving a vehicle she wasn't used to, and in front of someone no less. He let her be, busy with his own worries. He turned on the radio to a station that Rhys had programmed into the car, letting the music fill the vehicle.

"So, driving," said Brennan suddenly. She seemed to have relaxed a bit and had allowed herself to lean back against the seat, her shoulders not held so straight, and her grip on the wheel not so tight.

"I'm actually not a fan of being in cars in general," Jonas mumbled, his heart rate rising as if admitting this had given it permission to.

He didn't look at her, watching, instead, the scenery whizzing by as they flew along the interstate. They passed a semi, and he almost held his breath. *Stop being silly,* he admonished himself. *It's pathetic. What happened was a freak accident.* But he was sweating now, and he couldn't stop himself.

"Has it gotten any better? As time passes does it get better?" Brennan's voice was hesitant. Jonas wished she would stop asking about it. *It's fair. You know about her anxiety. It's fair.*

"Not really," he finally said. Agitated, he tapped his fingers against his socket, drumming out a haphazard rhythm. "I just feel so out of control in a car. It didn't used to be like this, but now—" He closed his eyes, forcing himself to lean back against the seat. "It's stupid, though. I can't do anything about it. And I got in a car and drove so many times before and it was fine. I'm fine. I'll be *fine.* I just have to make myself go places, I guess. It's just a car ride."

The car was quiet for a moment, except for the hum of the tires on pavement and the music from the radio in the background.

"It's okay, you know." Brennan broke into his thoughts, her words hesitant. "It's not something to be ashamed of. PTSD is a real thing."

"PTSD is for victims of abuse and soldiers returning from overseas. Admit it—it's rather pathetic for a kid who lost half a leg in a freak car accident." This was a little too deep, a little too much. The leg—that was off limits. *Rule number one. Don't talk about the leg.*

"It's not just for them, Jonas," she said quietly. "PTSD is for survivors of accidents too. Traumatic events. I don't know everything about your accident, but I think losing your leg in a car crash counts as traumatic. I know people who have been in car accidents where they weren't injured, and *they* didn't immediately want to drive or be in a car afterward. It's okay."

Jonas frowned, his fingers stilling their tapping, twitching. He clenched his fist. "It just feels so pathetic, you know?" He shook his head, closing his eyes and laughing bitterly. "I'm a college guy who's afraid to get in a car. I wasn't even driving when the accident happened!" The words were getting louder, like they were just begging to get out. Like he'd wanted to say this, and now he was saying it, and he couldn't stop.

"Don't be so hard on yourself," Brennan was saying. "I mean, you got in a car and drove to me when I was in trouble and that's—that's pretty brave. Or at least, I thought so."

"Do you think it's brave, Brennan?" He couldn't look at her. He was afraid that if he did, he wouldn't say anything. "Would you think it was brave if you knew I had to break it into steps to even start the car and drive? Would you think it was brave if you saw how I was soaked with sweat? Would you think it was brave if you knew I had to tell myself over and over *you have to drive, you have to drive*?" He whispered the last words.

Brennan didn't say anything. She stared straight ahead, her fingers gripping the steering wheel. She switched lanes and passed another semi, Jonas holding his breath until they were back in the slow lane. His hand moved to the center console and he was tapping again. He tried to focus on the smoothness of Brennan's movements as she switched lanes and switched back, weaving in and out of traffic. She was a good driver. *But so was Rhys.*

He stared out the window until Brennan spoke again.

"Hey," she said, sounding unsure, hesitantly putting her hand on top of his on the console. "Are you—are you okay?"

Jonas jumped at her touch, almost giving himself whiplash as he faced front abruptly. "Brennan!" he yelped.

"What?" exclaimed Brennan, swerving slightly, her right hand returning to the wheel and both hands resuming their tightened grip on the steering. "What's wrong?" she said again, her voice a little high pitched, her gaze going to all of her mirrors and gauges.

"Hands on the wheel," he said shakily as they passed another semi. Why did there have to be so many semitrucks on interstates?

"Really, Jonas?" Brennan said after a few tense moments. She sounded a little annoyed. "You know people can drive one-handed, right?"

Heat rushed to his face and he avoided her gaze. *Yes, I know. No, it doesn't help to tell myself that.* "I just—I don't *like* it," he muttered. He folded his hands in his lap. Unfolded them. Tapped the prosthetic socket.

"Okay," Brennan said. "I'll keep both hands on the wheel." He saw her glance sideways at him out of the corner of his eye. "Okay?" she said.

He let out a breath.

"All right."

brennan

They took the exit for I-55 toward St. Louis.

For a while, they continued to drive in silence. Traffic was a little heavy, so they went about five miles per hour less than the normal speed limit once they were on 55. Brennan watched Jonas in her peripheral vision. He hadn't seemed as nervous when he'd driven her around the night he'd come to get her, but she supposed adrenaline had helped him out in that case. She thought back to the accident, when she'd first met him, and how he'd told her, the day of the disastrous therapy session, that he hadn't been paying attention, but not for the reason she thought.

It made sense now, at least.

"It was a semitruck," he said suddenly, watching out the window as they passed another one of the big trucks. They were everywhere on the highway. *It must be torture for him,* she thought. Brennan loved driving; it always calmed her down, made her feel more in control, not less. She tried to imagine how it would feel for Jonas—how it would be to suddenly feel so out of control and helpless in an environment you had never had to be afraid of before.

She didn't say anything, just waited for him to go on if he chose to.

"I wasn't driving," he said again. "Rhys was." He shook his head. "I always went over all the—the what-ifs." He was silent for a moment, looking out the window. "You know, if I *had* been driving, would it have changed anything? If I had driven myself to school and left right when classes were out, instead of having to wait for Rhys to finish his basketball practice and give me a ride. If I'd taken my dad up on his offer to pick me up instead of telling him it was fine; I told him I only had to wait ten minutes until Rhys was done. No sense in him stopping by the school—going out of his way—just for ten minutes. *Ten minutes.*"

Brennan turned on her blinker and eased into the other lane. Jonas didn't even seem to notice.

"I hate winter," he said. "I hated it before. Always cold, chapped lips and dry hands, colds and the flu. Snow that's pretty the first time it falls and an inconvenience every time after that." His fingers were tapping against the center console again. "Ice," he said. "That's what it was. The light was at the bottom of a hill. It was just red. Ours was green. We were just starting through the intersection, maybe the third car going through, just two others in front of us. The truck came over the hill and he just couldn't stop. It was icy, they told us later. A big patch of black ice. The funny thing was, it was late snow. End of March last year. Do you remember it?"

They were on the exit for the zoo now. Brennan remembered it.

Her mom had kept her and Ayden home because of the roads, even though school hadn't been officially canceled. They'd watched movies and sipped hot chocolate. She felt guilty now for enjoying it.

"You know what's weird?" Jonas said absentmindedly.

"What?" she said, the one word quiet in the car, the music from the radio still playing in the background, forgotten.

"I remember it," he said. "I remember looking up, just in time to see that the truck wasn't slowing down properly, wasn't stopping. I was in the back seat. You know, maybe if I'd been in the front, I might have been okay. Or you know, better off. Rhys was mostly fine, after all. But he hit the back half of the car, and I remember it, and it's just weird, you know, remembering. Rhys was being a typical older brother, and we argued because I wanted to move his stuff off the front seat so I could ride shotgun. He wasn't going to let me, but then he was, but not, not *willingly*, you know. Sibling stuff. So I sat in the back, just to spite him."

Brennan stayed silent. They found a spot near the zoo, and she parallel parked along the street, a little clumsily. Parallel parking wasn't one of her strong points. Jonas didn't seem to notice. He didn't move to get out once they stopped, so neither did she.

"You know what's weirder?"

She didn't say anything, just turned to look at him. His jaw was clenched; he was staring straight ahead, unblinking. He looked as if he had left for somewhere else. Another car, another day, on another road in a different city.

"It didn't hurt, at the very beginning. I think it was the shock of it." He smiled slightly, one corner of his mouth moving upward. It didn't really reach his eyes. "Anyway, the weirdest thing was looking down and seeing blood everywhere, but not really registering that this stuff on your hands, all over your lap, staining your clothes—it's your own, because it doesn't hurt and the metal from the car door kind of blocked my view of the worst of it. Then the pain started coming, but I still wasn't quite sure what was going on. I passed out, anyway, because, you know, blood."

She laughed a little; she couldn't really help it after his last comment, and he did another tiny half smile.

"Next thing I *really* remember was waking up in a hospital bed. I didn't even know my leg was missing because it felt like it was there. I mean, it hurt like *hell*. Sorry, but, you know. And anyway, I guess I thought if it hurt that bad, it had to be there. So hearing that it wasn't was kind of a punch to the gut. Or the throat. Whichever feels worse. I guess the throat?"

Brennan shrugged. She turned the keys in the ignition, shutting the car off. Without the music playing in the background it was silent. Jonas stared out the front windshield.

"Most people think it should have been my right leg, since that's the side that got hit. I had my left leg propped up on my right knee. It's weird thinking about it—that it was, you know, the last time I had two legs."

Jonas's hand was resting on the center console once more, but he still didn't look at her.

Brennan moved her hand closer to his, hesitantly touching it. He glanced at her, and she gave him a small smile, which he eventually returned.

"You know, it feels a little better, having told someone." He frowned. "Everyone always wanted me to talk about it, and that made me want to talk about it even less. I already felt somehow less me because I was missing a leg. I was ashamed, and it wasn't even my fault. It wasn't anybody's fault. Not the semi driver's. He wasn't speeding or anything. Not Rhys's. He couldn't have stopped it. And certainly not mine, although I blamed myself for a long time. I couldn't have even done anything!" He turned to look at her. "Anyway, it's better, having someone know."

She nodded, unsure what to say.

Jonas watched her for a moment, before turning away and undoing his seat belt. "Anyway, let's do this. I want to see penguins."

35

JONAS

"It's like a really fat guinea pig."

They were standing in front of the capybara's habitat. Behind them, people moved around, off to see elephants and penguins and whatever other big exhibits that the zoo had. It seemed like Jonas and Brennan were the only two visiting the capybara, other than the occasional child who stopped by until their parents called them away. The capybara didn't seem bothered though. It was just sitting there, occasionally looking up at them disinterestedly.

"Hey," admonished Brennan. "It's cute."

"I said it was like a fat guinea pig. I wasn't negating its cuteness. Guinea pigs are cute."

"Aww," said Brennan, her voice teasing. "Jonas actually thinks something is cute?"

"What," he muttered, leaning on his crutches. "I'm not heartless." He rolled his eyes.

"You just don't seem like the type of person to think of anything in such trite terms as *cute*."

"That's not true," he argued. "I think plenty of things are cute."

"Oh really?" She crossed her arms and examined him, raising her eyebrows.

"Yes, really," he said. "Like the capybara. And some cats." He faltered for a moment, meeting her eyes and getting caught off guard. She looked happier than she usually did. Happier than she had over the summer, certainly happier than she'd been the night he'd come and picked her up from Road's Edge. Her eyes were alight, and she was smiling, so much so that it showed in her entire face. Strands of her brown hair blew across her eyes in the breeze, and she blinked. One of those rare times: Brennan at full brightness. She laughed, as if his momentary silence had proven her point. "All dogs," he finally continued, somewhat lamely. "But I really like corgis."

She laughed again, tilting her head back just enough to expose her neck, originally protected by the scarf, to the open air. "Is that an exhaustive list?" she said, still giggling slightly, covering her mouth with her hand. "Or is there anything else?"

Jonas swallowed and forced himself to return his gaze to the capybara, shifting his weight over the crutches from his left leg, which had developed a slight ache, to his right. "Nope. That about sums it up, I guess."

brennan

It was dark when they got back to Edwardsville, the late-fall days just starting to get shorter pre-end-of daylight saving time.

They'd stopped to get burgers in a strip mall, across from Jenny's Diner. In a corner of the parking lot, Jonas had opened up Gus's trunk and they sat there, legs swinging over the edge, while they ate their burgers.

The lights in the strip mall's parking lot were just starting to come on, but their spot was far enough away that the yellow glow didn't equal total light pollution.

Brennan finished her burger then cleared her throat. "For a moment, today,"—she swallowed—"I felt like I was fixed." *For once, not falling apart.*

She didn't look at Jonas, but she felt him look at her. "What—"

"Don't," she whispered. "Don't ask about it, because it will ruin it—I'll think too much, and it will be ruined." *You always think too much.*

"So what if we were fixed? Then what?"

Brennan thought about it. She thought about telling Jonas again that he wasn't broken. But if he wasn't broken, even with all his problems, what did that mean for her? It meant she wasn't broken, either, right? Or was it not so simple as if-then? Because she felt broken—wrong. Out of whack. Damaged goods, a malfunctioning human. Like on the manufacturing line of life, she was the one with a factory defect.

"Then I don't know," she said. She closed her eyes. When she opened them, she looked at the Jenny's Diner sign across the street. Neon. Familiar. It made her want to shrug off her insecurities and just be.

36

JONAS

Jonas stood in the bathroom, staring at himself. He looked deceptively the same as before The Accident, though maybe a few inches taller.

He hated it. Hated the fact that he looked so . . . same. *My head is messed up. Here it is, over a year post accident, and my head is still messed up.*

His leg hurt—had been hurting. He shifted his weight on his crutches and left the bathroom.

What if we were fixed?

He'd been in front of the mirror to try to psych himself up for five minutes: five minutes during which he planned to sit in Gus (not even put the keys in the ignition, just sit there) and get through the sweating, the hand tremors, and the heavy hand of panic constricting his airway.

Down three floors, then across the campus, then already at the parking lot before he was ready to be. It was dark out. The streetlights cast the cars in the parking lot in a bath of amber light.

The heaviness in his chest started as soon as he got in and closed the door behind him. He took his coat off (he was already hot).

This is fine. You're just sitting here. It's the same as sitting anywhere else. You're fine. He looked at the clock: 7:42. *Okay. Just until 7:47.* Five measly minutes.

His phone vibrated on the passenger seat. What are you doing? Brennan.

Jonas wiped his sweaty hands on his T-shirt and unlocked the phone, tapping back. Nothing, he said. What about you? His mind was suddenly replaying the crash—except instead of Rhys, he was the one driving. And the steering wheel wouldn't turn; the car wouldn't brake.

The phone buzzed in his hands again and he almost dropped it. There's this calzone place in St. Louis . . .

Jonas set the phone on the center console and tried out putting his hands on Gus's wheel, minus the hum of Gus's engine actually being on. Not so bad. He clenched and unclenched his fingers. *Relax, relax.* The solar dancing character on the dashboard ticked wildly, its happy little animal face grinning.

He picked up the phone again. What? Then, quickly, before he could chicken out—Brennan, what do you do when you're nervous? I mean, how do you calm yourself down?

There's this GIF, she said, not asking (thank God) why he wanted to know. It's this circle. It expands and contracts, over and over. You breathe with it. In through your nose, out through your mouth. Can you picture the circle?

I guess, he tapped out. His forehead was sweaty. His armpits were sweaty. His hands were sweaty.

He pictured Brennan's circle. He tried to breathe in through his nose—out through his mouth.

His phone buzzed. We should go sometime—to the calzone place. Have you ever had a calzone?

Jonas found himself half smiling, even as sweat dripped into his eyes.

It's kind of like a pizza folded in on itself? Like a crust pocket with fillings.

What are you doing?

Trying to distract you. Is it working?

Who says I need distracting?

The three dots. Then Your question was kind of odd. So . . . is it working?

I don't know. Sort of. Kind of. "Maybe?" Jonas said aloud, to himself. Jonas looked at the clock: 7:50. His heart beat faster, but this time not from panic.

I want to go there, Brennan sent. To the calzone place.

Then I want another night like the one at the zoo. A normal night. A college-student-going-out-and-doing-things night.

Jonas was worrying his bottom lip between his teeth. Not ready, he finally said, abruptly. For driving.

So don't. I can.

It's the first time I've said I'm not ready, you know?

Before Brennan could respond, he texted her again. Being not ready implies a readiness someday. Implies that there is a someday, somewhere, where I drive again. I . . . I like that thought.

For a few moments he just looked at his phone, and then he opened Gus's door and got out. The cold air felt like it was freezing every drop of liquid on his body, so he put his coat back on.

Then he started back to Umrath House.

He'd lasted from 7:42 to 7:55. A grand total of thirteen minutes.

He felt like pumping his fist and yelling, uncharacteristically. *Thirteen minutes!*

37

brennan

They were supposed to be studying for midterms. Brennan felt like she'd been spending all her spare time studying. Even her private library writing corner had turned into a study space, with no time to write.

Today she felt a little off. Her throat was sore and her head was stuffy. Not up to going somewhere else to study, Brennan had tried to go back to the dorm.

But Ambreen and her friends were all in the dorm room.

"Brennan!" Ambreen greeted her, laughing, as soon as Brennan came in the door. Brennan did her best to offer a small smile. Even though it was nine o'clock at night, all she wanted to do was relax in her room, and she'd just found out that Ambreen *and friends* were chatting and giggling in said room.

"Hey, Ambreen," she said, her tone a little off.

"Whatcha doing?" asked Calvin. He was sitting up on her bed. She shot a sideways glare at him, but he either didn't see or didn't care, because he didn't get off.

"I was *going* to study," she said. "I've got another midterm tomorrow." She hoped they'd all take the hint. Unfortunately . . .

"Oh, we're studying too!" Jen laughed from her spot on Ambreen's bed. "You can study with us."

"That's okay," said Brennan tiredly. She suddenly felt like crying and screaming at them all at once (mainly at Calvin: *Get off my bed!*). "I'm just picking up a textbook I forgot and then I'm headed back out."

"Stay warm out there!" said Ambreen. "Are you going back to the MUC?" Student center. The SIUE counterpart to Wash U's DUC, which Jonas had told Brennan about the other day.

"Yeah," mumbled Brennan. *I guess I am.* She wished her brain would give her anxiety permission to go away so she could hang out with them.

She left Prairie Hall behind, going out the back door. Instead of following the path to campus, she climbed one of the small rolling hills, punctuated with little goals for Frisbee golf. During the summer, students came out here all the time, to either play Frisbee golf or sit and relax, chatting.

In the chilly late October air, however, they were nowhere to be found.

Brennan sat down in the browning autumn grass, leaning back and staring at the sky. She didn't know where to go, exactly. She didn't feel like going back to campus, and she couldn't face Ambreen and all of her friends in their dorm room. Ambreen always referred to them like they were Brennan's friends, too, but Brennan always felt like she was just borrowing them—like they didn't really belong to her and she was just their surrogate friend, Ambreen's little tagalong. If they really liked her, they'd try to understand, wouldn't they? They wouldn't just sit on Brennan's bed in their street clothes and not care, would they? Brennan pictured the germs: *multidrug-resistant organisms—MDROs. Flu. A bad cold. Norovirus.*

From here Brennan could see the window to their dorm room.

Ambreen had the blinds open and the warm yellow light of every lamp and string of Christmas lights in the room spilled out over the grass.

Brennan knew she shouldn't be out. It was almost too cold to be out anyway. But she couldn't go inside. What would she do? Hide in the bathroom?

The worst part was, she wanted to fit in with them—with all the people in her dorm. But there was no happy medium. She would have to change who she was because they wouldn't change who they were. She didn't want them to change all that much, just meet her in the middle. *Understand.* But she figured it would just be like when she tried to explain her anxiety to Ambreen. They'd be sympathetic, but they wouldn't get it. They wouldn't leave her alone in the room when she needed it—wouldn't understand if Brennan needed to have her personal space.

Hot tears stung her eyes. What was she doing? Here she was, off at college, and completely failing as a college student. No new friends, no big college stories to tell, no nothing. Brennan was tethered to home while most everyone else was growing into themselves. She still texted her mom every night, for God's sake.

Brennan, you're in college now. How long will this go on? Are you taking your meds? Her mom, last night.

Yes, Brennan sent back, lying, trying to force hot tears back into her eyes at her mom's words. *I'd get rid of it if I could!* her mind screamed. *All I want to do is get rid of it!*

Brennan straightened her legs and pressed her body into the cool grass—blank, unmoving. She was stuck, well and truly.

She pulled out her phone, frozen fingers hitting Jonas's name on her contact list—on purpose this time.

"Hello?"

"Hi," she said, small and hoarse and sore throated. Her brain was freaking out a bit. *You called. You* called. *What the heck is wrong with you?*

"You okay?" he asked immediately. She almost did cry then. Because he knew her, understood her—*got* that everything wasn't all right. Unlike stupid Calvin, sitting on her bed, and Ambreen and Jennifer, acting like everything was just peachy. *Peachy.* Ambreen said that. Brennan thought everything was the opposite of *peachy.*

"No," she said. Just that.

"You called. What's wrong?"

"Just, everything. I feel like I'm the surrogate friend in my hall. The charity project. Like everyone just tolerates me, probably because Ambreen asked them to pretend to like me. They're all so cheerful. And here I am, feeling sick, wanting to go to the dorm room and study alone, and they're all there, because they're good college students. Normal ones, who hang out together, and laugh and have a good time, even when they're studying. I feel like a loser."

"What are you doing now?"

"Sitting outside, like a crazy person, because even though I'm half sick, I can't bring myself to go inside."

"Where?"

"Outside Prairie. The back, in the grass. I'm sure anyone who wanders by will think I'm nuts."

"Hang on a few minutes." Jonas hung up.

Brennan stared at her phone. About twenty long minutes later, it lit up in her hands. She answered. "That was rude of you. Abrupt."

"Come to the front doors and let me in. It's freezing out here."

Extremities frozen, Brennan stumbled up and to the back doors, slipping inside, dragging her backpack after her. She could see him—Jonas—through the front doors. He was hunching his shoulders against the cold, dramatically, and when she opened the doors, he pushed inside in a hurry.

"Wow, it's cold," he said into the phone, the words echoing in her own ear through their still connected phone call. She hung up.

"What are you doing here?" she asked him hoarsely.

"I just finished a study session at the MUC with my lab partner from A&P. Rhys wanted to hang out with his friend again, so he drove me."

Her eyes went to the two heavy blankets he was holding in his right hand, the crutches shoved under his left. "Did you drive over from the MUC? What are you doing with those?"

Jonas avoided looking at her, and she took in the way he shifted his weight off his prosthetic left leg. "I walked. That's why it took longer than a few minutes. As to these"—he managed to look at her again, now that they weren't talking about driving—"they're from the emergency kit my mom put in the back of the car. Just trust me. If you want to stargaze in the cold, this is how you do it." He glanced around. "Do you have a laundry room around here?"

Brennan pointed dumbly past the desk. "You have to give them a photo ID to get back there," she said lamely. Jonas took out his driver's license and handed it to the RA at the counter. Brennan gave them her student ID, and they paired it up with Jonas's license, marking him as her visitor.

Brennan led the way to the laundry room, and then sat down, hoisting herself onto a table at the back as Jonas found an empty dryer and stuffed the blankets inside. She watched as he dropped quarters into the slot, the *clunk-clunk-clink* of them rattling around the empty room.

The mechanical sound of their dryer hummed in Brennan's ears, joining the other running machines in the room. There was a detergent-y smell in the air, and something like citrus coming from an abandoned box of dryer sheets at the other end of the table Brennan was sitting on.

Jonas came and sat next to her. When she was silent, he nudged her knee with his—the good one, she noticed, not the prosthetic one. She wondered if he'd chosen to sit on that side of her on purpose. "Hey," he said.

"Hey," she said. She felt disheveled—her hair hadn't been washed since yesterday, and was half-up half-down, pieces of it loose on her forehead, falling into her eyes. The sweater peeking out from her unbuttoned coat was obviously wrinkled, and the T-shirt was a too-big one from her high school (*Go Knights!*) with a stain on the front (pizza grease that had never come out, circa three years ago) that she normally kept buried in her bottom dresser drawer.

"You're not the surrogate friend," he finally said. "There's plenty of reasons to like you."

"Name one," she challenged him, squinting at him.

"You're smart. You laugh easily, when you let yourself, and you have a nice laugh. You write *books*. Like, some fifty thousand–odd words come out of *your mind*."

"I've never actually finished a book, you know."

"Okay. You write stories that could be books someday."

"What are you doing here, Jonas?" She turned to look at him, hoping that the heat behind her eyes wasn't trying to turn into tears.

"You weren't okay."

They didn't say anything for a few minutes after that, listening to the tumble and clink of the washers and dryers currently running. There wasn't anyone else in the laundry room at the moment, but the other machines going hinted that they'd be back.

"I hate the way I feel sometimes," she said, her voice tiny. For a moment, she wondered if she'd said it at all.

Jonas moved just enough closer to nudge her with his shoulder, and she leaned her cheek against the sleeve of his jacket, which smelled like spice. He stiffened momentarily, like he hadn't been expecting it. Because she wasn't sure what to do, she stayed like that. He eventually relaxed, staring ahead at the laundry tumbling in the dryers.

Eventually, she stopped wondering about how long she should stay like that, because he wasn't moving, and just gave in to the comfort of it.

They sat there in silence until the buzzer on the dryer went off.

Jonas hopped down and opened it, pulling out the blankets. "Brennan Davis, you're about to be educated on the Nguyen-Avery method."

"Who's—"

"My mom and dad," he said, simply. "Come on." She held the blankets and followed him as he crutched out of the laundry room and back outside Prairie. This time, they went farther away from the street-lit path and the glowing windows of Prairie, until it was all stillness and silence and Brennan was conscious of *being alone* with Jonas.

He transferred his weight to his good leg and dropped the crutches before laying out one of the blankets and sitting down, patting the spot on his right. She sat down, hesitation pricking at the edges of her thoughts, and he covered them both with the other blanket. The remaining dryer heat pocketed between the blankets and around Brennan's skin. Jonas lay down and she followed his lead.

They were shoulder to shoulder and hip to hip. She stared at the sky, at stars that seemed to blink because she wasn't. She looked for the only constellations she knew—the Big Dipper, the Little Dipper, and Orion. The cold, empty air kissed Brennan's cheeks and her nose, but every other part of her was warm, wrapped in the trapped heat and the closeness of Jonas.

"I admit," she breathed, "that the Nguyen-Avery Method is superior to the Brennan Davis Method. And thank you, Gus—and your mom, I guess—for providing us with these lovely blankets."

She didn't look at Jonas because she couldn't look away from the inky black of the sky, but she heard him laugh softly.

All she could think about was how distractingly close he was to her. Close enough that she was imagining just how small the amount of space was between them—so small it was just invisible-to-the-human-eye atoms at this point; the amount of space that exists between all objects. Then she was thinking of atoms, her atoms and Jonas's atoms, and how she knew this line of thought was crazy, but he made her crazy.

The stars looked like paint randomly flicked across a canvas. This was dizzying, spinning—a beautiful out of control. Which was *crazy* because Brennan hated being out of control. But this—she liked this. How was it fair that Jonas had this power over her?

"You're my friend," Jonas said suddenly. "Not my surrogate friend, and probably the best one I've got. And here we are, hanging out together, having—at least, I like to think—having a good time." Brennan looked at him then. "So," he said. He was looking at her now.

"So?" she whispered.

"So you aren't failing as a college student." He grinned. "That's gotta be at least a C. And you know what they say: Cs—"

"Get degrees!" She was laughing then, and the knot completely untied. It felt loose and nice and *everything*. Everything at once. Intoxicating. "I like *this*," she said.

"Me too," said Jonas.

"This is one of those moments where I think, if time were to just stop and this was all we had, I might be happy."

"That's another nice thing about you—you have thoughts like that."

Brennan stared at the sky again because she didn't want Jonas to catch her staring at him.

He was staring at the sky too. "Does it ever make you feel small? Like, we go about our lives, and there's a certain space that we feel we occupy—in school, jobs, with our friends—but then you go outside on a night like tonight and when you stare at the sky, it all just starts to seem tiny, and you realize you're smaller than you thought." She wondered if his voice really did sound smaller—more unsure—than normal.

"M-hmm," she hummed. It felt like the tiny distance between them shrank a little more. "But I think it feels nice."

"Like all the things that trouble us are smaller too?"

"Exactly. I like knowing there's something bigger than everything that scares me."

"What scares you, Brennan?"

Being out of control. Being known. Not being enough. Being known, and having people find out she *wasn't* enough, *wasn't* what they thought she was. *Letting* herself be known, and still ending up alone, with no friends, no one to love her. No one. "Everything." She forced the word past her heart, which was working its way into her throat. "My own mind." She closed her eyes, swallowed her heart back down.

"What are you afraid of?"

Brennan looked at him. He had closed his eyes. "I think—" He took a shaky breath and Brennan wondered if he was cold or nervous. "I think, sometimes, that I'm afraid of being happy."

"What do you mean?"

Jonas was silent for a few moments. She moved her hand under the blanket and flinched when she accidentally brushed his. But when she went to move away, he grabbed her fingers. Held on tight. His hand was warm and it made her feel melty.

"It's just, after the accident—" It seemed like he was forcing the words out, the same way she always felt like she was forcing words out. "I've always sort of been afraid to let myself feel happy—to be alive—because what if I can never be as happy as I was before?"

Brennan thought for a moment, which was hard with his hand holding hers like that. "I think," she finally said, "that you're alive, and being alive is all that's required to be happy." She thought of herself. Was she alive, avoiding all the things she avoided? Wasn't living breaking and rebuilding and loving and losing and everything all at once? Everything she blocked off and tried to prevent, and it happened to her anyway. She still lost, in the end. *Let go,* she told herself. *Let go.* But her mind stepped in then: *Don't let go; don't lose control. This is what protects you. It might block everyone out, but it keeps the bad out too.*

Brennan closed her eyes. *Who am I without my anxiety? Take it away, and am I even the same person?*

"What are you thinking about?" Jonas whispered. His words floated on white clouds of breath in the bracing fall air. "I can almost *hear* the gears in your head turning away."

"Nothing," she breathed. "Everything, actually, but I want to think about nothing."

"Shut up, brain," he said. "Right?"

She closed her eyes, her lips turning into a tiny smile. Tiny, but there. "Speak for yourself." She felt some of the tension go out of the shoulder that was pressed against hers.

38

JONAS

Jonas lay on his bed, staring at the white, slightly bumpy ceiling of his dorm room, his English textbook forgotten at his side. He was supposed to be reading poems for their poetry unit. The problem was, he kept getting distracted.

Brennan laughing at the zoo.

Brennan leaning her head against his shoulder in the laundry room.

Brennan lying next to him under the night sky, making him feel so on edge he wasn't quite sure how he had managed to stay rooted to the spot.

Brennan hesitantly wrapping her fingers around his hand, which he hoped wasn't shaking.

Brennan. Just Brennan.

He shut his eyes and pressed his hands against them. "I'm a real mess," he whispered to the empty room. He laughed faintly, somewhat disbelievingly. "Brennan," he said, first as a whisper, and then louder. "Brennan, you messed me up."

He looked at his phone, sitting cold and silent on his nightstand.

She hadn't texted him since yesterday. Was she avoiding him? Had last night been too much for her? Should he have grabbed her hand? She didn't seem to like being touched much, by anyone really, but she'd let him back on the night of the fateful Road's Edge party, so he'd thought, well . . .

What *had* he been thinking?

He'd been thinking how much he liked being next to her. How warm and almost giddy it made him feel to lie close to her, to hold her hand. Just to be in the proximity of her, for goodness' sake. It was like suddenly becoming conscious of the world spinning, time passing, his own heart beating.

Beating, beating.

Beating harder. *What does it mean if she wants to be more than friends? What does it mean if you do? Do you? Yes. What then?* The leg. *How could you not think about the leg?* Stupid.

He pictured Brennan. Brennan made him want to forget about the leg and just focus on her.

brennan

For about the tenth time, Brennan picked up her phone and unlocked it, opening up her messages, before promptly darkening the screen and letting it fall back onto her bed. Her throat hurt, the scratchy feeling from the night before having turned into a raging sore throat that hurt every time she swallowed.

She buried her face in the blanket she'd had outside last night. Jonas had left it. It wrapped her in the smell of:

1. Cold air and starlight.
2. Jonas.

Like Jonas's cologne or shampoo, or whatever it was that smelled so nice if you sat up close to him.

She stared at her phone again. *Where is this going?* her mind quizzed her. *Where is this going to end up?* Brennan pictured herself and Jonas a few months from now. Would they still just be friends? Did she want them to only be friends?

The problem was, she thought that she might want something more. Maybe she wasn't content to just be friends with Jonas. She liked him a lot. She liked him more than anyone else she'd met at university, and anyone she'd met before, for that matter.

But what if Jonas didn't want anything more?

What if he does? she thought, her mouth turning dry. The thought that he might want more was almost scarier than the thought that he might not. Brennan swallowed, hugging her pillow to her chest. What if Jonas wanted *her?*

Would he want to kiss her? She didn't really think of herself as someone who was particularly kissable. She wasn't very attractive, and she was certainly way too awkward to ever know where to put her mouth, her nose, her hands. She pictured Jonas trying to kiss her, and her not knowing how to do it, never having kissed anyone and never having been kissed herself. She pictured him thinking she was weird— well, weirder. For sure he knew about kissing. For sure he'd kissed someone. *You're thinking crazy.*

Something turned in Brennan's stomach when she thought about someone else kissing Jonas. It was a weird sort of flip-floppy feeling. But surely he had been kissed before. Even with his leg gone, he was attractive. *Not that he was any less kissable after the accident,* she argued, inwardly defending Jonas's honor against her own mind's thoughts. *I mean, that doesn't matter.* She swallowed.

What if they kissed and then he figured out that she knew nothing about being in a relationship? What if he ended it, slowly at first, then all at once? One day texting; the next, never to be heard from again.

Besides, did *she* want to be in a relationship? It seemed like so much pressure. Constantly worrying about what someone else was thinking of her. Constantly worried about whether or not they were happy together.

Wasn't it why she had pulled away when a guy had asked her to homecoming in high school? Had suddenly clammed up? Been friendly, but not personal or relaxed? Afraid he might want something more than just friendship?

The Walls, her brain reminded her. *Remember the Walls.*

She buried her face in her pillow and stayed there. She no longer felt like texting Jonas. She felt like running and hiding.

Typical Brennan, her mind taunted her. *Always running away. Afraid someone will get to know the real you.* Brennan wanted to scream. *YOU'RE THE ONE WHO TOLD ME I SHOULDN'T LET PEOPLE IN. YOU'RE CONTRADICTING YOURSELF.*

Regular girlfriends don't have to constantly worry about anxiety, her brain continued. Brennan squeezed her eyes shut. *Don't be silly,* she told the anxious part of her brain. *Surely there are girls out there with anxiety who are in healthy relationships and are happy with themselves.* Of course, it was way harder to imagine those girls when she herself was such a mess.

She breathed in, smelling her own shampoo on her pillow, letting the floral scent calm her a bit. She was panicking. She shouldn't be panicking.

What if Jonas does want more? What if he does like me like that?

She was almost glad he hadn't texted her yet; she didn't want to face any of this. She wanted to go back in time, to last night—to the moment where everything felt lovely and nice.

A part of her was whispering, *What if you want more too?*

Followed by, *What if you want more but he doesn't?*

Her phone rang. She picked it up, hesitantly. *Jonas.* She swallowed, moving to hit Accept but hesitating, her finger poised above the screen. She dropped it on the bed and let it ring. Her phone lit up with a voice mail. She didn't listen to it.

The call was followed by two text messages.

Hey, Brennan, what are you doing right now?

Followed by I was trying to read for my English class . . . it's the elective I'm taking this semester . . . but I just couldn't concentrate.

Those text ellipses. That, and a hundred other little things about Jonas would be the death of her.

She stared at her phone as the screen went dark. Why couldn't Jonas concentrate? Was he thinking of her too? Did she want him to be thinking of her?

Anyway, I guess I'll leave you alone. You're probably actually doing your work like a responsible person. Talk to you later, I guess.

Brennan lay down, hugging her pillow close and attempting not to hyperventilate.

Stop panicking, Brennan, she told herself sternly, feeling like she might cry. *This isn't even something to worry about. It's just Jonas. You're comfortable with Jonas. Jonas is nice. He's great. Stop panicking.*

She took a deep breath but kept her face buried in the pillow.

Stop panicking.

She took a solazepram with her ramen that night. Solazepram. Sol-ER. The little logo had a little sun as the *o*. Like it would make everything happy and okay. Like it would solve all her problems. Maybe it would, if she just took it like she was supposed to.

She swallowed. She took a bite of her ramen. It was the last package. She'd been to the cafeteria a few times, but only to pick something up and take it back to the dorm. Maybe tomorrow she'd try actually eating a meal there.

39

JONAS

Brennan didn't text back that day. She didn't text back the day after that either.

Soon it was Saturday.

That night, Jonas thought about somehow unsending the messages he'd sent for Brennan, and how his phone didn't have that capability, and how that was a shame because he was sure he'd messed up, said the wrong thing.

It felt too hot in the room. It *was* too hot in the room. Sam was always cold, so the thermostat in the room next door was cranked. The heat practically bled through the walls. Jonas opened the window. Cold air pricked his face. He closed his eyes. *What are you doing?*

He'd stopped texting Brennan. He didn't want to look desperate, or stalkerish, and she clearly didn't want to talk. He wondered what she was doing. He wondered if he'd scared her off with the whole hand-holding thing.

Jonas didn't understand Brennan sometimes, but he kind of thought that was okay. She was like poetry, he'd decided after spending more time than he wanted to on his English homework: deep and often hard to understand, but with that *something* that stirred you and pulled you in until it didn't matter that you didn't fully understand why.

He pulled on a jacket and left his dorm, taking the elevator to the bottom floor. On the elevator, he fixated on the beep of each floor passing. Three, two, one, there. The doors opened.

Jonas crutched across campus. His leg hurt, and with each step the ache deepened. He continued to put weight on the leg but couldn't bring himself to try it without the safety of the crutches. "Why," he muttered aloud. "Why the fight and the back seat, why the late snow, why Paul Whitford, why *me*?" He felt out of control, and not because he was out of control in that *moment*, but because he'd *been* out of control. That day. He had been totally unable to control what happened. He thought that was unfair. He'd been stuck in the out of control ever since.

He reached Gus's side. The little CR-V sat cold in the light of the weak half-moon. His heart was already pounding. Jonas counted the beats for a while, just off the sound of it in his ears. He got in.

1. Hands on the wheel.
2. Keys in the ignition.
3. . . .

He couldn't do it; couldn't turn the key. He slammed his fist against the steering wheel. This was inescapable. He was stuck in a loop, constantly being slammed into by a semitruck every day.

Jonas tried to picture a future—an ending where he was a doctor, like he'd always wanted to be, and things were good. Where he was happy and whole. He felt like a book from which someone had ripped all the end pages out—like there was a black hole obliterating everything from the point of The Accident onward. *Bones of the human body.* Part of a picture obliterated where it shouldn't be. What was two years from now? Four years from now? The end of college?

He pulled down the visor, looked at himself in the mirror. Feathery hair that was back to being just-too-long and eyes rimmed with dark circles from too many late-night video games. But his grades were still good—his mom and dad would be happy. Maybe they'd worry less next semester. Maybe that was the key to the future—the illusion. Maybe if he kept the illusion up long enough, it would turn into reality.

He remembered the first out of control. He'd been in the hospital. His mom had gone home (Stop *it, Mom!* Jonas had yelled at her earlier, while she tried to fuss over his bandage, learning to do the dressing changes with the nurse. It hurt, it hurt, and he couldn't take it. *She* hurt, after that. He'd told her to go.) and he was alone in the room. He had picked up the call-light remote and hit the button for the lights. The alarm clock his mom had put on the bedside table read 8:48 p.m. Obnoxious glowing green numbers. Everything in the hallway too loud. *Clunk, beep-beep, creak,* wheels rolling, phone ringing—hospital at night. And then his chest felt tight and he couldn't get a breath that was deep enough to accomplish anything. He could see, from the bright crack of light spilling out behind the bathroom door, the clouds and stars and shapes on the ceiling (little-kid ceiling that he hated) and he stared at them. *You aren't you. You don't have control at all, or this wouldn't have happened. You're careening, million-miles-an-hour careening, through life on a crash course with who knows what. Slow your breathing. Slow your heart. You can't, can you? You aren't your own.*

Jonas turned the key. He was sweating. Gus's engine turned over, protesting the cold a bit with sluggishness.

He couldn't bring himself to put the car in gear, though, even though he told himself he wouldn't actually move it. Just the action of starting it, which for now, was the part that mattered.

But still. *Something.*

So he sat there, closed his eyes, and felt the vibration of the running car somewhere in his skull, behind his eyes. *It's okay. You're okay.*

Brennan was the first good thing his new, out-of-control life had brought him. Some part of him wanted to hang on to that, because it had to mean something. *Does it mean anything?*

He turned Gus off and leaned his forehead on the steering wheel, his hands still gripping nine and three.

brennan

Brennan sat on her bed, staring at her phone. She still hadn't gotten up the courage to respond to Jonas's texts. She froze every time she opened the Messages app, as if she was a skydiver about to jump out of a plane, intent on doing the thing at first, but then petrified at the sight of the ground so far below.

She wished she could be one of those people who just went along with things and waited to see where relationships led. The type to *go with the flow*. She wasn't; she wanted to control the whole scenario, to plan for every eventuality, to protect herself. *Walls.*

Jonas hadn't texted her in a while. Maybe he'd given up on her. Maybe he'd realized he had more important things to do.

She balled up her fists and drew her knees to her chin, eyes still fixed on the phone, which had become a symbol of everything she was afraid of.

She had messaged Emma. They'd had radio silence for a while— Brennan busy with her new college life, and Emma busy with hers. Can we talk? Emma hadn't messaged back.

Ambreen entered the room.

"Hey," she said. It was their customary greeting. Sometimes Ambreen tried to be friendly with Brennan, but Brennan got the impression that Ambreen would have rather been roommates with Jennifer.

"Hey," said Brennan back, trying to force cheerfulness that she didn't feel.

Ambreen paused in her hurried rushing around the tiny dorm

room. Brennan briefly wondered what she was getting ready for. With Ambreen filling all the space in the room personality wise, Brennan felt boxed in. "What's wrong?" Ambreen asked.

Brennan shrugged one shoulder halfheartedly. "Nothing," she said.

Ambreen cocked her head, her shiny dark hair falling over one shoulder. "Nothing?" she said skeptically. "Brennan, you kind of look like the bottom has dropped out of your world."

Brennan didn't say anything, but she was thinking plenty of things, mostly along the lines of *Why do you care*? Ambreen never showed an interest in Brennan's life, generally, other than in occasional attempts to help Brennan practice extroversion. The problem was, Brennan didn't want to give everyone the time of day. Some people she would rather not exhaust herself interacting with. She was happy being an introvert. It was her anxiety, her panic, her *mess* that she was concerned about. She was starting to wonder, though, if they were hand in hand inside her. Like maybe if she forced extroversion, her anxiety might eventually ease.

"Come on," said Ambreen. "You can tell me."

Can I? thought Brennan. She didn't really trust Ambreen (re: Road's Edge party), and this was something she was reluctant even to tell the people she trusted. She absentmindedly twisted the corner of the sheet in her hand, before untwisting it and retwisting it again.

"I just made a mistake, is all," said Brennan finally. "I think I'm pushing someone away. Like I always do in the end. It's—" She suddenly felt like she had been given a small push and had almost fallen out of the proverbial plane. This was too much; Ambreen didn't need to know this. She was busy with her own stuff; she didn't even care enough about Brennan to respect her stuff in the room and to keep her street-clothes-wearing, shoes-still-on friends off of Brennan's bed. *Petty of you to think of that,* thought Brennan. *Maybe Ambreen really is trying to help. It's not as if you've been honest with her about your problems; she's just trying her best.* "It's nothing," she finished. "I'll figure it out."

Ambreen studied her for a moment more, before shrugging and going back to getting ready for whatever or wherever it was she was off to. She was already chatting about what she and Jennifer had done, what parties the guys in the hall were having, etc. Brennan tuned it out until Ambreen left.

Then she lay down and cried. She'd always been too emotional. She cried at the drop of a hat.

But right now, she thought maybe she had a reason. She felt lonely, more lonely even than she usually felt. Brennan was happy being alone. She was happy reading a book or writing in her library corner, or being the only one in the study area in the MUC late at night. She was starting to figure out that alone and lonely were two separate things. That she could be both at once, or only one. Right now, she was both.

And it hurt like hell.

It's all YOUR fault. Her brain piped up more and more lately. *You can END this. TEXT HIM.* But if she went to text him, her brain was immediately in conflict with itself: *THE WALLS.*

Brennan took a solazepram. She ticked off a second day in her mental calendar. She stared at her phone.

She stared at it until she fell asleep.

40

brennan

Brennan was so tired that she felt like she was moving through her day underwater. Maybe coffee would help. Then again, maybe coffee would send her into an anxiety spiral. Fifty-fifty. Did she risk it? She decided on no and trudged into Peck Hall.

Post midterms, the number of students in the study area had shrunk. The past few days, Brennan had been climbing the steps to the second floor and finding a spot by the window, where she'd sit down and work on *Superioris*. Studying and her Jonas conundrum had distracted her the past few days, but it was time to get back on the horse (as her dad would say, if he was there). After all, she had about a hundred followers now, after a popular allfixx writer had added her story to their fic recs list—one hundred followers expecting her to write something for them to read.

Brennan liked writing at Peck Hall. On the second floor, home of the English department and all the students looking to pursue English majors, she felt more like a real writer. Here, there were other students, armed with coffee and their laptops, decked out in glasses and sweaters, spilling words from their fingers into computer documents or note-books. Not even fiction, necessarily, but she felt somehow less alone with all the other words flowing around her.

The scene she was working on was a charged one—Cas, who had an unfortunate somnambulism problem, had just been awakened by Ing, who was concerned because in his sleep Cas seemed to mistake her for someone trying to hurt him.

> *Ing didn't touch him. For some reason, where she might ordinarily offer a touch of comfort or closeness to anyone else, it felt like it would be an invasion. Cas's reaction to her touch while asleep—the fear that sparked in his unfocused eyes and the stiffening of his entire body as he recoiled from her—told her that a comforting touch on the shoulder might not be so comforting right now.*
>
> *Ing waited for him to talk—to do anything other than sit there, staring at the wall. His dark hair was sleep tousled and sticking up in the back.*
>
> *"Did I hurt you?" he finally asked, each word bitten out, like it was an effort to say them.*
>
> *Ing tried not to think about the grip of his hands on her wrists, trying to push her away, locked in combat with who-ever haunted his dreams, desperate to keep the ghosts away. She rubbed the skin over the bone on her wrist. "No."*
>
> *"I'm dangerous, you know. You shouldn't try to stop me if I sleepwalk. I've—I've hurt people before."*
>
> *"I can take it," Ing said. She wanted to take his face in her hands, trace the planes of his cheekbones. She wanted to whisper, "It will be okay."*
>
> *"Don't be silly!" Cas snapped. "You're an Ambivalent. I'm a bio-manipulator. I'm not just a healer. I was able to heal you because I can manipulate life, which means it's all too easy for*

me to take it. Do you know how easy it would be for me to
hurt you in my sleep? I don't see you. I see—it doesn't matter,
but I don't see you. And if I don't see you, you're in danger.
Close to me means you'll just be hurt down the road."

Brennan stopped, her fingers pausing in their flurried motion over the keyboard. She hadn't meant to write that line; it had just come out, like she was emptying herself through the words on the page. Maybe that was why she was pushing Jonas away. Because close to her meant hurt for him down the road, when she inevitably pulled away and threw her walls back up. *Or what if he pulls away? Hurt for you?*

Suddenly, it was like the flow of words from her fingers was cut off, dried up.

She shut the laptop and opened her phone. The message from Emma still sat in Messenger, unanswered (Brennan couldn't bring herself to respond right now). A little busy right now! Sorry! Maybe we can catch up over TG break? She stared at the words. Emma felt safe, and reminded her of the times when things were simpler and not so complicated. Now Emma was moving on, clearly. Why couldn't Brennan move on? Why was she stuck in the same negative feedback loop? Like her body's response to increased anxiety and life complications was just to reduce her moving-forward function even more.

Stop. Before the anxious side of her mind could tell her not to, Brennan grabbed her phone. JONAS AVERY.

Hey, sorry it's been so long! I've been pretty busy and not feeling well (sore throat). How have you been? Surviving? It's almost Thanksgiving break, and I can't wait to go home.

She hit Send.

Then she opened her laptop again and started writing, but every time she wrote about Cas—about his dark hair and eyes—she pictured Jonas, which was only *slightly* distracting.

JONAS

The last Friday before Thanksgiving break passed in a blur. Between

1. An organic chemistry test.
2. The increasing pain in his leg (he was *seriously* thinking neuroma again at this point) and
3. Packing things for break.

Jonas thought he wouldn't have time to think about Brennan.

He was wrong.

He sat in the passenger seat of the car, waiting for Rhys to get the rest of his stuff in the trunk. Just about on my way, he texted Brennan.

A few moments later, she texted him back. I wish I was. My dad's not coming to get me for another hour. Which I guess is okay, because I need to do some cleaning in the room before I leave so Ambreen and I don't fail room inspection. Brennan had been texting him again, so at least there was that. Jonas just got the feeling that she was avoiding seeing him in person. She always said she was busy.

He texted her back. So Ambreen is a slob?

Neither of us is very neat. I'm actually pretty messy. That's why I haven't let you see my dorm.

Rhys finally got into the driver's seat and they were off. Jonas sent Brennan a picture of the sign that said Welcome to Illinois. I went out of state to college, he joked.

Hardly, she sent. I'm not sure it even counts, really. Half of St. Louis is in Illinois, isn't it?

Jonas spent the first half hour of the drive staring out the window. Rhys didn't say anything. He hadn't said much to Jonas since the day after the Road's Edge party.

They passed Exit 23 for Edwardsville and Marine. A sign said

Southern Illinois University Edwardsville: This Exit. Jonas looked away as they passed the exit, facing forward.

Rhys glanced sideways at him. "You haven't said a thing since we've gotten on the road," he said finally, hesitantly. "Something wrong?"

Jonas wanted to retort that Rhys hadn't said anything, either, up to this point, but he just half shrugged. Then, remembering that Rhys couldn't see him when he was looking at the road ahead, he said aloud. "No. Not really."

"Come on, man," said Rhys suddenly. "I know you're lying."

Jonas didn't say anything in reply.

Finally Rhys sighed. "I've been wanting to apologize. You know, for when I yelled at you for taking Gus. I said some things I shouldn't have said. It was a little harsh." He laughed shortly. "I mean, it was a *lot* harsh. And I'm sorry."

Jonas didn't say anything for a few moments, focusing on the road ahead, the lines marking the lanes blurring as they passed them at seventy miles per hour. "You were right, you know," he said.

Rhys's surprise was almost tangible, but he didn't say anything, just waited for Jonas to continue, glancing at him once more.

"I've been really selfish," he said. "I've felt sorry for myself since I woke up in the hospital missing my leg. I've been selfish to you, to Dad, to Mom. God, I've been *so* selfish to Mom." He swallowed. He pictured his mom, trying everything to make him happy, to cheer him up. Missing work to take care of him in the days right after he'd first come home from the hospital. He pictured her always being willing to drive him to his appointments when he didn't want to drive himself. He pictured her just taking it when he got angry or frustrated and snapped at her. She shouldn't have just taken it. She shouldn't have *had* to choose to take it or not, because he shouldn't have acted the way he'd acted.

The car was silent for a while, both brothers focused on the interstate ahead of them. Road signs passed along the side of the highway but were paid no heed.

"I'm sorry," said Jonas. He massaged his leg absentmindedly, the pressure soothing the dull ache.

"It's okay," said Rhys. "I'm sorry too. For yelling at you for taking the car. If it was an emergency, it was an emergency." He glanced sideways at his younger brother. "Is your leg hurting?"

Jonas immediately stopped massaging his leg and rested his arm on the center console. "I mean, a little," he admitted. He shrugged. "Anyway, it's not terrible." *Most of the time.*

"You know, I have no idea what that's like," said Rhys. "Sometimes I would lie awake at night and wonder why it wasn't me. Sometimes I think it *should* have been me."

Jonas glanced at his brother. Rhys's jaw was tensed, his eyes staring straight ahead, and his back rigid. "Don't say that," said Jonas. "It wasn't your fault." He remembered the first time he'd been at school after The Accident—hearing the whispers and seeing the stares. It felt like everyone's eyes were following him, and everyone's words were gossip about him. But he'd heard, when he was in the little nook off the hallway where the elevator was, the sort of things people were saying about Rhys. *Did you see that Avery kid? Heard it was his own brother's fault.* And *I think I'd never talk to my brother again if he lost me my leg.* And, right before the gossip mongers stepped into Jonas's view, *Figures it would be the Asian.* Followed by snickers. Jonas always thought the stereotype of Asians being bad drivers was ridiculous. His mom was a great driver. Rhys was a great driver. It was just bad luck. Stupid bad luck. Remembering made him wonder how many of those comments Rhys had heard. "It wasn't your fault," he repeated to his brother.

"Did you ever blame me?"

Jonas didn't answer for a moment, and Rhys slumped a bit. "That's what I thought." Jonas felt guilt squeeze his stomach, that he *had* blamed Rhys.

"I hate it now, that I did. Even then, I knew deep down that I was just being selfish and making myself miserable; deep down, I knew it wasn't your fault. We established that I've been a selfish jerk. It wasn't your fault, Rhys."

Rhys didn't say anything after that for a few moments. "Thanks," he finally mumbled. He turned up the radio.

Brennan texted Jonas then. Finally leaving!

Jonas kind of wanted to ask Rhys what to do about Brennan. He just didn't know how to start that conversation.

He thought that mentioning his brother's girlfriend might be a good jumping-off point. "How's Madison? You happy to be back down at school with her?"

"She's good. It's great. What about you?" Rhys grinned. "Found anyone since you started school? Living up to Mom and Dad's legacy?"

Jonas tried to remember the last time his mom had told the story about how she and his dad had met at Wash U—when he'd spilled his illegal, uncovered drink all over her in the library and had managed to dumbly say, "At least I didn't spill it on the books," in an effort to smooth things over—but he couldn't. It had to have been before The Accident. Jonas wanted her to tell it again. She always told it animatedly, with a goofy voice standing in for Elliot Avery's.

"Well, I mean, sort of? Not really," he faltered lamely.

"So by 'not really,' you mean you have a crush on someone."

"Why do they call it a crush?" said Jonas grouchily. "It just seems like a weird term for it."

"It's a crush because they so often crush you. What would you call it?"

"I don't know; not that."

"So who is she?"

Jonas sighed. "She goes to SIUE. Remember the night I took the car?"

"Of course I remember. I mean, I did tell you I've been agonizing over it for a while now, didn't I? With the heartfelt apology and everything?"

Jonas laughed nervously for a moment before continuing. "Well, I went to pick her up from a party she'd gone to. Her roommate had ditched her, I guess, and she'd gotten into a . . . situation. Anyway, she left the party on her own but didn't have a ride back to her dorm. She called me, so I went and got her. We went to a diner in Edwardsville at one o'clock in the morning." He shrugged.

"You've seen her since then? And how'd you meet her in the first place?"

"I met her over the summer." Jonas suddenly recalled the embarrassing fender bender and frowned. "At the grocery store," he lied. "She worked at the deli over the summer."

Rhys laughed a little. "The grocery store?" He snorted. "Romantic!"

Jonas rolled his eyes. Then he fell silent. Talking about Brennan, out loud, brought back all the out-of-control feelings.

"I meant"—Rhys cleared his throat—"the grocery store is a fine place to meet someone."

Jonas looked out the window again. He could almost feel Rhys turning to look at him. He tried to ignore that and focus on willing himself not to start sweating or hyperventilating, because thinking about lack of control made him all too aware of being in a moving vehicle.

"Do you want to stop somewhere? We could get something to eat, walk around a bit—"

It was at once embarrassing that Rhys had noticed his verge-of-panicking state and also somehow grounding that he cared.

"No," he mumbled.

Rhys let them sit in silence for a while.

"It's just, she didn't text me, you know? For a while, she didn't text me, and when she did, it was like she was willing to text me, but wanted to avoid actually seeing me. I feel like maybe I scared her? I told her the leg story." He leaned his head back against Gus's headrest, closing his eyes. "Part of me hates this, this odd limbo, where she obviously wants to talk to me in some capacity, but maybe not in that capacity. But part of me"—Jonas's brain felt scrambled, and he wasn't sure how his thoughts were going to translate into words—"part of me thinks it's for the best. I'm afraid—" He stopped, couldn't continue for a while. Why was he telling Rhys this? It wasn't like they'd ever talked about anything like this before, and definitely not anything related to Jonas's leg. "I mean, I can't drive. Like, freaked out, panic attack can't drive. I'm not *normal* anymore. Nothing about this is normal. I don't walk normally, I don't have a normal leg.

"You know, when you think about being in a relationship with someone, being in it for the long haul, they're going to—to *see* you. And Rhys, *I* can't even look at *it*." He bit off the last word. He didn't say it, but it hung in the air, unspoken. *So how could I let anyone else see it?*

Jonas opened one eye to find Rhys staring straight ahead. His brother opened and closed his mouth a few times. "I wish I could tell you what to do," Rhys finally said. "But I don't know that anything I could say would help." Rhys's hands on the steering wheel tightened. "I can tell you it's okay, and that it's not a deal breaker. Okay? The leg isn't a deal breaker. But I can tell you that, and at the same time, I know if it were me, it wouldn't be that simple."

"Don't say anything then," Jonas said. "It just felt good to tell some-one." His stomach was still flipping. His brain was still rapid switching between relief and fear that he'd said too much.

41

brennan

The first day of Thanksgiving break found Brennan sitting in her room the entire day, laptop open and fingers flying across the keyboard, spilling all of her thoughts and emotions into angsty scenes between Ing and Cas. It was cheesy stuff, with lines like *Ing imagined that Cas's lips tasted like secrets, if secrets had a taste* and *When Ing thought about Cas, it felt important, like it mattered.* It was cheesy and mushy, and somehow the only thing that made Brennan feel better, even if it might not end up in the book at the end of everything.

The second day, it was as if all her inspiration had been drained and, even after trying several beginnings to a new scene, she couldn't get on a roll like yesterday.

She sat cross-legged in the middle of her bed, laptop open, fingers poised, and no words coming out. *One of those days.* Like there was a faulty connection between her hands and her brain.

"Brennan?" Her mom's voice was muffled through Brennan's closed door.

"Yeah?" said Brennan, closing her laptop but not getting up from her bed.

"We're going shopping for Thanksgiving dinner. Do you want to come?" She sounded hopeful. Brennan knew her mom had missed her, had had a hard time letting her first child go off to college. Half of Brennan wanted to indulge her, to get up and get dressed, and head into town with her parents.

However, the other half of her wanted nothing less than to go to the grocery store she had worked at and risk possibly seeing her old co-workers and having to make conversation.

She also had this fear that she might see Jonas there. Texting him was okay. That was good. Seeing him, it might undo her, and she couldn't let herself be undone.

"Sorry, Mom," Brennan called. "I think I'll just stay home—I've got a bit of a headache."

There were a few moments of silence, and then Brennan heard her mom sigh audibly through the door. "Okay," she finally said. "Just don't be spending too much time glued to your computer screen. Maybe you can make dinner with me tonight?"

Brennan didn't want to help make dinner. "Okay," she said, to please her mom for now.

She could hear her mom talking to her dad in the hallway. "I just don't understand. She's been away all this time, and now she's back but she doesn't want to see us. Just wants to spend all her time stuck to that computer. What is she even doing on it?" She couldn't hear her dad's low response, but her mom's words were enough. She shut the laptop, a sick feeling curdling in her stomach. Tears stung her eyes. It wasn't that she didn't want to see them. It wasn't that at all. It was just that right now, she felt like she was drowning, and this was how she was staying afloat.

She thought about Jonas again. She wondered if he thought she hated him, when it was actually the exact opposite. He made storms inside of her. She just couldn't tell him.

Brennan sighed, letting herself fall back against her pillow. She stared at the familiar ceiling above her bed. It was nice being home, at least. Her anxiety was a little less of an issue than it would have been at school. It freed up her brain to worry about Jonas more, though, so maybe it wasn't that much of a good thing. And there was a clear tension between her and her parents, who wanted to believe that she'd gotten better off at college when, in fact, it had been the complete opposite.

Her phone buzzed with an incoming text. Hey.

Jonas.

Hi, she replied.

How's the writing?

That made her smile slightly, at least. The words are a little stuck today, but I've got a few chapters in reserve so I've still got something to post for my fans.

Speaking of the fans . . . how many are there now?

Still sticking around 100. Seems like I've stalled out. I'm moving more backward than forward; a few people unfollowed me. Lately, Brennan had tried to tell herself not to worry about her follower count. She told herself things like "Writing is a journey," and "Use this time to improve," but they didn't really stick; it was too easy to focus on the number and its ups and downs when people followed or unfollowed her.

Jonas replied, Don't worry about them, Bren. They're the ones missing out.

Her face heated. Did you just call me Bren?

Sorry. Are you opposed? It just felt kind of . . . natural.

Brennan's stomach flip-flopped. No, I'm not opposed. It's just that no one outside of my family has ever given me a nickname.

So yes to Bren?

Brennan's fingers twitched, energy humming through her. Yeah, sure. Yes to Bren. I guess.

So, Bren . . .

Then . . . He was typing.

She frowned at her phone. What exactly was he going to send her? Her mind started picturing all the possibilities, and how she might respond to each of them. What if she couldn't think of anything to say? Would she just have to ignore him and drop off the face of the earth again, this time for good?

It took a few moments for his next text to come through. 418 W Westmor.

Her address. Like this summer.

??? she sent.

Tomorrow-ish? I think? If the delivery date is right?

Brennan's stomach twisted; there was a knot in her esophagus that she couldn't swallow around. What are you talking about? she sent, finally.

Just wait and see, he said.

I'm not a wait-and-see kind of person. Brennan bit her lip. Jonas didn't respond.

———

The next day, Brennan kept waiting for something to happen.

She thought about walking up the street to the library to distract herself. Then she decided not to. She felt a weird mixed ache—for the library she'd always loved and for her little writing corner in Lovejoy at SIUE. How could she want one place back and miss its replacement all the same?

She looked out her window at the sound of squeaking brakes. The UPS truck was parked in front of their house. Her heart was hammering. This must be what Jonas had meant by delivery date—he had shipped something to her.

She half hopped down the stairs, trying to beat her parents to the front door but also not look like she was too excited about whatever it was. *It might not actually be for* you, her brain reasoned.

"Who's coming down the stairs?" Brennan heard her mom yell from the kitchen.

"It's finally emerged from its cave," her dad joked from the living room around the corner, where he was playing something on the Wii with Ayden.

Brennan wanted to scream. *MAYBE I'D COME OUT MORE IF YOU DIDN'T MAKE COMMENTS LIKE THAT WHEN I DID.* She sat on the bottom step and focused on the UPS man getting closer to the front door. He set the package down and before he could ring the doorbell and alert her parents, Brennan opened the door, grinning awkwardly in an attempt to pretend like it was a coincidence.

"Oh, hi!" she said. "Have a package?"

The delivery man recovered a bit from the surprise and nodded, picking the package up and handing it to her. "Here you go." She thanked him, exchanged the necessary have-a-nice-day, you-too business—then rushed back up the stairs with her package.

"Already retreating," she heard her dad mumble.

"I heard that, Dad," she said, voice small.

"Oops!" Apparently not that small.

She wanted to scream. Then she was safe upstairs in her bedroom, door closed.

She looked at the box.

> *To Bren (You did say yes to Bren.)*
> *—Jonas*

Brennan stared at the box for a few moments, then tore at the flaps with shaky fingers. The desperation to get inside that rose up in her chest caught her off guard; her fingers slipped on the tape and she accidentally mangled the cardboard a bit in her hurry.

The first thing that she pulled out was a note. She sat down against her bedroom door and read it.

Brennan,

I debated with myself whether or not to deliver this in person. Honestly, I've not always been the greatest with giving gifts, so I decided to have it delivered so I didn't have to have the pressure of seeing your reaction in person. Maybe that makes me a coward.

Besides, I think you're probably more comfortable if I don't come. At least not now. It's okay, I think. I mean, I kind of get it. And it's okay. I like my non-surrogate friend the way she is.

Anyway, I think that getting holiday gifts from friends ups your college experience–grade from a C to a B (even though Cs get degrees, they don't keep scholarships or anything).

What am I even saying now?

Happy early Christmas. (Sorry—I couldn't wait to give it to you.)
—Jonas

The second thing was a T-shirt. Brennan pulled it out. It was from Jenny's Diner in Edwardsville. Peachy pink-orange. *Jenny's. Est. 1995. Famous for breakfast.*

Brennan hugged it to her chest, because *this mattered.* She wasn't even sure she could say why it mattered so much. Maybe it was just the fact that he'd thought of her. Had he thought of her when he'd seen this? Or had he thought of this when he'd thought of her? Either way, he'd *thought* of her.

Her shoulders slumped. How could this make the jumbled thoughts in her mind even more jumbled?

"Brennan!" From downstairs, her mom's voice was muffled. "I want you to help with dinner! Come down!"

Brennan closed her eyes. She was picturing the questions already. *How's school been? How are your grades? Have you made lots of new friends? Are you taking your meds?*

She pulled the old gray, fleece sweatshirt she was wearing over her head and slipped on the Jenny's Diner T-shirt before pulling the fleece back on. There. *Like armor. You're pathetic.*

"Brennan!"

"Coming!" She went downstairs.

42

JONAS

It was strange, the fact that it was almost like coming home when Jonas stepped inside his dorm room. He took in the shoe rack by the door, the bed under the window, and the desk with his textbooks all in a row.

At this point, it was almost as much home as home was.

His phone lit up. Brennan. It's weird, but I feel like I wasn't even really gone.

And then It didn't even have that funny not-home smell it had when I first moved in at the start of the semester. It's like I'm used to it now. Do you get that? I know it's weird, but I have this thing about how home smells.

Jonas took off his shoes and stretched across his bed. I get it, he sent. I was actually having thoughts along the same lines.

Brennan's next text was a picture. It was her, but just the reflection of her outfit in the bathroom mirror at her dorm. I'm wearing the shirt. Jenny's Diner. Famous for breakfast. Jonas kind of wished they were at Jenny's now. He'd gotten it the night after they'd lain outside under the stars. Then he'd saved it, because it never felt like the right time to give it to her. He'd second-guessed it a lot (what if it reminded her of a night she wanted to forget), but she'd liked it.

One and a half weeks until Christmas break, Brennan sent him. Isn't that crazy, that we just had a week off, and now it's a week of school and half a week of finals and we'll go home again?

It *was* crazy. He texted her back. Also, we'll be halfway through our freshman year. What is time?

Brennan was silent for about ten minutes, and then she texted him a picture of the desk in her corner of Lovejoy Library. *A&P sux* someone had scratched into the corner of the wooden surface. My true home, she sent. The picture thing was something she'd started doing over the break, after getting the package from Jonas. It had started with a picture of the Christmas tree Brennan's family had gotten the day after Thanksgiving.

Jonas texted her a picture of the periodic table poster above his desk, which served dual purposes of decoration and reference for his organic chemistry cram nights. Back in my element.

Brennan sent him a picture of a document that was blank except for a long line of *HAHAHAHAHAHA* cutting it in half. He grinned.

I have to write now, she sent him after another beat.

"Have to" is a strong phrase.

I have to.

Don't you "have to" study?

The words want out of me, she replied. "Help us, Brennan! We want out!" Studying will "have to" wait.

Finals are saying, "Study, Brennan! Lest you fail!"

Shhhhhhhhhh.

I'm going to study. Are you going to study? We could study together . . .

Jonas held his breath. What exactly was he asking?

I'll study later, she sent, after what seemed like too long. I promise.

brennan

"Um, Brennan?"

Brennan held up an index finger, halting Ambreen's questioning. Biting her lip in concentration, she hunched farther over her laptop, fingers moving more quickly than she thought they ever had, rushing to get to the end of the chapter.

She hit Period and slumped back against the wall, a little spent and a little ecstatic to do it all over again for the next chapter.

Ambreen was staring at her like she was crazy. Maybe she was. It had been less than a week, and Brennan's clean desk of pre-Thanksgiving break was already covered in notebooks and loose papers, and the odd sticky note with a scrawled idea for *Superioris*; her bed was unmade, and she was at the head of it, in her Jenny's Diner T-shirt, her sweatpants, and some candy-cane striped fuzzy socks (that her mom had sent her, along with a note that said, *Time to get into the Christmas spirit!*). Her hair was frizzing out of the ponytail she'd attempted to wrangle it into (it was just long enough to fit into a decent ponytail now) and probably was greasy, but still smelled like the dry shampoo she'd used yesterday before class.

"Did you go to psych today?" Ambreen asked her, dropping her purse on the floor at the end of her bed.

"Um, yes?" Brennan forced a too-toothy grin at Ambreen.

"No?" Ambreen sighed. Brennan was glad she and Ambreen, though sharing a physical therapy major, didn't share a psych class. If so, Ambreen's constant questioning would be even worse.

"No," she admitted. "I had to get this scene out before it evaporated. Like if I wait too long to write out an idea, it's gone. I've got to get it while it's there. I'm a slave to the words, Ambreen." Or a slave to anxiety, which had told her that morning that she most definitely shouldn't go to class.

Ambreen rolled her eyes and stepped around a sweater of Brennan's that had been abandoned on the floor after Brennan had gotten too hot in the midst of her writing frenzy. She propped her elbows on the lofted bed and peered at Brennan. "So what's this supersecret thing you're always writing?" Ambreen asked. Brennan's roommate had traded in the carefully applied makeup and perfectly coiffed hair of the beginning of the semester for a finals-week messy bun and sleepless nights, which she wore in dark circles. Ambreen was studying. Brennan should be studying. She ignored that thought.

"I, um, I'm writing a novel."

"Like, thousands of words novel?"

"Yeah," said Brennan. "Or at least, I'm trying to get there."

"That's actually really cool," said Ambreen.

Brennan stared at her roommate blankly, her glasses slipping down her nose a bit. "Really?"

"Really." Ambreen grinned. "You should let me read it. I feel like I have to read it now. I'm invested."

"I could send you a link?"

"Yeah! Do that!" Ambreen turned back to her desk and grabbed a few textbooks, tossing them into her backpack. "Now I'll have something to look forward to after finals." She mimed writing on the palm of her hand. "I'm penciling it in."

Brennan smiled at her roommate as Ambreen gave her a little wave and left the room once more, loaded down with textbooks.

She stared at her laptop, at her fingers, which were stiffening in the absence of her typing. She pulled back her comforter, revealing the psych textbook that she'd shoved under it earlier. Sighing, she opened it and started to read.

Twenty minutes later, she was typing again, the words flying across the page.

Later, she sent Ambreen a link via Messenger. She wondered if her roommate would actually read it.

She opened her chat with Emma, which had been long silent.

The last message was one from Brennan to Emma.

Are you excited about Thanksgiving break?

But Emma had never responded to that message. Brennan wondered if she'd ever gone to the allfixx site and read *Superioris*. Not that she needed to. *She's probably just busy,* Brennan told herself. *She said she'd read it, so she probably will, eventually.*

She closed her eyes and leaned back against the wall. *Don't be deluded,* that persistent little voice in the back of her mind whispered. *Neither Emma nor Ambreen will want to read your story, because it* isn't *good. Don't be silly.*

JONAS

Jonas sent Brennan a picture of the empty stage at the front of the lecture hall. If the professor doesn't show, do we have to take the final? It was the day of his A&P final (aka the last day he'd have an excuse to be on the SIUE campus, because he was taking the second part of A&P at Wash U).

Brennan texted him a picture of a goose on the sidewalk. About to be attacked on my way to class. The SIUE geese were everywhere, but they seemed to have somehow worsened in the past month. Jonas wondered if the goose in Brennan's picture was the same one he'd passed on the way past Peck Hall as he'd left the bus stop behind. It looked just as mean.

What are you thinking right now? Jonas sent her.

How I'm about to throw up, fail my finals, and flunk out of college, she responded, after a moment.

Jonas wished he could see her, stand in front of her and have more than just the blurry picture of her he kept in his head. You're going to be fine.

She didn't say anything, until Promise?

Pinky promise.

I'll hold you to that. Jonas didn't respond to that because his professor chose that moment to walk into class, just as the clock marked the top of the hour. *Just in time,* Jonas thought, turning his phone off.

43

brennan

Brennan sat at the table and stared out the window at the back patio; snow covered everything, and more was coming down. Finals had come and gone (Brennan had managed an A, two Bs, and a C—a C she was avoiding telling her parents about, considering the higher standards of her high school years), and she was home. She had a month. Brennan thought it was the longest and shortest amount of time she'd ever been given.

Her mom had lit a peppermint-scented candle and placed it in the middle of the counter, and the kitchen smelled like mint and the baking cookies in the oven.

Jonas had texted her earlier. I miss my best non-surrogate friend.

She'd wanted to text him back that she missed him, too, but her anxiety had held her back, worried that that might reveal too much about what her feelings for him actually were. *You can't tell him things like how he makes you feel like you're flying and drowning all at once, because that would be weird.* So she hadn't replied yet, but she couldn't stop thinking about it.

Her mom was putting away dishes in the kitchen, currently working on drying a mixing bowl (that would be put away in the cupboard on the right, above the stove, second shelf, under the strainer; it comforted Brennan to know that everything at home was exactly as it was before she had left for college). She tapped her foot and waited for the inevitable. When her parents had called her downstairs, the tone in her dad's voice had warned that this wouldn't be a pleasant catching-up chat.

Finally, her mom finished the dishes, and both her mom and dad came into the dining room and sat down across from Brennan. Dan and Rose looked tired. Brennan felt tired already, like just the thought of *serious conversations* was wearing her out.

"Brennan," her dad began, folding and unfolding his hands. "We let this go all the way through Thanksgiving break, but we feel like you're avoiding us. What's going on?"

Brennan looked at her mom, who looked like she was looking for an answer. When Brennan didn't offer one, she changed tactics. "How were your grades this semester?"

There it was. Brennan swallowed. "Fine," she said. Her mom raised an eyebrow. Brennan tried again. "I got a C in psych. It was just, the tests were always on stuff that the professor didn't talk about and—"

Brennan's dad closed his eyes. Brennan stopped. Her mom hesitantly reached across the table like she wanted to touch Brennan's hand, but she gave up and stopped halfway over. "How—how is your anxiety?" she asked.

Brennan wanted to disappear into the floor. Fall through it, maybe, and just keep falling—away and away and away from this conversation. She stared blankly out the window at the snow outside.

"Are you taking the solazepram?"

Brennan was hyperaware of her quickening pulse. Sounds started to feel distant and it was just *pound, pound, pound* in her ears.

"Brennan." Her dad. "Answer your mother."

"Yes," she lied. "I'm taking it."

She came back to herself and caught the way her mom's shoulders sagged in relief.

"So what did you think about your first semester of college?"

"I mean, I called you all the time, Mom."

"Yes," Rose argued. "To talk about what was going on here. What's going on there?"

"Nothing exciting," she lied. "As predicted, I don't have a lot of friends. I spend most of my time by myself in the library."

"You're not spending all your time talking to your online friends, are you?"

Brennan frowned at the floor. "They're not 'online friends,' Mom." Defensive.

"Then what are they? Brennan, what you're doing isn't healthy."

"I have a friend, Mom. Okay?" Brennan thought of Jonas. She thought about how she would never have pictured herself wanting to go back down to school, if only to stop being home (for her parents to look at her as a computer-addicted social recluse on pills). "I don't need a ton of friends. And I enjoy my writing. It helps with my anxiety."

"Brennan, your psych class—"

"It's fine, Mom. I kept my scholarship. Isn't that what matters?" Brennan's hands tugged at the edge of the Jenny's Diner T-shirt sticking out from under the old gray fleece.

Rose looked at Dan. "We're worried about you," she hedged.

"Don't be," Brennan whispered, doing her best not to cry and give it all away.

JONAS

Jonas texted Brennan a picture of the elevator-floor numbers while the elevator was busy charting a slow course from the first floor to the third floor. He tried to ignore the now-pinching feeling of putting weight on his prosthetic leg, relying more on the crutches than usual.

He had forgotten to caption the photo, but Brennan texted back all the same. Doctor's office?

Jonas left the elevator and checked in at the desk. He didn't know if it was a good thing or a bad thing that the receptionist remembered him. *Both,* he decided. He'd been there too often.

He sat down and texted Brennan back. Orthopedic surgeon's, yeah.

What's wrong?

Nothing. Just a follow-up. Just, nothing. He stood, shifted his weight to his left leg, and tried not to flinch when the fingers of pain traveled from his missing left toes up to his spine.

The list of words that are the biggest lies was now:

1. Fine.
2. Just.
3. Nothing.

How are you? he asked her.

Not amazing, she sent back.

What's wrong?

It's complicated. Parent stuff. Anxiety stuff, to be honest. It's hard to talk about.

Okay, he said.

Hey, Jonas?

Yeah?

Nothing.

What is it?

I just wondered . . . now that you've practiced putting weight on your leg for quite some time, are you going to try to walk without the crutches?

Jonas stared at the text. That was the question, wasn't it? The one he'd been pushing away over and over again because it was easier not to think about trying to walk again without the crutches. He clenched his left palm, trying not to think of the white scar that was still there—of him sitting on his kitchen floor, of glass shards, of blood.

Brennan sent him a text. Lovejoy Library. I'm free Monday and Thursday afternoons?

Jonas swallowed. He typed a response. He deleted it. His mom finished parking the car and came inside, sitting down next to him. "Are you okay, Bird?"

"Yes," he lied. Then he texted Brennan back.

I would, but I don't have a class at SIUE anymore. I've got A&P at Wash U now.

Brennan didn't say anything for a while. Then Oh.

Jonas wanted to scream at his stupid leg. He'd gotten pretty good at suppressing his anger that things weren't different. But now—not now.

———

"Move, Rhys," muttered Jonas from his spot slumped against the couch cushions, his leg propped up on the coffee table in front of the couch. He was wearing a sock on the prosthetic foot again. He still couldn't look at it.

"Geez, Jonas." Rhys rolled his eyes but moved out of the way of the TV and plopped down next to his younger brother, jostling Jonas's shoulder. Jonas wished Rhys would have chosen his right side to sit down on, rather than his left. He instinctively moved his prosthetic leg away from his brother's leg.

"How many times have you seen *A New Hope* now?" Rhys nudged Jonas's shoulder on purpose this time.

Jonas just frowned at the TV, watching Leia, Han, and Luke, and ignoring his brother.

Rhys snatched the remote from the cushion next to Jonas and hit Pause. "So," said Rhys. "Leg or girl?"

"How about both?" Jonas grouched.

"Yikes. Okay. That's a little more complicated than I was prepared for." Rhys sucked in an exaggerated breath. "But we'll deal. So what's wrong?"

"Dr. Akeson thinks that adjusting my prosthesis didn't permanently fix my leg pain problem. You know, the neuroma."

"So the next step—"

"Is surgery, if I want to get rid of it for good. And even then it could re-form; it could not. It's still a guessing game." Jonas closed his eyes, suddenly tired, and leaned his head back against the couch cushions. It was hard, and a little exhausting, suddenly thinking about the fact that he might have to deal with this for the rest of his life.

"That sucks," said Rhys softly, after a few moments.

"Yeah." Jonas kept his eyes closed. "I go back tomorrow and they'll let me know. If they do surgery, they're looking at trying to do it during spring break. Which means no missed school." He faked a smile and a thumbs-up before letting his hands fall to his sides.

Rhys was silent. Jonas wondered if he even knew what to say. He tried to imagine what he would say if it was Rhys missing a leg and him trying to come up with adequate words. Nothing came to mind.

"Sucks, right?" he supplied, opening his eyes.

Rhys nodded. Jonas took the remote and pressed Play on the *Star Wars* movie. Rhys stayed there and watched with him, even though Rhys didn't really like *Star Wars*. Somehow, that meant more than anything he might have said.

44

JONAS

Jonas peeked around the end of the cereal aisle. The girl with the messy bobbed haircut and big glasses was still there. No doubt about it; it was Brennan. Finally, after all this time. It felt kind of full circle, considering their history with this very grocery store.

He watched her for a short time, kind of amazed that he was really looking at her. The blurry picture in his head righted itself; the details he hadn't quite remembered correctly, like the shape of her nose or where exactly her hair came to now, correcting as he looked at her.

She was standing in front of the dairy section, scanning the selection of cheeses. He recalled their cheese conversation of the past summer. It felt like yesterday and last year all at once.

Jonas swallowed. Should he say hello? Say anything at all? Walk up next to her? Or simply wait until she had moved on and he could pick up the shredded cheddar that his mom had asked him to get (the shredded cheddar Brennan was currently holding in one hand while she used the other to do something with her phone). He considered just letting her be, continuing the slow buildup of texting that was killing him a little but letting Brennan, he guessed, feel more in control. Besides, texting was safe. Texting, he could easily dodge anything leg related. He ducked back around the aisle. She was wearing some of those mittens where the top part folds back to let you maneuver your fingers. Jonas had always thought those looked a little like little-kid mittens, but on Brennan they were cute.

Suddenly, his phone buzzed in his hand, a text covering the top of the note he'd written the grocery list in. He tapped the notification and was greeted with a picture of himself at the end of the grocery aisle. His face flamed. Stalker, the picture was captioned.

Jonas stepped sheepishly out of the aisle, the plastic shopping basket in his left hand clacking against his left crutch. Brennan was gripping the handle of her cart tightly in one hand and her phone in the other. Her eyes were wide behind her glasses, but she was smiling.

"Hey. Hi," Jonas fumbled, his pulse picking up to something that was pushing the upper limits of the average 60–100 beats per minute of the human heart. He could feel the blood in his residual left leg throbbing right along with it, and he shifted his weight off it a bit.

"Hi," she said softly.

"Hi," he said again, stupidly.

She didn't seem to catch his blunder. Maybe she was a little distracted. He tried to convince himself that he was only imagining that she looked a little trapped. She had moved on from gripping the cart handle to buttoning and unbuttoning the button on her left mitten. Jonas looked at the mittens now that he was closer. They had black and white panda bear faces and red cuffs.

"How has your break been?" she asked.

He thought about the surgery he was probably going to have to get and the worsening pain in his leg. "Okay," he said.

The list grew:

1. Fine.

2. Just.
3. Nothing.
4. Okay.

"Do you want to get coffee?" he blurted. "I'll pay."

Brennan stared at him for a moment. He noticed the T-shirt peeking out from under her half-zipped sweatshirt. Jenny's Diner. "Sure," she said. "Okay, I guess."

She followed Jonas to a Starbucks that had opened in the Kroger while they'd been away at school. "This wasn't here," Brennan said, looking around a little blankly.

"No, I guess not," Jonas remarked.

Brennan ordered a hot peppermint tea. "Decaf. Caffeine and I—we don't really agree," she muttered. "It just kind of makes me more anxious."

Jonas nodded before ordering another peppermint tea. He'd already had about half a pot of coffee that morning, at home. The last thing he needed now was more caffeine to push him over the edge from nervous to jittery in front of Brennan. If it wasn't for needing an excuse to see Brennan, he would have skipped the Starbucks—he hoped his ride, Rhys, didn't finish up at the pharmacy next door (where Madison was working for the holiday) for a while.

"Tell me something about you," he blurted. "A Bren fun fact. It was your turn, remember? I told you I wanted to be a doctor and you never told me your next fun fact."

She laughed then, attempting to cover an involuntary snort with a hand over her mouth.

"What?" he questioned her.

"I can't believe you've kept score like that." And there were her brown eyes, shining.

"I'm a meticulous keeper of scores," he said solemnly.

"Okay." She sucked in a breath. "I used to be on my school's swim team."

"Really? What was that like?"

"Awful. I loved swimming *for fun,* so I somehow thought I would like swim team. I was the slowest person on my team, and I—" She looked away, her face falling a little. "I had my first anxiety attack in the locker room during practice. Locked in a bathroom stall, hiding from everyone." She straightened, her shoulders lifting. "Anyway, it's clear, in retrospect, that I probably should have stuck with something like book club or writing club. You know, the things someone might actually *expect* someone like me to do."

Jonas offered her a small smile, unsure of what exactly to say.

Brennan broke the silence. "So now it's your turn."

It was Jonas's turn to suck in a breath and try to fortify himself for what came next. "I'm having surgery the first day of spring break."

Brennan kept her head downturned but lifted her eyes a bit so that they just met his. "What for?" she asked.

"My leg," he said. "I have a neuroma. It's been making it kind of painful to walk. Even with the crutches."

Her eyes looked worried. "Neuroma," she said, like she was testing out the word. "What's that?"

"Just a tangle of nerves. Hard to explain. It just makes it hurt pretty bad to put pressure on it walking."

She let out a breath. "Thank God," she said. "I heard neuroma and the first thing I thought was some kind of cancer."

"Aww," he said. "You were worried about me? How sweet." He immediately regretted it when her face turned bright red and she avoided looking at him again. She took the lid off her tea and blew on it a bit to cool it; the mint scent wafted across the table.

"I'm just glad," she said, "that it isn't anything harmful in the long run. It will be fine after the surgery, right?"

"They hope." Jonas shrugged. "But they've told me that these things can reoccur. They technically didn't tell me I *had* to have surgery, I just—" Jonas sighed in frustration, his fingers absentmindedly tapping the table's edge until he noticed and clenched his fists in his lap. "They gave me some things to try. I've already been doing the massage and the percussion—the finger tapping thing I do sometimes on my leg? I'm not sure if you've noticed, but anyway, I've tried, and it didn't help. Maybe the surgery works. Maybe it doesn't. But if it does, I'll be able to walk without pain again—maybe. Even if the neuroma re-forms, that's still time pain free."

"Oh," she said. "I get it now. Why you won't walk without the crutches. It must hurt pretty bad."

Jonas swallowed, not wanting to correct her. He ended up just nodding.

They were both silent for a little while, Jonas unsure how to continue the conversation, and unsure whether Brennan even wanted to. Her hands worried the hem of her sweater, and she wouldn't look at him.

"Well," Jonas finally said. "I suppose I'd better be getting on to the checkout. I have to get these things home to my mom." He hoped he hadn't kept Rhys waiting. He hoped his mom wouldn't be upset that they were a little later getting home than they'd said they'd be.

Brennan didn't say anything for a moment, so he turned to go. "Okay," he heard her say quietly, quickly, as though she'd had to gather up her courage to say it. "See you later?"

See you later. Not "Text you later," or "Talk to you later," but "*See* you later." Jonas's heart was beating faster again as he waved and started to crutch away (silly shopping basket clacking away at the side of the crutch).

"See you later," he said.

See you later, and *she'd* suggested it.

45

brennan

So could I catch a ride back to school with you?

Brennan swallowed as she read Jonas's most recent text once more. Her mind was currently trying to convince her to stall by ignoring the text (she could just say she hadn't gotten it somehow when he inevitably asked why she hadn't responded).

She was disgusted with herself. *You disgust me,* she thought.

Jonas had texted her that morning, telling her that Rhys had gone back to school early and he needed a ride back to Southern Illinois. He'd said that Rhys could come get him in Edwardsville if Brennan could get him that far.

I understand if you can't, he'd said. *I'll figure something out. I just thought we could ride together. It might be fun.*

Brennan exhaled. It could be fun. She wanted to believe that it *would* be fun. But it could also be the biggest disaster of her short life.

Or maybe saying no would be a bigger disaster.

Her brother opened her door and walked into her room.

"Ayden!" she muttered, frustrated. "I told you to knock if the door is closed."

Ayden rolled his eyes slightly but didn't look up from whatever he was doing on his phone. "Mom says it's time for dinner."

Brennan sighed, looking back down at her own phone, the screen still frustratingly black, providing her with no answers.

"You coming?" asked Ayden.

"Yeah," she said. "In a second."

Ayden turned to leave. Brennan watched him go, the T-shirt he was wearing from their high school's retreat reminding her that he was much braver than her. She'd convinced her parents to let her stay home from the retreat because she couldn't bear staying in another state for a week, sleeping in strange beds and eating food not prepared in her own kitchen. She'd pictured herself having an anxiety attack in front of all the people in her class. Pictured it, and immediately done what she had to do to avoid it.

"Hey, Ayden?" she said suddenly.

Ayden paused just outside her doorway, not turning around, still engrossed in his little phone game.

"Tell me to stop being such a coward."

Ayden sighed. "Stop being such a coward, Brennan. Although, you aren't, you know? Not really." He finally looked up from his phone, letting the screen fall black and turning to face her. "You may be a different sort of brave than, say, me, but you're brave all the same. I don't think I could deal with what you deal with every day."

He kept looking at her for a few moments while she digested his words. Was she really dealing? Skipping class and avoiding seeing Jonas?

She gave her brother a small smile because he'd managed to make her feel at least a little better. "Thanks, Ayden."

He rolled his eyes, back to being just her annoying younger brother, and turned to go once more, his words trailing after him as he walked away. "Geez, Brennan. Don't get all mushy or anything. Get down to dinner before Mom wonders if you've gone missing up here."

He was gone. Brennan stood up and stretched, pulling tension from her muscles and loosening her cramped limbs before heading out of her room to go downstairs for the meal.

She stopped, her hand on the doorknob, and looked back at her phone. She closed her eyes for a moment. *You're the author, Brennan,* she argued with herself. *Decide your own story.* She stepped quickly to her bedside and picked up the phone, unlocking it and opening her messages, even as the words *You are brave enough; you can do this* raced through her mind on repeat, to the rhythm of her hammering heart.

Check your pulse, her brain told her. Brennan ignored it long enough to type Sure and hit Send. That's fine with me. She hit Send again.

Then she closed her eyes. She'd done it. *In. Out. Anxiety is a wave.* She brought two fingers to the spot under her neck where her pulse pounded beneath her skin. A little fast, but okay. Alive. *Anxiety is a wave. It always recedes. You'll be okay.*

spring semester 2015

46

JONAS

Jonas zipped up his duffel bag, slinging the strap over his shoulder and standing, taking a moment to steady himself and shift his weight cautiously to his left leg, testing. The pain wasn't too bad today, a fact that he was thankful for considering that most of his thoughts were occupied with his imminent return to school. *And the car ride with Brennan.*

He wasn't quite sure what had made him ask Brennan. His mom could have taken him—probably wanted to take him. But he wanted to see Brennan, even if it meant seeing her in a car. Did that make him crazy?

He picked up his crutches and took his weight off the prosthesis. His mom came in as he was trying to position the crutches around the duffel bag. "Do you need help with that?" she asked hesitantly.

He felt a little guilty at the slight falter in her voice. She'd always only wanted to help him, and he'd always snapped at her in frustration at himself and his own inadequacy.

"I'm okay," he said. She simply nodded and looked away quickly, which he only noticed now that he was watching her, paying attention to it. "Mom?" he said softly, putting his hand on her arm to stop her from leaving the room. She turned and met his gaze, giving him a half smile.

"When did you get so tall, Bird?" she said quietly, as she reached up and brushed to the side a floppy piece of dark hair that had fallen over his forehead. "You're all grown up."

He took her hands, smaller than his now, and squeezed them. "I'm sorry, Mom," he said, and the words caught in his throat before he could continue. *Sorry for not being a good son. Sorry for changing. Sorry for being a mess. Sorry for everything.*

His mom had tears in her eyes now. "What are you sorry for?" She took her hands from his and put her arms around him instead, holding him tightly. "I love you, Jonas. It's okay. We're okay. I'd do it—this—all over again if you needed me to. I'm always here for you. You don't have to move on all at once." Jonas blinked rapidly, his eyes wet. Even now, inches taller than her and far from a child, there was that mothers'-arms safeness, like no matter what happened, she loved him and she was there, and real; her love for him was real. For a moment, he felt small again.

"Jonas, your ride is here!"

At the call from his sister, his mom pulled back and looked at him. She smiled. "Ready to go back?"

Jonas nodded. "See you spring break?"

She nodded back and squeezed his hand, then turned and left the room.

Jonas looked around his bedroom, which had become his place of refuge and his prison all in one—childish glow-in-the-dark stars on the ceiling, PlayStation, and TV, with his *Star Wars* movies in a neat stack next to it, messily-made bed.

He took a deep breath and stepped out, bag in hand, ready—really ready—to see Brennan. *Even with the car.*

brennan

Brennan breathed in and out and loosened her grip on the steering wheel as she pictured the GIF with the expanding circle again. She ducked in her seat and craned her neck enough to see out the passenger-side window. The Avery house was nice—it was a smaller two-story accessorized with still-hanging Christmas lights and the light dusting of snow that had fallen last night.

She was nervous. (Then again, when was she not?) She'd thought maybe she'd gotten a little better, but now that the new semester was here, she felt like she was on the verge of throwing up or passing out when she thought of going back to school, away from her comfort zone at home.

Brennan swallowed, breathing in through her nose to avoid the nausea squeezing her throat. *Don't throw up, don't throw up, DON'T THROW UP,* her brain taunted her. The voice had been quieter over the break, like it was on vacation, too, but it was back in full force again. Before it could overwhelm her, Brennan forced herself out of the car and up to the front door, making prints in the previously undisturbed snow on the sidewalk—snow that crunched under her feet and stuck to the bottoms of her shoes. She pressed the doorbell and stood back, awkwardly shifting from one foot to the other. She was early. *Too early?* The whole way there it had been *What if you don't find it* and *You're going to be late,* but here she was. *Will they think it's too early?*

Other than the grocery store, it had been before Thanksgiving break when she'd last seen Jonas. Part of her wanted to see him, in a way that made her ache somewhere in her chest. The other part wanted to run. *Why are you standing here?* her mind said. *Turn and run the other way. Leave while you still can. It's best for you. It's best for everyone.*

Before she could even entertain any thoughts of running away, formulating excuses, and getting out of there, the door opened.

"Brennan!" The woman at the door was smiling and familiar—her dark eyes were warm and friendly. "I'm Mrs. Avery. But you can call me Elise. You might recognize me from the deli?" She stepped back. "Do you want to come in? Jonas will be out in a second."

Brennan forced a smile. "Sure," she said and stepped inside. While Mrs. Avery busied herself with going to the hallway and yelling for Jonas ("Jo-nas! She's here!"), Brennan tried to calm her nerves by slowing her breathing (*In. Out. Picture the GIF*). She found herself looking at the photos on the wall next to the stairs.

A smiling toddler grinned up at her from one of the frames, all fluffy dark hair and chubby toddler hands. The eyes told her it was Jonas. She found herself smiling back at the picture. The next one was of Jonas with a little girl who must be his younger sister. She felt like she was an observer, peeking in on Jonas's family through picture windows. His brother, Rhys, with Mrs. and Mr. Avery, probably before Jonas was born. A slightly older Rhys holding a baby Jonas. Their sister, Taylor, as a baby. Jonas, on a middle school soccer team, grinning at the camera, gap toothed. A portrait that was probably Rhys's senior picture. Jonas, with braces. And Jonas, in what was probably his own senior portrait. He looked more like Brennan knew him, not smiling and looking off slightly into the distance, like he was contemplating life and happiness. *This was after, then.* From the pictures, she could see that Jonas took after his dad more, while Rhys looked more like their mom. But when Jonas did smile, it was *all* his mom's—warm, comfortable. An everything-will-be-okay smile.

"Hey."

Brennan jumped about a foot and whirled around to face the hall, where Jonas stood at the end. A thousand things to say ran through her mind at once, tripping over one another. A hey-hi-how-are-you-I'm-sorry-ready-to-go-I-missed-you mess. "Hey," she said, finally.

Jonas walked down the hallway and paused for a moment in front of her, his eyes going to the pictures for a few seconds. "You ready to leave?" he asked her, meeting her eyes while she blushed and looked at her feet, self-conscious to have him standing so close and suddenly more nervous than ever to be in an enclosed car with him for three hours (the storms in her stomach had started before she'd even gotten up to his porch, for goodness' sake). She just nodded.

Jonas went into the other room and Brennan heard him telling his mom good-bye. "She's cute," Brennan heard Mrs. Avery say in a loud whisper. "I mean, I should have known; she was cute even in the deli uniform!" Brennan's cheeks blazed red.

"Mom, really?" Jonas's whisper sounded exasperated, and Brennan pictured him rolling his eyes.

"Good-bye, Bird," Mrs. Avery finished, before releasing Jonas back into the hallway.

Brennan eyed his one bag. "That's all you had home for the break?"

"Rhys already took back the rest of it." Jonas shrugged.

They made their way outside in silence. "You can, umm, put your bag in the trunk? Or the back seat? Or, wherever," she muttered, trailing off.

"Brennan?"

"Yeah?"

"Relax."

She didn't know whether to feel warm about the fact that he knew her well enough to know when she was starting to spiral out of control, or to feel embarrassed that it was that obvious. She forced a lopsided grin. "Back seat?" she offered.

"Perfect," he affirmed. Once Jonas's bag was in the car, he got into the passenger's side and she got into the driver's. She sat there, hands clenched around the wheel, while Jonas moved his prosthetic leg to a more comfortable position and settled back in his seat. He turned to look at her after a few quiet moments. "Shall we go?" he asked.

Brennan snapped out of her trance and started the car, pulling into the road. The silence was awkward, but she didn't want to talk. She didn't want Jonas to ask about the semester, because the classes she'd skipped weighed on her mind. Her New Year's resolution was to skip no classes this semester, but she was already thinking about breaking it to avoid the no-good-seats-on-first-day predicament. Syllabus day, after all. She didn't want to explain that her anxiety hadn't really gotten better—had, probably, actually gotten worse.

"I got you a gift," Jonas said suddenly. "For Christmas." His eyes dodged away from hers. "I mean, another one. Besides the diner shirt. Or maybe that was just a normal gift? An extra? And this is post Christmas so—"

"That's really nice," Brennan rambled, interrupting him. "You really didn't have to—"

"I wanted to," he interrupted her back. "It's in my bag and I didn't think to get it out before we left." He paused as she accelerated onto the interstate. They were really on their way now, too late for Brennan to make her excuses and get out of this. She wished her mind wasn't always immediately jumping to making excuses to get her out of things; she always felt like garbage afterward.

"I guess it doesn't matter because I didn't wrap it anyway," Jonas continued. Then, mumbling—"It's a candle."

Brennan looked slightly sideways at him, keeping most of her focus on the road.

"It seems like a silly gift, now that I say it out loud. Mom got Taylor a day at a candle making shop for Christmas—Taylor likes that kind of stuff, creative stuff—it was for her and a friend, but Taylor is pretty shy, so she asked me to take her instead." He was tapping the fingers of his left hand on his left thigh, the place where his real leg would meet prosthesis under his jeans. She noticed it, noticed so many things about him that she wouldn't notice about anyone else. Did it mean *he* was nervous? Maybe because of the car? Maybe it was creepy that she noticed. Jonas was continuing. "So I spent the day at a candle making place. It was weird. A lot of smells. Good smells. I don't know. Anyway, the lady who was instructing us on how to make the candles was telling us what all the different scents were good for and she said that lavender is good for stress relief and can make you feel less anxious, so that's what I made. I made a lavender candle for you. It's a little crooked, because I set the mold on an uneven surface, but it smells good. I mean, I hope you don't actually hate the smell of lavender."

She loved lavender. Brennan felt like crying. She didn't deserve Jonas—didn't deserve his kindness, didn't deserve the fact that he'd thought of her while making a candle. She didn't deserve to feel warm when he talked to her, or like her heart was beating faster in a *good* way. Not when she had thought so often about running in the opposite direction. Her stomach twisted; she didn't know what to say, didn't know what to do. How could she tell him how much it meant to her?

"You okay?" he said, his words slicing into the chaotic swirl of her thoughts.

She nodded, barely holding on to her currently-spinning-out-of-control mind. "Thanks," she said. "For the candle." *What if he thinks you don't really like it? What if your reaction didn't quite make it clear that it's the best thing you got this Christmas?*

"You're welcome," Jonas was saying. "It's a pretty nice candle, other than the whole lopsided thing. It's like me—pretty nice, except for the lopsided, missing-leg bit." He looked away.

Brennan found herself blushing for what seemed like the millionth time since she'd first seen Jonas that morning. "Yeah," she said stupidly. "Yeah."

"You think I'm nice?"

"I mean, God, Jonas." Her grip on the steering wheel tightened again, the blush on her cheeks spilling over to her neck and forehead. Her ears were hot; she tried not to think about how red they were.

"Am I making you nervous?" The speed of his fingers tapping on his leg increased. "I'm sorry."

"I'm always nervous, Jonas," Brennan whispered helplessly. "I'm always nervous, and I don't know how to stop being nervous." The words were spilling out of her all of a sudden, and she couldn't stop, couldn't stop. "Sometimes, I wonder if I'll ever *not* be nervous." She couldn't breathe; her head spun and her face was hot. "You know, my parents wouldn't even let me take my car down my first semester because they were afraid I'd—" She laughed shortly. "Afraid I'd show up on their doorstep before the first week was over. I only get to take it now because they *think* I'm getting better. I mean, there's a lot you don't know about how crazy I actually am. I'm medicated, Jonas. Or at least, sometimes. I always forget to take it, or I'm actually *afraid* to, which is the craziest part. I'm afraid of getting the side effect of nausea, so I don't take it regularly. It's stupid."

She sucked in a breath dizzily. "And you know what my medication is called? Solazepram. Its brand name is Sol-ER. Like the sun; seriously, part of its logo is a little sunshine, like it will make everything sunny and better." There were tears on her cheeks now, and the road blurred a bit before her, black pavement bleeding into white lane markings. "Sometimes I think that I'm strong enough to do this without medication. But others I—what if I'm not actually strong enough?" She felt embarrassed to be crying in front of Jonas, and tried to look straight ahead and pretend that her watery eyes were just a symptom of her anxiety, like her flushed face and dizziness, like her symptoms were a neat little list:

1. Flushed face.
2. Dizziness.
3. Watering eyes.

and not really her breaking down in front of Jonas.

"Hey, Brennan," he said softly, his voice breaking through the chaos of her thoughts. It sounded a bit echoey in her head. "Take this exit up here."

She glanced sideways hesitantly, before signaling and getting off the interstate.

JONAS

At Jonas's direction, Brennan turned somewhat shakily into a Walmart parking lot and pulled into an open spot. It struck him that, before, he might have been worried about her driving, upset as she was, but now he was only worried about her.

"Come on," he said, getting out of the car and crutching to her side to open the driver's-side door. Brennan was still sitting with her hands on the wheel, staring blankly out the front windshield, but at his words, she turned slowly and looked up at him. Her helpless expression made something in his stomach clench. He put both crutches under his left arm and held out his right hand. She took it, after glancing back and forth between it and him a few times.

Her grip was loose on his fingers at first, but she eventually held on more tightly. He gave her hand a squeeze, hoping it made her feel better somehow. He wished he knew what to do for her. All he wanted to do was *everything*—everything it took to make things better for her.

"Are you all right to go inside?" he asked her.

She shrugged slightly but nodded.

They walked slowly into Walmart, Brennan slowing her pace to walk next to him as he crutched inside. Her hands were fidgety with nervous energy.

They walked through the store for a while in silence.

They were in the kitchen aisles when Brennan spoke suddenly. "When I was younger, my dad used to take me with him to Walmart every time he needed to change the oil in the car. It would always be a Saturday, and early in the morning, and he'd always let me look up what kind of filter our car needed in that—it's almost like a phone book, with all the different types of filters for each car in it—he'd let me look it up, then find it on the shelf. Then he'd get me some kind of candy, whatever I wanted."

Jonas looked at her.

She blew out a breath, looking at her feet. "A Bren Fun Fact. It was my turn, remember?"

He chuckled softly. "Now who's keeping score?" He led her to the automotive section.

She wandered over to the filters. "They've upgraded, I guess," she said, running a hand over the little electronic database attached to the shelf. She pressed the start button, as if testing it out. *Welcome,* the screen said. *Choose your vehicle's make.*

"Honda," said Jonas. Brennan pressed the button next to Honda on the screen.

"Odyssey," he said. Brennan pressed the next button.

"This is the Bus, isn't it?" she said, a tiny smile tugging up the corners of her lips. It didn't quite reach her eyes yet.

"Yeah," he said. "2002."

She pressed the button. They raced to see who could find the filter with the proper number the fastest. Brennan won. "I guess all that practice paid off," Jonas remarked.

They left the automotive section, wandering a few aisles down to the clearance aisle in the back of the store. It was mostly deserted, the shelves full of discounted Christmas items.

"Do you want anything?" Jonas said. "Some Christmas lights? Inflatable Santa?" He picked up an item and held it up. "Reindeer antlers?" He put the headband on and offered Brennan a small smile, all while mentally kicking himself. What weird part of him was this that came out when he was around her?

He banished that thought immediately when she laughed softly. This time her smile reached her eyes. "I think they suit you," she whispered.

God, her smile was so pretty.

"Anyway," she said, turning and fiddling with a box containing icicle lights. "Your turn. Jonas Fun Fact."

There were so many different things he could have said, but when he looked at her, they all scrambled until there was nothing but one thought, big and unwilling to let him ignore it.

"Brennan," he blurted, suddenly.

"What?"

Brennan. She was perfect.

"I think I'm falling in love with you."

For once, she didn't immediately break eye contact with him. Her eyes widened even more, her eyebrows rose in surprise, and her lips parted. "W-What?" she stuttered.

He curled his fingers tighter around the crutches, suddenly nervous. "I . . . like you, Brennan. I like you a lot. I've never been in love before, so what the heck do I know, but I think maybe this is what it feels like." Head spinning, out of control. He'd thought that maybe part of what he was so scared of was the feeling that things could happen, out of the blue, and he might not get to *live*—to experience something wonderful and exciting and *good*—but here he was; here *she* was.

"Jonas, I—" She closed her eyes. "Look at me," she whispered. "Look how much of a human disaster I am. Why would you . . . how could you—"

"I don't care, Brennan," he said, and the words were earnest. "This, as painful as it is for you, is—it's a part of you. And I like all the parts of you. What you think is good *and* what you think is bad."

"What if I think it's all bad?" Her voice was so quiet he could hardly hear her, even in the empty aisle. "What if I think I'm all cons?"

"You'd be wrong." What if he was all cons? Did it matter right now? Somehow, it seemed like it didn't. He felt less like a boy with one and a half legs, and more just like a boy standing in front of a girl.

She looked up at him. Her eyes were huge behind her glasses. Her face was pale, aside from the bright-red flush on her cheeks. Up close, he could see the spattering of freckles peppered across her nose like the stars in the sky. How had he not noticed them before?

"Most people would—would kiss now, wouldn't they?" Brennan whispered, her voice a little shaky.

"Do you want to kiss me?" he asked, his eyes meeting hers.

"I do," Brennan said. "But maybe . . . not now. I'm a little nervous for all that. I don't know how; I've never done it. I want to though, in the future. With *you*, if you want to?"

"I'd like that," he said. His mouth was dry. His heart was hammering.

Then Brennan was closing her eyes, her fingers going slack and relinquishing their death grip on her sweater cuffs as she put her arms around him, tightly. For a moment, his thoughts were jumbled—*Can she feel the prosthesis against her legs? Can she feel the plastic, fake part of me? Does it matter?*—but then he leaned into her and put his own arms around her, pulling her close. She hugged him tightly, like if she let go, he might run away and leave her alone in the clearance aisle of Walmart, like maybe she didn't quite believe he was real. Her head came just perfectly to his chin, which he thought was a little clichéd, but did *that* matter? No.

"I think I'm falling in love with you, too, Jonas. And it scares me and excites me all at once. Are you—are you okay with that?"

They stayed in one another's arms as he answered. "Yes," he said. "And Brennan?"

"Hmm," she hummed against his chest.

"It ends, you know? The bad stuff. Good stuff comes. I have to believe it, even if I don't, if that makes sense. Because I'd go completely crazy if I didn't, in some hidden part of me, believe things get better."

She pulled back and looked up at him, searching his face. Finally, Brennan smiled. Brown eyes shining; Brennan at full brightness. "Okay," she said.

She looked away, face red. "Wow," she breathed. "I think—I think if it was possible to win at the fun facts game, you would have just won."

"Yeah?" He felt wonderfully, deliriously happy. And warm,

somewhere in his chest and the pit of his stomach. *Is this the end? Is this the good?*

He could hear the grin in her voice without even looking as she added. "Don't forget to take those antlers off."

His face flushed hot, but he grinned and pulled the headband off. Rather than putting them back on the shelf, he kept them in one hand as they headed back toward the front of the store.

"What are you doing?" Brennan asked. She laughed. "Don't tell me you're buying them!"

"Why not?" He grinned. "It's a commemoration."

47

brennan

Brennan stared at her reflection in the mirror, taking in her boring brown eyes, currently wide behind her glasses, and her hair, which was stubbornly refusing to stay tucked up in pins. She adjusted the collar of her dark maroon dress, trying to relieve the choking feeling in her throat, to no avail.

She jumped as the door opened and Ambreen trudged in, makeup smudged and hair escaping a messy bun after a long day of classes. "Brennan!" she exclaimed, brightening a bit. "What are *you* all dressed up for?"

Brennan couldn't help but notice the slight emphasis on the word *you*. Of course Ambreen would be surprised to see Brennan going out; she usually saw her roommate holed up in their dorm room, curled up in a ball on her bed watching Netflix or tapping away at her laptop in her own fictional world.

She forced a smile. "I'm going out." Out. The word felt funny on her tongue, but nice. It was nice to be able to say she *was* going out. *She* was going out.

"On a date?" Ambreen's smile spread across her face. *God, she's beautiful,* thought Brennan. *Even in day-old makeup and a messy bun. Why can't I look that good? I just look like a little girl trying to play at being an adult.* She sighed.

"I guess," she said out loud. "Yeah, it's kind of a date." It *was* a date. There was no kind of about it. Jonas's text had said, Will you go on a date with me? Short and to the point, so there was no doubt that *this was a date.*

She'd almost said no. She'd almost let herself be too afraid to go. But the part of her inside that wanted nothing more than Jonas was louder than the parts of her that were scared, for one of the first times ever, so she guessed that she owed it to herself to try. Before the feeling ended.

"Anyone I know?" teased Ambreen. She was wiping her face with a makeup wipe—half-on half-off, like Mulan having a when-will-my-reflection-show moment.

"No. He goes to Wash U in St. Louis." Brennan picked up her phone from her desk and scrolled through her photos until she found the one she was looking for. A sort-of-creep shot she'd taken of Jonas at the capybara exhibit. He was backlit by the autumn sun, which highlighted the angles in his face and his straight nose. She had almost texted it to him as a joke, captioned *Capybara exhibit, Saint Louis Zoo,* but she'd chickened out because *WHAT WOULD HE THINK ABOUT THE FACT THAT YOU SNUCK A PHOTO OF HIM??* She showed the picture to Ambreen now.

"Oooo! He's *cute!*"

Brennan forced a smile, although her belly flipped a little at the fact that Ambreen had called Jonas cute. To hear someone else say it just reminded her of the fact that other people knew Jonas was cute and that he could have any one of them instead of *her* (*uncute, plain Brennan*).

Outwardly, she smiled just a little. Ambreen stepped up behind Brennan. "Let me help you with that." Before Brennan could argue,

Ambreen had stolen the pins from her hand and deftly pinned up the unruly hairs in the back.

"Thanks," said Brennan awkwardly.

"No problem," said Ambreen. "You look really nice. What time is he coming to pick you up?"

"I'm supposed to meet him out front in ten minutes." She clenched her fists. "I don't know if I can stand to wait ten minutes, Ambreen. My stomach is already doing flips; I'm so nervous."

"Do you like this Jonas?"

Brennan hesitantly nodded.

"Then just see. He obviously likes you, too, or he wouldn't have asked you out on a date. And the way you're dressed up, it's a fancy one. He wouldn't go through all this effort if he didn't like you."

Brennan's face flushed with heat. "Really?" she said. "You think so?"

"I know so," said Ambreen, and her voice was softer and more serious than usual. "You're going to be fine." Then she hugged Brennan, in one of those hugs that Brennan normally tried to avoid because hugs were awkward, but this time she hugged Ambreen back.

"Thanks, Ambreen," she said. She stepped back and smoothed her dress, taking herself in in the mirror one final time. From her long-sleeved maroon dress to her black tights and heels, she was more dressed up than she had ever been around Jonas, and yet she was still worried it wasn't dressed up enough to hide *her*. But *her* was supposedly what Jonas liked. *Don't be silly,* her brain scoffed. *You know that isn't possible.*

"I guess I'll head out now," she said.

Ambreen handed Brennan her coat. "Have fun!"

———

Brennan took a big gulp of the crisp February air, filling her lungs with a snap of cool relief—like being in the deli cooler times one hundred. She started toward campus, trying to slow her steps and her racing heart.

She looked up at the sky, where a few odd snow flurries were just starting to fall. She stopped for a moment, closing her eyes and focusing on breathing in and out. The cold stung her cheeks and the snowflakes landed in her hair. In that moment, in the silence on the pathway behind the dorm, with snow falling softly and silently past the lighted windows and the nearby streetlights, Brennan felt small. Like being under the stars. Like being in silence.

She reached the bus stop. This part was her idea. *Why?* her brain scoffed. *You're going to be confined to a bus, out on the highway, in front of a bunch of strangers. What if you get car sick? Throw up? Can't get off?*

But it had been the first thing that had come to her mind when Jonas had offered to come pick her up. It had surprised her—this new and strange thought. When had she started to worry about him? When had someone else's anxiety started to matter as much—more, in the moment she'd texted, *What about a complicated combination of foot, train, and bus?*—as her own?

Two buses pulled up at once—one from Cougar Village (the on-campus upperclassmen's apartments) and one from St. Louis. Brennan lost herself in watching the lights come on in the bus. One by one, the passengers stood up—gathering backpacks, adjusting head-phones, offering the driver little waves and thank yous as they spilled out into the February cold. She closed her eyes, willing her heart to slow as she pictured herself getting on the bus and finding a spot. Sitting down.

"Hey."

She smiled and opened her eyes, her heart continuing its breakneck pace. "Hey," she said, a little breathlessly. For a moment they just stood there, looking at one another as the snow fell gently around them. Jonas was wearing a suit, a real black suit with a tie and everything, and shiny black shoes. Brennan felt a little underdressed next to him, just as she'd feared. The people leaving the bus streamed around them and off onto campus to do whatever they had come to do.

"You look beautiful," Jonas stammered, leaning into his crutches, his face turning a little red. *A lot red*, at least for Jonas.

Brennan smiled shyly. "You too. I mean handsome. You look—you look nice." She cringed inwardly. *Stupid, stupid,* her brain said. *Shut up, brain,* she told it.

"You ready to go now?" said Jonas. "Because when you're ready, we'll go. Just tell me if you're not, and we'll wait."

"I'm ready," she whispered, even though her stomach was doing flips at the idea of going to a fancy restaurant. She wondered if she'd even be able to get anything past the knot in her throat.

Then he was standing closer to her. "Are you sure?" he said. Brennan closed her eyes, swaying a little, the lilt of the other bus goers' voices and the chill of the evening breeze wrapping around her.

When she opened her eyes she looked at Jonas; a few snowflakes had yet to melt completely and still adorned his hair like small stars in a dark sky. "Where are we going?" she asked him, not wanting to answer his question. *What does it mean if I'm not?*

"It's a surprise."

"I don't even get a hint?"

"Nope," said Jonas. "You'll see soon enough." He was silent for a moment before asking, "Are you nervous at all?"

She hesitated.

"Are you afraid you'll hurt my feelings if you tell me?" Stupid Jonas, knowing her so *exactly*.

"No," she lied. "I mean—" She let out a breath. "It feels stupid to be nervous when I know you, and I *like* you, and I'm comfortable with you, but I am nervous. I'm really nervous. For some reason, the idea of being in a restaurant with a ton of people—what if I mess up? What if I spill soup on myself? Or trip in my heels?" She laughed anxiously. *Food poisoning,* her brain added. *But don't tell him that or he'll think you're weird.*

Jonas was quiet for a moment. The driver of the St. Louis bus opened his doors one last time. "You coming?" he called.

Brennan moved to step forward, but Jonas took her sleeve and tugged—not hard, not like he was forcing her to stay, but just like he maybe wanted to see if she would; thumb and forefinger, testing. She stopped.

"No, sorry," Jonas said. "Thank you for checking."

The driver nodded, closed his doors, and was gone.

Brennan started to feel hot and anxious again. What was going on? She tried to slow her breathing. *In. Out. Anxiety is a wave.*

"Do you trust me?" he asked her, switching both crutches to his left side and shifting his weight to his right leg.

"What are you . . ."

"We aren't going to the restaurant."

"W-What?" she stuttered. "No, Jonas. Don't change plans just because of me. Did I ruin this? I'm so sorry for ruining this." *Stupid, stupid, stupid,* her brain chanted.

"You didn't ruin anything," said Jonas.

"But we aren't going—"

"I know," he said.

"Is the date over already?" She nervously did and undid the clasp on the little clutch she'd brought as the bus into Edwardsville pulled up. "Jonas, I'm sorry."

"There's nothing to be sorry about," he said, using his left hand to navigate the crutches while offering his right to her. "The night's not over. Just wait and see."

She stared at their hands for a moment, before taking a deep breath and taking his, holding on tight. "Okay," she whispered.

The bus's doors opened and they got on.

48

JONAS

They found seats near the front.

The other passengers boarded the bus. A boy with headphones on, his spare hand drumming his thigh in rhythm with an unheard song as he found a seat in the back. A couple laughing at something on the girl's phone. A girl hunched against the cold in a too-light jacket, hands shoved deep into pockets.

Jonas told himself the seat at the front was because he didn't want Brennan to feel trapped in the back. *Don't kid yourself.* He didn't want to feel trapped either.

The lights in the bus went out and Jonas watched Brennan's face get cast in the yellow of the streetlights.

———

"Walmart?"

Jonas couldn't help but smile at the confusion in Brennan's voice.

She looked sideways at him as the bus pulled away from the stop behind them. "What are we doing here?"

"Gathering supplies," he said, shrugging. For a moment they stood in the parking lot, before walking to the entrance, snow crunching under their feet (and crutches, in Jonas's case).

"So," Brennan said. "What sort of supplies?"

"Oh, just a few odds and ends," he answered nonchalantly. He felt giddy. Silly. They were going into a Walmart in *dress clothes*. They made it inside and Brennan pulled out a cart. He glanced sideways to watch her face as they approached the deli, her pushing the cart slowly to keep pace with his crutching.

"What are we—"

Jonas grinned as they came to a stop in front of the counter. "One pound of oven-roasted turkey, please," he said to the worker. "And a half-pound of Muenster cheese."

The guy behind the counter nodded and pulled out the turkey, preparing to slice it.

"Can we get that sliced on a two?" Brennan suddenly blurted.

Then, to Jonas, "The cheeses."

"The cheeses." Jonas looked at Brennan and raised an eyebrow. "What about them?"

"It was one of our first conversations," she said. "And I had you try the Muenster." She was looking at him with some sort of unreadable emotion on her face. It was almost like wonder. "So you remembered." Wonder, like she didn't think she was important enough that anyone would remember what she said.

"Yes," he whispered. "Of course I did, Brennan. Do you have any idea how many times I've played our conversations over and over in my mind? Wondering if I should have said something different, done something different."

"Now you sound like me." Brennan blushed red and looked at her feet. Jonas noticed her hand twitch toward his, but she quickly pulled it back. So he took her hand himself and held on. Her hand was warm and small in his and he thought he could hold it like that forever.

The meat and cheese were done. "Have a good night," said the deli attendant as he handed them the packages.

They went on their way to the bakery, and Jonas let Brennan pick out a nice bag of ciabatta rolls.

"What about dessert?" he asked her.

"How about cheesecake?" she said, after a moment of consideration.

"Cheesecake it is."

They moved to the checkout after picking up some paper plates and cups, and Jonas paid.

Outside, Brennan turned to face him. "So what now?" she asked. Her smile was less forced and she seemed more comfortable.

Jonas smiled as they reached the bus stop once more. "Do you trust me?"

"I think that I do," she whispered, as if surprised.

"Have you taken the St. Louis Metro before?"

She shook her head.

"What is the combination of bus, foot, and train without the train?"

"Boring, probably."

The Edwardsville-St. Louis bus pulled up. "Right. The train is the fun part."

They boarded, and this time, they sat in the middle.

———

Jonas opened the door to the hallway and held it for Brennan as she ducked under his arm, bearing her burden of cheesecake.

He noticed that she gripped the cake a little tighter as they made their way farther and farther into the depths of the Washington University dorm. "So this is your home away from home, huh?" she said, glancing around at the posters people had taped to their doors and the announcements randomly posted on their walls. Music curled lazily down the hall from someone who was probably getting in their last bits of noise before courtesy hours went into effect.

"This is it," he said, gesturing at a handmade poster on the wall that said Home of the Whales—featuring a red whale on a blue background. "Not much different than the dorms at Edwardsville. I guess all dorms are kind of the same. Maybe that's the point of them."

"Yeah," Brennan said. She pointed at the poster. "The whales?"

"Umrath and South 40's mascot. On my first day, I got a T-shirt with a whale on it." He stopped at a door. "Well, here we are." He shifted one of the Walmart bags to his other arm and pulled out his key, working at unlocking the door.

"Is your roommate home?" she asked. Muffled music could be heard in the hall.

"Nah," he said. "I don't have a roommate anyway, just next-door neighbors. I think that's Sam's music. Travis is my other suitemate. He's on a date though. Or, well, he's always on a date."

Brennan laughed slightly as Jonas finally got the door open and they went inside. "Just toss the stuff down on the desk," he said. "I'll get the sandwiches made." He noticed her watching him as he carefully took his shoes off, dress sock covering his prosthetic foot. She took off her wet shoes as he stepped inside.

Brennan sat down on the edge of the bed, and Jonas watched out of the corner of his eye as she looked around his room. It was pretty bare, other than the stuff his mom had gotten for the bed. He did have a couple posters on the walls though—one from *Star Wars* and one, more recently, from Harry Potter. Then there was the periodic table, the one from his text. He noticed that Brennan smiled a bit when she saw it. Besides that, there was a string of lights that was half burned out—a joke gift from his dad, who'd replaced the Christmas tree lights that year. Jonas had hung it up anyway, because it had made his dad laugh like he hadn't laughed in a while.

Jonas fixed up the sandwiches, even sticking a toothpick through the top like it was a fancy restaurant. He brought Brennan her plate and presented it to her with a flourish of his hand. "Your dinner, mademoiselle." He smiled when she laughed as she took the plate.

He sat down next to her.

She paused in the middle of bringing her food to her mouth. "Jonas?"

"Yeah?"

"I'm glad this is our first date."

He looked at her, taking in her wide brown eyes rimmed with long lashes. The lashes were something he hadn't noticed before. He liked that; that she was familiar and new all at once. "Me too," he finally said, after a moment.

They ate in silence for a little while more, before he remembered something and jumped up. "You know, Rhys got me a pretty great gift for Christmas. I thought we could find something to do with it." He pulled a set of the Harry Potter movies from his desk drawer.

Brennan grinned. "You haven't watched them yet?"

"Well, I *have* hardly finished the books," he said. "And I'm a believer in not watching movies until you've read the books—"

"I approve," Brennan interrupted.

"Anyway, I suppose I wanted to see them with you. Because without you, I probably never would have read them."

Her face turned red, but she didn't say anything.

Jonas put the first DVD in and turned on the TV. The opening music started playing. Brennan was sitting on the bed, leaning against the headboard, her legs curled up under the skirt of her red dress.

Jonas sat down carefully next to her, suddenly hyperaware of how close she was. *Her left side—your right against her left.* He stretched his legs out because he didn't want to deal with the logistics of bending the prosthetic one.

Harry was waking up under the stairs at the Dursleys for the first time.

"You know," he whispered, barely audible over the movie. "You look really nice in that color."

"Shush," she said, even as she messed awkwardly with the hem of the red dress. "Watch the movie."

But she leaned her head against his shoulder anyway and put her hand on top of his. Just like that, it was suddenly a lot harder to concentrate on the movie.

49

brennan

Brennan woke up to Jonas saying her name and shaking her shoulder.

"Brennan? Movie's over."

She blinked and sat up, trying to banish the lingering grasp of sleep from her heavy eyes and foggy mind. "What time is it?"

"Only nine," said Jonas, moving to get up now that she was awake and had removed her face from where it had been plastered to his shoulder. He went to the window and frowned as he looked out. The half-burned-out string of Christmas lights flickered. "The snow's gotten pretty bad though, so if we want any chance to get you home, we'd better leave."

"Okay." She yawned as she stood and grabbed her coat, shrugging into it and wrapping her scarf around her neck. Jonas pulled on his coat and repositioned his crutches as he awkwardly got his shoes on.

Once they got outside, it became clear that the snow was even deeper than it had looked from the window. Brennan glanced at Jonas; he seemed a little tense, one hand gripping the bus pass against his crutch. Her sleep-addled brain finally caught up and she shook her head. "I'm sorry, Jonas," she said. "I know—the snow—" Her gaze flicked to his left leg (she noticed he had shifted to his right to keep his weight off of it) and then up to his face. He was still staring ahead as if in thought. They were still a ways from the Metro station—not even off campus yet.

"Jonas?"

Without acknowledging her, he just turned and started walking in the opposite direction of the parking lot. "Rhys has a sleeping bag," he said over his shoulder as she struggled through the snow in heels behind him. "I'll sleep on that and you can take the bed. It's too bad to drive tonight—bus or not. It's just not safe. You can stay with me."

"Wait, Jonas—" He stopped and she caught up to him. "You don't have to sleep on the floor," she said. "I'll take the sleeping bag."

"Don't be silly," he said. He seemed nervous, a bit unfocused.

"Really—" she said.

He frowned at her heels. "It's a long walk to Rhys's dorm," he said. "Why don't you take the keys and go back to the dorm room. Do you remember how to find it?"

"It's okay," she said. "I want to come with you." She didn't want to be alone with her thoughts. This was an eventuality she hadn't prepared for, hadn't thought about. Hadn't been given notice of. Sleeping anywhere other than her own bed was bad enough (she thought about chickening out of her high school retreat) but doing it on short notice—best to push those thoughts away and occupy her mind with something else for now.

Jonas looked at her for a moment before shrugging. "Okay," he said, simply. Brennan shoved her hands deep into her coat pockets and continued walking next to him.

The snow fell silently around them, making her feel small again. She closed her eyes and turned her face toward the sky.

"You know, I had a good time tonight."

Brennan looked up as Jonas broke the silence. He seemed a little nervous, like he was worried about whether or not she'd had a good time also. "Me too," she said. She frowned, looking into the distance. "Jonas?" she said hesitantly.

"Hmm?"

"Why do you really like me? Because I'm so . . . me?" She sighed. "I just still can't quite believe—"

He stopped short under a streetlight that stood next to the sidewalk, a silent sentinel in the snowstorm, casting the snow beneath it a mellow orange.

"Forget it," she said. "It's a stupid question. And you kind of already answered it when we stargazed but I just—"

"No," he said, turning to her. "It's not stupid. It's just a complicated answer. Or at least, I thought it was. But now—" He met her eyes. "You make me want to get better. You are possibility."

Brennan smiled slightly, not asking what he meant because she understood. He was possibility to her too—the possibility of better, and normal, and something good.

She bumped her left shoulder against his right. "Hey."

"Hey." Then, after a moment. "This is good, right?"

"This is good," she said. Then she shoved a handful of snow down his back, which made him gasp, hunch into his crutches, and then laugh.

———

"So . . ." Brennan watched as Jonas spread the sleeping bag on the floor and fluffed a pillow, placing it at the head of the makeshift sleeping space. "I didn't exactly bring pajamas." She laughed awkwardly. Her tights were soaked through, and her dress wasn't doing so well either. She shivered a little and wrapped her arms around herself.

Jonas frowned for a moment, before crutching to his dresser and pulling out a pair of shorts and a sweater. "The shorts have a drawstring," he said, "so you'll probably be able to make them fit. And you look pretty cold so—" He shrugged. "Sweater."

Brennan took the things from him and held them to her chest.

"You can change in the bathroom across the hall," he said.

She nodded and escaped to the bathroom. Alone, she stared at herself in the mirror. Her hair was messed up from sleeping and then walking (and some running on her part after the snow incident) through the snow with Jonas. Her dress was soaked at the hem and down her back (he'd gotten her back), and her tights were sopping. *You're a mess.*

She stripped off the soaked tights and dress and quickly pulled on the shorts and the sweater, which was so large on her she might as well have not even been wearing the shorts, since it hung to her knees. She found that odd, because Jonas wasn't exactly very big. Then again, he was tall, and she was short.

She shook her head, halting her mind's foray into focusing her anxious thoughts on sweater logistics. She pulled her arms into the sweater sleeves and wrapped them around her chest, still staring at herself in the mirror.

Brennan imagined how Ambreen would tease her once she figured out that Brennan had spent the night at a guy's place, even if it hadn't been in *that* way. She tried to think about what Ambreen might do in her situation. *Be confident, like Ambreen,* her brain said.

She did her best to push her anxiety into a ball in the pit of her stomach. She took a deep breath and turned out the bathroom light, before peeking out to make sure no one was in the hallway and practically leaping the few steps between the bathroom and Jonas's room.

She shut the door behind her, a little too loudly. Jonas looked up from his sleeping bag, where he was lying on his stomach, scrolling through something on his phone. "Lucky it's not courtesy hours yet," he remarked.

Brennan didn't say anything, just sat on the edge of the bed.

Jonas watched her for a moment. "You nervous?"

"When am I not?"

"Wanna watch another Potter movie? I know you're obviously tired since you fell asleep during the first one, so maybe it would help you to relax and fall asleep."

"Worth a shot," she said.

Jonas got up and put in the movie, turning on the TV. Brennan climbed into bed and pulled the covers up over her. The pillow smelled like Jonas's shampoo—pine, peppermint, something she didn't quite recognize. She yawned, even as the movie started to play.

She looked down at Jonas, watching as he crawled into the sleeping bag. "Don't you—" She paused sheepishly. "Never mind."

"What?" he said, looking up at her from the floor.

"Don't you take your prosthesis off to sleep?"

He looked away slightly, not making eye contact. "I mean, usually," he muttered. "But I don't usually have people over to see me sleep."

They were both silent for a few moments.

"You know," said Brennan. "You can't wear it all the time. I'm gonna see it eventually. Why not just get it over with? It's not like it will make any difference for me to see you without it. I already know you only have one and a half legs. There's not some secret that's going to be suddenly out there if you take off the plastic and metal part of your leg."

Jonas didn't say anything, and he avoided looking at her. "I've kept it on before; it's not a big deal."

"Jonas . . ."

"Stop, Brennan."

His tone was sharp-edged. Brennan swallowed. "I'm sorry. I'm an inconvenience."

What felt like an eternal sixty seconds passed. "You're not an inconvenience."

Brennan didn't reply, just got up and turned out the lights before returning to bed. She looked at the ceiling as the dialogue of the movie swirled in and out of her thoughts.

"Jonas?" she whispered sleepily.

"Hmm," he muttered. She wondered if he had already been asleep.

"Good night," she said.

"Good night."

The snow outside made shadows on the wall as it fell past the street-light outside the window. Brennan watched *The Chamber of Secrets* for a while. Jonas had his back to her now. She watched him for a moment, the rise and fall of his side as he slept, the tousle of his dark hair against the pillow, already mussed.

She closed her eyes and breathed in Jonas's shampoo smell from the pillow, letting herself relax and fall into unconsciousness, even as Harry first heard the voice in the pipes in the movie still playing in the background.

30

JONAS

When Jonas woke up—for the tenth time or so, he'd lost count—Brennan was still asleep. He lay there for a few moments, listening to her quiet breathing, the only sound in the room.

The prosthesis was uncomfortable. He should have taken it off. *You should have taken it off. She wouldn't care. She* said *she wouldn't care.*

You are this. The words repeated in his head. He remembered when it had first happened. He remembered that people suddenly forgave him for any little argument, because all they saw was him, almost lost, and now altogether different. Special circumstances from his teachers; special consideration from his parents. He could no longer be Jonas, normal teenage boy, because he was now Jonas, teenage boy minus half a leg.

He picked up his phone and hit the email notification on the home screen, looking to distract himself. His eyes scanned the email.

—due to inclement weather, school facilities will only be open a limited amount of time today. Please visit the cafeteria, the bookstore, library, or student center as needed before they close.

Jonas glanced at the clock. Nine. The cafeteria closed at noon. *That's still three hours.* But it felt stifling in the sleeping bag, prosthesis still on. As much as he hated the stump, he didn't like begrudging it the chance to breathe—taking off the prosthesis was as good as taking off your shoes and socks at the end of the day. He glanced at Brennan. No need to wake her. She looked so peaceful, her wavy brown hair loose on the pillow and her eyes closed, one hand tucking the blanket up to her chin.

He stood, propping himself up on his crutches, and grabbed a pair of sweatpants, a sweater, his coat, his shoes, and his wallet and keys, before slipping out of the room, shutting the door quietly.

After changing in the bathroom, he headed downstairs and out into the cold.

The snow that had been so beautiful and serene last night was still falling, but it didn't have quite the same magical feeling in the daylight. There were a few students out, trekking to the cafeteria for food or to some of the restaurants within walking distance for takeout. The snow on the sidewalks hadn't been cleared yet, but the feet of the students had plowed a makeshift path, churning dirt into the snow and browning it a bit.

Jonas started down the path, making sure to place his feet and crutches carefully as he went.

He ignored the burning in his leg and thought about Brennan instead. If it didn't stop snowing soon, she'd have to stay here another night. Not that he particularly minded—he'd sleep on the floor any night for her, even if his back had hurt a little this morning from the lack of a mattress.

He thought he'd better get enough food for two in case.

"Jonas! Hey, Jonas!"

Jonas turned around just as Sam practically skidded into him and almost knocked both of them into the snow as he grabbed Jonas's coat to steady himself, pulling Jonas down against his crutches, sending shocks of pain through both his armpits (it reminded him of back when he'd first started using the crutches and he'd walked on them wrong—weight carried through armpits and not wrists). *Ouch.*

"Headed to the cafeteria, Sam?" He winced, straightening and regaining his balance.

Sam nodded, pulling his stocking cap a little farther down over his ears and blowing on his hands. "God, it's cold."

Jonas shrugged. "It *is* winter."

Jonas didn't mind the cold much as long as he was only out in it to walk somewhere with the promise of warmth at the end. Sam, on the other hand, acted like he was dying from hypothermia every time he set foot outside.

"You haven't played video games with us lately," commented the shorter guy, falling into step with Jonas and taking two steps to match Jonas's one. "Busy?"

Jonas nodded. He *had* been busy. With school and with Brennan, whom he still had yet to tell his suitemates about. He guessed he'd better do that, in case they happened to run into her this weekend.

"I'm seeing someone," he said. "We've hung out before, but our first official date was last night. I think it went pretty well. Although with the snow, we didn't make it back to Edwardsville, where she goes to school. She stayed over last night."

"Dude! Is she hot? Did you tell Travis?"

Jonas rolled his eyes. "No," he said. "About telling Travis. Come to think of it, I haven't seen Travis. Wasn't he out on another date last night?"

"He was," said Sam. "Came back drunk, though. Apparently, he walked back from her dorm in the snow." He was muttering now, as he added, "Without a coat, like an idiot."

Jonas sighed. He'd been exposed to drunk Travis enough times to be surprised he hadn't been woken up when Travis got in. Normally, there was raucous singing involved, or at least a lot of banging next door when Travis gave up on trying to get in the door and started yelling for Sam to open up.

"He's his normal self this morning, though, or at least he will be once I get some food and water into him." Sam frowned at the ground.

Sam seemed almost like the protective mother of the suite, in the absence of real mothers. He was always admonishing Travis for his drinking and bad habits with girls, trying to get Jonas to go to bed early the night before a big test instead of pulling an all-nighter, and insisting that all three of them take their vitamins. It seemed at odds with Sam's own bad habits of playing video games and eating junk food all weekend, but as Sam would say, someone had to do it.

Sam, who had fallen behind Jonas, caught up once more, puffing a bit. "Hey, so after I get Travis back to the present, we were planning on playing some video games."

"Sam, I told you I had someone over. And with the snow expected to continue, I don't think she'll be going home tonight either."

"So? Bring her," said Sam. "The more the merrier. Beating *three* people at *Super Smash Bros. Brawl* is even better than beating two."

Jonas rolled his eyes yet again as they reached the cafeteria and trudged inside, stomping the snow off their shoes on the rug outside the door first. "Okay," he said. "Maybe. I'll see if Brennan wants to."

"Brennan?"

"My guest, Sam."

"Oh. Yeah. Your *girlfriend*."

Jonas sighed and the two continued into the bustle of activity that was the cafeteria. Jonas's leg hurt.

brennan

Brennan jolted awake when her phone rang.

Vision still blurry from sleep, she looked at the screen. Ambreen. "Hello?"

"Brennan? Is that you?"

"Yeah," said Brennan, voice groggy. "Who else would it be? What's—" She yawned. "Up?"

"You didn't come home last night. I mean, to the dorm. Calvin said you'd probably just stayed over, but I wasn't sure. I was worried. I mean, you know, things happen."

Brennan's eyes widened. She wondered if she was imagining the strain in Ambreen's voice. Almost like her roommate might cry. "No, nothing like that. Everything's fine. We just got snowed in, so I slept over at Jonas's dorm." She stumbled out of bed, doing her best to untangle herself from the comforter one handed and managing to only trip a little bit. She went to the window and pulled the shades up, revealing the still falling snow outside. "How is it still snowing?" she mumbled.

"Anyway," said Ambreen, her voice losing the tremulous quality. "As long as you're fine. That was all I wanted to know."

"Thanks, Ambreen. Really. It was nice of you to be concerned."

"No problem. Let me know when you're coming back. It's still pretty bad out there. The plows aren't even out on campus."

"Okay. I will. See you."

"Bye."

Brennan set her phone down on the bed and sat back down on the edge of the mattress, the springs of which creaked beneath her, strikingly similar to her own dorm bed at SIUE. Where was Jonas?

At least with him gone, she had some time to think, mostly about the fact that she had slept in a boy's room last night. And no, nothing had happened, but for her, this was an accomplishment. She'd slept in the same room with someone she didn't normally sleep with, and with the boy she really liked no less. And she hadn't even been that nervous.

Brennan lay back down and pulled the blankets to her chin; it was pretty cold in the dorm room. She stared at the ceiling. Then she pictured Jonas staring at the same ceiling, since he normally slept in this bed every night. She thought about not having her laptop, and the fact that it was still snowing and she probably wouldn't make it home today either. Which meant the count of days not writing was just going to go up. Brennan wondered if Jonas would let her borrow his laptop. It wouldn't be her own trusty document, but she could type directly into the allfixx editor and make do.

She closed her eyes, willing away the knot in her stomach that was busy retying itself in the light of day.

JONAS

When Jonas got back to Umrath, he took the elevator up to the third floor. Then he ignored his own room and went into the bathroom. He set the food on the counter. Then he lowered himself to the floor.

He rolled up his sweatpants and took off the prosthesis. Then the liner. He didn't look at the stump but just sat there for a few minutes, just to be prosthesis-less for a while. He thought about Brennan seeing the stump. He thought about her looking at it. He thought about being sick to his stomach.

There was banging on the door. "Heyyyyyy!" slurred Travis. "I gotta pee!"

Jonas sucked in a breath. "Just a minute! Almost done!"

He put the liner on. Then the prosthesis. Sock and shoe. Then he stood up, grabbed the food and his crutches, and left the bathroom behind.

In the dorm room, Brennan was awake.

Jonas set the bags down on the desk. "Hungry?"

"Starving."

"I've got some normal cafeteria food—pizza, chicken tenders, sand-wiches—and I walked down the street to my favorite Vietnamese place and got some pho. Great for cold days. I thought we could have it tonight."

"Sounds good," she said. "I guess I'll have pizza for breakfast."

"Good choice. Very healthy."

"Nothing you brought is exceptionally healthy."

He shrugged. "Touché."

Brennan took a bite of the still-warm pepperoni pizza. Jonas caught her looking sideways at him. "Jonas?"

"Hmm?" he mumbled around a mouthful of food (chicken ten-ders, dipped in honey mustard).

"Thanks for all of this. For the pajamas, the food, for sleeping on the floor—for letting me stay over, I guess. For making me feel comfortable."

Jonas swallowed, before offering her a straight face. "What did you think I'd do? Kick you out into the snow last night?"

Brennan smiled around her pizza and took another bite.

"You're welcome," Jonas said.

51

JONAS

Jonas finished the last sip of beef broth from his pho, setting down his bowl and leaning back against the footboard of the bed with a sigh. "I'm stuffed," he said. He glanced at Brennan. "Did you get enough to eat? There's more in the fridge."

"Yeah," she said. They'd spent a bit of time playing *Mario Kart* with Sam and Travis. She was quieter now that they were once more in Jonas's room, the next-door duo having hiked to another dorm for some impromptu video game tournament.

"So," he began, breaking the silence. "You're pretty good at *Mario Kart*, huh?" She'd handily beaten Sam and Travis, much to Sam's frustration as self-proclaimed video game champion of the suite.

A small smile crossed her face. "I guess," she said. "I find video games pretty fun. They distract me from my thoughts for a little bit." She seemed like she was getting into uncomfortable territory—like she hadn't meant to say that—and she fell silent once more.

"Jonas?" she said suddenly. "What's your favorite color?"

He glanced at her, surprised. "What?"

"Your favorite color. I feel like we're dating now but we've had such big issues, what with your leg and my anxiety, that we've never gotten to just focus on the little things."

He frowned, her answer not quite satisfying him. Though it was no doubt true, she wasn't fully looking at him, and he guessed that perhaps she was trying to awkwardly transition to some other bigger question.

He'd let her though, if it helped.

"Green," he said. "Or blue. I don't actually really have one favorite."

"You have two siblings?"

"Yeah. Taylor and Rhys, both of whom you've met in passing. Taylor has anxiety, though it's not the same as yours. Everyone with anxiety tends to feel it differently." He paused. "Of course, you know that. I didn't mean to—sorry. I didn't want to make it sound like you didn't know or like I was trying to act like I knew more about anxiety than you." He ran a hand through his hair, no doubt messing it up even more than it already was.

"No," Brennan said. "You're fine. Go on." She crossed her legs and wrapped her arms around herself, leaning back against the headboard. They were sitting directly across the bed from one another now. Face to face. He saw her eyes go to his left leg, and then he couldn't look at her.

"Okay," he forced himself to keep going. "Taylor has anxiety, but it doesn't make her feel sick like it does for you. She just feels dizzy and claustrophobic, or at least that's all she's told me. She loves sports though; she plays soccer and basketball and does cross country. Not sure how she manages with the schedule she has, but apparently keeping busy helps her.

"And Rhys, he's a pretty normal older brother. He *thinks* he's pretty cool, though I beg to differ." He smiled as Brennan giggled. "We fought like cats and dogs until the semitruck hit us and I lost my leg. Then we fought like cats and dogs again, after an initial period where he felt guilty, and now we're better friends than we've ever been. It's been a roller coaster." He looked at her. "What about your brother?"

"Ayden's pretty good as far as brothers come. We sort of operate in different orbits most of the time, but every once in a while we connect, I guess."

They fell silent again, before Brennan spoke up, her eyes flitting to and from his like she was trying to make eye contact but couldn't quite make herself do it. "Jonas?"

"Hm." He absentmindedly massaged his leg above the prosthetic socket, gritting his teeth a bit against the pain. He honestly couldn't wait for surgery, if it only meant they'd get rid of the neuroma pain. He wasn't keen on the idea of surgery and subsequent rehab and recovery otherwise.

"Are you afraid to show me your leg?"

There it was, the harder question she'd been trying to ask. He wasn't expecting that, though. Of all the things he'd expected her to ask, that was last on the list. "W-What?" he stuttered, doing his best to regain his composure. *No. No, no. Not this question. Anything but this.*

"Are you afraid to show me? Without the prosthesis and such, I mean."

He opened and closed his mouth a few times, trying to formulate a response. *Yes* was the short answer. He sighed. "Can I ask you something, Brennan?"

She looked up and a flash of what almost looked like fear crossed her face, before she smiled hesitantly and said. "Okay."

"You don't have to answer if you don't want to."

"I'll try to answer."

"Are you afraid of *me*?"

That seemed to catch her off guard. "W-What?"

"Do I make you nervous?"

"I mean, yes. A little. I don't know. *You* don't, specifically. But maybe the idea of being with someone is a little scary to me. I just—I feel so needy. I feel like I'm always seeking assurance, validation. And I don't exist in my own little orbit now; there's someone else to consider."

She picked at the sleeve of his red sweater. *That sweater,* he thought. *I didn't like it much until she wore it.* She continued softly. "Like I need to be told over and over that we're okay, that I matter, that I'm not just a temporary passing thing in your life. And I'm afraid that you'll get tired of always having to be assuring me, of always having to be the strong one because I'll always be the weak one, the hesitant one." She sighed, and he could see tears welling in her eyes. "I wait for the bad, Jonas. Even when things are good, I'm sure it will all be bad around the corner."

Something in him wanted to go to her—move to sit next to her at the head of the bed and pull her into his arms gently, like she was something fragile that he was afraid of breaking. He pictured her burying her face in his chest, her tears wet against his T-shirt, like that night he'd come to get her out of the playset at Road's Edge. Part of him felt selfish because he couldn't—he was too worried that, in this close contact, she might brush his leg, hit plastic and metal instead of skin and bone.

He was fighting with himself. *Go to her. Stay.*

"I'm sorry," she said. "I always cry too easily. I feel like you see me as someone who's always breaking down, who's whiny and not confident enough in herself and who she is to stop being such a crybaby."

"I don't think of you that way," he whispered. "I don't think of you that way at all." *If you saw me—the way I can't drive, the way I sit in Gus and don't go anywhere, the way I can't sit next to anyone on my left.*

"But I think of myself that way," she whispered back.

"People see you differently than you see yourself." The half-burned-out Christmas lights flickered.

Brennan was silent for a while, avoiding looking at him. He decided that she was the opposite of fragile; she was strong to survive after breaking and breaking and breaking. He wished he could stop her from breaking, even just once, because he knew that the breaking hurt her. *I wish I could stop breaking.*

"Anyway," he said. "I had a point—I wasn't just avoiding your original question about my leg." He sighed. He stared at the wall across from them. Brennan stared at her lap. Maybe it seemed easier than acknowledging the conversation they'd just had; were still having.

"I'm afraid of you, Brennan. And it's weird." He laughed shortly, surprised at his own admission. It had just come out. *Fact: you wouldn't usually say that.* "I'm scared I'll mess it up with you somehow. I'm afraid I'll scare you away, and that's the last thing I want. I've never done this before—dating. Having a girlfriend. I mean, I took a girl in my class to homecoming for the first three years of high school until the accident, but it wasn't the same. It wasn't something I was wanting to last. And I would like it to last with you, Brennan.

"The newness of it, you know, is intimidating. It's never been something that was on the table, showing my leg. Friends don't exactly care about that, but it's different with you. It's not very fair of me to ask you to share yourself with me if I'm not willing to share myself with you, and I know that, but I'm still scared."

He broke off when she crawled to his end of the bed, reached up and held her fingers to his mouth, effectively shushing him. "It's okay," she said. Her fingers were soft, distractingly so. She pulled her hand away, leaving him wishing she'd put it back. "Don't be scared. I mean, you can be scared. I'm scared. Isn't it okay to be?"

"Yes. No. I don't kn—" She shifted slightly and Jonas sucked in a breath as her hand neared his left knee—the prosthesis, the fake, the missing one. He found her hand with his and stopped her. "Brennan."

She pulled away, like she was hurt that he couldn't let her be part of that part of him. He should let her. She was good. *How broken are you that you can't even let the good happen?* She sat by him—*on the left*—but didn't look at him, worrying her bottom lip with her teeth.

Do you think there are perfect moments? His mom had asked his dad this, when he was younger—*before*—when they'd gone out for ice cream as a family. *Yes,* his dad had said. He'd clarified: *There's no such* thing as a perfect life, but definitely perfect moments. Then I wish, she'd said, that there was some way to know you were in one, before it's gone, and not so perfect anymore. He wished he'd known that it was his last time with two legs before that moment was gone and the rest of his story was irrevocably thrown into this alternate ending. Maybe there was another alternate universe where he had two legs and he was happy. But do you meet Brennan in that universe?

"I like being your friend," he said. He shifted a little, stretching the remaining part of his left leg to dispel the pins and needles a bit. "I like being your boyfriend. I like . . . you, you know?" And he did. And if he did, he liked this story line. He liked knowing her. He was torn. A world with two legs probably meant no Brennan. Because if no accident, no fear of semitrucks. If no fear of semitrucks, no fender bender. If no fender bender, no Brennan—deli-uniformed, hole-in-her-left-shoe, I'm-going-to-make-you-walk Brennan. He closed his eyes and tried to picture the world where he had two legs, but all he could see was the semitruck hitting their car, over and over again.

So he opened his eyes, and Brennan was there. She was smiling slightly, but she wasn't saying anything; she just closed her eyes, her eyelashes brushing her cheeks in what Jonas found to be a very distracting manner.

"Are you tired?" he asked her.

"Yeah," she whispered.

"I'll let you go to sleep now," he said, moving to get up.

"No," she said. "I mean, stay. You can stay. It's okay."

"I don't have to."

"I actually really want you to," she whispered. "I mean, if you want to."

He smiled slightly. "Okay, just let me go to the bathroom really quick." He crutched out of the room and into the bathroom. He looked at himself in the mirror. Breathe, he thought. It's not that big of a deal. You want Brennan to stick around, right? Yes. Then these things will *happen. You can't just hold her at arms' length. That's not how it works.*

He left the bathroom. He thought of Sam and Travis. *How long do you have to be on crutches for your ACL, man?* More people at arm's length.

He lay down across from Brennan. Somehow, it felt too close. He lay on his right side, watching her while she looked back at him, wide eyed. He tried on a smile, hesitantly, and she smiled back, a smile that reached her brown eyes and warmed them.

"Remember Road's Edge, when you told me that just because I had a thing to deal with that's different from some of the other people I know, it doesn't make me broken?" She touched Jonas's cheek and his jaw tensed.

"The leg thing doesn't make you broken, Jonas."

"But I—"

"I'm okay with it. Are you afraid I won't be okay with it? Because I know, and I'm okay with it, I promise."

"You haven't seen it," he argued. *I haven't seen it—really seen it. I can't look at it. How will you?* "I'm sure you grew up picturing yourself with someone who had all their limbs. Even if you say you'll be okay with it, you don't *know*." When his mom first looked at it, post-op and still held together with stitches, the skin red and angry, she'd had to look away, tears in her eyes. His dad had done the first dressing change. He knew it was just the overwhelming feeling of seeing her child maimed, and the idea of having to hurt him by cleaning the wound and rebandaging it (and he didn't hold it against her) but still, the idea of having anyone else see it, even now that it was healed . . .

"So let me see it." Her voice was earnest. "Let me see it, Jonas. I'll be fine. This is the career I'm going into after all."

"Brennan, I—"

"Come on, Jonas. It's okay. Really it is."

What if.

What if he let her? What if she was okay? What if she wasn't? And if he didn't let her, then where was this going? Why was he even letting himself lay across from her; think about her?

"I saw another amputee earlier that day, the day I shadowed my aunt—"

"No. I can't. Stop." *I'm afraid you'll hate it the way I do. That you won't be able to look at it, just like I can't.* "I look in the mirror every day and I look the same, but I have to *know* that it's missing. I hate thinking about it." *But it's all I can think about.*

"Keeping the prosthesis on makes you feel a little less different from the person you were before." She smiled hesitantly, the corners of her lips just turning up. "But you're a good person now, Jonas. And I didn't know you before. I know you now."

"You know me with two legs! Even if you know I have—" *The stump.* "*It,* you see the prosthesis every day. If I take it off, there's no going back to that."

"Do you really think I would turn on you the moment I saw it and somehow see you differently?"

Yes. "How can I know? You already backed away before!"

She looked taken aback. Instantly, it seemed like part of her had closed off. But she tried one more time: "Jonas, I'd be fine. I really would. I was scared to tell you about my anxiety but now—"

"Brennan, no! Okay?" He closed his eyes. He didn't want to see her look hurt again. "I'm really tired. I'm sorry." *I'm sorry, I'm sorry.*

"It's okay," she said, but she turned over, like she couldn't look at him right now. Still, she curled into him, tucking herself under his arm.

"I'm really sorry, Brennan," he whispered again. "I shouldn't have said that. It's just—I can't." *Showing you my leg feels like facing it.* He said it again, felt like he couldn't stop saying it. "I'm really sorry."

"Jonas, it's okay. Maybe someday. And that's fine."

"Still . . ."

"Stop," she said. She touched his hand with hers, her skin soft on his. "It's okay. Go to sleep. Okay?"

———

Jonas lay awake for two hours, until midnight.

He couldn't sleep. He couldn't relax. His entire body was tense. *Don't relax. Don't let the prosthetic leg touch her. Is it touching her? How would you know? It can't feel anything.* And *You already backed away before* ran through his head. *How could you say that to her?*

At midnight he slipped out of bed, careful not to disturb Brennan. He took the elevator down to the first floor. *You can wish for the alternate story line where you have two legs, but the fact is, you're here, living in this one.*

He crutched across campus, through the thick wet snow to the parking lot outside Rhys's dorm.

He unlocked Gus and got inside. He started the car.

He sat there for about fifteen minutes. No sweat and his heart rate was relatively normal. *Progress.*

When he put his hand out to shift the car into reverse, however, tachycardia and sweat.

52

brennan

"I miss you."

"I miss you too."

Brennan lay back on her bed, staring at the ceiling, the texture of the surface burning itself in her memory so that when she closed her eyes, she could see it on the backs of her eyelids. She pressed the phone to her ear as Jonas started talking again, like it might make them closer. Next to her, her laptop sat, the allfixx site open in one window and her document for *Superioris* open in another.

"You been busy?"

"Yeah," she said with a sigh. "All my teachers decided to assign a lot of homework, all leading up to tests the week before spring break. That, and I've been trying to get somewhere with the end of *Superioris*. I've been a writing fiend, according to Ambreen, the past few days." She groaned. "I should study, shouldn't I." Not a question, but a statement. She really needed to study.

"I wish I could see you."

"I wish you could too." Brennan picked at a piece of lint on her sweater. It was the red sweater Jonas had let her borrow the week-end she'd spent snowed in at his dorm. That weekend, it had felt like they were the only two people in the world. Brennan had been *happy*, and *truly happy* was something she never would have said about herself at any given time. Needless to say, she still hadn't returned the sweater, because when she put it on, she put herself back in that moment.

"Are you nervous about your surgery?" she said after a few moments of silence. She felt like, as his girlfriend (*girlfriend!*), she should ask. Then again, judging by his reaction when she'd brought up his leg the other weekend, he might not want to be asked. She felt again that tiny inkling of hurt—that tiny bit of you-don't-trust-me that her anxious brain had been taunting her with ever since that night.

"Not really," Jonas said, but he didn't say anything else.

"What are you thinking about?"

A few moments of silence. "Nothing," he said. "Just—it's nothing."

Brennan changed the subject. "How are Sam and Travis?"

"Same as normal. Sam is acting like a grumpy mother because Travis came home blackout drunk last weekend. How's Ambreen?"

"She's fine. Normal. She has all her friends and she always goes off with them, which is honestly fine by me, I guess."

"Is it?"

"Is it what?"

"Fine for you. Don't you ever want friends, Brennan?"

"I have you."

"More than me, though I can't help but be a little proud of my status as your best friend."

Brennan sighed and closed her eyes, letting the darkness embrace her. "Maybe," she finally said. Then, "Sometimes. But in the end, I'm always okay." For a while, Jonas didn't say anything, and Brennan just let herself revel in the comfortable quiet (she tried to remember when she'd become comfortable with his silence, when she'd always felt the need to fill it before; she couldn't).

"You did tell me you shouldn't rely on one friend, or did I imagine that?"

Brennan frowned before remembering that Jonas couldn't see her over the phone—that he wasn't really there. "You didn't imagine it. But I don't know what to do about it, Jonas," she said. "I've always been a one-man show. I had really started to feel like I was meant to be alone. Every best friend I made, always had a better best friend, or always left me in the end. I don't have a very good track record when it comes to friendships."

"Nobody is meant to be alone." Jonas's voice was a mere whisper in her ear.

"I'm not alone, though, not now," she whispered. "I have you." Brennan wrapped her free arm around herself, snuggling into the sweater and imagining it was Jonas hugging her instead of just her own arm.

She could hear the smile in his voice when he responded. "But I'm only one person," he said.

Brennan changed the subject. "Are you going to let me come visit you in the hospital after your surgery?" she asked.

"I suppose so," he responded. "After I've come down off the drugs and regained some semblance of alertness."

She laughed breathlessly. "What if I want to see you before then? What if I can't wait?"

"Probably not a great idea. Apparently I was falling asleep in the middle of conversations after the first surgery."

Brennan laughed again. The door opened and Ambreen entered the room. She gave Brennan a little wave. "I have to go, Jonas," said Brennan, after waving back.

"Okay," he said. "I'll see you later then?"

"Yeah," she said. "At the latest, I'll see you spring break."

"Bring chocolate to the hospital," he said. "And pho. And maybe pizza. Hospital food ought to be deemed unfit for consumption."

"It's not *that* bad."

"I suppose not," he said.

"Is this just an excuse to see me?"

"I don't know. Is it working?"

"I would come anyway."

"I'm sorry, you know."

"For what?"

"The other night. I just—"

"You don't have to explain. It's okay."

For a moment Jonas hesitated, as if he might say more. Then, "All right. Talk to you later."

"Bye." Brennan heard the click of Jonas hanging up sound in her ear. She sighed.

"Hey," said Ambreen, coming to stand next to Brennan's bed. She wiggled her eyebrows. "Talking to Jonas?" she teased.

Brennan shoved her in the arm. "Stop," she said, smiling slightly and blushing. "Of course I was."

Ambreen grinned. "You two are adorable," she said.

"Yeah, yeah," said Brennan, her eyes going back to the ceiling. She frowned.

"What's wrong?"

"I just . . . nothing. Sometimes I worry that I've got so much good that something bad is going to happen to even things out."

Ambreen was silent for a moment, then she sighed. "Sometimes you just have to believe in the good. The bad's going to come, yeah, but we have to believe that the good will outweigh it, you know? Even if we have to look hard to find it."

Brennan just stared at the ceiling.

"You're somewhere in your mind, aren't you?" Ambreen said.

Brennan just nodded, closing her eyes.

"Don't stay there too long. Here." Brennan flinched as Ambreen dropped something on her stomach without warning. She opened her eyes. It was a chocolate bar.

"Eat it," said Ambreen. Her roommate smiled slightly, the corners of her mouth just turning up. "It's part of the good."

———

Dear @b-rennan,

Your story, *Superioris*, was chosen for our March Fic Feature!

What does this mean? It means that, out of all the stories on the allfixx site, and all the nominations we've received from hopeful authors or their fans, yours stood out to our moderators.

Congrats! You've earned it.

—the allfixx Team

53

JONAS

Paul Whitford.

Jonas had been thinking about him that morning, after another failed attempt to drive Gus somewhere (to even back the little Honda out of his parking spot). The only thing about Paul that Jonas could remember was two fuzzy shadows outside his hospital door on the pediatric floor. The first, his mom. The second, taller, shoulders slumped.

The things he knew about Paul Whitford could be counted on one hand:

1. He was a truck driver.
2. He was old—about ready to retire at the time of *The Accident*.
3. He lived in Wisconsin.
4. He'd stayed with Jonas and Rhys (Jonas too out of it to remember this) until the police, the firemen, and the ambulance had shown up.
5. He'd tried to apologize.

Jonas's phone lit up with a new text. Brennan. JONAS.

His chemistry professor was saying something about the Diels-Alder reaction. Jonas was trying to remember what he'd said.

His phone lit up again. JONAS GUESS WHAT.

He gave up on Paul and Diels and Alder (and their reaction), and texted Brennan back. What?

It took her a moment, but she finally texted him back a screen-shot of a note. Your story, *Superioris*, was chosen for our March Fic Feature! This message was followed by another with a screenshot of what had to be Brennan's follower count—it had shot up to over a thousand. In one day! she texted him. And still rising! Her next text was just a lot of exclamation points—!!!!!!!!!!!!!!!!!!!!

Jonas couldn't help but smile—he pictured her smiling her full-brightness smile, with her brown eyes shining and hands ani-mated. What did I tell you? he sent her. You're amazing. You've always been amazing.

She was silent for a while, as if she didn't quite believe him and therefore couldn't formulate a response. Finally, those three dots, and then her message. You're amazing. This is amazing. You—this—it's all more than I could have imagined when I thought about going off to college or post-ing my story . . . any of it. I can't believe it.

Jonas thought of Brennan, of her hand on his and her arms around him. Even of Sam and Travis, of playing video games late into the night with them. Of friends. *It's all more than I could have imagined when I thought about what life would be like with one and a half legs.* Any of it. All of it. It felt like *possibility* and *moving on*, when it had felt like the end of the world—Jonas's Great Tragedy—before.

He wondered if he still had the piece of old hospital menu with the name, number, and address written on it. He wished he could call and get his mom to search his room for the paper without telling her what he wanted it for, but there was no way, and no chance that she wouldn't know what it was if she found it, considering Ellis Whitford,

Paul's wife, had given it to *her* in the first place, after Jonas had refused to see any visitors.

At the front of the lecture hall, the professor was wrapping up their lecture. The auditorium filled with the sounds of shuffling papers and zipping backpacks as students unfolded themselves from their chairs and prepared for a mass exodus.

Jonas shouldered his backpack and took a deep breath before standing up, supporting himself with the crutches, and gingerly putting weight on the prosthetic leg (not too bad today).

Was this moving on?

I'm tired, he thought. *It's unfair, but unfair things happen every day. Is it fair that Brennan has anxiety? Is it fair that Rhys was the one driving when* The Accident *happened? IS IT FAIR YOU LOST YOUR LEG? NO.*

So. *So.*

Jonas hated this churning, mind-whirling feeling. He was so tired, but he couldn't sleep. In his bed at Umrath, he would look up at the ceiling and see that stupid playful patterned ceiling on the pediatric floor. He thought about Brennan, and lying next to her, and when he thought about that, he thought about his fear that she would see his leg and be what he was: disgusted.

Brennan. *His girlfriend.* If he'd let her be.

Three alternate endings:

1. Jonas lets Brennan go because he can never show her his leg—never trust anyone with that part of himself.
2. Jonas shows Brennan his leg, she is disgusted, she leaves, and he lets her go anyway.
3. Jonas shows Brennan his leg, and she stays.

His mom: *Do you think there are perfect moments?*
Jonas wasn't sure, but he had to find out.

He called Brennan.

This time, she picked up. "Jonas!" she exclaimed, and her voice sounded just how he'd imagined it would sound.

54

brennan

Brennan stared at the black computer screen in front of her. Last time, she'd gotten as far as opening the document for *Superioris* before giving up. This time, she hadn't even managed to turn the computer on.

Don't be silly, she admonished herself. *Don't be silly. Just write. Like you used to, like when it was fun. Don't worry about what anyone else thinks about it.*

She tried not to think about the myriad messages on her profile. *Write more!* and *When will a new chapter be up?* They were starting to feel like demands even though Brennan knew they just liked her work (many of them were among her new five thousand followers). She stretched her fingers; she almost hit the Power button before giving up, shutting the laptop in frustration.

Ambreen swept into the room. "If it isn't the famous writer!" Ambreen gushed. "How are you on this fine day?"

Brennan flopped backward onto her bed, staring at the ceiling. "The famous writer has written the same scene three times over, trying to get it right. The words are stuck," she moaned.

"Still?" Brennan's roommate sighed. "It's no different than before, you know," she said.

"It feels different," groaned Brennan. "Like it matters a lot more now. Like the stakes have changed."

Ambreen slouched into her desk chair. "You know, a lot of the pressure you're feeling? You're putting it on yourself. Your readers love what you've already written. They already love *you*. This new pressure is unnecessary pressure."

Brennan didn't say anything, just stared at the ceiling. She wondered how Ambreen would know since she'd never actually read the story when Brennan had sent her a link. She hadn't even mentioned it until Brennan had told her about getting featured, practically bursting with the news and desperate to tell anyone, even her roommate.

"I'm going next door to Jen's room," Ambreen finally said. "You seem like you need some alone time to think."

"Ambreen." Brennan rolled over as Ambreen turned around, her hand poised on the door handle. Brennan sighed. "I used to think being popular—being noticed for something—would be the best thing that could happen to me. And I'm grateful, but at the same time—"

Ambreen didn't say anything, just waited for her to go on.

Tears pricked at the backs of Brennan's eyes. She blinked a few times, dispersing them as best as she could. "I actually hate how everything has changed at once."

Ambreen hesitated, like she might say something, but Brennan shook her head. "Never mind," she said. "I'll figure it out."

Ambreen left and Brennan was alone. Again.

She waited until the sounds of laughter next door trickled out into the hallway, a door slammed, and the voices faded off and out of the dorm.

Brennan stood, wrapping herself in her jacket and picking up the throw blanket from the end of her bed. She walked to the laundry room and put it in an open dryer, scanning her student ID and hitting start.

Then she sat on the table at the back and waited, the hum of the dryer buzzing in her ears. She started to text Jonas. I— She stopped. How could she even explain what had happened? She'd gone from the top of the world to the lowest low she'd ever experienced in her writing.

The dryer's alarm buzzed, and she deleted the text, grabbing the blanket and making her way outside.

Darkness had just fallen, and the stars weren't all out. Brennan spread her blanket and lay down on top of it, staring at the sky like maybe there would be answers there. She lay flat, her outstretched arms spanning the blanket, her puffy coat cushioning her.

Suddenly, she just wanted tomorrow to be over, so break would be here and she could go home. Maybe at home, in the room she'd started writing in, everything would go back to the way it was before.

55

JONAS

He had to find Paul Whitford. Logically, his brain had created this course:

1. You are having a hard time moving on.
2. You are having a hard time moving on because you have issues (could maybe be called PTSD) related to semitrucks and standing on your own two (one and a half) legs—which really interferes with your normal-college-student daily activities because it really puts a damper on walking and driving.
3. You are having these issues because of *The Accident*.
4. Paul Whitford was the other driver in *The Accident*—the other party in a terrible, horrible event that no one wanted to make happen; it just happened.

When Jonas called Brennan at nine o'clock the evening before his surgery, he thought he might be crazy. God knew his mom thought he was crazy. ("You need to go to sleep! You have *surgery* tomorrow, Bird!"

Then she'd smacked him in the back of the head with the towel she was using to dry dishes.)

He watched for Brennan out the blinds because he didn't want his mom to make a big deal when she arrived. When she pulled up, he crutched to the front door and opened it, just as she was about to knock.

"Hey," she said blankly, momentarily caught off guard.

"Hey." It had almost become their customary greeting (Jonas wondered how many times they had to greet each other like that before it officially became a custom). He looked at her for a few moments. What would she think? What would she think of his sudden odd preoccupation with Wisconsin and Paul Whitford, moving on, and perfect moments. Finally, he stepped aside and held the door open for her. "Come on in," he added.

Brennan stepped inside, into the entryway. For a moment, Jonas just stared at her, and she stared at him. He wanted to hug her (should he hug her?) or say something, but he eventually just gestured back toward the hallway and led her into his room.

"Door open!" his dad yelled. Jonas bit his tongue and left the door open.

He watched as Brennan took in his room, and took it in as she might see it—*Star Wars* poster on the wall, clutter of paper and books and folders (and the reindeer antlers from Walmart) on his desk, glow-in-the-dark stars stuck to the ceiling. And then he watched her gaze pass over and go back to the poster on his closet door—*Bones of the Human Skeleton*. Good-bye tibia and fibula.

He sat down on the edge of the bed. Brennan sat down next to him. *On the left. On the left.* He tried not to think about it. He was in the business of moving on now, right? This was what this was all about, right? So he didn't say anything and didn't move. For a few moments, silence hung between them. Finally, Jonas spoke. "Thanks for coming over," he said, not really looking at her.

"Sure," she said. He watched as she picked at a loose thread on her sweater. "What's going on?"

"I—nothing, I guess. I just wanted the company. Someone other than my mom, who's been fussing over me since I came back here for break." He sucked in a breath. "It's the surgery."

"Oh," said Brennan.

"I thought maybe we could watch *Star Wars*."

"Okay. Sure."

Jonas stood and crutched to the DVD player. He put the disk in. Brennan's hands clenched the edge of the bed. Jonas sat back down next to her and picked up the remote.

The movie started.

Jonas thought about Paul Whitford again. *I expect that everything after meeting him won't live up to my expectations. I expect that I'll just be disappointed. What if I wasn't? I could be happy.*

His leg was cramping, as if it felt his mental turmoil and wanted to contribute. He winced and massaged the spot just above the prosthesis with his thumb, teeth gritted.

He noticed Brennan watching him and stilled his hand. "This is the first in the original trilogy," he explained, drawing her attention away from his leg and gesturing at the TV. "You pretty much have to watch it first."

"Is it bad today?" Brennan whispered, reaching out a hand. He flinched as she neared his leg. She noticed and diverted her hand, clenching her fingers and looking away. "Sorry," she muttered.

He closed his eyes. Admitted something he normally wouldn't have admitted. "Yes," he said.

They watched the movie in silence for a moment. Brennan swung her left leg against the bed a bit. "Jonas?" she finally whispered again.

"Hmm."

"Are you nervous about tomorrow?"

Yes. No. Not for the reasons you think. "No." he said. "I mean, not really. I've just—I've been thinking."

Brennan watched her feet. His feet. Then back to hers. "What about?"

He could feel her watching him. "Do you ever feel like there's something you should do? And it just, you have to do it, before anything else? Your brain won't let you think about anything else?"

He caught her moving her fingers to her neck. Carotid pulse? "I guess that makes sense," she said. "Why?"

He looked back at the TV. "Nothing. It's nothing."

Brennan seemed like she didn't quite believe him, but she let the subject drop.

56

JONAS

Jonas stood outside of Brennan's house, pacing back and forth on his crutches.

Four hundred and eighteen W. Westmor. Six o'clock in the morning. He'd sent her the text last night at about midnight. *She probably didn't even get it. It's a weird text. Why did you send it?* He should have explained, maybe. Probably. He stopped pacing and stared at her front door, trying to decide if he should go and knock on it after all. "No, this is crazy," he said aloud to the six-in-the-morning empty neighborhood. "You've officially lost it Jonas."

Maybe he had.

That morning, the crazy had started with an argument with his mom. He'd called and left a message to reschedule his surgery last night, after Brennan had left. A couple of weeks wouldn't hurt; he'd been dealing with the pain in his leg for this long. "What *in the world* were you *thinking*, Jonas Elliot Avery?" Jonas had almost missed "Bird," what with the scathing way she said his first, middle, and last name. Then, judging by the way his father raised his eyebrows (his father had picked up quite a bit of Vietnamese over the years he'd been married to Jonas's mother), she muttered what must have been some equally scathing statements in Vietnamese. Even Jonas recognized a few of the words—mostly she went on and on about his lack of consideration and how crazy he must be. She seemed most upset at the fact that, by rescheduling the surgery, Jonas would have to miss some school. At this point, Jonas didn't care. Rhys had done so many crazy things at the beginning of his college career. Jonas figured it was about time he did something to disappoint his parents (something a little bigger than hiding in his room the majority of the past year and a half).

Not that he *really* wanted to disappoint them; he just knew it wasn't realistic to make it through life without doing it at least a few times. When he'd explained to his mom why, she'd actually been a bit more understanding (after yelling at him again). *That still bothers you, Bird? I'm sorry. I didn't know.*

Jonas crutch-paced a few steps back and forth in front of Gus. That was the second part of the crazy: Rhys had told him to go ahead and take Gus, because the Bus wasn't fit for long trips (*The Bus is hardly fit for trips across town*, Rhys, 2015). So Jonas had gotten into the driver's seat. He'd started the car. He'd put it in reverse (heart pounding, sweat dripping). He thought about driving to get Brennan from Road's Edge. He thought about the fact that he had to do this thing he was going to do, and only he could do it. So he backed out and he drove (about five miles per hour under the speed limit, but still), all the way to Brennan's house.

Jonas pulled his phone from his pocket before he could stop himself. He went to his recent calls and hit Brennan's number. He waited. It rang. And then rang some more.

This was stupid. He knew she'd be asleep, and he should just do this himself. No use dragging her into it. Her voice mail picked up. He took a deep breath. Now, or never?

Now.

"Hey, Brennan," he said. "I know you'll think this is crazy. I've gotten a lot of that this morning. I've canceled my surgery. Well, rescheduled, not canceled completely. Anyway, the point is, I have something I want to do—need to do, really—before I get the surgery. And I can't explain why I want to do it all of a sudden, but I've got to." *To be with you.* "So I'm going to Wisconsin to find the guy who was driving the semi when, you know. Just for a couple days. I just want to tell him it wasn't his fault and everything, because I completely refused his apology and anything to do with him back when it first happened." *I need the closure.* Jonas's fingers were tapping on his leg again, out of habit—nervous habit. "I was going to ask you to come with me, but I guess you're probably still sleeping. So I'll see you in a few days."

Jonas was just getting back into the car when the front door opened and Brennan stumbled out, almost tripping over the bottoms of her too-long pajama pants. "Jonas!" she called. "Wait!"

He rolled down the window and she came up next to him. "Hey," he said. "I figured you were asleep."

"I woke up, but apparently not enough to manage to answer my phone in time." Her hair was tousled and sleep disheveled, which he thought was really cute. She was studying him. "Why are you doing this *now*, Jonas?" she asked. "I mean, couldn't it have been after your surgery?"

Jonas bit his lip and averted his gaze from her slightly.

"You *are* afraid of this surgery, aren't you?"

He shrugged. *Afraid to let myself move on. Afraid of you. No. Not of you, but of me and what you'll think of me, what I'll do when you want to see me and I'm too scared to let you.* And he was scared of the surgery too. He had been too traumatized and out of it for his first surgery to even have the ability to feel scared. Now he was nervous. And even though the logical part of him said that everything was going to be perfectly fine, he couldn't help but think of the risks. He'd been putting some thought into finally declaring a premed focus of study; unfortunately, his renewed interest in reading medical textbooks in his spare time was putting all the risks at the forefront of his mind. *Increased pain, nerve damage, D-E-A-T-H.*

Brennan sighed. Behind her eyes, he could see her brain working through this, the imaginary cogs turning in her head. "Okay," she suddenly said. "Let me go in and pack a few things and talk to my parents."

Jonas waited what seemed like an eternity before she came back out, a small duffel bag thrown over her shoulder. She tossed the bag in the back and got into the front seat. He watched as she strapped in and then nervously folded and unfolded her hands in her lap. He could read her well enough to tell that she was nervous.

"You okay?" he asked her.

"Fine," she said. She laughed sheepishly. "This is just the first trip I've taken in a while, and with anyone other than my parents and my brother. But I trust you. So let's get this show on the road, I guess."

Jonas couldn't help but smile slightly, one corner of his mouth curving up almost against his will.

He took the crumpled paper out of his pocket—an old menu sheet from the hospital. On the back, the address. He smoothed it across his thigh a bit and then used the clip-on air freshener to put it on the visor. Whitford. Wisconsin.

He went through the steps:

1. Start the car. Check.
2. Put it in drive. Check.
3. *Go.*

And he did, even though his heart rate still picked up and sweat still beaded on his brow. Brennan touched his arm. Comfort, without saying anything.

They headed for the interstate.

North, to Wisconsin.

brennan

They'd been on the interstate for about a half hour now. The knot in her stomach was tying itself more tightly the farther from home they got.

She hadn't told her parents.

Here was the problem: they'd argued last night.

Her mom: "Brennan, I'm tired of having you come home from school just to be in your room the entire time. Is there something going on that you aren't telling us? Are you taking your meds?"

Her: "It's just that I have to have a chapter done by Friday." She was out of reserve chapters to post and the writer's block was still strong. *Ignore the part about her meds.*

Her mom: "I'm not sure I like that you're putting all this time into an internet site that we've never heard of." *Because you don't get on the internet much?*

Her: "Mom, I'm eighteen. And you know me. I wouldn't do something if I didn't think I was safe." *Anxiety makes sure of that.*

Her mom: "I know. You're all grown up. But you still live here. We pay your bills. Doesn't that count for something?"

Her: "Yes, Mom. I just—I have to write, Mom. I have commitments."

Her mom: "What about your commitment to us? Your family? You can't spend your whole life *writing*." The way she said writing—something about it was jarring. "It's fine as a hobby, but you can't let your hobbies get in the way of your life, Brennan. I just want what's best for you. Come downstairs and help with supper."

She'd left then, and Brennan had shut and locked her door. She'd looked in the mirror over her dresser. *She's right. It won't get you anywhere. You're probably not even good. It was probably a fluke that you got featured. You put all your effort into this for what? For nothing.* And her brain scoffed: *Look at you, little college girl. Failing.* She set the timer on her phone. She allowed herself to cry for five minutes. Then she wiped her eyes and went downstairs, where her dad was on her mom's side.

She didn't tell them about the feature. She didn't tell them about thousands of followers.

She didn't tell them she was going to Wisconsin with Jonas—they were still sleeping, so she just left a note. *Remember when I told you about Ambreen and some people from the dorm going to Colorado for the weekend? Well, I'm going to Wisconsin. I'll call you.* And then, because they were still her parents, and she still loved them—*I promise. I love you.*

Brennan glanced sideways at Jonas. She could tell he was occupied with his own thoughts. His two-handed grip on the steering wheel was tight, and he stared straight ahead except when switching lanes.

"Jonas?" she said, wanting to voice the question that had been on her mind, mostly because she wondered if he had considered it too.

"Hmm." He didn't look at her, just the road. The white, dashed lines separating the slow and the fast lanes flashed by.

A semitruck started passing in the left lane and Jonas tensed. She didn't say anything until the truck was done passing.

"What if you, you know. What if you get there and he's not there? It's been a little while, hasn't it? A year and a half?"

"Two years, end of this month."

"Two years." Brennan adjusted her seat belt so it didn't press so much against her neck (the pressure made her throat feel gaggy). "A lot can change. He could have moved." She stared at the yellow hospital menu paper with the scribbled writing on the back. Paul's name and an address in Door County, Wisconsin, stared back.

"I—I don't know for sure," he sighed. "I just want to try." He laughed shortly, tapping his fingers against the steering wheel. "Maybe he doesn't even remember me. Maybe he doesn't even think about the accident anymore. I mean, he seemed like the type who would care. At the time, he was really broken up about it, my mom said. I wouldn't even see him, of course. I was pretty rude." He frowned. "I guess I just want to try to find him, on the slight chance that he does still think about it, or does still feel guilty, to let him know . . ." He trailed off, like he wasn't sure what he was going to let Paul know.

The sun reflected off the road far ahead, turning the spot hazy, like water. Brennan nodded. "I get it," she said. "You don't have to explain it. You're good," she said. "You know that, right? You're so good, Jonas. And sometimes I don't think you even realize it."

His fingers moved alternately between gripping the steering wheel and tapping the edge of it, anxiously. "This is a change," Brennan said wryly. "I'm usually the nervous wreck."

One corner of Jonas's mouth turned up in a slight smile.

"Whatever happens, I'll be there with you."

He reached over to squeeze her hand, but quickly returned his hand to the steering wheel.

"And no matter how it goes, whether you get to talk to Paul or not—" Brennan paused, took a deep breath, and continued. "I just want you to know that it's really really good of you to try."

"Thanks, Brennan," he said. "And really, thank you for coming with me." He let out a breath. "You really didn't have to. Maybe it was crazy of me to ask you."

"Maybe not so crazy," she whispered, leaning back against the seat's headrest and closing her eyes. She blew out a breath. "I didn't actually talk to my parents. I just left them a note."

Jonas didn't say anything, so she continued.

"They think my writing is silly. That the internet is silly and no one on there can be trusted. I used to tell them things? But I haven't told them about being featured and stuff. Because I'm afraid that they'll be happy, I guess." She laughed. "It sounds so bad when I say it out loud. Basically, I'm afraid they'll be happy, but when I increase my commitment to writing to please those followers, they'll go back to saying *writing* like it's something nasty they don't want to touch with a ten-foot pole. It's almost worse than if they were never proud of me at all."

She looked out the window—the grass along the highway blurring into the blue of the sky. "I haven't told them about losing Emma, how we really haven't had a substantial conversation since the beginning of the semester, about how having a roommate is hard for me, skipping classes, not taking meds, finding you—I mean, I'm not ashamed of you. I'm sorry if it sounds that way. They know about you, I mean, they know you're my friend. I didn't tell them about the fender bender though; the grocery store. About falling in love with you."

Jonas let out a breath, a slow, small smile spreading across his face. He shifted a bit in the driver's seat, letting some of the tension in his shoulders go now that they had been on the road for a while. "I guess I got out of some of that parental disapproval with *The Accident*. It's weird. I hate what happened, but I guess there are some benefits to it." He grinned, and she punched his shoulder lightly, laughing.

"They love me," she said. "I know that. That's important. I just wish, sometimes, that they could step back from their parental wisdom a bit and just be my friends. Maybe they're trying. I guess I haven't let them. What with the anxiety and everything, I've always been a needs-monitored child. Are you taking your meds? Did you get enough sleep last night? Did you do your homework?"

A semitruck passed. She watched Jonas's hands tighten on the wheel—felt Gus swerve just the tiniest bit. Kept talking. *Distract, distract, distract.*

"I guess it's just got too easy to lie about being okay."

57

JONAS

When they stopped at a gas station, Jonas took the opportunity to walk off the cramp that had set in in his left leg, crutching back and forth a few times next to the car and stretching. Brennan pumped the gas.

When she wasn't looking, he watched her. She pushed a stray hair behind her ear, the spring breeze only blowing it loose again as she watched the numbers climb on the pump, frowning as she counted the gallons that went into the car.

He was so glad she'd come. With her there, he'd been able to distract himself from some of the anxiety he was feeling.

He hated the nervous feeling in the pit of his stomach. And Brennan had to feel that almost every day. He shook his head, somewhat amazed. She had to feel that almost *every day*, and yet she kept going. Even if she didn't always face things perfectly, she got back up and tried again the next day. If she could do it, couldn't he?

Brennan turned to remove the gas nozzle from the car and caught him looking at her. She gave him a little, hesitant smile, and a small wave. "You ready to go?" she called. "The phone GPS says we'll be there soon."

"Yeah," he said. "Just let me run inside and grab some water and snacks."

"Okay," she said, screwing the cap back onto the gas tank and shutting the fuel door. "I'll come with you."

They walked inside, their footsteps falling into an even rhythm.

Once inside, they moved to the comfortably quiet back aisle and studied the drink options. They both ended up simply picking water—the cheapest one, one of the smaller brands that Jonas didn't ever see except at gas stations.

"Brennan," he said hesitantly. "Do you think he'll be mad? That I blew him off back when it happened, I mean."

"Jonas," she laughed. "Don't worry about that. If he is, that's his problem. You were going through your own personal hell back then. You'd just woken up from surgery with an entirely new identity to grapple with. I'm sure he'll understand." She smiled and squeezed his arm. "It's a good thing we both don't have anxiety; I feel like we'd probably implode. I'm not used to both of us being nervous."

Jonas smiled slightly and wrapped his arm around her shoulders, comforting himself in the closeness of her.

Once they were back on the road, he managed to relax a little. Brennan was driving now, giving him an opportunity to close his eyes in an attempt to recover from the lack of sleep last night. The neuroma was sending shooting pains up the remaining portion of his leg as if it somehow sensed how agitated he was and wanted to do its part to make it worse.

Even with his eyes closed, sleep wouldn't come for Jonas. He figured it was probably a side effect of being in the car. He supposed he probably wouldn't be able to sleep in a car again, at least not for a while.

He shifted slightly, propping his head on his fist and keeping his eyes closed, as if that might help in his efforts to sleep. Eventually, he felt the slowing speed of Gus leaving the highway. And then—

"Jonas," said Brennan softly. "We're here."

Jonas sat up, opening his eyes and ducking to peer out the window better. They were driving through a neighborhood populated with well-kept houses with trimmed lawns and gardens that were just beginning to blossom with spring flowers and greenery. It looked like one of those neighborhoods that got featured in the home magazines his mom used to like to read.

He looked down at the piece of paper clutched in his hand. It was now creased in the middle from where Brennan had taken it down off the visor—folded and refolded it over and over, before they'd traded seats, and he'd taken over the job of nervously fiddling with the paper. "Three hundred and sixty-eight," he said. He scanned the passing houses, counting down addresses until: "That one," he said, his mouth going a bit dry. "On the left."

Brennan pulled the car into the driveway. The house was small and gray, with a blue door. A porch swing rocked slightly in the breeze. Jonas glanced around, looking for some sort of personalized sign or a name on a mailbox. Anything that would tell him the Whitfords still lived here. Nothing.

He took a deep breath and got out of the car. Brennan also got out and stood for a few moments, looking up at the front door. At full-grown height, he was as tall as his dad. Now, he felt like a child again. He felt like maybe his parents should be here—like go-betweens.

Brennan cleared her throat. "Do you want to go up by yourself? Or do you want me to come?"

Jonas swallowed. "You can come," he said. He crutched up the front walk and onto the porch. He tried to purposely slow his breaths—in through the nose, out through the mouth—to prevent hyperventilating as he knocked on the door: once, twice, three times.

"Coming!" a woman's voice called. The sound of the door unlocking was too loud in Jonas's ears. The door was opened by a lady even shorter than Brennan. Jonas looked down at her blankly.

She smiled up at him. "Can I help you?" she asked. Her blue eyes were friendly and sharp; her silver hair was pulled into a bun. Jonas found his mouth frustratingly dry. He opened it; closed it again. Luckily, Brennan spoke up. (He could have kissed her right then.)

"We're, um, looking for a Paul Whitford?"

The woman's smile turned slightly confused, and she tilted her head to look at Brennan quizzically.

"Are you Ellis Whitford?" Jonas interrupted, dragging the woman's attention back to him.

"Yes?" she said, more like a question than a statement. Jonas shifted his weight to his good leg as he stepped forward slightly, supporting his shaky right leg with the crutches.

"I don't really know how to start this." He gave her a small smile and pulled the paper with Paul's address on it from his pocket, handing it to her. "My name is Jonas. Jonas Avery? I don't know if you remember me. You gave this to my mom in the hospital."

"You're—you're the boy—" The older woman looked at him in shock, one hand going to her mouth. He saw her eyes go to his legs, and then his crutches.

He nodded. "Yeah," he said. "That's me." He gave her a reassuring smile. "I know that I wouldn't talk to Paul back when it happened, but I wanted to—I just wanted to see him and apologize for that."

Ellis gave him a sad little smile. "He still talks about you, you know. He wonders what happened to you. I know he'd like to talk to you. He's out on an errand right now—he'd probably say I'm a bit of a slave driver, sending him out left and right—but he'll be back in about twenty minutes, if you want to stay? I could give you something to eat and drink while you wait."

"Sure," said Jonas. "That would be great. Thank you, Mrs. Whitford."

The woman laughed and shook her head. "Friends get to call me Ellie," she said, smiling as she stepped back and held the door open for both of them. Jonas exchanged a glance with Brennan and she gently touched his arm, encouraging him to go in.

"Who's this?" said Ellie, smiling at Brennan.

"This is my girlfriend, Brennan," he said. Brennan, blushing, gave the older woman a little wave. *Girlfriend,* thought Jonas, a bit stuck on the word (in a good way).

"Hi," she said.

Ellie led them into the cozy kitchen, the windows of which were open to the spring air. She gestured for them to have a seat at the counter and then went to the cupboard and pulled out a package of cookies. "Do you like Oreos?" she asked, setting the package on the counter. "They're our grandkids' favorite, and I'm afraid we don't have much else around at the moment."

Brennan nodded her thanks and took an Oreo, even though Jonas noticed she didn't actually eat it. His stomach was still doing flips, and he didn't want to eat either. Ellie brought out a jug of cold milk and poured two glasses, passing one each to Brennan and Jonas.

Jonas sipped his, the cold liquid contrasting with the heat in his face. He nervously tapped his good foot against the leg of the stool he was sitting on.

He heard the front door open, the creak of it reverberating somewhere in his skull. "That would be Paul," said Ellie. "I'll just go catch him and tell him you're here. You can talk in the living room, just through there."

Jonas nodded. Brennan looked up at him as Ellie retreated to the front door. "Do you want me to come in with you?" She shifted slightly, her shoulder touching his.

"I think—I think I'll do this part by myself," he said. "The last time he saw me—he was the one who waited with me and Rhys, you know. Until the ambulance showed up?" His mind had painted a picture of the scene—Jonas, in the jeans and NASA shirt he'd been wearing that day, with blood all over, Rhys crying, the tone of the traffic lights signaling walk as the lights changed. And Paul Whitford trying to help them, even when he didn't have to. Even when he must have wanted to run away or at least try to ignore the fact that he'd just been in an accident. "I haven't seen him since then; I wouldn't see him. I just want to talk to him now."

Brennan gave his hand a reassuring squeeze. "I get it," she said. "It's okay. I'll wait here with Ellie. She seems really nice."

Just then, footsteps alerted Jonas that Ellie and Paul were coming back.

He stood quickly, hurriedly gaining his balance between his prosthetic leg, his good leg, and his crutches as Paul entered the room. The older man's eyes immediately went to Jonas. Jonas wondered if he imagined the hesitancy, the almost fear, and the sadness that flashed across his face.

"Paul," Jonas said. "Mr. Whitford." He swallowed. "I was—I was hoping to talk to you?"

"Of course," said Paul, his voice almost a whisper. He gestured to the living room and Jonas gave Brennan's hand one final squeeze before he followed Paul.

Once in the living room, Paul gestured to the chairs and the couch. "You can sit wherever," he said. "If you want."

Jonas nodded and sat down on the couch. Paul sat down in the chair next to him. For a few moments, the older man just sat there silently, his gray head bowed and his brown eyes sad. Paul Whitford was a tall and weathered man; his face held lines that Jonas could only assume came after The Accident.

He looked up and met Jonas's eyes. "What—what made you decide to come find me, after all this time?"

Jonas tucked his hands under his legs to stop them from nervous-shaking. "I—I wasn't in a good place when it happened," he said. "And I wasn't in a good place for a while. But I'm trying to *be* in a good place now. I thought—" He looked at his feet, identical inside his shoes— no evidence of a missing leg, other than the pins-and-needles tingling somewhere around his nonexistent shin. "I guess I thought—" He sighed in frustration. He looked at Paul. The old man just waited.

"I wanted to hear what happened," he said. "And not from the reporters, or from my parents, or the doctors, or the police, or the paramedics. From you. Besides my brother, you're the only person who was there. You're the only other person who was in that crash. So you know what it was like."

Paul was silent for a few moments, and Jonas wondered if maybe he wouldn't say anything.

"It was a late snow, but I'm sure you know that part."

Jonas looked up. Paul bowed his head. "I had picked up my cargo about a half an hour north of town and had to go through town to get back to the interstate. They talked about black ice on the radio; had just talked about it minutes before the crash.

"I'd been driving for forty years. I've driven other winters. Seen some worse snows than the one your town got that day. I was going slow. I was watching. But when I came over that hill, the light was red, and the trucks don't stop as fast as you want them too. In the moment, it felt like slow motion, like I wasn't slowing down at all. I tried to turn, but the wheels just skidded on the ice and it hardly changed trajectory."

He closed his eyes, like he was remembering. Jonas pictured it from Paul Whitford's side, looking down over Rhys's car from the cab of his semi.

"When we both stopped, I sat for a minute—shell-shocked. I thought about insurance, and retirement later that year, and my wife, and how she would do if I was gone, even though I was sitting there, clearly fine and able to move all extremities.

"You were both stuck in the car, so it was hard, at first, to see if there were any injuries. I got out and I walked over. They say all this stuff about not admitting fault in an accident—I think I just said 'I'm sorry, I'm sorry,' over and over again. I talked to Rhys first. Even though he couldn't get out, he said he could still feel all his toes and fingers. I told him not to move his neck, just in case. I took a napkin out of my pocket and wiped his forehead, because there was a small gash there that was bleeding into his eyes—most head wounds do, even if they're small—and I didn't want him to move. He was a little in shock for a moment, but it didn't take him long to remember you. I kept telling him not to move—I'd check on you."

Paul swallowed, and Jonas wondered just how bad he'd looked when Paul first walked around the side of the car.

"You weren't really awake. You kept trying to open your eyes and look at me. 'What's his name?' I asked your brother, and he told me. I kept saying your name, but you kind of passed out, but not really. You would open your eyes, but not for long, and not long enough to focus on me or answer any questions. So I knew something was wrong. I moved what I could out of the way, but the door was covering most of your lower leg. I tried to put my hand down to move some of it off, and came away wet with blood. I did my best to put pressure on it. I don't know how much it helped."

"How long do you think it was? Before anyone showed up."

"Probably less than ten minutes. But it felt like forever. I just kept holding pressure as best as I could. Your brother—"

"Rhys."

"Rhys was crying. He kept apologizing to you. Telling you to hold on. That it would be okay. I didn't tell him how bad the bleeding was, but I think your lack of a response sort of put him onto the fact that you weren't doing great. When rescue workers showed up, they cut you out of the car first. Rhys told them to get you first. He wouldn't let the other team work on him at the same time. Said he didn't want to leave you if he got out first. They got you out. Sped off in the ambulance, and that was the last I saw of you. They got your brother out next. They checked me, cleared me, I talked with officers—

"I went to the hospital to try and see that you guys were okay. I know if it was my kids or my grandkids—I didn't know if you had family coming, or what was happening. I just wanted to make sure you were okay. I met your mom. It was pretty emotional. I think we both started crying at some point. I wanted to apologize to you. She wanted me to be able to, but you didn't want to see me. I didn't want to force an apology you weren't ready to hear yet. I guess I've finally got the chance to apologize."

"No," interrupted Jonas. "I should apologize." He let out the breath he'd been holding. "The accident wasn't your fault. You tried to stop. You shouldn't feel guilty."

"But I have—"

"And that was my fault," Jonas pressed on. "I made you feel like it was. I did blame you for the accident for a while. I feel ashamed that I did, because deep down, I knew that it was just that—an accident. I knew you couldn't have helped it. And then you stayed with me and my brother until the ambulance showed up, even though you were probably scared. I want to say thank you, actually, for that."

He looked up from his feet and met Paul's gaze. Paul gave him a sad smile, his warm brown eyes glistening. "I'm glad you came, Jonas," he said. "I never expected you would. I admit I've felt very guilty for what happened. I always wonder if I could have stopped it somehow. When I went to the car after the crash—I thought I had killed someone, honestly." The weathered truck driver got a faraway look in his eyes. "There was just this—this fear." Paul stopped, closing his eyes.

Jonas thought about Rhys. He had never thought about what it would be like to see his brother hurt—unconscious. To not be sure if he was dead or alive. He'd never stopped to wonder what it was like for Rhys, to be *present*. After all, being unconscious had its benefits; Jonas didn't have to remember anything other than flashes of the actual accident. Rhys hadn't left him. Rhys wouldn't leave him.

Paul was continuing. "You were so still, I thought you were dead. I've always wondered what happened to you, after. I'm sure Ellie told you I ask her sometimes, what she thinks happened after we left the hospital and came back to Wisconsin."

Jonas gave the old man a small smile. "I've graduated high school. I was pretty bitter for quite some time." He pulled up the leg of his pants, letting Paul see the prosthesis. He looked at it too—plastic and metal. Everything he hadn't been able to really look at for months. "I wouldn't even wear this thing," he said quietly. "I moped around on crutches for the rest of high school. To be honest, I've still kind of been moping around on crutches."

He smiled slightly. "The summer before I started college, I met Brennan. She's the girl who's out in the kitchen with Ellie. To make a long story short, she's kind of why I'm here."

Paul smiled hesitantly.

"I go to Washington University in St. Louis," Jonas continued. "I've been undeclared, but I think I'm going to actually do this premed thing, finally. I always wanted to be a doctor, but after the accident, I kind of had this messed-up thought process, where I figured I had changed, so the things I wanted had to change too. But maybe I can help people.

"I just—I don't know how to explain it. I felt like I had to come here and talk to you before I could finally move on. I needed to hear you tell me it was an accident. I needed my stupid brain to really hear that, and maybe stop being so messed up about everything. Because Brennan, she makes me want to move on."

Paul really smiled then, placing a weathered hand on Jonas's arm. "You know I"—Paul ran a hand through his thinning hair—"I stopped driving trucks after. I was set to retire that fall, so I just went a little early. I'd always loved driving trucks, but when I hit you and your brother, I guess I got scared, knowing I could kill or hurt someone so easily without even trying. I felt so powerless when I was sliding on that ice. I kind of wished it was me. I had lived long enough. I had a good family support system. Why did that crash take your leg and not mine?"

Jonas looked at his feet, slightly less uncomfortable in the moment with the thought of the prosthesis inside his left shoe. "I don't know," he said. "Sometimes I imagine this alternate universe where my leg isn't gone. It's there. I'm happy. But with that ending, I miss out on some of the good things I've gotten in this one. It doesn't mean I don't miss the leg or wish I had it, but I also know I would miss the things I have here if I didn't have them." *Like Brennan. Do you believe there are perfect moments?*

Paul met Jonas's eyes as they stood, Jonas leaning on his crutches. "Do you think you've moved on?"

Jonas thought for a bit. "Maybe not yet." He smiled slightly as Paul rested a hand on his shoulder, and they started to make their way back to the kitchen. "But I want to now." It felt like he hadn't really been breathing this whole time, and he suddenly could. It felt like seeing his new life for the first time. It felt good.

58

brennan

Brennan watched Jonas from the end of the convenience store aisle. She couldn't really concentrate on the labels of the soup cans as she listened to the conversation he was currently having on his cell phone.

"Hi, Uncle Ethan," he said. "It's Jonas."

Silence while Uncle Ethan talked.

"Yeah, I'm in Wisconsin. Listen, I would have asked you before, but this just kind of happened."

Silence. Uncle Ethan's turn again, passing the conversation off like passing notes back and forth. Brennan absentmindedly picked up a can of soup, her stomach roiling. *Overnight. Staying overnight.* With *Jonas. I mean, what did you think was going to happen? You were just going to get up here and then drive right back?*

"I came to find the, you know, the truck driver?"

Insert Uncle Ethan's line. Brennan blew a stubborn piece of hair out of her eyes, waiting. It was storming outside, rain pounding on the roof. They had tried to get a hotel for one night, but the cost for a room was more than Jonas had brought (after factoring in the gas for their return trip) and she hadn't thought to bring any money. Uncle Ethan was Jonas's solution. She wondered if Ethan was Jonas's uncle on his mom's side or his dad's side.

"Really? That would be amazing. Thank you." Silence then. "Lake Michigan Drive? Okay. I'll wait for the text. Really, thank you so much."

Jonas hung up the phone and Brennan hurriedly picked up a can of soup, pretending like she hadn't been eavesdropping. Jonas glanced sideways at her. "We've got a house. My Uncle Ethan rents vacation houses and he's letting us stay in one of the vacant ones."

"That's nice of him," Brennan smiled.

"Yeah," said Jonas. "Picked out some soup yet? We can go to Walmart later for some more substantial supplies."

"Chicken noodle." Brennan grabbed the first can her hand came across.

Jonas nodded. "Chicken noodle." He grabbed his own can. "So listen. We can have the house for up to three days. I don't know if I want to go back right away, you know?"

Brennan paused, then nodded. She did. Part of her didn't want to go back, didn't want to face her parents (*I can't believe you would just leave without even telling us in person! It's not like we wouldn't have let you go, even if we might not have wanted you to. You're eighteen. But leaving in the middle of the night?*) and their disappointment in her life choices (*writing*—insert an appropriate amount of scorn here), but she was also on the verge of having a panic attack at the thought of staying even one night in an unfamiliar place. *Jonas is here. You trust Jonas.* Thunder boomed outside. "Well, we can't drive back in this weather," she said feebly.

"So we stay a night. Reevaluate tomorrow." Jonas put both of his crutches under his left arm and wrapped his right around her waist (which somehow felt more intimate than when he just wrapped his arm around her shoulders—level one, shoulders; level two, waist). "Are you okay?" he asked her.

"Just tired."

"Anxious?"

Always. "Yes."

Brennan watched as Jonas set their items on the counter and the gas station clerk started ringing them up.

He turned to her. "Do you need anything else?"

She swallowed. Again, like a wave that had just receded and was now being wind-driven back into shore, it hit her that she was here in Wisconsin, with Jonas, overnight for several nights (or at least one) and there was nowhere she could escape to if she did something stupid, or messed up and embarrassed herself. *Don't be silly,* she told her mind. *I've stayed an entire weekend with Jonas before. This is no different.*

"Brennan? Do you need anything?"

Brennan forced a grin. "Yeah. My head checked." She laughed, like it was a joke. It wasn't, but she didn't want Jonas to know that. *Shut up,* she begged her brain, which was currently telling her stomach that it should be sick, that the world was somehow ending.

———

The cottage was on the shore of Lake Michigan, which was currently decorated with breeze-tossed waves. It was almost like being at the ocean, minus the salt in the air. Brennan crossed the lane and stood on the path that led through a thin strip of trees to open beach. The rain had lulled momentarily. She closed her eyes and breathed in, forgetting the anxious knot in her stomach for a moment.

She heard the house's screen door bang closed behind her, and then Jonas was at her side. She leaned her head against his arm. For a moment, they were both silent.

"I feel like I can think here," Brennan whispered. "Like my head is clearer."

Jonas didn't say anything, just leaned against his crutches.

"Does this make you nervous at all?" she asked. "Or is it just me?"

He hesitated. "You make me nervous," he said. "But good nervous. I don't want to mess things up with you. I want to stay here. Part of me is—ugh!" He raked a hand through his hair. "It's hard talking about these things. But I feel like I should? I want to, for the first time, really—" He looked at the ground. "I told Paul Whitford that I wanted to move on. And I do. I think I have for a while, but now it's like I've given myself permission to. But part of me is afraid that if I go back home, the feeling will fade. Here, I feel like it's easy to be the different, changed person that I have been since the accident, but I'm kind of afraid that, at home, it will be too easy to dwell on the *before* again."

When she didn't say anything, he spoke up again. "So I want to stay here, for the whole three days. But I also don't want to mess things up with you. And if you don't want to, I don't want to. So, like I said, I think we just take it one day at a time?" He rubbed the back of his neck.

After a while, Brennan straightened. "I guess we should go inside and make our soup and set up our beds."

She didn't say what she thought about staying yet, because saying something committed her. No way out.

———

Brennan stood in the shower, closing her eyes and letting the warm water cascade through her hair and down her shoulders, washing soap suds down the drain. She turned off the shower, then grabbed a towel and wrapped it around herself. She stood in front of the mirror, staring at her fog-blurred reflection for a few moments before hastily dressing in her pajamas. She yawned; from the early start to the time they had finally said good-bye to the Whitfords, gone to the gas station for supplies for the night, and reached the vacation cottage, it had been a long day.

She brushed her hair and left it down to dry, shutting off the light and leaving the bathroom.

Jonas was sitting in the living room, absently flipping through channels on the TV. He'd started a fire in the fireplace, and the open window let in the cool spring air, which mingled with the heat in blissful coziness. Brennan turned to Jonas, her heart beating wildly. "Anything good?" she asked. He was slumped against the couch cushions—posture relaxed, eyes sleepily half-closed.

"Nope," he said, yawning. "Nothing much." He flipped off the TV and set the remote down.

"So you feel better?" she asked him after a few seconds. "After talking to Paul, I mean?"

He nodded, closing his eyes. "Yeah," he said. He yawned again. "And now I'm absolutely exhausted."

"Are you going to go to sleep?"

"In a little bit," he said. "I think I'll take my turn in the shower first."

"Okay," she said. Jonas stood, grabbed his crutches, and departed the room. After a few moments, Brennan heard the shower turn on.

For a little while, she just stood and stared at the fire, then pulled out her laptop and charger from her duffel bag, returned to the couch, and booted it up. The blank document stared up at her. Apparently, the lake's magical ability to clear her mind and let her think didn't apply to *Superioris*. She couldn't even think of where to begin.

In the other room, the shower turned off. Jonas came out of the bathroom. She started to move over—to let him sit on her left side so his right was next to her, like always—but he sat down quickly on her right. He didn't look at her, just stared at the fire. Her heart sped up. She touched her fingers to her wrist, feeling her pulse hammer. *Seventy-two, seventy-three, seventy-four,* and climbing.

JONAS

In the moment, it had felt right.

Now, he wasn't so sure. *Heart rate. Jitters. Sweat.*

Brennan hesitantly inched closer to him. Then a little more.

He took a deep breath and scooted the last inch himself, until their legs were touching. He couldn't feel his socked prosthetic foot against hers, but he *could* feel the way his heart beat faster and his head spun and the blood thudded in his ears.

brennan

Brennan held her breath, and reached out her hand—rested it on Jonas's knee. She felt him tense next to her. "Sorry, I'm—"

JONAS

He set his hand on top of hers, and she went quiet.

brennan

Jonas leaned back into the couch cushions and closed his eyes. Brennan closed her laptop with her spare hand and leaned into him, curling her legs up underneath her.

"Don't let me interrupt your writing," Jonas mumbled, eyes still closed.

"I can't write," she whispered. And saying it out loud to Jonas, she almost felt like crying about it. Heat was already building up behind her eyes, threatening to send tears spilling down her cheeks.

Jonas opened his eyes, turning to look at her. "Why not?" he asked gently.

"I haven't been able to since I was featured. For a while, I felt like

I'd peaked, you know? Like I was good." She tilted her face into his side to avoid having him see her start to break down. She shouldn't be breaking down, not about this. *Get it together,* her brain admonished her. "I'm actually nauseated by the recognition," Brennan said. Then she laughed bitterly, and it came out kind of as a snort. *God, you're so embarrassing.* "That makes me so weird, don't you think?" she said, staring unfocused at the orange flames in the fireplace.

"Not weird," he said.

She breathed. In, out. *Anxiety is a wave.* "I second-guess everything I write now. Like it isn't good enough, like it won't live up to what my new audience expects of me, and they'll all leave."

Jonas moved his arm from her hand on his knee to put it around her, running his fingers through her hair comfortingly. With his other hand, he gently pulled her laptop away from her. "Take a break," he said. "Don't force it. Just think about being here for a while, in this moment."

She started to protest, but he turned and leaned his head against hers, whispering in her ear. "Don't force it. It will be okay."

Brennan closed her eyes. She listened to the pop and crackle of the fire. Through the open windows, she could hear the lake's waves on the beach. Her hand was still on Jonas's knee.

Jonas shifted so that she was cradled against him. Somewhere outside, in the distance, thunder rumbled. Soon, gentle rain was falling again.

Brennan could still hear the waves as she fell asleep, just like that— on the couch, curled into Jonas.

———

When she woke up, she felt the familiar disorientation of being not in her own bed.

The fire had dimmed, just embers now, among the ashes in the fireplace.

Jonas was sleeping, easy breathing soft against her hair. She stared at his hand, loosely resting on hers at his left leg, hip to hip, knee to knee with hers. *Invisible-to-the-human-eye atoms.*

What have you done to deserve him? her brain scoffed. *You'll just mess it up. Human disaster. That's what you are, remember?*

Brennan's stomach twisted.

Outside, the rain had stopped again, like it couldn't make up its mind. The waves still beat against the shore.

Brennan gently moved Jonas's hand and shrugged out from under his other arm. She watched anxiously as he stirred a bit, but he just shifted and fell into deeper sleep once more.

She slipped out the front door, careful not to let the screen door bang in its wooden frame.

Outside, the rain-fresh air was cool. A light breeze pricked her skin as she stepped barefoot across the lane and between the thin trees. Her feet hit wooden slats, traversing the wooden walk across the marshy ground leading to the beach. Then her feet were in the sand, and she was silently crying.

She hugged herself, looking up at the clearing sky, clouds already scudding off into the distance.

Stupid, stupid. Why are you out here? Why are you crying? Why are you running away?

BECAUSE YOU TOLD ME TO, Brennan wanted to scream at her mind.

We, my dear, are one in the same.

HOW DOES THAT WORK? WHY AM I LIKE THIS?

You let me. You let yourself get like this. Tell me no, why don't you? You can't, can you? You're weak. It's just you, your mind. Take control. Or can't you?

Brennan's fingers worried the hem of her pajama T-shirt.

Shut up, brain, she said. *Shut up. Shut up. Shut up.*

59

JONAS

Jonas woke up to darkness.

Well, not complete darkness. Orange pricks of light still glowed in the fireplace.

Brennan was gone. That was the first thing he registered, after the darkness. Her spot was cold, and he was cold where she was gone and the breeze from the open window now found a place to wrap around him.

He wondered if she'd gone to bed.

He grabbed his crutches and made his way carefully up the stairs to see if she was in one of the upstairs rooms. Every step with weight on the prosthesis was painful. He reached the top.

Empty, beds made.

Back downstairs, he noticed the quiet creaking of the screen door in the breeze.

He stepped into the night. In the sky, the stars and moon offered light to the ground. Jonas moved across the lane and through the trees, until he could see the beach.

There was Brennan, sitting on the sand, hunched over with her arms wrapped around her legs.

He hesitated, then slowly walked up next to her and gingerly lowered himself to the wet ground. He didn't say anything at first. Brennan glanced sideways at him.

Finally, he put an arm hesitantly around her and, after a moment, she leaned her head against him.

"What's going on in there?" he said, patting her head.

"Too much," she whispered.

"Shut up, brain?"

She nodded, took a shuddery breath, but didn't say anything.

"I'll stay," he said. "I'm here, Brennan. I'm just going to stay here until you want me to go, okay? I'm here."

brennan

She couldn't think of anything to say.

So she just nodded again and buried her face in his side.

60

brennan

Brennan sat on the couch the next day, laptop on her lap, finally writing.

She still couldn't pick up where she'd left off in *Superioris*, but she was at least writing a scene.

> *Ing looked at Cas's face, in the moments when he wouldn't look at her. Tired, it said. So tired. He was too young to be this tired.*
>
> *"Cas?" A beat. "I'll stay," Ing said. "I'll stay for as long as you want me to. I'll be here."*
>
> *His face contorted a bit, as if he might cry, but he only nodded and let out a shuddery breath. Then his hand found Ing's, and he squeezed, and he didn't let go for a long time.*

Brennan leaned sideways enough to peer into the tiny kitchen, where Jonas was busying himself making burgers in a cast-iron skillet he'd found in a top cupboard. If she was less self-conscious, she might show him the scene. *Look, what you did last night really meant something to me. Meant so much, I wrote it into a scene.* Then she'd probably laugh awkwardly. *Funny, huh?*

She groaned inwardly. It would just sound stupid, wouldn't it? In the kitchen, Jonas was finishing the burgers, carefully arranging them on wheat buns, his brows knit in concentration.

Brennan's heart rate picked up. *Check your pulse,* her brain said, and it wasn't excitement this time. And she couldn't resist it; her fingers found her wrist. *Beat, beat, beat.* Fast. *You're fine,* she said.

—

Brennan stared at her computer screen. She'd gotten out that one scene earlier, but it was, once more, frustratingly blank, the cursor blinking up at her mockingly.

Jonas crutched into the room. "Having difficulties?" he asked. She glanced up at him. He was smiling.

"Yes," she groaned. "I wrote some earlier, but I'm stuck. Again."

He held out his hand. She stared at it. "Come on," he said. "Leave it. Don't force it. Come to bed. Everything looks better after a good night's sleep."

She put her hand in his, but still, she protested—albeit weakly. "Jonas, I can't—"

He held a finger to her lips, almost losing his balance on his crutches with both hands engaged. "Come on, Bren," he said.

When he said Bren. "Can't—"

"Come to bed." He stuck his lower lip out.

"Jonas." It took real *effort* to force his whispered name up her throat and out her mouth.

He was backing up. "Come read me some of your story. Or we talk. Something. But you don't think about making any new words." He stumbled a bit on his prosthetic leg, winced, and then half laughed. "You're leaving me hanging."

She watched as he backed down the hallway to the bedroom and sat down on the edge of the bed. "I'll just keep bugging you until you're sick of me—"

"I couldn't be sick of you," she said, the words almost painful in her throat.

"Let me read some of your story," he said. "I'd like to read some if you'd let me?"

A blush crawled up Brennan's neck to her cheeks and ears, heat filling her. Her pulse was racing again. "I guess," she said, surprising herself. "I mean, I don't usually let people I know read my writing. It's just, I'm more afraid they won't like it, or they'll think it's bad, and then what will they think of me—" She cut herself off; she was rambling now. Jonas was just watching her, a slight smile curving up one corner of his mouth. "I'm crazy, aren't I?" she whispered.

Jonas patted the bed next to him. She crossed the room—sat. He flopped backward onto the bed, and she lay down next to him (hip to knee, electric—her head against his shoulder).

She opened the allfixx app on her phone. "Are you sure about this?"

He just nodded his head, against hers. (She was starting to feel like she was all heartbeat and rushing blood—in her chest, in her ears, to her brain.)

She opened her allfixx profile. And then *Superioris*. "I don't know. Should I start—"

"How about the beginning?" Jonas whispered, against her ear.

"I guess I should explain—I mean—it's set in the future and . . ." Her voice choked. She couldn't manage to get words to come out past the knot in her throat. Reading aloud felt weird; it felt like sharing a part of herself that she always kept hidden.

"Brennan?"

"Yeah?" She turned to look at Jonas helplessly.

"What if I read it?"

"Oh. I mean, okay, I guess." She helplessly relinquished her phone to him.

He shifted slightly next to her and began to read aloud, his voice humming in his chest, where she now rested her head.

"Sometimes, Ing thinks too much.

"She starts to think about the fact that there are sixty seconds in a minute, but each of those seconds can be divided into infinitely smaller and smaller increments, until they are so small that people can't comprehend them, but they're there.

"And the people—Ing—they're there, living in them."

Brennan thinks her words sound better, somehow, coming out of Jonas's mouth. Like he speaks them, and they're magic. Now, he's a few paragraphs down.

"Time is a funny thing, Ing thinks. If you become too aware of it, you start to drown—drown in the infinite number of moments. People say that forever is a long time, but even a second is a long time when you think about how many tiny moments went into that one second.

"Time, no matter how infinite, is always moving, never stopping.

"Except twice, Ing felt like it stopped."

Brennan felt like it was stopping now.

"The first time, a lady in a dark suit, pressed and tailored to perfection, her hair dyed white and severely bobbed, told her that there had been an accident, and then gave Ing her father's wedding ring, because it was all that was left of him.

"And time stopped. Ing drowned in the seconds.

"The second time, she wrote her name down, letter by letter—Ingrid Wei—and folded the slip perfectly in half before dropping it into a huge stone bowl, which already held hundreds of other slips just like hers, and watched it fall until time stopped, until she started to feel like she was watching herself from some great height and the slip wasn't moving anymore, it was just suspended halfway down, until she started thinking about her name being one in a thousand . . ."

Brennan thought about being one in a thousand. It didn't mean she was unique; it just meant that the rest of the thousand hid her.

"Until it did eventually hit the bottom, and it was finished.

"Ing had put her name in for the Santos Games.

"I'm one name in hundreds. I'll never be drawn—she thinks.

"Sometimes Ing thinks too much."

Brennan yawned as Jonas finished the prologue. Somewhere along the way, she'd forgotten to be worried about what he thought.

"Ready for bed?" Jonas whispered.

"Yeah," she said. "I think so. What did you think?" she asked as she took the phone back from him.

"I think I want to read more," he said softly.

JONAS

It was like Brennan was his superpower. He was hyperaware of his surroundings. Every little noise in the little house—every crash of every wave on the lakeshore outside.

She pulled her legs up onto the bed and sat up—cross-legged, staring at him. He sat up, too, so that she was between his legs—fake one and real one.

"Brennan," he whispered.

"Jonas," she whispered back.

And then her hand was on his left ankle tugging the edge of his plaid pajama pants—and he was covering her hand with his. "Brennan."

"Jonas." And he let her. She tugged his pant leg up until it was at his knee, then over his knee. Plastic and metal. She touched it. He closed his eyes.

Then he was taking it off, for some unexplainable unthinking reason. The prosthesis, then the sock to make the fit right, then the liner. Brennan met his eyes, as if waiting for him to tell her it was okay. When he nodded, she looked at his stump. He looked too—really looked, for maybe the first time. The scar, the suture marks—all laid bare. She touched it, and her fingers were cold. He winced.

"Are you all right?" she asked him. "Does it hurt?"

He shook his head.

brennan

Brennan traced the line of Jonas's scar, before becoming suddenly hyperaware of Jonas watching her. "I love you, you know," he whispered. She met his eyes and found herself unable to look away.

"Do you believe there are perfect moments?"

"What?" she whispered. "I mean, maybe. Maybe that's subjective. Maybe one person thinks it's a perfect moment, and the other doesn't." He was staring at her. Her lips parted slightly, and she found herself leaning toward him. His eyes closed, and she felt her own shut as she moved closer.

Jonas bowed his head and his lips brushed the corner of her mouth, like he wasn't sure yet if he should kiss her full on. Something sparked inside her, and she was conscious of her heartbeat in her ears, and her hand on Jonas's chest. He pulled back, and she kept her eyes closed, as he traced the curve of her jaw with his hand. "Brennan, I—" She held a finger to his lips and he stopped talking, taking her hand in his and kissing her fingertip.

*YOU'RE—I MEAN, A BOY—YOU AND A BOY—WHAT IS HAPPENING—WOW WOW WOW—*her brain was broken, unable to keep up and comprehend what was happening. Overwhelmed. Beautifully overwhelmed.

Until it couldn't take the lack of control anymore. *STOP STOP STOP. WHAT ARE YOU DOING?* Fear jerked her back.

A sick feeling tugged in her stomach, and nausea squeezed her throat. Tears wet her eyes. Why couldn't she do this? What was wrong with her? She loved Jonas, didn't she? He'd sat there with her last night, through her anxiety, not saying anything—just being there. He'd be there. Didn't she love him?

Yes. Yes, she did. But her brain screamed, *CONTROL,* and this was the opposite of control—this was her stomach flipping, heart racing, insides turning to mush, can't keep up, *can't keep up.*

She pulled away, trying to look away from the question in Jonas's eyes. "I'm sorry Jonas—I don't know—" The tears in her eyes blurred her vision, but not enough to make her miss the look of hurt and disappointment on his face.

"I'm sorry." she whispered, again.

JONAS

Jonas covered his stump with his pant leg. It felt stupid now, having it visible. *Stupid, stupid, stupid.*

"Brennan, I'm trying to understand. Sometimes, I start to think that I *do* understand you. But I don't understand *this.* This backing away thing you always do. It's not like kissing you is some make or break thing. I can wait until you're ready."

His mom: *I wish there was some way to know you were in one before it was gone, or not perfect anymore.*

"Haven't I been patient with you, Brennan? Haven't I tried to give you the support you need?"

"It's nothing you did. It's me."

"That is such a clichéd thing to say," he snapped.

brennan

Maybe she was a broken record. She kept repeating "I'm sorry."

SHUT UP, BRAIN, she shouted inwardly.

CAN'T SHUT UP. I'M YOU. I'M YOU, it mocked her.

JONAS

"I love you, Brennan," he said, almost desperately. "But I'm starting to feel like it's just going to be this over and over again. When you wouldn't text me, when you backed away. I can see it in your eyes. We'll get back home and you'll push me away because you think it will make you safe. You'll text me, but you'll come up with reasons not to see me. So is this it? Because, for God's sake, Brennan! If this is going to be that all over again—if this is it—why don't you just pull yourself together and say it to my face!" He didn't mean to sound this angry. He wished he could take the words back—reel them back in and close his mouth around them so they wouldn't get out. "And if it's not—" His voice was earnest. "Tell me that too."

"You don't understand," she said, and her eyes flashed—with hurt, with anger (at him, or at herself?). "I will always have doubts. I will always need to be constantly reassured that you're not going anywhere, that you're here, that you won't leave me. That's too much of a burden for anyone. I'm too messy for someone else."

Jonas wished she would go. To the other room. Outside. Somewhere where he didn't have to see her face—watch them fall apart over and over again.

brennan

Jonas let out a shaky breath and ran a shuddering hand through his dark hair. *Feather hair.* It was sticking up in the back again, and that little detail alone made her feel like breaking.

Doubt ate at Brennan's thoughts. *Maybe he's only with you because he thinks he owes you,* the anxious voice in her brain whispered. *This won't be enough for him. Someday he'll realize he can't deal with the constant reassurance you require. Then he'll leave, because he can't take it anymore. Better leave now. Leave now. It hurts now, but it would only hurt you both more in the future. You're not good for him, Brennan. You're not good for anyone. You're a disaster area. Dangerous.*

"I'm sorry. This is it," she said.

She hated that the nausea twisting her stomach disappeared as soon as she said it.

Outside, it was raining.

JONAS

Jonas went to leave. Couldn't (leg still off). "Go away," he whispered, trying not to make his voice break. "Please, go away."

When he looked up, she was gone. He heard her footsteps on the stairs.

It was stupid. He had wanted her to stay—to argue for her staying.

61

brennan

She was numb.

"Brennan? Hey. You okay?"

Brennan shook her head just slightly, still staring at her closet door. Back in her dorm room after spring break, she felt emptied—like she'd lost all of herself and was nothing but an empty shell. Ambreen eyed her critically.

Brennan flopped back onto her bed, staring at the ceiling. Jonas hadn't texted her. Of course he hadn't. Why had she half expected him to? She'd been the one to break up with him, after all.

Broken up. That's what they were.

She hated it.

The morning after she'd told him this was it, they'd both gotten up and packed, leaving the little vacation cottage behind. Neither of them had said anything beyond cursory comments regarding their trip. (*I'll drive,* Jonas had said. *Okay,* Brennan had replied.) She had wondered if he had even slept; the dark circles beneath his eyes seemed to say he hadn't, and he'd been sitting out on the front steps when she'd gotten up in the morning.

Not that she had been much better off, having cried half the night. Her head hurt now, somewhere behind her eyes. What was wrong with her? She could have ended her own misery, and yet, she was too afraid to.

"Brennan, seriously." Ambreen pulled Brennan's arm until she was sitting and facing her. "Tell me what's wrong."

Brennan snapped. "What's *wrong* is that you always let people sit on my bed and I don't like it!"

Ambreen frowned. "I didn't know," she said. "I'm sorry? I'll tell them not to?" She eyed Brennan. "That can't be *it* though. What's actually wrong?"

Brennan hesitated, then sniffed before she could stop herself. "Jonas and I aren't—we aren't together anymore."

Ambreen's pretty face fell. "Oh. Oh no. I'm so sorry, Brennan." Brennan's face crumpled all over again. Ambreen climbed up onto the bed and sat next to her, putting her arms around her roommate. Brennan spent the next ten minutes ugly crying.

"I'm sorry," Ambreen said again softly. "Breakups suck." She rubbed Brennan's back while she cried. "What happened?" she asked.

"I don't—I'm not ready to talk about it yet," Brennan hiccoughed.

"Okay," said Ambreen. "We don't have to."

They spent the next few days not talking about it.

Brennan skipped her classes. All of them.

She spent a lot of time in the bathroom, staring at her reflection in the mirror—hair in disarray, puffy eyes, red face. *I hate you,* she told her reflection. *I hate you. I can't do this anymore. Anxiety is in me; it is me. I can't live like this anymore.*

You can fix it, part of her mind said. But she couldn't bring herself to text Jonas. It was too late, wasn't it? She'd irrevocably put it out there. It was her fault. *Un-take-back-able.*

Brennan checked her phone again for texts. There were none. *Of course not,* she told herself. *You broke it off.*

She felt like her heart was ripping in two. She had lost everything. Jonas. Her writing. What did she have left?

It's your fault, her brain sang. *It's your fault, because I am you. There's no voice in your head that tells you what to do. You tell yourself what to do. You let me do what I want—you let yourself do this. You were afraid that it would end, just like your other friendships, and you'd be heartbroken because it's more than just a friendship this time. So you thought you'd be better off if you just broke it off yourself—before Jonas got the chance to.*

Brennan closed her eyes. "But what if he never would have?" she whispered.

JONAS

"Seriously, man?" Jonas glared at the TV, where Sam had just pelted him with a blue shell in *Mario Kart*, passing him for first place at the last second.

"Maybe you should call her." Travis took a handful of popcorn and leaned back against the wall. "Maybe she's changed her mind."

Jonas frowned. "If she'd changed her mind, she would have told me by now." *I basically told her to break up with me, didn't I?* He had told them the whole story. The whole story had necessitated telling them about the leg. Surprisingly, it hadn't been a big deal—they actually thought the prosthesis was cool.

"Guess the ball's in her court then." Travis sighed and threw a piece of popcorn at Jonas's head. "Even if it's the end of things, relationships end sometimes, man. You won't help yourself by moping around playing video games." He sat forward. "You've got to move on."

Jonas closed his eyes. "Easier said than done," he snapped.

"True," said Travis. "But still no less important."

Sam took the controller out of Jonas's hand and set it aside. "A lot of first relationships don't work out anyway, so you're not exactly abnormal."

Jonas glared at his shorter suitemate. "Thank you," he said. "That's very helpful for my time of heartbreak."

"I think you need a break now," said Travis. "Go do some homework. The video games will be here when you get back."

Jonas shook his head in an effort to clear it. Travis was right; he was letting all his schoolwork fall to the side. "You're right. I'll see you guys later."

He left their room and went next door to the bathroom first. He looked at himself in the mirror. Same crutches. Same hair sticking up. New dark circles rimming his eyes. When he forced a smile at himself in the mirror (an action startlingly similar to when he'd done the same in front of his closet mirror at home, the day he'd taken Taylor her permission slip), he looked slightly unhinged (the same as he had that day).

Jonas left the bathroom behind for his own room.

He sat down in his desk chair and stared out the window. Out on campus, spring was in full bloom, trees heavy with buds and grass growing green after the long winter. Jonas sighed. He remembered walking those same paths, covered with snow, with Brennan. He frowned.

You need to push Brennan out of your mind, the logical part of his brain told him. The emotional part, however, seemed to think it would be a good idea to ignore the logical part and drown him in some sort of contrived depression.

Here are the facts:

1. You and Brennan are broken up.
2. You basically told her to break up with you.
3. How could you, how could you, how could you?

62

brennan

It snowed again. Late March, like the year Jonas had had his accident.

Brennan tried not to think about Jonas as the white flakes fell thickly past her window. She tried not to think about how she'd tried to write but still couldn't. She tried not to think about the messages from her followers: When will there be a new chapter? I can't wait anymore!

Ambreen was outside. She, Jen, and some of the guys down the hall were sledding down the big hill on campus with makeshift sleds that were really the lids of plastic storage bins.

Brennan lay on her bed and stared at the ceiling. *Empty. I am empty. I can't even feel anything anymore.* She didn't hurt, didn't cry—she just lay there and didn't do anything, because she couldn't bring herself to.

Suddenly, the door to their room slammed open and Ambreen came in, clumps of snow falling off her boots and out of the hood of her coat.

"Get up!" she yelled, startling Brennan.

"Why?" Brennan asked, incredulous. She lay back and looked at the ceiling again.

Ambreen grabbed her arm with wet, cold gloves. "You're going outside. We're going outside. You're going to slide down the hill, and you're going to scream a lot, and when you're done, you'll feel a little bit better."

"I don't want to." Brennan turned and stubbornly faced the wall.

"Do it or I'll put snow down your back."

Ambreen dragged Brennan down from her bunk and tossed clothes at her—sweatpants (two pairs to layer), sweater (and a T-shirt for underneath it), two pairs of socks, and rain boots ("Rubber keeps the wet out better than anything," Ambreen insisted).

Outside, dusk was starting to fall. Brennan felt heavy and clumsy in her layers as they trundled down the slick path out back of Prairie. It took longer than usual to get past Woodland Hall and onto the edge of the main part of campus, where the big hill towered above them. The thing was a nightmare to get up when it wasn't snowing—sweating, and puffing, and standing on your bike pedals to get more leverage—but getting up it when it was slick was almost comical.

When they reached the top, Brennan refused to go. "You go," she told Calvin when he offered her his container lid. "I'm okay." They were all running around like children, tossing snowballs and laughing and shrieking. Calvin went down the hill.

Ambreen came up behind Brennan with another lid. "Get going," she demanded.

"Stop being bossy, Ambreen," Brennan snapped.

"That's what you need right now," Ambreen snapped back. She threw the lid on the ground. "Now sit down."

Brennan obediently maneuvered herself onto the lid, holding on to the sides tightly. She was suddenly nervous. The hill was tall, and this was a plastic lid. There wasn't much keeping her from falling off, and she pictured herself losing a tooth or breaking an arm.

"Ready?" sang Ambreen.

"No," whispered Brennan.

"Go!" Ambreen gave Brennan a shove, and then she was sliding, slowly at first, and then picking up speed. The snow stung her face as she rode into it, frozen flakes hitting her cheeks.

And then she went from feeling nothing to feeling everything at once, and she was dizzy, and screaming, and before she knew it, at the bottom of the hill.

She trudged up, and went down three more times. Her glasses were smeared with melting snow, her cheeks and nose were numb, and she was on her way down again.

At the bottom, she tumbled off the sled, rolled a few times, and stopped, facing the sky, letting the snow hit her face.

She was crying now, and her nose was running, and she was laughing. She imagined that she must look like a crazy person. Ambreen ran over to her. "Brennan! Are you okay?"

Brennan had to take her glasses off to see, they were so blurred with wetness.

"What's wrong?" Ambreen asked, concerned.

Brennan laughed, insanely. "Nothing. Everything. It's all wrong, and all right! I feel—" She sobbed. "I feel alive, and normal, and warm—and everything. And—" She sobbed. "Awful—all at the same time."

"It's going to be okay!" shouted Ambreen, taking her by the shoulders. "You will be okay. It's going to be okay!"

Then she hugged Brennan, and Brennan felt like a tiny piece of her was fixed.

63

brennan

"PEEL!" yelled Ambreen, a little too loudly in the silent dorm room, startling Brennan enough to drop the letter tile she was holding. "I win! I win! FINALLY!"

Week two of being broken up with Jonas meant leaving behind the feeling of momentary freedom she'd felt sliding down the hill on a plastic container lid, and starting to give in to her mind again. Ambreen had been trying to distract her. From Monopoly to trips for ice cream to, now, Bananagrams, Brennan felt like Ambreen was babysitting her like a child who needed watching. It felt nice, weirdly.

Jen looked up from her words, glancing at Ambreen's assembled tiles. "Are you *sure* those are all words?" she complained, upset at being dethroned from her status as queen of Bananagrams.

"Yes!" insisted Ambreen. "I'm sure!"

Jen eyed the tiles, frowning. Then her face lit up. "Ha! Breakup is two words, not one."

"No," mumbled Brennan. "It can be both. Breakup is a perfectly valid word choice." *Trust me, I know.*

Ambreen started doing a little victory cheer with her hands while Jen rolled her eyes. "Yeah, yeah," she said. "Soak it all in. You won't win the next round."

Brennan pushed her tiles into the center of their little circle and stared at them glumly as Ambreen began flipping them over. Her roommate glanced up at her. "Brennan? You okay?"

"I'm just—" Brennan shrugged helplessly. *Furious with myself.*

Ambreen got up and went to the minifridge, digging around in the freezer portion for a few moments. Jen stood up and pulled Brennan up by her arm. "Come 'ere," she said, pulling Brennan onto Ambreen's bed. Ambreen came up from her search in the fridge with a pint of mint chip ice cream.

Grabbing some plastic spoons from a drawer, she hopped onto the bed on Brennan's other side. "Here," she said, handing a spoon to Brennan and pulling the lid off the ice cream. "The best breakup cure."

Brennan took the ice cream and had a small bit, the frozen treat cold as she gulped it down past the knot in her throat. *You're going to cry. Don't cry. Don't cry.*

Her suitemate patted her shoulder. "There, there," Jen said. "He should never have broken up with you. Boys just don't know what's good for them."

The dam broke, and Brennan was bawling and hiccoughing all at once.

"Oh no," said Ambreen, shooting Jen a look. "That's a sensitive subject."

"He *didn't* break up with m-me!" blurted Brennan. "*I* broke up with him. It's all *m-my* fault. I blamed m-my anxiety, b-but really, I was just plain scared, so I didn't commit."

Ambreen frowned. Brennan had always said she didn't want to talk about it before. "Really?" she said, incredulous. "Then what the *hell* are you doing just sitting here? If you want to be together, for God's sake, *do* something about it!"

"I want to!" Brennan sobbed. She was coming unglued. "But I don't know what to do! How can he want me back after I'm the one who ended things?"

"You don't know what he wants!" lectured Ambreen. Jen seemed freaked out by the crying and was currently sneaking out of the room. Brennan didn't blame her. Then again, maybe she just wanted to go to bed, considering it was now one o'clock in the morning or some such ridiculous time—she'd sort of lost track.

"Look at me," ordered Ambreen. Brennan shifted so that they were sitting cross-legged across from one another on the bed. She turned watery eyes to Ambreen, the mint chip still held tight in her grip, freezing her hands.

Ambreen placed her hands on Brennan's shoulders, maintaining eye contact that was, in Brennan's opinion, sort of terrifying. "Do you love Jonas?"

Anxiety burned in her stomach. *Yes,* her mind yelled. *Yes, you do!* She looked into Ambreen's sincere eyes, and she suddenly was tired of denying it, tired of pushing it down, tired of being so afraid that she couldn't say what was in her mind out loud, as if she was embarrassed about it. Because she wasn't, embarrassed about it, that was. So why in the world hadn't she been able to say it to Jonas when it mattered? "Yes!" The answer suddenly burst out of her, and it was like the knot in her throat had been untangled, and the burning of nausea in her stomach dissipated. She blinked.

Ambreen smiled, her dark brown eyes glinting. "Then, and seriously, Brennan, please, for God's sake. *Tell him.*"

Brennan forced a watery smile at her roommate. "Yeah? Do you— do you think he'll still want to be together?"

"I don't know," said Ambreen. "I can't tell you how people will react. You did hurt him, after all. But I *do* know this. You will regret it for the rest of your life if you don't at least try to fix things. You clearly love him; I've seen it on your face since the day I found out you were going out with someone.

"People are complicated beings, Brennan. We break, we fall, we piece ourselves together again. We tear relationships apart, and we glue them back together. Maybe it's not always perfect, and by nature, happy endings come after a lot of *unhappy* crap. But that doesn't mean there *aren't* happy endings. And you'll never know if you don't try, because the happiest endings always require some effort on our part."

Brennan nodded, smiling through her tears, the first real (not unhinged) smile she'd had since the breakup (one word). "Yeah?" she said.

"Yeah." Ambreen pulled her into a hug. "And if he doesn't want to get back together with you, I'll be here with a tub of ice cream and we'll glue your pieces back together ourselves. You'll learn from this, and you'll move on, eventually."

"Okay," said Brennan. When Ambreen pulled back, she jumped down from the bed and started throwing things into her empty backpack.

"What are you doing?"

"I'm doing it. I'm doing it now before I freak myself out too much and back down and chicken out. Jonas has his surgery tomorrow, well, today, I guess," she said as she glanced at the clock that now said three o'clock. "I have to tell him. I want to tell him before he goes back for surgery."

"Okay." Ambreen stood up and grabbed her keys and wallet off her desk.

"What—what are you doing?" asked Brennan, slightly confused.

"I'm taking you." Ambreen grinned, flipping her dark-brown hair over her shoulder absentmindedly. "You're emotional and nervous, and I'm here to make sure you get to the hospital to confess your love in one piece."

Brennan dropped her backpack and threw her arms around Ambreen, almost ready to cry again. "Thank you, Ambreen," she said.

"You're welcome!" Ambreen pushed her off. "But let's go!" she said. "You said his surgery's at seven didn't you? If you want to make it there before then, we've got to get this show on the road!"

64

JONAS

7:00 a.m. It seemed like everyone should be just waking up, and yet the hospital had already been busy for an hour—techs checking blood pressures and pulses, nurses passing medications, shifts changing.

Jonas took a deep breath as he lay back on the transport bed that would take him to surgery. He blinked at the lights that suddenly seemed too bright. They put the rails up on the stretcher and placed a cap on his head to cover his hair. It reminded him of the caps Brennan would wear at the deli. Like medical dramas. Like shower caps.

He felt silly.

"We're ready," said the OR nurse who had come to take him. She came around by his head to push the bed. "You'll be in and out in no time."

"Yeah," he said, his throat tight around the word. "Thanks."

His mom appeared at the rail and smiled down at him, her wide eyes a little teary. Behind her, his dad placed a comforting hand on her shoulder. Jonas gave his mom a small smile. "Come on now, Mom," he said. "Don't cry."

She squeezed his shoulder. "I'm just worried. It's a mother's job to worry, you know," she said.

"I'll be all right," he said. "You and Dad go get some breakfast while I'm gone and I'll see you later, okay?"

She nodded. "Okay," she whispered, before bending down and kissing him on the forehead.

"Mommmmm."

She laughed. "Okay, okay. I'm going. Don't give them any trouble in there," she joked.

"Oh, you know me," he quipped for her benefit. "I'm so much trouble that even the *anesthesia* can't keep me down." Joking with her felt good. His stomach unclenched a little.

She laughed and then stepped back, giving him a little wave. "Bye, honey," she said.

"Bye, Jonas," said his dad, stepping forward to squeeze his son's shoulder. Jonas's dad was awkward with emotion, but Jonas supposed the surgery of one of his children was an exception, because the older man's voice was slightly choked up. "See you in a little while, okay? I'll watch out for your mom."

"See you, Dad."

"I love you, you know? I'm proud of you." His dad gave him a tight smile, and then stepped back, putting his arm around Jonas's mom.

Jonas gave them a weak wave as they wheeled him off.

"Your family seems more worried than you," chuckled the nurse from her spot by his head as they left the nursing unit and entered the hallway, heading to the elevator.

"Yeah," said Jonas. "I guess they are." *Or maybe I'm just better at hiding it—burying it.*

They were getting onto the elevator when he almost convinced himself he heard Brennan's voice around the corner. But the doors closed, and he decided he'd just imagined it.

brennan

Brennan ran (she had fully committed, no halfway) onto the medical-surgical floor where she knew Jonas would be staying for the brief time before and the time after his surgery. She'd been running since the parking lot. Not wanting to wait for the elevator since it was so close to seven, she'd even taken the stairs. Ambreen, huffing and puffing behind her, almost ran into her when she stopped in front of the nursing unit desk.

"Hi," she puffed, out of breath. She leaned on the desk. "I'm looking for Jonas Avery?"

"Are you related to him?" A nurse with curly red hair eyed Brennan.

"I—I mean, no. I'm not."

"But she wants to be," whispered Ambreen in Brennan's ear, unhelpfully. Brennan turned beet red.

The nurse glanced back and forth between Ambreen and Brennan.

"I'm sorry," she said. "I can't give information on a patient to someone who isn't—"

"Brennan?"

Brennan whipped around to see Mrs. Avery and someone who had to be Jonas's dad (he looked like Jonas, but with lighter hair and glasses). "M-Mrs. Avery," she stuttered slightly, her heart hammering against her chest. "Mr. Avery."

You can do this, she told herself.

Mrs. Avery was frowning, but not unkindly. "I don't understand, Brennan," she said, giving the nurse a little gesture to show she had things from here. She led Brennan over to the visitors' waiting room. "Why are you here? I thought—"

"That I broke up with Jonas."

Mrs. Avery nodded.

"I did. I did, and I've regretted it every moment since. I shouldn't have. Your son is amazing, Mrs. Avery." She glanced awkwardly at

Jonas's father, whom she hadn't met until now. "Mr. Avery." She swallowed. "I have anxiety. I have an anxiety disorder." She felt giddily free saying it out loud to people she hardly knew. Two words, right next to one another. Anxiety. Disorder. "Jonas has been so patient with me, and this is how I repaid him. I backed away when he needed me to commit." The words were spilling out of her. Ambreen squeezed her arm, encouraging and supporting her. "I know there's a chance he might not want me back. This is my fault; I realize that I messed up. But I also know I can't be happy with myself if I don't at least try to fix things. If I don't at least apologize."

Mrs. Avery was holding Mr. Avery's hand, her eyes not leaving Brennan's face.

"So I just—could I have your permission to see him?" Her heart was hammering so hard she was sure they could hear it beating against her rib cage.

"I'd let you," began Mrs. Avery slowly. "But I think it should be his decision whether or not he wants to see you. He's been—he really loved you, you know, and you hurt him." Brennan's own heart was hurting. "But I will ask him for you," finished Jonas's mom. Mr. Avery nodded his support of the decision.

"Okay," she said. "I'll wait." She waited for Mr. and Mrs. Avery to get up, but they didn't move. She looked at Ambreen, and then back at them, a question in her eyes.

Mr. Avery cleared his throat. "He just went down to surgery before you got here," he said. "It will be a few hours before he's out and up to seeing anyone. If you would like to come back then, I'll let you know if he's willing to see you."

Brennan wanted to shout inwardly in frustration. She was *so* close! Waiting would only give her time to feel anxious and run away.

NO, she ordered herself. *You've come this far.*

"Okay," she said. "I'll come back."

She hooked her arm into Ambreen's as they walked out, mostly to support her shaking legs. They got on the elevator and headed down.

"What a roller coaster," breathed Ambreen. "But you're here! You did it. You're halfway there. *I'm* proud of you, at least."

Brennan let Ambreen hug her. "Thanks," she said. "For everything, Ambreen. For getting me here in more ways than just driving."

Ambreen gave her a comforting smile. "No problem. I've honestly been feeling kind of bad lately because I—"

Brennan's eyes widened, and she frowned at Ambreen. "You what?"

"I'm the one who submitted your story to the allfixx moderators for them to consider for a feature. I feel—I thought it would be great, that you'd be so happy. But I feel like I've wrecked you, somehow. Like I broke Author Brennan."

Brennan stared at her roommate blankly. "You—you liked my story that much?"

"I did. I did like it that much." Ambreen smiled slightly. "You're talented, Brennan. I'd buy your book in a heartbeat, if it was published. Even one of those expensive hardback editions they always come out with first, leaving us poor people to wait to borrow it from the library or until such time as a paperback finally comes out." Ambreen winked. Then she grinned, "There's a lot you're going to have to get to know about me if we're going to become best friends. And"—she grabbed Brennan's arm—"you're stuck with me now. I'm invested."

Brennan laughed. "I'm actually okay with that," she said. "I'm learning that 'No man is an island' became a saying for a reason."

Somehow, she thought she could even write a new chapter for *Superioris*, if she had her computer there and a document open.

JONAS

"Count backward from one hundred."

Jonas stared at the ceiling. Bright OR lights. White. "One hundred, ninety-nine, ninety-eight, ninety-seven, ninety-six . . ."

He pictured Brennan and stopped counting.

Eyes closed, brain off.

brennan

This is a silly idea. This is a silly idea. This is a silly idea.

It was like the anxious part of her was trying to regain some control of her mind.

Maybe it was a silly idea. *No.*

Brennan got out of the car. Ambreen had stayed at a café in the hospital to charge her phone. This was something Brennan had to do herself.

She took the steps up to the porch all at once, knocking on the door before she could stop herself.

She'd never actually met Rhys Avery in person, but she knew it was him when he answered. "Hi," she said. "I'm—"

"Brennan," finished Rhys. He frowned down at her. Jonas's older brother wasn't as tall as Jonas was, but he was taller than Brennan. "What are you doing here?" Taller and annoyed.

"I don't have a lot of time. I know you're probably angry with me, if Jonas told you anything about what happened, but I'm trying to make things right. I just—I need something that Jonas has in his room."

Rhys watched her warily for a few moments. In the background, Brennan heard Taylor yell, "Who is it?"

Rhys opened the door just enough for Brennan to get inside. "Go ahead, I guess," he muttered.

"Thank you!" Brennan called over her shoulder as she hurried down the hallway to Jonas's room.

She opened the door and stepped inside. It looked just like it had when she'd come over and watched the *Star Wars* movie.

Exactly like it looked that night. Which meant that, at least so far, her crazy half-formed plan was on track.

She looked at the skeleton poster on the closet door and thought of Jonas. She wondered, not for the first time, why she hadn't just said *no. No, this is not it. I'm going to try.*

She closed her eyes and repeated to herself the few statements she'd been repeating to herself all the way to the hospital with Ambreen.

1. You are not your anxiety.
2. It is part of you, but not all of you.
3. You can still have the things you want, anxiety notwithstanding.
4. Guess what? Lots of people have anxiety, and they're out having the life they want to have. They're doctors, they're writers, they're *living*.
5. You have the *choice* to let *it* rule you or to force it to coexist with the rest of you in your head.

She got back in the car. Maybe now she'd finally be better. She felt sunny. Like Sol-ER. Like things might end up okay, even if not right away.

There was one more thing she had to do. She picked up the phone. *Deep breath*. The phone rang in her ear.

"Brennan?"

"Hi, Mom. There's—there's a lot I have to tell you."

65

JONAS

Jonas heard his parents' voices before he opened his eyes.

So he just lay there with his eyes closed, still drowsy post-anesthesia, and listened to his mom and dad talk.

"I just don't know," said Mrs. Avery. "Do you think he'll want to see her? After she broke things off? Backed away?"

Her? Brennan? Brennan was *here*? He tried to shrug off more of the fog of anesthesia. He'd been awake (briefly) when he'd arrived back on the post-surgical unit, but sleep had been easy, and he'd gladly given in at the time.

Mr. Avery answered, with what sounded almost like humor in his voice. "Perhaps," he said. "If he's anything like his old man."

"Oh stop!" hissed Mrs. Avery. "We were different."

"You backed out on me several times in our relationship. How is it different?" His dad was laughing now, and then his mom must have elbowed her husband because he exclaimed, "Ow!"

Jonas forced his eyes to open against what felt like a huge weight keeping them closed. "Mom? Dad?" he mumbled. His head hurt, and everything was a little foggy.

"Jonas?" His mom was at his side so quickly he wondered how she hadn't fallen over in her haste. He met her eyes, blinking a few times as his own adjusted slowly to the light. "How do you feel, Bird?" she asked anxiously.

"Finnne," he moaned, almost slipping back into sleep. The drowsiness was something he remembered—familiar—from after his first procedure. He refocused on her. "Did you—did you say . . . is Brennan . . ."

He watched as his mom glanced back at his dad before looking back at him. "Yes, Bird, she is. I didn't know if you wanted—"

Jonas swallowed, his throat dry. He wanted to see her. He wanted to see her so badly that it hurt.

But he was afraid that seeing her would make it hurt worse.

"Yes," he said, ignoring the part of his brain that told him to say no. "Yes. I want to see her."

"Now? Or do you want to wait a little bit? You still seem tired . . ." His mom sounded a little worried.

"Now," he said. "I want to see her now."

———

Jonas closed his eyes again while he was waiting for his parents to find Brennan and bring her to see him. The light was hurting his head, or was it the knowledge that Brennan was here? He fumbled for the remote with the light control on it and switched off the overbed lights, leaving the room a little darker.

Everything was giving him a headache. Brennan here? To see him? What did she want?

He tried to relax, letting the pillow cradle his head. He tried to stay awake, when all he felt like doing was sleeping for a year.

A knock on the door made him tense up all over again.

"Jonas?"

Brennan.

"Can I come in?"

He swallowed, opening his eyes and focusing on the door once more. "Yes."

She entered the room, looking small, like she was trying to shrink into herself. She was carrying a plastic bag, which she held with two hands, as if she might drop it. Her hands were shaking. "Jonas. Hi. How are you?"

He blinked. "I just had surgery?"

"Right. Right." She shook her head. "God, I'm an idiot. I'm sorry."

He just watched her, distractedly twisting his hospital armband. "What do you have to say?" he said flatly. "Clearly you've got some-thing on your chest, so get it off. Unburden yourself. Do what you have to so you can leave and I can go to sleep." He knew from the stricken look on her face that it was harsh. He tried to dislodge the anesthesia heaviness further from his mind, needing to be fully present.

"First, I brought you something." She set her bag on the over-the-bed table, pulling out a container with a familiar Vietnamese logo on the side.

"You brought pho?" he stuttered, blinking, caught off guard and surprised she'd remembered after everything that had happened.

"Yeah," she said, placing it in the room's minifridge. "Hospital food sucks, right?"

He just stared blankly at her.

"If you're still trying to wake up, I can come back later."

"No," he said. "I'm fine." His headache was growing. When he closed his eyes, it helped.

So he closed them for a few moments, gathering himself, before he refixed his gaze on her. "So go ahead?" he prompted.

She nodded, wringing her hands. "I'm sorry, Jonas," she said. "I've been selfish, this whole time I've known you. I've always given the impression that my problems were bigger than yours, probably because, deep down, that's what I was unconsciously thinking. I—"

She sucked in a breath, her voice a little shaky and higher than normal. "I messed up. I made a mistake. I shouldn't have pushed you away. I was only thinking of myself. Of how scared I was to commit, of how worried I was that everything would change if I admitted what I felt for you, if I let us become even more entangled in each other's lives than we already were. I didn't think of you, I thought of me. And I was wrong. I was so wrong."

She stood there, swaying a bit. "So I'm putting myself out here because it's worth it, to me, to be with you. I'm done," she said, a little loudly, firmly. "I'm done letting anxiety run my life and be my excuse. That's why I'm here." Her voice shook a bit.

The room was plunged into silence. Jonas watched Brennan. Dark circles rimmed her eyes, and her face was pale. She was shifting her weight from one foot to the other like she always did when she was nervous, and she was biting her lip. "And I'm not saying I won't ever be nervous again, because I will. I'll always be anxious. It's part of me. I'm always going to need reassurance that I matter to you—to anyone—because that's how I am. But I will try to give a little—be a little more not that way."

Silence again.

He was so tired suddenly. Missing her was exhausting. Jonas wanted her back. He wanted to say so, but some small part of him held back, urging him to protect himself from the possibility of being hurt again.

"And I have one more thing to say." She shakily opened the plastic bag again to reveal a familiar pair of reindeer antlers.

"How did you—" Jonas started. Stopped.

Brennan placed the antlers on her head with trembling hands, a tendril of her dark hair escaping the headband and flopping across her forehead. She seemed too nervous to notice it.

He held his breath.

"Jonas Avery," she said, her voice small, steadier than it had been this entire time. "I am in love with you." Her words picked up speed, like she was afraid he might stop her before she could get it all out. "I am so in love, in fact, that it might be ridiculous how in love I am with you. I am standing here, asking for a second chance. A different ending. And I want to kiss you, if you'll let me?" He blinked in disbelief as her voice trailed off into nothing, and she stood there, looking small and exposed. He could tell she was uncomfortable.

He was wide awake now, the fog gone from his mind. "Yeah," he whispered. He nodded, the pain in his head forgotten. "Yes."

So she stepped forward and sat on the edge of the bed, closing her eyes and leaning into him so that their lips met. The kiss was tentative at first, then sure. Jonas lifted a hand to her cheek, tilting her head a bit, and Brennan brought her hands to his shoulders, grasp tight. She paused for a moment, pulling back just slightly and letting out a deep breath. Her eyes were wet as he cupped the back of her neck and she bumped her forehead against his. "I'm sorry," she whispered, her breath feather soft against his face. "For everything. I'm so sorry."

"It's okay," he said. "It's going to be okay." She kissed him again, like she couldn't get enough. *He* couldn't get enough. She pulled back just slightly, but still touched him; forehead to forehead and nose to nose. She smiled against his mouth. He moved over in bed so she could sit next to him. She leaned back against the hospital bed, her fingers wrapping around his and holding on tightly.

He closed his eyes again, a contented smile on his face. "Wow," he breathed.

"You should get some rest," Brennan whispered, leaning against his shoulder (falling together, not apart).

"You should too," he mumbled sleepily, without opening his eyes. "You look like you haven't in ages."

"Not since spring break. Not really," she replied as she got up. "I'll let you sleep."

Jonas tugged at her sweater sleeve. "Stay. Please."

"You need to sleep—"

He grinned. "Brennan, come to bed."

She laughed, but climbed back up and rested her head on his shoulder. He tangled her hand in his once more, watching as she closed her eyes.

"Brennan?"

"Hm?"

"Maybe take the antlers off?" Jonas moved his head to the side to avoid being poked in the eye.

She laughed drowsily against his shoulder and reached up, taking them off and setting them on the nightstand. He rested his head against her own, her soft brown hair overwhelming him with the scent of her—floral shampoo, and vanilla, and everything good. "I'm glad," he whispered. "That we're an us again."

"Mm-hm," she hummed.

"We may be a mess, but we're our mess, and everything we are is pretty perfect, in the end."

"All three and a half good legs of us," Brennan laughed breathily, nudging Jonas's good leg with her foot.

Do you believe there are perfect moments?

Jonas closed his eyes. Smiled. Maybe not a perfect life, but perfect moments? *Yes.*

acknowledgments

Well, here I am: Thanks and Acknowledgements. I have always dreamed of reaching this moment, but I have, at the same time, always imagined it as the great dream, and not something that might actually happen to me some day.

I don't even know quite where to start. (Deep breaths, deep breaths.)

In the summer of 2016, I was frustrated with writing. I was anxious. I didn't know what I was doing with my life. That summer, I wrote a pretty-much-autobiographical essay in which my self-character was also frustrated with writing. She wanted to write something that meant something to people—that meant something to her. A little over a month later, I started writing *Three and a Half Good Legs*, now known as you know it, if you are holding this book, *The Opposite of Falling Apart*.

It's been a long process—the longest part of my life I've ever given to a book. It was inevitable in a process like that—a process that was such a big part of my life for the past several years—that people close to me became intertwined in some way.

Thank you, Mom, for teaching me to write (literally, teaching me my letters, and then sentences, and then essays and stories, and then . . .). Thank you both, Mom and Dad, for being there for me even when I'm me. Thank you Kaeli, Sawyer, Kadin, Josiah, Mariah, Joshua, and Isaac. To the rest of my family—aunts who read to me, uncles who chatted about my story ideas, cousins who let me read to you—thank you for being my first supporters and encouraging me to read, which, in the end, helped me to write.

To Jane and Rebecca, my editors—thank you for working with me to turn this story into what it is now. To Sam—thank you for so graciously gifting this story with your insight and perspective. I am grateful to all of you for catching my mistakes, offering suggestions, and truly making this story better.

Aunt Kari—thank you so so much for taking my headshots on such short notice, and for keeping my secret back before I could tell everyone.

There are so many people I would like to thank on Wattpad, but I don't think I've got access to the number of pages I'd need to list them each by name, so I'll try to hit the high points.

To Wattpad user kittencatten and my sister Kaeli, for being the first two to really read and follow this story. Thank you for all your comments. Thank you, Kaeli, for continuing to read and comment even when I was annoying and begging you to read. It meant a lot to me that you did.

To my brother Kadin, for listening to stupid brainstorms while walking—a dual purpose exercise resulting in a clearer head and a clearer story vision.

To Wattpad user trivialpotter, who has been my support through writing ups and downs. I've loved getting to share a writing journey with you.

To Nick, Leah, Monica, and Deanna. Nick and Leah—thank you for inviting me to Paid Stories, and supporting the story through that.

Monica—thank you for tolerating all of my (sometimes stupid) questions during the publishing phase. Deanna—thank you for being a part of my publishing story.

Amanda. You are amazing. You were integral in making me believe that my work could be liked—even loved by people other than me. You have continued to believe in me, to support me, to push for *this* story to be on bookshelves. I firmly believe that my publication story wouldn't be what it is without you.

To all the people who have read this story—in any of its iterations—during its time on Wattpad and left comments, feedback, and votes. You are a part of this.

HUGE THANKS to the people who purchased the story through Paid Stories. You made me believe that people might actually buy my book (or at least, partly. I still hardly believe it sometimes!).

To my high school writing club—thank you for letting me read my notebook-paper-back-of-chemistry-class stories and encouraging me to keep going.

To Tori—you got me through some of the toughest times in high school, and you were part of my writing journey back when I was writing fan fiction and participating in spur-of-the-moment role-plays. To Sigfrid and Astrid, Loki and Thor.

To my freshman dormmates (and my sophomore roommate, because I was a slow learner in this respect)—this is a complicated dedication, because I wasn't the best roommate, by all accounts. Like Brennan, I pulled away, withdrew, hid. Unlike Brennan, I didn't learn from it until it was too late. So I'm sorry. Also, thank you. Thank you for showing me college friendships—for being open and encouraging and lifting one another up through mistakes, through imperfections, through good times and bad. Thank you for the times you tried to do the same for me. I'm sorry I didn't let you.

To SIUE, for being the first place I got to go out on my own and the place where I started to learn a lot about myself.

To Julia, Erendira, Destiny, Delaney, and Airyn—for all being part of keeping me sane over the years during which this book was written, even if you didn't know about it for all of them. You've all helped me to come out of my shell, each in your own way, and I am so, so thankful for all of you.

To my anxiety—I never thought I would say this, but thank you. Thank you for making me stronger. Thank you for being a powerful lens to help me relate to people, and for making me a more empathetic person.

Thank you, God. I never believed any of this was possible.

To younger me, anxious me—thank you, for not giving up.

PS: Hi, Grandpa! I love you.

about the author

Micah Good has been writing since middle school. She's been post-
ing stories on Wattpad since the summer before her freshman year of
college. Her work has been featured and has won a Watty Award, and
she was invited to participate in Wattpad's Paid Stories program. She
currently lives in the midwestern United States, where she is pursuing
a career in nursing. She loves getting lost in a book, which might make
her relatable, or at least someone who you now know likes reading.

Fresh off the heels of an awkward breakup, Samar has to come to terms with unexpected feelings for her sworn enemy, Benjamin.

Read the Free Preview on Wattpad

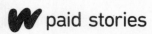 paid stories

Check out the latest titles from Wattpad Books!

Available wherever books are sold.

wattpad W
Where stories live.

Discover millions of stories created by diverse writers from around the globe.

Download the app or visit www.wattpad.com today.

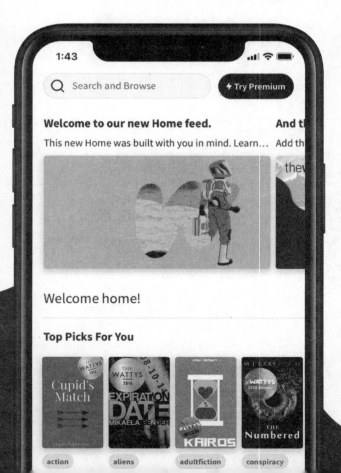